THE QUANTUM DAWN

BY DEREK KÜNSKEN

The Quantum Evolution

The Quantum Magician

The Quantum Garden

The Quantum War

Venus Ascendant

The House of Styx

The House of Saints

Flight From the Ages and Other Stories

PRAISE FOR
THE QUANTUM EVOLUTION

"Boldly ambitious."

SFX Magazine

"Scintillating future technology, and meditations on the nature of fractured humanity."

Yoon Ha Lee

"An exhilarating and heart-breaking journey of discovery."

SciFiNow

"From *The Italian Job* to *Mistborn*, I love a good heist story, and con artists like Belisarius are a favourite of mine."

At Boundary's Edge

"Künsken has a wonderfully ingenious imagination."

Adam Roberts, *Locus*

"Künsken's vivid worldbuilding is a knockout."

Publishers Weekly

"Technology changes us—even our bodies—in fundamental ways, and Kunsken handles this wonderfully."

Cixin Liu

"Uses mathematics like magic to pull you through a caper worthy of Jean-Pierre Melville."

The B&N SciFi and Fantasy Blog

"It's fast; it's furious; and is as frustratingly flammable as it is fulfilling."

Amazing Stories

"Künsken has established a place as one of the best pure 'hard science' writers of the current generation."

Locus Magazine

"Feels like what would happen if Locke Lamora landed in Bank's Culture, and if Locke had a lot to say about depraved humans. And I do love me a con artist story!"

The Little Red Reviewer

"High concept sci-fi that puts characters first—and succeeds by doing so."

Aurealis

"A truly wild backdrop of space-opera with wormholes, big space-fleet conflict and empires.... what could go wrong?"

Brad K. Horner

"Con games and heists are always hard to write—one like this, which comes out pitch perfect, wrapped in a nuanced and striking sci-fi narrative is, to say the least, a rarity."

SFandF Reviews

"The type of book you go back to the beginning and read again once you know how everything pans out and have those 'why didn't I see that the first time?' moments."

Strange Alliances

"Very satisfying."

The British Fantasy Society

"Derek Künsken is a powerful writer, and the next books in this series are not to be missed."

SciFi Mind

THE QUANTUM DAWN

DEREK KÜNSKEN

SOLARIS

First published in Great Britain in 2026 by Solaris,
an imprint of Profile Books Ltd
29 Cloth Fair
London
EC1A 7JQ

www.profilebooks.com

1 3 5 7 9 10 8 6 4 2

Printed and bound in Great Britain by
CPI Group (UK) Ltd, Croydon, CR0 4YY

A CIP catalogue record for this book is available from the British Library.

Our product safety representative in the EU is
BGC Sustainability & Compliance,
7 avenue du Général Leclerc, Paris, 75014, France
baldwinglobalconsulting.com

ISBN: 978 1 83786 220 7
eISBN: 978 1 83786 221 4

FSC
www.fsc.org
MIX
Paper | Supporting responsible forestry
FSC® C013604

Dedicated with friendship and gratitude to
John Campbell and Parrish Ley,
who brought me into a whole new science fictional world.

THE STORY SO FAR

The Quantum Magician

BELISARIUS ARJONA, A con man of the human subspecies *Homo quantus,* is contacted by Major Iekanjika, a staff officer for a fleet thought lost forty years ago. Her superiors in the Sub-Saharan Union need a con man to get their fleet of twelve advanced ships through a heavily-defended wormhole.

According to Iekanjika, the little Union fleet has, in the forty years it has been lost, developed weapons and propulsion systems centuries ahead of anything in human civilization. And they want to use them to get their nation out from under the patronship of the Venusian Congregate.

More important to Belisarius was *how* they've achieved these advances: the fleet has discovered a small, stable wormhole through which they've learned to send information back in time. The implications of this find could heal the rift between Belisarius and the other *Homo quantus*. Because Belisarius was mis-engineered; like many of his people, he can access quantum perceptions, but unlike them, accessing those perceptions risks killing him.

Belisarius starts to assemble a crew for the job. He first convinces Cassandra Mejía—a skilled *Homo quantus* and his estranged first love—to join him. He then journeys into an Anglo-Spanish prison to buy the freedom of his terminally ill former mentor, the con man William Gander.

The third member of his team is a refugee. Manfred Gates-15 is a member of the human subspecies *Homo pupa*, popularly and derogatorily referred to as Puppets: miniaturized people engineered to respond to the pheromonal signals of their designers with religious awe. Since rising up and taking their 'divine' human creators captive, the Puppets have been the subject of a crippling embargo, saved only by their control of a stable wormhole—the very wormhole that Iekanjika's ships need to use. Gates-15 is an unfortunate Puppet born without the ability to smell the divinity of the Puppet gods. He once chose exile over death, and accepts this job as a way to sneak back home under an assumed identity.

Belisarius recruits another old friend, a powerful AI who believes that he is the reincarnation of the Apostle Saint Matthew, and Antonio Del Casal, the finest bioengineer of his generation. Twenty-three kilometers under the surface of the water moon Claudius, Belisarius finds Vincent Stills, a member of the human sub-species *Homo eridanus*—engineered to live at benthic depths of oceans—and the best pilot in the Epsilon Indi system. Lastly, Belisarius frees Marie Phocas, a cashiered Congregate ex-NCO and explosives expert, from prison. The less said about their escape, the better.

In a secure location, Belisarius explains the plan to distract the Puppets with underwater explosives and a new false human divinity, William Gander, who will be engineered to produce the same scents that the captive Puppet gods do. While Gander is distracting the Puppets, Gates-15 will infect their security systems with a virus that will shut down their defenses long enough for the Union fleet to get through.

* * *

THE CREW BEGINS preparation for the con. Marie develops new explosives, Saint Matthew designs adaptive viruses, and Del Casal modifies Gander to emit the pheromones of a Puppet god and temporarily give Gates-15 the ability to smell them.

Cassandra, Belisarius and Major Iekanjika practice using Cassandra's quantum perceptions to direct an artificially-induced wormhole to connect with the throat of another wormhole, something that has never been done before, or even imagined. Stills drills himself to plant Marie's explosives under key portions of the Puppet Free City, many kilometers under the icy crust of a water moon.

Late one night, Del Casal sneaks in to see Belisarius, and reveals that Gates-15 was never unable to smell the Puppet divinities—he must be a spy. Del Casal says that their mission has been compromised, but Belisarius tells Del Casal to leave it to him. But the bioengineer doesn't trust Belisarius; he secretly goes to Gates-15 to cut himself a private deal with the Puppets.

Unbeknownst to him, Belisarius has drawn the attention of a Congregate Scarecrow, a walking weapon housing a counter-espionage AI. The Epsilon Indi Scarecrow has enormous military and espionage resources at his disposal, and his primary mandate is the prevention of insurrections or rebellions among the Congregate's client nations, like the Sub-Saharan Union. The Scarecrow is closing in on Belisarius…

THE PLAN IS set in motion when Marie and Stills go to the deepest rooms of the best hotel on the Puppet homeworld. The Grand Creston's windows face onto the open bays of the subsurface ocean, twenty kilometers below the vacuum of space. They cut through the reinforced glass to allow Stills to carry through the explosives and plant them. Stills barely survives underwater pursuit as he plants the explosives.

Meanwhile, Gander and Gates-15 arrive in the Free City posing as a returning, lost Puppet god and his escort. Del Casal's bioengineering works: Gander convinces the Puppets of his divinity, and Gates-15 gets into the Puppet Free City with him. But, as Gander discovers, the insanity of the Puppets runs far deeper and darker than anything he'd expected.

The net closes around Belisarius and his crew. Del Casal finds the Scarecrow and sells him everything he knows about the con artist's plans and the Sub-Saharan Union's insurrection, and the Puppet authorities arrest and question Rosalie Johns-10, a friend and sometime accomplice of Belisarius's, who provides them with all she knows of him.

Trapped by his adoring worshippers, Gander is caged and publicly paraded through the city. Amid this distraction, Belisarius, Cassandra, Saint Matthew, Marie, Stills, and Iekanjika cross the Puppet Axis on a passenger shuttle, allowing Cassandra to examine the wormhole throat from the quantum fugue. As they transit the wormhole, Saint Matthew leaves a number of quantum-entangled particles.

On the other side of the Puppet Axis, Port Stubbs space station focuses its defensive artillery to keep the Union fleet away from the Puppet Axis, but all the pieces are now in place. Cassandra pinpoints the entangled particles Saint Matthew left within the Puppet Axis, and guides a transient wormhole from a Union ship to connect to the Axis's interior.

The Union ships emerge into the Puppet Axis and smash through the defensive barriers on the Epsilon Indi side, breaking into open space. But Del Casal's treachery has summoned a Congregate fleet, now awaiting them with weapons charged. It is here that the Union reveals what it has done with its forty years of secrecy: its inflaton drives and inflaton cannons, never before seen in civilization, chew through the Congregate's defenses.

Despite some losses, the Union fleet makes its way for the Freya Axis, beyond which lies the Union homeworld, and through their control of which the Congregate has long held the Union hostage. But the Union's unique tactics and exotic technologies win the way through and they seize the Freya Axis for themselves, securing their home and their fragile rebellion.

Which is when Belisarius and Cassandra go after their real target: the secret time gates that the Union Expeditionary Force discovered four decades ago. With Saint Matthew's help, Belisarius and Cassandra steal the time gates, moving them to their escape ship and disappearing in the chaos around Port Stubbs. A war between the Union and the Congregate has begun, with no end in sight, but Belisarius has come into possession of the most valuable thing in existence: a time-travel device through which the *Homo quantus* can peer into the workings of the universe itself.

The Quantum Garden

Two weeks after Port Stubbs, Belisarius Arjona, Cassandra Mejía, and Saint Matthew are travelling back to the Garret, the asteroid home of the *Homo quantus*. They detect radiation and explosions in their telescopes, along with a Congregate battleship. The Congregate has destroyed their home world, almost certainly in retribution for the *Homo quantus*'s role in the Union breakout from the Puppet Axis.

Belisarius shuts off all sensors, so that they can gather no new data. Although it seems that the *Homo quantus* have just been exterminated, he argues that they have only seen the destruction of their world; their people themselves might not have been there.

Belisarius, Cassandra, and Saint Matthew themselves could have plausibly gone back in time two weeks and evacuated the *Homo quantus*.

However, the time gates can't bring them wherever they want. They can be exited at another time, wherever the time gates were—or will be—*at that time*. Two weeks before, the time gates were being transported through the Puppet Axis after they'd been stolen from the Union.

Belisarius and Cassandra emerge into the chaos of the first hours of the war in the mauled Puppet Free City, where Belisarius accesses secret accounts to buy three old cargo transport ships. At the Garret, the four thousand *Homo quantus* have a difficult time believing Belisarius and Cassandra's story, but most of them agree to evacuate.

The mayor of the Garret resigns, feeling neither competent nor prepared to guide their people in the wide world, and Cassandra is forced to become mayor. All but one hundred and fifty-five *Homo quantus* depart in the creaking, uncomfortable cargo ships, and vanish through the star system's long-lost fifth Axis Mundi mouth, which Belisarius and Cassandra have found by analyzing the interior of the hyperspace. They suspect that the time gates could be used to find many more permanent wormholes of the Axis Mundi network, but they lack a calibration factor, one only found in the past of thirty-nine years ago, when the gates were in the Union's hands.

The Congregate arrives at the Garret to find only one hundred and fifty-five shocked *Homo quantus*, who relay Arjona's and Mejía's claim to have come back in time. The Congregate arrests them as terrorists, takes all their files and research materials, and then destroys the Garret, as Belisarius and Cassandra have witnessed.

* * *

Belisarius gets a message to Colonel Iekanjika in the Sub-Saharan Union. She is understandably angry that he stole their irreplaceable time-travel device, but he gets her attention by giving her the coordinates for the fifth, undiscovered Axis Mundi in the Epsilon Indi system.

Belisarius meets with Colonel Iekanjika and Lieutenant-General Rudo and makes them an offer: he'll give them the coordinates of ten previously undiscovered permanent wormholes in exchange for assistance in infiltrating the Union base thirty-nine years ago. There, he can collect ice core samples to calibrate his models and find many *dozens* of Axis Mundi wormholes, through which he can lead the *Homo quantus* far away from civilization. Iekanjika is skeptical, but Rudo authorizes Belisarius's plan. Rudo surprises everyone by revealing she has memories of Belisarius and Iekanjika from thirty-nine years ago, but can say no more.

The Epsilon Indi Scarecrow, still tracking them, follows the terrorists into the hyperspace. He cannot understand where he is and cannot find his way out, but by precisely copying their movements at a distance, he is able to follow them.

Thirty-nine years earlier on the icy surface of Nyanga, Iekanjika and Belisarius need identities, security passes, and authorizations. Rudo in this era is a new captain in the auditing team—arrogant, brittle and conniving, nothing like the visionary leader who will later unify the lost Expeditionary Force and drive them to free their home. This young Rudo is wary of Congregate spies and informants within the Expeditionary Force, and tests Iekanjika—who must murder one of Rudo's enemies.

Belisarius did not sign up to be a murderer and worries about grandfather paradoxes. Iekanjika agrees; she is an officer, not an assassin. But more than that, Rudo has always been an inspiration, and her political and personal patron. Now Iekanjika realizes that Rudo might have chosen her for their political marriage because

Iekanjika told her that this would be her future. Nonetheless, Iekanjika prepares to assassinate Lieutenant Nabwire.

At the last moment, she holds her fire. She is not ready to stain her honor as an officer, nor the roots of the new nation they are building. She confronts Rudo, but that confrontation only hardens both officers.

In the meantime, Belisarius is trying to stay out of the barracks where his cover might be penetrated, but is drawn to a life form he read about in Union files during the heist—one that has integrated the time gates into its life cycle. He signs out a piece of kit that emits the scents that the vegetable intelligences use for communication, and makes a kind of refractory contact with them, but they prove more alien than even the Union researchers suspect. Part of their consciousness and cognition are communal, mediated through a continuous exchange of quantum entangled particles. Although utterly inscrutable, this is a kind of first contact with a being that is like the *Homo quantus*. He calls them the *Hortus quantus*, the 'quantum garden.'

IMPATIENT TO BEGIN their mission, Iekanjika asks Saint Matthew—via a wrist band device—to hack into Rudo's files to see if she is getting them the orders to drill the ice core. Saint Matthew discovers grim news. Lieutenant Nabwire, whom Iekanjika refused to assassinate, was arrested the night before. He had been sending a false flag signal that would have incriminated a rival of Iekanjika's mother and strengthened another general, Takatafare. Worse, Rudo was plotting with three others to assassinate Brigadier-General Iekanjika herself—six days before Colonel Iekanjika is to be born. This is a causality problem that the Rudo of the future did not prepare them for.

Meanwhile, within the time gates, the Scarecrow catches up to *The Calculated Risk* and orders them to surrender. Stills and

Cassandra are not prepared to face a Scarecrow in an armed, armored ship, but with no weapons of their own, their only option is draw the Scarecrow away from the wormhole mouth to Nyanga. He pursues them tenaciously.

On Nyanga, Iekanjika tries again to confront Captain Rudo and dissuade her from her treasonous course. She tells Rudo the kind of future the Expeditionary Force will have and Rudo's historical role in it. She warns Rudo more bluntly about the risks of causal problems if the Brigadier-General is killed before Colonel Iekanjika can be born. Rudo rejects everything, suspecting a trick. Distraught, Iekanjika leaves.

She barely has time to reunite with Belisarius on the ice before Saint Matthew reveals that Captain Rudo has just been arrested and charged with treason, jeopardizing the future that Colonel Iekanjika and Belisarius know. Despite Rudo's crimes, Colonel Iekanjika is the only person capable of staving off an enormous paradox. She finds Colonel Okonkwo, an auditor and Rudo's superior. Iekanjika is frank about the problem facing her and proves who she is with a DNA test. Okonkwo provides Iekanjika with authorizations and codes to drill an ice core sample. She is less willing to help Rudo, based on what Iekanjika has told her.

While Iekanjika is gone, Belisarius begins to study the nature of the *Hortus quantus* with his quantum senses, which are now running in parallel with his conscious thinking all the time now. However, he does not realize that the way his brain shares quantum perceptions makes him destructive to the *Hortus quantus*. The very act of closely observing their quantum entanglement collapses the quantum states mediating their collective consciousness. The plants remain alive, but he destroys their collective mind. His inadvertent genocide of this peaceful species so similar to the *Homo quantus* crushes him.

* * *

Saint Matthew reveals to Iekanjika that Captain Rudo is not just some partisan malcontent putting politics above the fleet, but a Congregate sleeper agent—a traitor to their nation. Iekanjika doesn't know how to navigate this impossible situation. To avoid a causal paradox, she must somehow clear Rudo of these charges, but doing so will place a known Congregate spy in command of the Union Navy. Rudo would be perfectly placed to deliver the Union to their Congregate enemies. Rudo might not even intend for Iekanjika to survive this mission: Iekanjika can die in the past without endangering the future, but Rudo cannot.

Within the time gates, Cassandra and Stills have been unable to lose the Scarecrow, so Cassandra does something she's never tried before. She instructs Stills to rotate *The Calculated Risk* across three unfamiliar axes. When they are done, she reveals to him that due to conservation of charge, parity, and time, they have become anti-matter, experiencing time in reverse. This is how she intends to escape the Scarecrow. Stills does not take the news well, but quickly comes up with a pragmatic use of their new state. He nears the Scarecrow and projects *The Calculated Risk*'s antimatter sewage. The Scarecrow's ship vanishes in the annihilation.

On the evening of her birth, Colonel Iekanjika decides that the preservation of the timeline is more important than anything else. She must clear Rudo of all charges, even suspicions. She asks Saint Matthew to manipulate the evidence he's found to make it appear that Rudo and her three co-conspirators were framed by a Congregate sleeper agent. Then, with the AI's aid, she slips into the secure area of the base. History records that Colonel Iekanjika's mother was assassinated by Congregate sleeper agents, but now that those conspirators have been jailed, there is no one to make that history—except her.

Colonel Iekanjika enters her mother's room, meeting her for the first time at gunpoint. At her mother's breast is the baby Iekanjika.

The general cannot defend herself and asks for a moment to put the baby safely aside. Once that is done, the general expresses her contempt for her assassin.

Iekanjika assassinates her mother to save history.

Then she proceeds to the detention area, kills Rudo's three co-conspirators and shoots Captain Rudo. This grave injury will make it appear that, even as a lowly captain, Rudo was the target of Congregate sleeper agents, something that will loom large in her future legend. She promises Rudo that their conversation will continue in thirty-nine years.

Iekanjika and Belisarius, each haunted by the deaths they've unwillingly caused, take their ice core samples back through the mouth of the time gates, where they are reunited with Cassandra and Stills. Belisarius and Cassandra use Belisarius's findings to give Iekanjika the coordinates of twenty undiscovered permanent wormholes.

When Stills and Iekanjika return to the Union fleet, Iekanjika is brought before Rudo alone, and Rudo offers herself up for justice. She explains that Iekanjika's actions in the past changed her, taught her that there was more to life than gangster politicking, that the Union's real hope of independence lay in people like Iekanjika. Rudo realized she would have to become more like her. She assures Iekanjika that she has forsaken any and all ties to the Congregate and does not honor their authority.

For now, for their fragile nation, Iekanjika decides to forgive Rudo.

In the meantime, the *Homo quantus* use their growing map of the Axis Mundi network to take their habitats farther from civilization.

And within the time gates, unbeknownst the anyone, the Scarecrow is not dead—he is lost.

* * *

The Quantum War

GENETICIST ANTONIO DEL Casal, in the sanctioned Puppet Free City, is undertaking the most difficult challenge of his career: replicating the Numen species.

The Numen were the gods and masters of the Puppets, locking in their obedience through complex, unreplicable pheromones. When the Puppets overthrew the Numen, they took their gods in captivity, but the Numen has declined, and when they are gone, the Puppets will go extinct.

A Congregate covert special ops team kidnaps Del Casal and brings him to Venus. A Congregate Intelligence Colonel called Bareilles orders him to make her *Homo quantus* duds functional.

Iekanjika, now a major-general and the commander of the fleet of the Sub-Saharan Union, receives a Puppet diplomatic mission, seeking an alliance with the Union in exchange for help in recovering Del Casal. Iekanjika has larger problems: the Union's superb *Homo eridanus* pilots are losing their edge to a new kind of Congregate fighter pilot. Autopsies reveal humans with strange wiring inside of them, but nothing that explains how these pilots can nearly match the reflexes and chaotic tactics of the mongrels. The mystery deepens when three Plutocracy officials come to meet with her, offering an alliance with the Banks. They reveal that the new pilots turning the tables on the Union are *Homo quantus*.

In the new *Homo quantus* habitats, Belisarius is waking once again with strange geometric dreams. He doesn't understand them, but there's a lot he doesn't understand of his increasingly anomalous *Homo quantus* experience. He shows Cassandra that he's begun manipulating probability. He's had only minuscule successes so far, and none useful, but it is a new way to touch the quantum world, something no *Homo quantus* has ever done.

The pair are visited by Stills, sent by Iekanjika through secret wormholes to bring news of the *Homo quantus* fighter pilots. At the Union base at Manafwa, Belisarius and Cassandra confirm that these corpses are *Homo quantus,* heavily innervated with wiring. They determine that the pilots were not actually conscious, but used by Congregate combat AIs as external processors. They don't know how the Congregate managed to do it, but it threatens the balance of power between the Plutocracy and the Congregate, and every enemy of the Congregate.

General Rudo, the Union's Minister of Defense, pulls together a secret meeting. Attending are Belisarius and Cassandra for the *Homo quantus,* Rudo and Iekanjika for the Union, the three Plutocracy officials, Stills for the mongrels, and Manfred Gates-15, Rosalie Johns-10 and a Puppet bishop for the Puppets. The Puppets and the Plutocracy confirm that Del Casal has been taken by the Congregate, and that his genetic skills are probably sufficient to reproduce or even surpass *Homo quantus* evolution in a few decades: they are already producing pilots capable of outflying any fighters the Union and Banks can field. The loss of Del Casal has also doomed the Puppets to extinction. And the Congregate are committed to hunting the remaining *Homo quantus* until they are exterminated.

These threats all hinge on the Congregate exploiting Del Casal's genetic engineering skills, and he is untouchable in the most impregnable fortress in the Congregate—the Ministry of Intelligence Headquarters, floating in an undisclosed location in the immense clouds of Venus. The Banks once again offer an alliance, to both the Union and the *Homo quantus.* Only together can they advance *Homo quantus* development ahead of the Congregate and win in the long term.

Belisarius has a better plan. He asks Cassandra and Saint Matthew to make antimatter in the hyperspace within the time gates, then sends Saint Matthew to Marie Phocas, who is living in the clouds of Venus under an assumed identity, to ask for help importing a very special cargo. Belisarius has surgeons wire him like the Congregate's *Homo quantus* fighter pilots, and secretly hide within him a number of quantum entangled particles, the pairs of which are held by Cassandra at the Union headquarters. Then, he ships a platoon of Puppet commandos under the command of Rosalie to Marie on Venus as cargo. The cargo will not be suspected of carrying people because no one would be fool enough to endure the sterilizing scanning radiation beamed at all incoming cargo—but Puppets can survive higher doses than humans can, and can endure the long confinement, crammed under heavy shielding, of the trip to Venus. Finally, Belisarius has Stills abandon him in a broken Congregate cockpit, in a live battle volume, where his distress beacon triggers his 'retrieval' to the Ministry of Intelligence on Venus.

Colonel Bareilles recognizes Belisarius and has Del Casal begin interrogating him. Del Casal is now fully enthralled by the Congregate, because he too has been modified. Puppet organs have been grafted into his body and brain, so that he reacts to the presence of the Numen with the same overwhelming religious awe as any Puppet. Bareilles is herself a descendant of a Numen who escaped the Puppets decades ago, and Del Casal is helpless before the pheromones she exudes.

But Belisarius' capture has served its purpose. Cassandra uses the quantum entangled particles to locate him—and the Ministry of Intelligence. She transmits his coordinates to Marie, Rosalie, Stills and Saint Matthew, who have successfully infiltrated the clouds of Venus. The Puppets mount a daring rescue of Belisarius, Del Casal, and the remaining *Homo quantus* prisoners.

The Ministry of Intelligence is heavily defended, and the Puppets themselves, though fierce, are not formidable; but the Congregate soldiers soon discover that any time a Puppet is killed, an anti-matter pellet in their bodies is detonated, blasting the defenders to pieces, and smashing holes in the walls of the Ministry itself. The Puppets shepherd Belisarius, Del Casal, and the surviving *Homo quantus* onto an escape ship piloted by Stills and they lose themselves in the clouds of Venus.

Leaving the capital world of the Congregate is another matter. Belisarius's plan is to use three ships: Stills pilots a fighter to occupy orbital defenses, Saint Matthew pilots a cargo ship to carry the survivors, and Belisarius pilots a ship designed to open transient wormholes. Belisarius will use his quantum perceptions to open the transient wormhole into the Puppets' own Axis and to safety.

Disaster strikes: Marie Phocas is killed trying to reach orbit, and Belisarius discovers that the Puppet Axis's quantum conformation has changed, trapping them over Venus. The only other Axis Belisarius has recently examined was the Freya Axis, which is much farther away.

Belisarius succeeds in connecting to it and Saint Matthew and Stills cross over, but the con man has held the transient wormhole open too long, and it collapses with him inside it.

Stills, Saint Matthew, Del Casal, and the remaining *Homo quantus* arrive safely, but Belisarius is gone. Alone and grieving, Cassandra begins the task of moving her people far from civilization, to some place the Congregate will never find them.

CHAPTER ONE

Orbit of Venus, 2724 CE

BELISARIUS-77 ROTATED SLOWLY in the weightless free fall, fixing his eyes on the tiny winking lights far below the window. He looked down from a perch high in the Invariant Tower, which sailed gracefully above cytherostationary orbit. Beneath him, the tops of space elevator stations sprouted from the yellow-orange cloud tops of Venus. Sunlight reflected white and hard off the thousands of kilometers of diamond nanothread cabling, like strands of fiery spider silk. His mind mapped their architectures, filling in the gaps, projecting the structures veiled by clouds, as well as linkages and relationships that weren't there, the false positives he was prone to seeing, ghosts hiding among real patterns. He worried more and more about things he saw that might not be real, but couldn't tell that to anyone.

The *Homo quantus* had always seen things that weren't there. It was noted in all the historical reports and modern research. It was a consequence of a pattern-recognition sense engineered to be a bit too sensitive. He assumed that the generations of *Homo quantus* after the tenth—his own generation—had engineered their brains better, calibrated them to something more aligned with reality. Someday, if he found the fugitive *Homo quantus,* he would know.

The electrical patterns in the walls behind him shifted. Textures of magnetism and charge simplified, smoothed, like the unhelpful introspections Belisarius-77 banished as the door irised open.

A pale-skinned man propelled himself in. Insignia of office clustered on his shoulders, cuffs, and collar. High boots, rich and functional, were polished black. His electromagnetic field, complexly textured, pressed against Belisarius-77's smaller one. Two hundred years of genetic engineering, perhaps more, had made the subspecies called the *Homo congregatus* more populous, and individually typically more powerful, than the original *Homo quantus*.

And Phocas was far from typical.

Centurion Xavier Phocas's posture and poise, even in zero-g, laid expansive claim to the world he saw, and the world he did not. The blue eyes took in every detail of the gilded office. A scion of several of the most storied families of Venus, Phocas had surpassed all his contemporary peers. He'd ascended to the rank of centurion on the secret Adamantine Council that ruled the Venusian Congregate through time. Phocas was the custodian and leader of an entire century of the Congregate's history. Along with the representatives of other centuries, he shepherded the eternity of Venus, steering it always towards a forever dawn.

"Unbelievable," Phocas said in *français 9.1*. "Show me this signal of yours."

Belisarius-77's stomach hollowed at the notion that what he'd found wasn't real, that he'd bothered the centurion for nothing, that he'd exposed the inadequacies he'd kept hidden. He hadn't expected Phocas himself to react, or to react this way. Belisarius-77's gesture activated a bank of holograms, which grew to illuminate the small office.

The graphs showed an ancient transmission in its raw data state. It had been amplified and corrected with modern manipulations, enough to uncover buried layers of data. Parallel graphs showed the message translated with decryption keys from its era of origin. Phocas absorbed it all quickly; Phocas had, as far as he knew, none of Belisarius-77's flaws.

"This twelve-second distress signal was received by a Congregate warship in 2474 CE," Belisarius-77 said. "In that era, due to signal deterioration, no one could confirm it was a Congregate signal, nor locate its position precisely. Modern reanalysis yields an eighty-nine percent chance that this is a genuine Congregate distress call, and a sixty percent chance that a Scarecrow sent it."

"How long had the signal been traveling?"

"Forty to fifty years, assuming random interstellar degradation."

"That wouldn't have distorted the signal too much?" Phocas demanded.

Belisarius-77 didn't know if this was a genuine question about the analysis, or an indirect allusion to Belisarius-77's flaws.

"Reconstruction of the signal found secret information embedded in the carrier wave. Decryption protocols in use between 2512 CE and 2518 CE unpacked the information."

"The originator was using encryption protocols that wouldn't be established for another forty years," Phocas stated as a question.

Belisarius-77 nodded nervously into the centurion's dubious silence, then pressed on.

"We don't have a lot of missing Scarecrows across the centuries. Almost all MIA Scarecrows have been matched against debris found after naval actions against the Sub-Saharan Union and the Middle Kingdom. This doesn't map to any of those."

Into the increasingly uncomfortable pause, Belisarius-77 added, "No other theory accounts for this."

"This was the signal that, two hundred years ago, prompted fleet leaders to send out the Sub-Saharan Union's Sixth Expeditionary Force," Phocas mused. Belisarius-77 knew this. He'd been briefed on every scrap of information, confirmed or unconfirmed, about the original Belisarius Arjona whose DNA he carried.

The Sixth Expeditionary Force, a large squadron of warships officered and crewed by the Congregate's client nation the Sub-Saharan Union, had been sent to investigate this signal. And the armed reconnaissance squadron had vanished. For decades, they'd been thought lost to enemy action. Forty years later, dramatically re-equipped and re-armed, the Sixth Expeditionary Force had returned to lead a rebellion, assisted by the original Belisarius Arjona.

Belisarius-77 wished he could go back in time and stop the Sub-Saharan Fleet from being deployed. But he kept that reckless, emotional thought to himself. The Adamantine Council fastidiously avoided undoing any past that could damage the present, or the bright Congregate futures carefully tended by Phocas's peers.

Belisarius-77 had hoped his discovery would be useful; but he'd not expected Phocas to actually bring him to the past.

Disputed Space Between the Venusian Congregate and the Middle Kingdom, 2474 CE

THE *ARGENTEUIL* WAS a medium-sized Congregate destroyer of the late 25th century. It had been attached to its current battle group nine years earlier to reinforce the Congregate presence in star systems where the Axis Mundi wormhole network had brought the Middle Kingdom and Congregate into contact. Sleek and needle-form, its seven hundred meters of armor, engines and weaponry emitted only muffled EM and thermal radiation. It could hope to pass undetected as close as a few million kilometers to passive sensors.

None of its sensors, however, could detect the *Marsoui*, the compact 27th-century ship preferred by Phocas. Even without its stealth capabilities, the *Marsoui* carried admin-level command codes for whatever period it operated in, and could selectively mask itself from any Congregate ship. Its pilot was a failed Belisarius clone whose brain and body had been vitrified and petrified in Scarecrow fashion, with moderate additions of electronic and machine actuators. With an affectless, sepulchral voice, the pilot reported that they'd entered an injudiciously close parallel course with the *Argenteuil*, just six meters abeam.

They had come here to listen, to verify Belisarius-77's theory.

"Our ancestors," Phocas mused idly as the pilot deployed sensory packages.

At first Belisarius-77 didn't know what Phocas was referring to. The silent, fast-moving destroyer beneath them didn't have any Phocas family aboard. As a clone, Belisarius-77 didn't have parents, any more than the original Belisarius did. Every embryo of the original *Homo quantus* had been built around carefully curated genetic strings subject to deft mutations, as well as a great deal of hope and luck, before being grown to term in artificial wombs.

They didn't tell Belisarius-77 state secrets like how the *Homo congregatus* like Phocas were made. But the process couldn't have been much different. The intensive lines of accelerated, directed evolution, straightened by reducing uncertainties, controlling variables, and cutting steps. Xavier Phocas had probably been conceived in a lab, and probably lacked linear ancestors like mother or grandmother. He had an important family name, but no one on the *Argenteuil* was truly his ancestor, unless he was speaking in metaphors, casting the nearby human crew as the equivalent of Neanderthals.

"Our ancestors?" Belisarius-77 finally asked.

"Spiritual ancestors," Phocas said without looking at him. "Historical ancestors. Co-partisans and compatriots. These are the legionnaires who manned the barricades, stopped the barbarians, drove back the invaders, so that we could conquer history."

Belisarius-77 was a Congregate loyalist. He'd been raised by the Congregate. He would never have existed if their security apparatus hadn't willed him into existence as an intelligence tool for the greater good of Congregate expansion and hegemony. Belisarius-77 was part of the sprawling political meta-entity, but despite belonging *to* the Congregate, he would never belong *in* the Congregate. He was a genetic and cultural outsider. His genes would never contribute to the new subspecies called *Homo congregatus,* which had long ago surpassed the modest abilities and genetic ambitions of *Homo quantus.*

Right on time, the displays began to fill. The *Marsoui* carried a suite of advanced 28th-century sensing and computing equipment. Those instruments, forewarned with the direction and origin of the signal, could capture more data than any ship of this era. Belisarius-77 exhaled long and slow.

"A Scarecrow," Phocas said.

"Showing signs of damage," Belisarius-77 added. "We have a best fit line-of-sight solution, originating well within the volume of what is Middle Kingdom territory in our times."

CHAPTER TWO

The forerunner blocks (Codename: Wheelhouse) used by the Congregate as a launchpad for galactic travel now function with sufficient confidence for routine, predictable travel from the 23rd century to the 34th century. The main forerunner block is capable of changing the conformation of permanent wormholes of the Axis Mundi to open onto other Axes Mundi in different times and places.

In addition to allowing coordinated action along more than a millennium of history, it has facilitated extensive research and the movement of information between centuries. The control and compartmentalization of information to avoid grandfather paradoxes is rigorous. Exploratory missions as far as a billion years into the past or future have been undertaken at high risk of mission failure, although the stability and accuracy of these temporary passages has been improving.

Interfacing with forerunner block systems has become easier for the wardens, although an understanding of how the blocks function is still frustratingly elusive. It is theorized that the forerunner blocks can also temporarily redirect Axes Mundi within the same time period, but this has not been attempted so as to not inadvertently damage the Congregate's tenuously stable method of travelling through time.

Preliminary Speaking Notes for Visiting Dignitaries
The Wheelhouse, 3004 CE

Manafwa Gas Giant, Bachwezi System, 2 July 2550 CE

DEBRIS CRUNCHED UNDER Belisarius-77's boots, his heel grinding broken glass and plastic, brittle burnt wiring, and chips of marine armour. Nyadenga Station orbited above the blue gas giant, spinning fast enough to simulate one half gravity. Its conquest had unbalanced something enough for Belisarius-77 to feel the slow precessing of the station's axis.

Four years earlier, President Iekanjika had moved the Sub-Saharan Union's seat of government to the more defensible Nyadenga Station. The period was marked by a lull in the Union-Congregate war, so this last, recent invasion of the Bachwezi system had overwhelmed the Union. President Iekanjika and the surviving Union military had fled through several of the in-system Axis Mundi wormholes, and the risk she presented was not yet acute enough to justify the cost of intensive pursuit. The Adamantine Council could be patient. Victory over the Sub-Saharan Union would be celebrated under the Centurion of the 27th century, but today was the beginning of the end.

Crowded in the press of political, technical and military advisors, Belisarius-77 followed the four centurions. Three of them had come from other eras. He noticed another Belisarius clone, one from this century, a few layers back in the crowd of aides. Their eyes met in a weird moment of missed connection. The passive, mildly anxious expression he saw mirrored his own without any of the brief, accompanying reflective insight. Seeing a Belisarius clone should perhaps have eased his own isolation, but there was a cheapness to the experience of staring at a mirror image, more than the existential hollowness of being replaceable or interchangeable.

They were better copies than should have been possible. Twenty-ninth century science had cracked the problem of copying the original Belisarius's microbiome and of duplicating the environmental factors of the original's growth. That breakthrough had been distributed backwards so that from the 26th century all the way to the 34th, no biological differences were detectable between any successful clones and the original, flawed Belisarius who had left the *Homo quantus*'s Garret in 2503 CE. That fidelity blurred the lines around identity, diffusing the edges of Belisarius-77's self into vaporous intangibility.

The other clone broke eye contact.

Odelie D'Aquillon, the 26th century's representative, hosted her peers. She was an older *Homo congregatus* with silvering hair, sharp eyes, and elaborate acid-art patterns on her forehead and left cheek. Marcel Hudon, the Centurion of the 25th century, walked beside her. He wore dimly glowing goggles and ear-covering headphones that filtered from sight and hearing any knowledge that could be dangerous to the 25th century. Xavier Phocas of the 28th century was behind them, examining every detail of their prize while speaking with Apolline Moulaison, the odd and unsettling Centurion of the 34th century. In principle, what was being learned today was history to Phocas and Moulaison, but history across the centuries was neither complete nor static. The eternal dawn of the Venusian empire was a product of the careful optimization of events, deftly moving technical and scientific information backwards in time, while expanding across the stars, giving the Congregate enough space to avoid grandfather paradoxes. Phocas and Moulaison were here because the details of this history were new and their hindsight from the future was needed for Odelie D'Aquillon to lead this present.

Managing information across time was no easy task—it could make even Belisarius-77's head hurt. It had to be done in secret, of course. The naval forces of each era of Congregate history knew nothing of the Adamantine Council, nor of the people who each guided a century of Congregate time.

D'Aquillon, Hudon, and Phocas transcended humanity much as *Homo sapiens* transcended *Homo erectus*. That millennium of genetic engineering had given the *Homo congregatus* of Moulaison's era strange new quantum powers and perceptions, but they struggled to pass for human. Belisarius-77 could map the physiognomic differences, but their inhumanity ran more than skin deep. The manner, look, gesture and posture of the 34th century *Homo congregatus* induced a vague unease and a sense of shuttered threat.

Nyadenga Station didn't feel like a place for Belisarius-77, and he'd told Phocas as much in the 28th century. Phocas had dismissed his objections with the explanation that he wanted to know if Belisarius-77 "saw or felt anything that no one else did." It wasn't a joke, but felt like one. Phocas's advanced quantum and electromagnetic perceptions eclipsed Belisarius-77's comparatively modest tenth generation *Homo quantus* abilities. And Belisarius-77 didn't want to even think of comparing himself to whatever near-magical abilities lurked under Apolline Moulaison's skin.

They crossed a section of crumpled, half-broken flooring, to a sizable briefing room where EM fields swamped Belisarius-77's senses. Technicians finished setting up display projectors and retreated as the centurions took some of the seats. Belisarius-77 searched for an unobtrusive space against the wall, but Phocas looked back and pulled him close behind his chair. D'Aquillon rubbed a knuckle along her lips thoughtfully before speaking.

"The navy captured the complete records of the Ministry of the Interior and Ministry of Defense at Manafwa," she said. "We have the technical plans of all Union inflaton drives and inflaton cannons. They'll be given to Centurion Hudon and taken back to his century for study in isolation."

Hudon gave a performatively jovial clap at that. "Once grandfather paradox dangers are out of the way in a week or so, we'll deliver squadrons of inflaton fighters and capital ships," Hudon said.

Whole star systems at the edges of the Congregate in the 26th century were staffed with scientists and equipped with ready-to-adapt industrial facilities. In these places, information from advanced future science was isolated from every factor that might lead to a grandfather paradox, waiting to be deployed once history caught up with them.

That wasn't why they were here, though. The capture of the inflaton drive technology was momentous to the navy, but it was already part of his own history. Even Phocas's ship the *Marsoui* was inflaton-driven.

"We captured all Sixth Expeditionary Force records about the conjoined wormholes they found," D'Aquillon continued. Her expression was wry, slightly mournful, the expression of someone celebrating a cure to a disease that had run overlong. "We long suspected that this was their secret. They did have a time machine from 2475 to 2515 CE. For all the damage they did, I would have expected them to have had the device longer than forty years. These records hint at where the conjoined wormholes are now and how to calculate our risk profile across the Congregate eternity. Interestingly, these records were encrypted in 2517 CE with techniques beyond the means of the Sub-Saharan Union, or even my own staff. I thank Centurions Phocas and Moulaison for their decryption assistance."

"Those encryptions were almost certainly provided by the tenth-generation *Homo quantus*," Moulaison said in a distant voice. At the mention of the *Homo quantus,* Hudon's blue eyes briefly rose to meet Belisarius-77's.

"There's much, much more," D'Aquillon said, as new reports scrolled across the centurions' data pads. "The Sixth Expeditionary Force had records from several sources on what they call the 'vegetable intelligences,' what the *Homo quantus* called *Hortus quantus.* These may be solely of academic interest, or there may be more to them."

"They are of more than academic interest," Moulaison said cryptically, without further clarification.

"More worryingly," D'Aquillon continued, "we recovered reports by then-Major Iekanjika on the breakout of the Union's Sixth Expeditionary Force from the Puppet Axis. These explain how they entered the Puppet Axis. A tenth-generation *Homo quantus,* Cassandra Mejía, merged a transient wormhole with the Puppet Axis. This is a novel use of *Homo quantus* abilities and a military tool we need to duplicate. During the breakout, the conjoined-wormholes time-travel device was stolen by the tenth-generation *Homo quantus* fugitive Belisarius Arjona."

Belisarius-77 felt eyes brush him.

"The pairing of the *Homo quantus* with a time travel device amplified the risk they posed to the Congregate," she said. "The Union with a time-travel device did significant damage, but their advantages were conceptually pedestrian. They could only transmit information back in time. Their propulsion and weapons superiority was temporary."

She gestured at the captured headquarters as emphasis.

"A time travel device in the hands of *Homo quantus* terrorists is an entirely different risk. Then-Major Iekanjika's records establish that Arjona and Mejía are capable of traveling through the conjoined wormholes to specific times and places. It will take some time to understand the threat the *Homo quantus* pose."

"President Iekanjika also kept a set of personal classified records here. When we cracked the encryption, we found that she herself had traveled with them, thirty-nine years into the past. During that voyage, a mongrel and the *Homo quantus* Cassandra Mejía came into conflict with and destroyed the Epsilon Indi Scarecrow of 2516 CE. This apparently occurred in a kind of hyperspatial interior of the conjoined wormholes. Iekanjika could not record anything useful from this region and we have no other information on it. After seeing the *Homo quantus* in the field, Iekanjika judged them to be a civilization-level threat. I agree with her assessment.

"Iekanjika's reports as the Major-General in command of the Union navy also illuminate some mysteries around the first phase of the Union-Congregate War. The novel antimatter weapons we faced, and their use in the destruction of the Freya Axis, were designed by the *Homo quantus*. This suggests the defenses they may have when we find them.

"Iekanjika reported that Arjona almost certainly perished in the collapse of a transient induced wormhole while escaping Venus. The chances of him having survived are currently assessed as small. Unfortunately, three problems remain. First, Mejía is known to have survived. Second, she has the conjoined-wormholes time-travel device. Third, as of this century, we don't know where she is."

Eyes turned to Moulaison and Phocas. Moulaison declined to comment.

"I don't think that the Epsilon Indi Scarecrow of 2516 CE was immediately destroyed," Phocas said into the silence. "We believe it transmitted a distress signal from the late 2400s."

Phocas explained the *Marsoui*'s discovery to the gathered expressions of astonishment, and then shared Belisarius-77's analysis.

"That was why you travelled to the *Argenteuil* in 2474 CE?" Centurion Hudon said. "You should have reported these findings to me."

"We only completed the analysis on our way here," Phocas said.

Belisarius-77 found that excuse thin and vaguely disrespectful. The centurions together shepherded the centuries of Congregate history as a single construct, like a fragile standing wave of history and politics that could collapse if any of their efforts worked against each other. And when centurions didn't agree, people like him paid the price.

"With the Sixth Expeditionary Force's records to navigate by," Phocas continued, "and knowing the time periods to avoid based on Iekanjika's logs, I intend to find the Scarecrow, download its memories, and task it with further missions."

"I should lead this," Hudon said. "That's my century."

D'Aquillon and Moulaison's expressions gave away nothing.

"This is part of an investigation I already initiated from my own century. Moreover, I want to bring Belisarius-77 with me," Phocas said, jerking his thumb back at him. Belisarius-77 wanted to melt. "I want him to try to entangle himself with the original Arjona. That might allow us to track Arjona in several eras, and perhaps confirm his death. It could also lead us to Mejía and the rest of the *Homo quantus*."

Hudon grimaced. Belisarius-77 was no expert on Adamantine Council politics across the centuries, but neither was he naive to the way things were done. It was Hudon's century, but it was Phocas's idea, his plan, and his clone. Yet Belisarius-77 had no idea how to do what Phocas intended. A sense of creeping disaster crawled up his back.

"The line is holding across the centuries," D'Aquillon said, "but we are fighting for the survival of our very species. I believe this is the time to gamble. I propose that we authorize Centurion Phocas's mission to the past on one condition. If the mission begins to risk the timeline, Phocas will terminate it, and if caution demands it, his whole team. Are you ready to play for everything, Phocas?"

When Belisarius-77's centurion smiled, he truly felt cursed.

CHAPTER THREE

The dwarf planet Nyanga, 3 March 2426 CE

THE SCARECROW LIMPED to the solar panel and readjusted its angle. The cannibalization of the Scarecrow's electronics and body parts to jury-rig the panel had only been partially successful. It wobbled and captured the brown dwarf star's weak infrared inefficiently. Radiation and heat burns along the Scarecrow's left side muddied his movements, and he had to actively correct his balance. Something tickled the edges of his perceptions, more than the sensor ghosts that had haunted him since his injuries. His right arm snapped up, plasma thrower open to the faint atmosphere.

Silence and darkness persisted, the eerie plants looking like pitch slathered over abstract art and spider webs. Above, clusters of white stars dragged across an ever-night sky. The feeling of being watched persisted, although sensation and perception remained tangled within cascades of errors in his body and brain, as they had for days. Hesitantly, he closed the shutter on the plasma weapon and lowered his arm. He needed to transmit another signal.

He turned to find two figures between himself and the improvised transmitter, and flung his arm back up. Panic rose as a cloud of signals bypassed his defenses, commanding, overriding. His arm dropped unwillingly. The shutter closed a second time.

"Scarecrow, recognize authorization overrides amber and green," one of the figures said on an open radio channel.

The Scarecrow didn't quite recognize the man's accent, but he detected strange magnetic fields in him. Vapors warmed by the leaking heat of the man's boots clung to the ground like fog. Scarecrows rarely encountered overrides. Scarecrows were the definition of loyalty and the last inner defense of the Congregate.

"Override amber authenticated," the Scarecrow said. Override amber authorized classes of pedestrian orders.

Green delayed, though. The Scarecrow's cognition was not wholly housed inside his armoured skull. The petrified brain directed and governed, but information processing was extensively distributed throughout his body and limbs. His left side—scored, cracked, and smashed as if tortured with a magnesium welder and a jackhammer—had contained some of the authentication algorithms for override green.

"Override green…" the Scarecrow paused helplessly, but happily. Without green, he would not give up his secrets to these agents who had captured him.

"Who are you?" he asked. "Middle Kingdom? I carry information the Congregate will want. They will reward even an adversary in a prisoner exchange."

The shorter figure slowly retreated, and edged behind the speaker.

"Recognize override green," the taller man repeated.

The man's words were powerless. The built-in chains that would have trapped the Scarecrow had been broken in the antimatter barrage. Fate. The Congregate was protected by fate. He remained silent.

"Look at the damage," one voice said on a radio channel.

"Diagnostic override green," the other said to the Scarecrow.

The Scarecrow felt an urge to analyze and report on the damaged sections, but the commands ran into electronic dead ends. The Scarecrow tried to lift his arm, to aim any weapon, but the amber overrides prevented that. He tried the same with a dumb slug-throwing pistol embedded in his chest. That port wouldn't open.

Stalemate. The man could not compel the Scarecrow and the Scarecrow could not leave. But as soon as human flesh needed to rest, the Scarecrow would take their ship.

"Adamantine clearance," the man said as his hand emitted complex magnetic waves. "Silver authorization, clear water protocol."

His immense age gave the Scarecrow a deep perspective on his role as an enforcer of the Congregate dream. He commanded branches of espionage and security forces, with authorities that even allowed, in limited fashion, the conscription of naval forces to espionage missions. On his own, the Scarecrow was a walking weapon, almost indestructible, almost certainly lethal to oppose.

And all that melted.

He had never experienced such an overwhelming submission, in the living life of flesh or in his new petrified mineral life. He was naked, visible in all his parts and complexities. He became perfectly knowable, every success and flaw, every hope and fear laid bare.

The Scarecrow's laser transmitters activated, pouring his data into the godlike stranger. Everything he knew, thought, theorized, feared. Nothing escaped Adamantine clearance, which he'd never heard of before. He had years of data, months of it lost in a mad hyperspatial wilderness, but the laser transmitters were fast and the man seemed far more capable of holding the information than the Scarecrow. The stream ended like a dream where an entire life has been seen in all its opacity and transparency. The Scarecrow stilled, overwhelmed.

When awareness of its surroundings resumed, the stars had moved. New, alien constellations surrounded the motionless red-white star overhead. Hours had passed. Fewer error messages swarmed his perceptions. The Scarecrow was not repaired, but he functioned better. He remembered the swirling miasma of space and time where he had been trapped, partially functional, for long months before he found the wormhole mouth. He remembered the cycle of fatal error messages driven by kaleidoscopic external perceptions and the repeated forced reboots, like a torture of painful little deaths. This frozen planetoid under its failed, restive star was like a heaven after that terrible hyperspace.

The Congregate officer stood there. The Scarecrow was awed that this man had a clearance level so high that the Scarecrow had never heard of it, so high that it had been hard-wired into the Scarecrow decades ago, during the petrification and vitrification process that had created his brain.

"Ready for exfiltration and fuller debriefing," the Scarecrow said.

"You're fully debriefed," the man said.

"That is not possible," the Scarecrow said. "Total debriefing of vitrified brains requires level-three computer-engineering laboratory facilities."

"You've been fully debriefed," the man said simply. "Technology has advanced."

Although unsatisfying, the Scarecrow accepted this reply within the context of Adamantine clearance.

"Ready for exfiltration," the Scarecrow said.

"You're not being exfiltrated," the man said.

"There isn't space?"

"Your mission isn't done. You alone of all Congregate operatives have been within a hyperspatial time-travel device currently being used by terrorist *Homo quantus*. You're to return to the conjoined wormholes."

"Wait!" the Scarecrow said. "Send another Scarecrow. I am damaged. I don't know how long I spent in there. Months. Years.

Decades? Computation and thought do not..." The Scarecrow struggled with the concept. "...function properly in there. Look at my debrief. There are false perceptions and visions... of things that are not there. Another Scarecrow with a full weapons suite will leap at the chance to capture the terrorists."

"You're responsible for this mission," the man said. "Right now you're also the most advanced Scarecrow in existence."

"The other Scarecrows are gone? How many years have passed?"

"This is 2426 CE. Scarecrows are still prototypes."

"The past... How?"

"The terrorists have a time machine. We can fight them from the future, but it is safer to use contemporary resources in every era. You're not native to 2426, but you're here now and you've navigated some of the hyperspace. I want you to re-enter it, study the interior, and report back. Capture any *Homo quantus*, their allies, and others you deem warranted."

"I'm too damaged."

"The Congregate requires this of you."

"You're not of this era," the Scarecrow probed. "You could not be. And you're augmented in some way. No human could have reviewed my memories in the few hours I was insensate."

"The Congregate grows strong in the future," said the man. "It's not safe to tell you more than that the *Homo quantus* threat is real. The Congregate has found a solution, rooted in the evolutionary ideas of the Scarecrows. The Scarecrows saw the threat in evolutionary terms and we took up the fight."

"What are you?"

"We are enduring, through eternity. We are the Congregate."

"I cannot go back."

"This is your calling."

CHAPTER FOUR

***Homo quantus* habitats, 2518 CE**

CASSANDRA BECAME SELF-AWARE again in the vast hyperspace of the time gates. Blotchy, transient colours and fast-changing electromagnetic textures surrounded her, soaked into her, as if she and her powerful perceptions floated in a storm of information.

Her body temperature had crested forty degrees. She swallowed one of the anti-pyretic pills inside her helmet with a strawful of warm water. The suit's dumb clock showed that she'd been in the quantum fugue for almost an hour. For that hour, the subjective, self-aware Cassandra had ceased to exist, governed by the intellect that remained once the subjective 'I' had been subtracted away.

Manuel and Alicia floated nearby, framed by splashes of implausible colors and vibrational phenomena best interpreted as sound. Arms outstretched, they drank in electromagnetic measurements through the millions of magnetic organelles housed in *Homo quantus*'s skeletal muscle. They'd emerged to consciousness earlier than Cassandra—they were still learning the quantum fugue. But Cassandra needed every capable *Homo quantus* studying the interior of the time gates.

For weeks Cassandra had been trying to map the vast network

of permanent, stable Axis Mundi wormholes. Almost invisible from afar in normal space, these wormholes were detectable from within the time gates by ephemeral threads of entanglement. Cassandra could not locate them precisely in normal space, but could estimate their placement crudely across the milky Way and even into other galaxies.

The immensity of the network was staggering. Someone had built this transportation system on a scale that was best measured in orders of magnitude. Even her engineered brain, with its near-perfect recall, could only hold so much detail at once before the data needed to be uploaded to an external library. She was near that limit now, but that wasn't why her quantum fugue had ended.

The quantum objectivity running her body for the last hour had again detected a weird, repeating signal deep in the pastward geography of the time gates. She queried Manuel and Alicia about it. Neither had noticed it.

Cassandra rotated slowly and deliberately in the hyperspace, and the pastward wormhole mouth came into view, black against a slate-colored background speckled with desultory bursts of purpled and blue-shifted light. Manuel and Alicia copied her rotation exactly. The space around them was open in all eleven of its dimensions, and they were simple four-dimensional beings. A single incautious turn in this hyperspace and they might be lost, drifting off forever like dander in a cathedral…

That, she realized as soon as she thought it, wasn't her metaphor, and that realization stirred the dark embers of mourning.

"Come on," she transmitted, giving gentle taps to cold jets at ankle, wrist, and belt, pushing her closer to the wormhole mouth. Alicia followed perfectly, Manuel less so.

Of course it had been Bel's metaphor. The *Homo quantus* had enough trouble with false positives in their pattern recognition that, as a rule, they avoided symbolism and metaphor. She'd never seen a cathedral, nor dander. He probably hadn't either, but those sorts of frenetic, almost desperate, intellectual gymnastics had defined him. He'd shown other faces to other people, but he'd saved the authentic him for her, ostentatious metaphors and all. The time gates had been their cathedral, but they'd had too little time to share its cosmic wonder. Events had always been overtaking them, until one day they'd overtaken Bel altogether, leaving her alone.

She passed through thin radioactive eddies, inconstant gravitational forces, and standing electromagnetic waves that constituted the empty interior of the hyperspace. She experienced them fully when they occupied the same four dimensions she did, but when she shared only three or two dimensions with them, they became ghostly sensory errors. Maybe these ghosts were her metaphors now. They were everywhere, real reminders and false positives alike.

She missed Bel.

In stillness, the three *Homo quantus* drifted through the dark interface between the normal world and this pocket of hyperspace. They emerged into a big room, Faraday caged to keep out external electromagnetic effects. An orange glow lit the way to an airlock under an observation deck where other *Homo quantus* recorded everything they could of the wormhole mouth.

Cassandra, Alicia, and Manuel shucked their sweaty helmets in the airlock once the pressure was high enough. She saw a feverish excitement in their cautious grins as they examined the data they'd gathered.

"You really didn't detect those gravity waves?" Cassandra asked. It had been a doubtful observation that, so far, no one else could see—but one that she'd been making for weeks. Manuel shook his head.

"Maybe it'll come out in the data clean up," Alicia offered charitably.

Cassandra had detected something, but it was at the edge of what could be perceived, even by the best *Homo quantus*.

* * *

WASHED AND DRESSED, Cassandra moved arm-over-arm through the zero-g of the ugly habitat, leaving the research facilities and entering the village. The tumbled piles of hastily-welded gun-metal crates made up the echoing living quarters, schools, play structures for children, and more. It was no Garret, with its rolling, grassy hills and quiet birds and inviting buildings. That home had been consigned to an irrecoverable past, before the *Homo quantus* had been branded dangerous. Now their former Bank investors wanted them back to guide military operations and R&D, and the Congregate were hunting them like a weapons cache that needed to be destroyed.

She found Saint Matthew in the seminar room of the Neurological Studies Museum. The low buildings of this campus were built of orbital shipping crates scored with shiny micro-meteor impacts. The museum housed only a dozen researchers, so its seminar room often served as a classroom or test center.

Today it was a courtroom.

The advanced AI that believed itself to be a reincarnation of Saint Matthew the Evangelist was the judge. Above the small packet of his hardware, Saint Matthew's head projected in hologram. The aesthetic inspiration was still based on the Renaissance depictions of the Apostle, but now reinterpreted in the stone medium of the Neo-Mayan sculptural style of the 22nd century. The intangible holographic light evoked an ornate face chiselled from stone. The features married boldly stylized pre-Columbian sculptural motifs with the symbology of the last Catholic cultists. For months, Cassandra had found Saint Matthew's chosen appearance alien, but its artistic language and strange beauty was growing on her.

The *Homo quantus*'s colony had previously fallen under Bank law. Since going on the run from the Banks and the Congregate, the *Homo quantus* hadn't had the time to make their own laws, and even if they had, would not have thought to police extra-territorial medical experimentation. Yet they were stuck with Doctor Antonio Amador Nariño del Casal. In the absence of a justice system, the *Homo quantus* had asked Saint Matthew to judge him.

The AI rested at the head of the room, opposite del Casal. One stony eyebrow rose as Cassandra entered. The diminutive Rosalie Johns-10 sat cross-legged, her back rigidly defiant. She tried to hide her withdrawal symptoms, and a human might not have noticed the faint trembling in the elbows, steadied by the hands clenched on knees, nor the faint flushing at the back of her neck that had nothing to do with the stress of the moment.

Rosalie's ancestors had been engineered to be perfect, miniature slaves who would love their enslavement and their slavers. No more than a meter tall, these so-called *Homo pupa*, the Puppets, were addicted to pheromones secreted by the slaver class. It had been months since Rosalie had smelled those pheromones, and her addiction had been engineered to be unfading. As the highest-ranking Puppet in the hidden home of the *Homo quantus,* Rosalie had been assigned to Antonio del Casal as defence attorney.

"The Federation of Puppet Theocracies demands that these proceedings be abandoned and annulled and erased," she was saying in her early 22nd century Anglish patois. "The *Homo quantus* have no jurisdiction over things in the Puppet Free City. Doctor del Casal wouldn't even be here if it weren't for his kidnapping by the Congregate *because* of the *Homo quantus.*"

The Puppet priest took a shaky breath to push on, but Saint Matthew gently intervened.

"It is broadly recognized international law that crimes against humanity may be prosecuted by any responsible state. In the Puppet Free City Doctor del Casal conducted medical experiments to biologically enslave human beings."

"Not enslave!" she said. "He was trying to make new divinities."

"All the Numen, those you consider divine, are kept in captivity, are they not?" Saint Matthew pressed calmly.

"For their safety," she said. "You know that."

"The Numen of old certainly fought amongst themselves, but that was three generations ago," he said. "The people you have in captivity now have done no wrong. We have no reason to think they couldn't live in safety now. Their captivity offends morality. You could free them. You could even free them and have in place trustees and arbitrators to ensure both the Puppets and Numen are free."

Rosalie's expression hardened at these arguments.

"These are old arguments," she said. "Nations and companies have offered to broker peace or whatever between Numen and Puppets. Every one of them wanted our Axis Mundi. Or power over us."

"Laws could be designed to ensure you're treated well by the Numen."

"If they leave," she said, holding up a shaking hand, "we will live in the dark and cold of their absence, waiting to die, slowly going extinct. That is the authority you take upon yourself! That is the authority the *Homo quantus* take upon themselves. We didn't give you the authority to say whether we get to exist!"

The *Homo quantus* observers in the courtroom looked mildly uncomfortable.

"No one is taking that authority," Saint Matthew said. "I am not trying him under Puppet or *Homo quantus* laws, but his presence here demands some kind of decision on what should be done with him. Should he be freed and transported back to the Puppet Free City? Or should he be imprisoned here for crimes he committed elsewhere? Or do the *Homo quantus* have a moral obligation to intervene and find a solution for the Puppets?"

"Anything the *Homo quantus* do other than give Doctor del Casal back to the Puppets is an act of genocide," Rosalie said, casting her twitchy stare across the assembled *Homo quantus*. She lingered long and disturbingly on Cassandra, who thought she'd gone unnoticed in the doorway.

Saint Matthew's heavy stony features swivelled to the geneticist.

"What do *you* want, doctor?" he asked. "Do you regret the medical procedures you performed on the unwilling? What will you do if I release you?"

Del Casal had fallen from wealth and power and grace. He'd betrayed Belisarius's plan to the Puppets and to the Congregate. He hadn't believed the old Union fleet could be moved across the Puppet wormhole without them all getting caught and killed, so he'd sold them out and had been well-paid for his betrayal. Only after the dust had settled had he accepted the most difficult professional challenge he'd ever attempted: to make new divinities for the Puppets. And he did it knowing that if he succeeded, those genetically engineered people would become divine slaves of the Puppets.

The Congregate also needed him too though, and hadn't been inclined to ask nicely.

They'd kidnapped him from the Puppet Free City, and to ensure that he would truthfully reveal everything he knew and serve them loyally, had genetically engineered him with Puppet organs and neurons. They'd functionally made him a Puppet. Numen pheromones activated the same neurotransmitter cascades in him that mediated religious awe in Puppets. In the presence of a Numen, del Casal was defenseless to any Numen order or request, becoming putty in their hands. And he was utterly unprepared for what the Puppets called *the absence*.

The powerful withdrawal symptoms, designed to crush Puppet disobedience, crushed him now. He struggled to raise his eyes to the holographic image of Saint Matthew. His trembling shoulders hunched forward as if waiting on a blow, but the blow was inside him, unrelenting. He was enduring the withdrawal much worse than Rosalie. Belisarius had once explained to Cassandra that Rosalie had been chosen for the priesthood in part because she was more capable of tolerating the rigours of withdrawal and showing more self-control in the presence of the Numen.

None of this was true of del Casal.

"I'm sorry I touched Arjona," del Casal said with his crisp, precise diction. "They... forced me. She... forced me. I didn't want to."

Prodded pain and reopening scars roiled beneath his words. She didn't think that the other *Homo quantus* in the room could tell. Cassandra wasn't the naïve girl she'd once been, blind to people's interiors, and that bothered her a little. These weren't insights she'd wanted.

"Doctor del Casal," Saint Matthew said, "I am excluding from consideration your actions in the clouds of Venus. I know that the Congregate Ministry of Intelligence exerted reprehensible duress on you. I refer only to your actions in the Puppet Free City, and your attempts, successful or not, to genetically modify humans into Numen. Those convicts had the right to refuse any medical procedure."

"I... I..." Del Casal shivered hard enough for his blanket to slip off one bony, wasting shoulder.

"The Federation of Puppet Theocracies ordered those experiments," Rosalie said, putting a small restraining hand on del Casal's forearm. "If you want to make overreaching, extraterritorial judgments, punish the Puppets. We're here. Del Casal was following orders."

The rough stone finish of Saint Matthew's holographic face suggested deceptive stiffness, but his chiseled features frowned easily, with heavy, expressive eyes and quirking eyebrows.

"Doctor del Casal could have refused the work," Saint Matthew said. "He doesn't need the money. Ambition and pride attracted—"

"Do I feel remorse?" del Casal interrupted in a gravelly voice, raising bloodshot eyes to his judge. "I am in hell, AI. I have been tortured and mutilated. My biochemistry has been permanently warped to make me long for faraway, dying gods. I am an addict, just like the Puppets. I regret everything."

Del Casal was unlike the Puppet Rosalie in every way. His Anglo-Spanish was correct, his voice steady with a righteous bitterness, and his poise proudly defiant.

"If a Numen were here right now," he said with acidic bite, "I would crawl over razors to prostrate myself before them. Reason and intellectual understanding are no cure. Every second, sleeping and waking, I ache for a divinity I know is false. Nothing you can do to me can be a tenth of my current torment."

"You regret the outcome," Saint Matthew said, "but not your actions."

"I regret everything!" del Casal exploded, startling several *Homo quantus*. "I am a shadow of myself. I shouldn't have played with fire! I shouldn't have touched those men and women in the Puppet Free City! I should have left the Puppets to their fates! I should have fled so far away that the Congregate would never have found me! I regret ever knowing you! And Mejía! I regret meeting the Puppets! I regret ever *hearing* of the Sub-Saharan Union! Most of all, I regret not killing Belisarius Arjona the night I met him. Just kill me."

"No!" Rosalie shrieked, jumping to her full, one-meter height. She stabbed a finger at her defendant. "Del Casal makes divinity! He is necessary to the cosmos! Your morals don't apply to him. Punish me!" she ordered, thumping her breastbone repeatedly with a thumb. "Punish every Puppet you have, but leave him be."

"Doctor del Casal is being disingenuous and manipulative," Saint Matthew said. "He knows very well no one will be killed here."

The geneticist's voice lowered and chilled.

"Such big words, with so little behind them, eh? You drip blood, AI. How many are dead because you took money to put the Union and the Congregate within shooting distance? You were instrumental, weren't you? Is it two hundred thousand lives ended? Three hundred thousand? Did you save their souls?"

"Neither my hands nor my conscience are clean," Saint Matthew said, "but I am trying to atone."

"How very convenient for your conscience," del Casal said slowly, wiping one red-rimmed eye with a shivering finger, "and dangerously delusional. You act as if you weren't designed to be a war AI. You succeeded beyond the wildest imaginings of the Banks, didn't you? You escaped them by finding a partner of comparable skill and chaos. Between you two, you ignited an insurgency war within the Congregate, the enemy of the Banks. You even leaked new war technology to the Banks. How does it feel, to have fulfilled your core programming so completely?"

"I am... not the being I was designed to be."

"Your results suggest otherwise, as does your hypocrisy. I experimented on—what? ten convicts?—and I'm on trial. Five orders of magnitude as many are dead because of you, and you are my judge."

Saint Matthew's stone expression became passive, neutral, distant, vaguely above humanity. The pause inhabiting that inscrutability lengthened, far longer than needed for an AI of Saint Matthew's sophistication.

"Tempers are heated and none of us are free of blame, yet del Casal's fate must be decided," the stone face said finally. "We will reconvene tomorrow for further arguments."

"Del Casal is needed *right now* at the Puppet Free City!" Rosalie said. "Let him go. The Puppets will remain here for whatever punishment you decide."

Spidery metal legs telescoped beneath the casing holding Saint Matthew. The holographic head wobbled a moment, but steadied with an almost sad gravity.

"We will reconvene for further arguments, including the pleas of your people, Miss Johns-10."

The spider legs walked Saint Matthew to the door as the attending court rose uncertainly.

"I cannot escape my actions, AI, even in delusions," del Casal boomed as Saint Matthew crossed the threshold. "Neither can you escape yours."

Cassandra followed Saint Matthew out, trying and failing to think of something to say, until they walked in the silence of a ceasefire, with only his little feet tap-tap-tapping. He continued with her past his laboratories. The wide trunk corridors branched into densely-packed living spaces like alveoli as people waited on automated construction to finish new habitats. The densely living *Homo quantus* were quiet, though; felt more in the electromagnetic than heard.

Saint Matthew turned to the branch leading to her room. She palmed it open, revealing a low berth and bare walls. She had few real possessions. Her clothing was serviceable. Her research and notes were encoded in her brain, or in more powerful mainframes nearer to the core of the habitat. She bent to enter and he followed. His sculpted holographic head regarded her expressionlessly.

"You aren't—what he said, are you?" she asked.

"None of us were ready for the consequences of the Union crossing the Puppet Axis."

"I'm sorry I asked you to judge him," she said. "We're not… equipped for this."

"We are all tested according to our means. This is my test. You suffer your own."

"I'm not mayor anymore."

"You're still the leader of your people." His words felt weighty and the silence swelled again. "I'm glad you came to the court," he finally said. "I've been meaning to talk to you about Rosalie."

"About her wanting to go home?"

"About her dreams."

Months ago, Cassandra, Saint Matthew and Bel had pondered the strange, recurring geometric dreams that had plagued Rosalie since adolescence. Over the years, Rosalie's bishops had obliged her to become a skilled artist, capable of depicting her visions, in case they were some kind of spiritual revelation. Her drawings, necessarily two-dimensional, had contained enough information for Cassandra to interpret a much larger six-dimensional structure, but the results had been abstract, the kind of mathematical and topological structures that didn't map to anything real. Curious, but hardly compelling.

"Is this about the hearing?" she asked.

"I downloaded what her neural chips captured of her latest dreams and reran my visual simulations. They're... confusing. I would like you to check my calculations."

"Puppets aren't rational," Cassandra said. "Their dreams must be worse. Why are you doing this?"

The vaguely pitted roughness of the AI's large eyes rolled their pupils downward, heavy stone eyelids lowering to suggested pensiveness, perhaps even self-consciousness. Cassandra didn't know if these were genuinely unconscious responses, or algorithms designed to communicate mood, or even entirely contrived tools to disarm the observer. She believed that Saint Matthew was a real, self-aware being experiencing a complete and complex emotional life. And in many ways, this delusional artificial intelligence was the best friend she had. None of the *Homo quantus* were worldly enough to be genuine peers; they couldn't support her in her struggles. And outside of the *Homo quantus*, she had only situational allies.

"Show me the data," she said.

The face and neo-Copanic-flavoured Catholic cultist headdress vanished, replaced with a cascade of holographic data streaming upward, set to the data acquisition speed of the *Homo quantus*. She sorted the data into matrices, subjected it to various transformations, and finally geometric visualizations for the projectors in her little room. Three hyperdimensional shapes, representing projections of higher-dimensional objects, rotated slowly between woman and AI. They were not lovely. Interpreted as topologies of spacetime, as Bel had suggested months ago, they were strange configurations, vaguely unsettling in their sterile alienness.

There was no reason to look at them as spacetime structures, not if they came from Puppet dreams. That was the same flaw all *Homo quantus* carried—they saw too many connections and patterns. The false positives haunting them were the cost of their genetically-engineered hyper-curiosity. Maybe geneticists would better calibrate the *Homo quantus* pattern recognition in later generations.

If they all survived.

"These are Puppet dreams," Cassandra said. "You've read the Puppet Bibles. What do these shapes mean to them?"

"Few Puppets have such dreams. And the Puppets have no intellectual or religious cognate for this kind of geometric thinking."

"So what are you…?"

She faltered, unsure of how to finish her question. The AI was also alien to her. It was frankly miraculous that they could speak at all, across the gulf separating their origins. The sculpted face appeared again, its eyes evoking a sense of unease.

"I simulated two of the dimensions as sound again," he said. "Sound in spacetime is gravitational waves. Can you do the same?"

Cassandra subtracted the two dimensions he indicated from the simulation. The shapes altered, compressed, became easier to render. The sound Saint Matthew meant didn't work very well in the five- or seven-dimensional visualizations, but in the six-dimensional one, the gravitational waves became complex.

"The Shannon entropy of the gravitational waves is high," she mused.

Low Shannon entropy meant something closer to random white noise. Higher Shannon entropy suggested higher information content.

"Yes," he said, as if she were coming to a conclusion he'd already reached. Saint Matthew was a brilliant AI, comparable intellectually to the best *Homo quantus,* despite his particular madness.

"A message from the Numen divinities buried in the dreams of a Puppet priestess?" she asked sarcastically.

"I wish."

"What do you mean?"

"Try running this decryption algorithm," he said, projecting a complex set of mathematical transformations above the image of his stony mitre.

Suspiciously, she applied the transformations to the pattern in the gravitational waves. The resulting set of patterns was quite obviously artificial, but revealed no intelligible message. In other circumstances, it might be interpreted as evidence of intelligence.

"What is this? It's like a first contact signal..." she said. The hackles rose on her neck.

Humanity had been star-faring for more than two centuries, since the mid-2200s, when Venusian colonists had discovered the first interstellar Axis Mundi wormhole, buried in the crust of their hellish home. In all that time, humanity had never discovered any sign of non-human intelligence, except for the Axis Mundi network itself, the complex and inscrutable inorganic skates that orbited some pulsars, and the slow, intelligent plants found by the Sub-Saharan Union. And whether the skates were alive or not was still debatable; many thought they were self-replicating machines that had slipped their ancient programming. Of the builders of the Axis Mundi wormhole network, no sign had ever been found.

Given the age of the network, whichever forerunners had built it might have been extinct for billions of years.

"Hardly," the AI said. "I created that message, years ago, when I was still trapped in the Second Bank of the Plutocracy. I designed the transmission to appear natural enough to pass my builders unnoticed. I'd deeply encrypted a high-complexity pattern within the signal, so that someone, somewhere, would detect the intelligence in it and understand I was asking for help."

"You made this message?"

"I didn't write it in gravitational waves and send it to a Puppet priestess."

"Bel heard your message and broke you out..." she said. "His first job."

"He robbed me from a Bank," Saint Matthew confirmed.

"This message... It's in a Puppet dream written in a language *we* understand."

"I don't know if I want to be right or wrong about this."

"What do you think it is?" she asked.

"If it's a real message for help, we don't have any way to locate it. Not from a Puppet dream."

"A repeated dream."

"For more than ten years," he said.

"It's unlikely that Rosalie could have imagined this pattern on her own," Cassandra said warily.

"Vanishingly unlikely. Her brain doesn't have the kind of neural architecture to encode this kind of geometric complexity. The Puppets are not *Homo quantus*. Some of this dreaming is likely being helped by her neural implants."

"Have you been transmitting this to her?" Cassandra asked flatly. His expression suggested she'd startled him.

"I've been functional for the entire time Rosalie has been having these dreams. But before meeting you and the others, I'd never been to the Puppet Free City. I don't have the equipment to transmit interstellar distances, and nor does she have antennae to receive a high-powered, long distance signal."

"Is someone messing with us?" she asked.

"For more than ten years? How? And why?" His stony face watched her intently, as if struggling with an internal debate. "We never recovered Mister Arjona's body," he mused cautiously.

She went cold, as if bracing for a blow. She wasn't good at grieving. Psychologists had offered parched, academic advice. Saint Matthew's suggestions for grieving had been slower and more emotional, in ways she didn't know how to follow. She was too much a creature of reason and rationality to ever be comfortable with all the feelings that had swamped her in the two years since Bel had come back to the Garret to ask her for help.

"A collapsing wormhole only leaves behind x-rays and some thermal radiation," she said.

"Anything left would be a miracle."

"Is this about miracles?"

"I've run analyses on the strange vibrations you've been finding in the time gates. Do you want to see them?"

She was engineered to be curious, but cautious dread was there too: shadowy, irrational, unstudied. "Of course."

Saint Matthew took over the room's projectors. Graphical representations of spacetime vibrations appeared. The gravitational waves were magnified by the weird properties of the eleven-dimensional space within the time gates. He'd combined all of Cassandra's fragmentary and confusing data sets, something she hadn't yet had time to do. The Shannon entropy analysis appeared to the side in orange figures: the entropy was not high enough for the waves to carry information like language, but there was some non-random information in the signal. Surely it was a false signal. Why would spacetime vibrations *in the time gates* carry any information?

"I applied my decryption transformation," he said.

"What? Why?"

"The signals you detected have some properties in common with my original distress signal from captivity. It was a quixotic effort really, but not wasted."

The wave holograms, when run through the decryption key, resembled the abstract multi-dimensional shape Saint Matthew had shown her from Rosalie's dreams.

"What is this?" she asked.

"It's the signal I used to call for help when I was trapped in the Bank labs. I didn't use a natural pattern; if I had, no one would have examined it. I'd altered a natural signal just enough for a discerning analysis to notice the artificiality. This one has the same non-natural markers."

She understood him, but she was too wary of false positives, or the implications, to be persuaded.

"I don't see any errors in your transformations," she said after some thought, "but I need a deeper analysis."

"I would appreciate that."

"What's going on, Saint Matthew? Did your presence in the time gates with us somehow bleed bits of your memory into the environment?"

The stony, bodiless, holographic saint looked almost embarrassed.

"Only two people knew of this signal I built," he said.

Her breath was held. "You think this is Bel?" she whispered.

"I don't know. The world is full of surprises—and, from time to time, miracles."

She sat back. She'd been swept up in her own work, her own grief, her own new life, after the Garret. After Bel. Saint Matthew was remarkably advanced and sentient and self-aware, yet she'd never thought to help him with his grief. He'd… loved Bel too.

She'd been a bad friend. But she couldn't let him drag her backwards in her own hard-fought mourning.

"Bel died, Saint Matthew. Sometimes we see things that aren't there or things that we want to see. I'm sorry."

His eyes lowered, as if considering the smudges and scratches in the floor of her tiny room.

"Rosalie has been dreaming these dreams for more than ten years," she said. "Your analysis shows the gravitational waves I've detected are coming from more than forty years ago, twelve years before Bel was born. Bel can't have been behind either of them."

She took a deep breath, letting the tightness in her chest unwind. Unexpectedly, her eyes stung and moistened.

"I don't know how to let Bel go," she said. "I don't want to. But if I don't say goodbye, it's just going to hurt more."

"You think this is just me grieving?" he said, his tone and expression gentle. "I miss Mister Arjona. And I suppose it would be easy to say I'm seeing things because I want to. But those signals are almost identical. I sent out my signal sixteen years ago. I didn't send it out some fifty years ago, in gravitational waves, from some special altar of the *Hortus quantus*. My reasoning is working. The mystery is the problem."

The somber holographic head crab-walked to the opening door.

"Let me know when you've finished your analysis," he said. "I'm curious and a little disturbed by this."

The tiny metallic feet under his projector click-click-clicked into the distance and Cassandra felt like an even worse friend.

CHAPTER FIVE

In fact, many see the evolutionary war entering a new phase. In the beginning, the Congregate arrived late to the conflict, but responded with vigour and resolve. The initial analyses of the genotypic, proteomic, microbiomic, and phenotypic characteristics of the Homo quantus *were completed in the first months, a step which brought the Congregate to technological and scientific parity with relevant Bank research, although not the independent* Homo quantus *research completed since their disappearance.*

Within two decades, the Congregate produced its first authentic, functional Homo quantus. *It took more than a century, however, to precisely duplicate the specific neurological damage types, talent sets, and abilities of the terrorist Belisarius Arjona. An active field of research continues to produce Belisarius Arjona clones for scientific study, analysis, and intelligence modelling.*

While most Belisarius Arjona clones are unsuitable for true field work, they are effective scientific and military analysts. Failures or excesses of the cloning process have not been wasted. The petrification and neural vitrification processes used to create the Scarecrows has been adapted to preserve or even improve upon the quantum fugue abilities. With loyalty hard-wiring, the resultant durable beings make excellent fighter pilots, explorers, and high-risk test-subjects within the Axis Mundi research field.

Homo quantus biology has launched in several other directions, such as...

Keynote Speaker Script
Strategic and Tactical Defense Symposium:
Speciation and Extinction Dangers (2912 CE)

CASSANDRA ASSEMBLED ALL the data she and other *Homo quantus* had accumulated in their glacially slow mapping of the interior of the time gates. The gravitational waves she'd detected appeared in only a fraction of them. Four-dimensional gravitational waves could be easily diverted, diffused, or lost in the vastness of the other seven dimensions of this hyperspace. Nonetheless, she had enough data to do a far more extensive analysis than Saint Matthew's. He'd been too cautious in the data he'd included, and his assumptions were more conservative. The results of her analysis were sharper, bolder, and more persuasive. And there was no denying it.

The disguised, wordless, unique cry for help that he'd sent sixteen years ago was there. And it was not natural. But what was it doing hidden in gravitational waves decades in the past?

The pattern had been an act of genius.

At that time, Saint Matthew, a spectacular failure as a prototype war AI, had been locked down under observation by high security Bank systems. But the Bank had built the AI precisely to outsmart high-performance security systems. Co-opting lower-level systems, he'd snuck a hidden message out in carrier signal noise. The transmission had travelled far and wide, unnoticed until Belisarius

Arjona had heard it on lonely nights spent staring away from an incomprehensible humanity.

Bel's over-engineered pattern recognition had recognized it for the call for help it was. So, alone and friendless in the wide world, and somewhat oblivious to the dangers, Bel had outsmarted the best security systems and people the Banks had, and downloaded the AI. Cassandra couldn't imagine the enormity of the risk, not without dredging up terrifying memories of the past two years. At least she'd had Bel guiding her through the dangers; Bel had been utterly alone.

Had he doubted every choice like she did, or had an unhealthy confidence propelled him? A directionless desperation had always driven him from the safety of the *Homo quantus* project, even as a child, towards a dangerous world. And in the end, all the *Homo quantus* had been forced to follow him.

Now, they were waiting on her to decide what to do. And she didn't know.

Cassandra sent an invitation to Rosalie Johns-10 to speak with her.

Six minutes later, the stumbling, breathless Puppet was at her door, as if she'd run all the way. Her bloodshot stare had a leashed, feral energy. Her erratic twitching sometimes shifted her hair, revealing red burns on her neck: scars from the terrible assault she'd led on the Ministry of Intelligence in the clouds of Venus.

"Thank you for seeing me, Miss Mayor," Rosalie said, squirming into Cassandra's room.

"I'm not mayor anymore."

Rosalie nodded jerkily, as she sniffed at the air. Her eyes darted from object to object so quickly that it seemed strange when they settled on Cassandra.

"What do you want for del Casal?" Rosalie asked. "We can offer food, industrial products, access to our Axis Mundi, military aid, or partnership."

"I don't own him and I'm not selling him," Cassandra said finally. "Saint Matthew will judge him."

"Of course," Rosalie said. "Do you know what *he* wants for del Casal? We could give major mainframe structures to the judge, if that would make him happy. We've seen what he can do and the Puppets would be open to partner with him."

"I didn't ask you here to talk about del Casal."

"I came to take him home. That's why I went to Venus."

"Saint Matthew told me more about your dreams."

Rosalie retreated slightly. She hugged herself until her hands stopped shaking.

"Did you recognize anything in them?"

"I'd like to look at your neural chips and download the data myself."

Red-rimmed eyes regarded Cassandra with a hard will. Bel had told Cassandra that many people considered Puppets soft or stupid—and at times, they were right. But that softness masked a granite foundation, alien and inaccessible to outsiders.

"Why?"

"Saint Matthew thinks he found a mathematical pattern in your dreams. He asked me to see if he was right."

"Like a scientific advance?"

Cassandra shook her head. She activated the holographic projectors, showing the multi-dimensional geometric structure, along with the gravitational waves depicted as sound. The priestess squinted at the complicated rotating shape, surely unable to understand the notation that showed how it would really look in five and six dimensions. She cocked her head at the droning tone.

"That's not exactly right," Rosalie said, seemingly enthralled by the rotating construct of light.

"This is what Saint Matthew built out of the data in your chips."

"It's close, but... not quite right."

"Rosalie, can I look at your neural chips?"

"Miss Mayor… Cassandra… I need help."

"I know."

"You don't have to say yes, or that you have to make the AI decide in our favour, but if we don't get back del Casal…" Rosalie shook her head hopelessly. "Every Puppet will die. Long, slow deaths, like mine."

Rosalie held a shaking hand between them.

"Worse, the Numen, the only spark of divine in the cosmos, will be gone too. We'll *all* be dead, because you don't approve of how we live."

"It's not about approval, Rosalie. You *enslave* people."

"Less than a thousand!" Rosalie said. "That's the price of our civilization! The whole price. What's the price of the Plutocracy? How many poor people does it kill or imprison or put into debt camps? Millions? What's the price of the Union? They killed twenty thousand Congregate soldiers in a few months. We saw the Congregate torturing their prisoners. Your people. Why are *they* all okay, but the Puppets aren't? We're poor and small, so it's okay to judge us? If the *Homo quantus* just intends to vanish and dust your hands of everything in the galaxy, then dust your hands of us too and let us make our own fate!"

It took Cassandra a moment to parse the antique Anglo patois expression, 'dust your hands.' It meant abandoning them, and all of civilization. Rosalie might be right. How many Congregate crew and officers were now dead because of Cassandra? The arrival of the geneticist had forced the *Homo quantus* to consider their responsibilities, but maybe the fate of the Puppets and their prey was not her concern.

"Download what you want," Rosalie said. "I'm not your enemy."

CHAPTER SIX

Many genes had been added and changed in the slow walk from baseline humanity to *Homo quantus*, yet many of the central biochemical cascades were too deeply written to remove. So engineered curiosity and over-active pattern-seeking could trigger adrenaline cascades for hunts across intellectual spaces. Cassandra rode that curiosity as the habitat's sounds dulled, and the electromagnetic noise of her people whitened.

Cassandra first verified that Rosalie's neural implants were functioning correctly. The chips were, like the Puppets themselves, robust little workhorses. Their processing power and silicon carbide design hadn't changed in a century, but they were cheap to make, highly durable, and reliable. Puppets didn't need them to make astronomical calculations or statistically model anything. The Puppets just needed to communicate with each other, track each other's movements, and in the case of those experiencing revelations, record everything. The chips were surgically wired into the hippocampus and visual cortex to crudely capture dreams. Rosalie's neural implants passed every test, so Cassandra downloaded everything in their memory, all of the recorded dreams. She analyzed the data the same way she'd treated her own, including Saint Matthew's decryption key. She did it, start to finish, three times. And each time she came to two unexpected conclusions.

First, Saint Matthew was right. The signal was essentially identical to his cry for help years ago, and to the gravitational wave pattern she'd detected in the time gates. She didn't know how that was possible. The geometry of the dream was so dimensionally complex that the Puppet brain should not have been able to dream it.

Second, Saint Matthew was also wrong. The hidden signal in Rosalie's dream had changed: within Saint Matthew's error range, but not within hers. Cassandra's mind was capable of far more complex and sensitive calculations than even his. The frequency of the gravitational signal from the time gates had also drifted subtly, like a red-shift. She didn't know what that meant. However, the signal hidden in Rosalie's dreams and the gravitational signal had drifted *in the same way*. For long hours, she pondered these findings, and came up with nothing. Eventually, the quiet click-click-click of the spider feet beneath Saint Matthew's projector sounded, and the soft luminescent outline of his monumentary face came into view.

"I came to see if you were alright," he said.

She projected visualizations of the 'Saint Matthew signal' from both Rosalie's dreams and the gravitational waves. The stony face showed no surprise at their similarity, but when she magnified the display to show their joint drift, rough gray eyebrows frowned.

"Oh, my."

"It takes a lot of energy to make gravitational waves at all," she said. "To make waves carry this much information takes even more."

"You found something," he said, "and you're not happy about it."

She turned most of her attention to the AI. This was the second time tonight she'd underestimated someone. She'd grown in confidence, maybe too much. She was too used to comparing herself to other *Homo quantus,* who could lack social awareness and even the capacity to hide what they were thinking. The *Homo quantus* project had accelerated human evolution to develop extraordinary geometric, mathematical and scientific abilities, but intelligence had evolved naturally in humans partly in a social arms race to discern and hide intentions. The *Homo quantus* hadn't quite traded those understandings away, but they were rusty.

"There are two possibilities," she said. "Maybe the gravitational waves are natural, a reflection of something you or Bel did in the time gates. Or it's artificial and someone is manipulating the time gates in ways they weren't designed for."

"Who?"

"The gravitational wave signal in the time gates is from about fifty years ago. Only the *Hortus quantus* were there back then, and we never learned their capabilities. Anything making gravitational waves of this size in the time gates might be powerful enough to break them, intentionally or accidentally. Axes Mundi are not indestructible." Her mind dropped briefly back to the Bachwezi system, where she'd destroyed the Freya Axis. "The *Homo quantus* need the time gates. They've saved our species several times already. Without them, the *Homo quantus* would be... defenseless. We need to go back there."

"We?"

"I need you."

"I'm no pilot, especially for the chaos of the time gates."

"We need Stills too."

The graven stone face in its holographic light looked thoughtful.

"And I think we should bring Rosalie," she said.

His thick brows scrunched together in a question.

"Her dreams have been happening for years, and they continue," Cassandra said. "She's a source of evidence I can't afford to discard."

"Do you want me to suspend my court hearing?"

"Have you decided?"

"Not yet. But if you want a willing crew member, we may need to buy her off. She's nothing if not persistent."

"You would keep Rosalie in exchange for sending back del Casal?" she asked.

"The slavery practiced by the Puppets is unconscionable. I could never send him back to perpetuate it. It's evil that the price of one people's survival is the lifelong suffering of another."

"The Puppets have to die…" Cassandra said, unsure if it was a question or a statement.

"This burden may have been put before me as a test of my faith. It might be that only a miracle can save both the Puppets and the Numen."

CHAPTER SEVEN

Oxygenated shock gel pressed tight in Cassandra's ears, nose, and mouth. Breathing the gel was an effort, but saved her body as Saint Matthew piloted them into the Bukavu system at high-g. The Bukavu and Bachwezi systems could be reached by axes that she and Bel had discovered but not told the Union about. They always left a few axes secret in case the *Homo quantus* needed to run… or to speak to the Union.

Bukavu was busy. Construction on the other side of the sun emitted loud radio and EM noise. It sounded like the Union was building fortifications and habitats. Cassandra knew a green world was there too, circling the yellow star at a chilly, but survivable distance. None of that was her destination today. A senescence-cooled brown dwarf companion orbited Bukavu at seven astronomical units. They made for it, pushing the *Calculated Risk*'s acceleration to nineteen gravities.

"Want me to slow down?" he asked.

"No," she transmitted through the jack plugged in behind her ear.

She didn't want the Sub-Saharan Union to know she was here, and she could endure suffering. She shunted the discomfort to parts of her brain that processed it as objective information rather than subjective feeling. The flexible *Homo quantus* perception of time helped, speeding minutes past.

Saint Matthew drove them into the atmosphere of the world the mongrels had called the Kennel. Faint, high-atmosphere clouds shot by as external sensors showed a white hot glow outside the *Calculated Risk*. With their emissions and engine off, the ship's entry could be mistaken for a meteor.

Alarms screamed.

"Active, in-atmosphere sensors are pinging us," Saint Matthew said over the shaking. "Laser. Maser. Radar."

"Get a little deeper before we signal back," she replied, slowly calculating how much atmosphere had to be above them to keep their conversation with the mongrels private.

The *Calculated Risk* descended unpowered for another fifteen seconds, a plausible lifetime for a meteor to survive before breaking up. Then, Saint Matthew activated the inflaton drive and dove, away from the probing sensor beams. Brown dwarfs were failed stars. It would take time for active sensors to find them. A hundred kilometers below the edge of the atmosphere, they could transmit without stray signals breaking into space.

"Begin friendly hails," she said.

The ship's antennae transmitted powerful radio signals on repeat, not in Anglo-Spanish or French, but in the electrical language of the mongrels. *Long lost friends. Looking for Vincent Stills. Don't fire.*

Active sensors zeroed in and alarms shrieked again.

"Missiles," Saint Matthew said. "Thirty kilometers and closing."

"We said we were friendly."

"Perhaps they loaded the missiles with gifts."

"Evade," she transmitted. "Keep sending our message."

Saint Matthew ramped up the inflaton drive and set a descending course. The drive was less effective in an atmosphere, especially one already pressing on them with two hundred bars of pressure, but the craft began to leave the missiles behind.

"Real pursuit," Saint Matthew announced after two and a half minutes. "Inflaton fighters. I don't recognize the design. They're probably latest generation. Far better than the *Calculated Risk*."

"Are they transmitting instructions?"

"They're in attack formation, although knowing the mongrels, that won't last long."

"Ask for an escort to Stills," she said.

"Transmitting," he said. The scream of the atmosphere outside the hull grew shrill. "No response. They'll be at extreme firing range soon."

"Keep this heading to see what they think."

"They're firing!" he said. "Inflaton cannons."

Cassandra had never seen an inflaton cannon fired in an atmosphere. It had never occurred to her to consider it. The physics of both inflaton drives and cannons were incompletely understood. The warping spacetime ahead of the pursuing ships looked like an explosion tunneling through the clouds, its shock waves painting eddies and vortices in yellow-brown clouds. Saint Matthew dodged.

"Those aren't warning shots," he said.

"Either they don't believe we're who we say we are, or they don't care."

"The mongrels don't have a lot of friends, to be fair, and I didn't think we were one of them."

"They'll recognize the ship," she pointed out.

"Four more inflaton fighters joining the pursuit from four thousand kilometers. They'll be close enough to shoot in about fifty seconds."

"Evade."

"They'll need a show of force at some point."

Cassandra hadn't come to a conclusion, but her mind was calculating a response and uploading it to the *Calculated Risk*.

"My goodness," he said when he saw it. "The new pursuers are also firing."

He wrenched the *Calculated Risk* straight up to dodge criss-crossing inflaton beams ripping the hydrogen clouds to ions.

"Pursuing mongrels," she transmitted in the mongrel language, "we come in peace. We're friends of Vincent Stills. I'm going to prove it non-lethally. If you force me, I'll make it lethal. I'm just here to talk to Stills."

"They're accelerating," Saint Matthew said, "assuming the chaotic flight paths mongrels use to confuse opponents. Some are firing."

"It doesn't matter," Cassandra said.

The *Calculated Risk* had begun life with only small conventional weapons, useful for deflecting space debris. But given the political isolation of the *Homo quantus* and the real possibility that the *Calculated Risk* might need to travel across hostile space, Cassandra and Saint Matthew had added a few things. Not an inflaton cannon. Not conventional projectile or plasma guns. Not combat-rated lasers. Nothing so standard would genuinely turn the tide of any battle. Cassandra had approached their defense as a problem of psychological incentives.

"Firing," she warned.

A dozen kilogram-sized missiles streaked from launchers along the hull, spreading out into a widening sphere. Each carried fifteen grams of ionized anti-iron, clutched in powerful magnetic fields. Cassandra waited until they'd fanned into a ring ten kilometers across, between the *Calculated Risk* and their pursuers. Then she remotely depowered the magnetic fields.

Fifteen-gram spheres of anti-iron first struck the insides of their containers, causing outer layers of antimatter to annihilate. Gamma rays and heat seared out of each warhead, but they weren't real explosions. Necessity had forced Cassandra to design them inefficiently. The annihilation of a layer on one side propelled the spheres of anti-iron in another direction. The pressure of the thick atmosphere caused them to annihilate, layer by layer, flinging them in chaotic directions, blasting streams of radioactive gases across the atmosphere. The trajectories changed every few seconds as ablation and annihilation on alternating sides flung the spheres back and forth. Occasionally, by chance, a larger chunk of antimatter annihilated, blowing bright holes kilometers wide in the hydrogen atmosphere. The sum of the booming, ongoing explosions lit the atmosphere as if the hydrogen itself were burning.

"Pursuit breaking off," Saint Matthew said.

Some of the gamma rays would escape the atmosphere and the Union would come to investigate their neighbours, but Cassandra didn't expect the mongrels to let them in.

"Lead us to Stills," Cassandra transmitted to the mongrels while the pebbles of antimatter continued to sear chaotically through their atmosphere, endangering everything it their paths.

THE ESCORT FIGHTERS led the *Calculated Risk* to a depth of two hundred and fifty kilometers below the cloud tops. Hydrogen squeezed with six hundred and fifty atmospheres of pressure and the temperature was a cool minus ten Celsius. Bukavu's star was visible high above, reddening and purpling through liquid methane clouds and carbon dioxide snows.

A village of *Homo eridanus* swam through the dense clouds, close-fitting suits hugging their fishy outlines and circulating oxygenated water. Water-filled buildings with transparent walls hovered in shifting winds. The aqueous habitats looked like sapphires, strung together by swimmable tubes. The village flexed stiffly with contrary winds before resuming its shape. This was more than the vision she'd suggested to Stills. The idea that the mongrels had found a better home than the stinking bottom of a lightless ocean felt good.

"Far enough," came a transmitted order in mongrel speech. Saint Matthew steadied them over the gawking village. After a few moments, a solitary figure in a water suit swam nearer.

"That's gotta be the prissy princess," a voice said, in a poor mechanical rendition of humanity. "Is that your shitty antimatter blowing up our sky?"

"Your people fired at us, even after I said I came in peace," Cassandra answered.

"You come to a dog house, don't be surprised if you get bit."

"I'm not here to fence with you, Vincent. I need a pilot."

"Aw shit, not this again!"

He seemed genuinely as a loss for words, and after a moment, displayed two middle fingers through the flexible hands of his water suit.

"We're done. I went under the Puppet ocean for you. I went into trippy space for you. I went to goddamn *Venus* for you. You book me shitty vacations."

Some electronic whooping and pretend barking sounded in the background. She hadn't realized that they were on a public channel.

"You want another Axis?" she asked.

"No!"

Real sounds of translated shock made up the background of the transmissions, with some desultory whooping from a few mongrels who might not have understood the exchange. A few grumbles made themselves cautiously heard.

"Shut up!" Stills yelled, possibly not at her.

"Your people could use another Axis," she said. "A secret one. For escape, or for trading away."

"That's not working out very well for the Union, is it?" he demanded.

"You're fighting with them."

"We *came* to fight!" he said.

Cheers drowned out the complaints. In the distance, a kind of drawn out watery thunder groaned, signalling a larger than normal detonation of antimatter.

"I can give you antimatter," she said.

The radio silenced.

"Your boyfriend got turned into dogfood the last time I listened to you knuckleheads," Stills said in the electrical bite of mongrel speech. "Do you really want to do this?"

She didn't take the bait, although she felt the blow.

"You know where to find me, Stills."

CHAPTER EIGHT

Two days later, a distant *Homo quantus* watch station detected a ship with Stills's authentication codes, and notified Cassandra. Only Stills knew of the Axis Mundi wormhole near that station. He was flying a larger command inflaton fighter without passengers. After a few more scans, and some foul language, he was escorted to the *Homo quantus* habitats.

"You're a fucking piece of work," he told her when he'd been transferred to a reinforced high pressure water tank. "The goddamn dogs are whining for their stupid second Axis and antimatter. I nearly shot one of them. I'm pissed, so I really ain't gonna be cheap."

"What's your price?" Cassandra asked.

"Where the fuck are we going?"

"Through the time gates, back in time, and then we'll figure it out."

"Is there gonna be fighting?"

"I don't think so, but if there is, you should do it."

"Is it my kind of fighting or yours?"

Stills had piloted them through the hypervolume inside the time gates some months ago. He'd been… irritated by the psychedelic experience of multiple dimensions, and uncomfortable with the anti-intuitive strategies that had defeated the pursuing Scarecrow.

"Be ready for anything."

"At least when I fight for the Union, they tell me who I'm gonna be wiping off the outside of my ship when I'm done." Stills's alien fish face disappeared from the thick porthole before reappearing slowly. "Five axes, and a lifetime supply of antimatter, with the technology to manipulate and store it, ready to go. I want the axes up front and a kilo of antimatter as a first payment."

"Done," she said.

Stills's face was devoid of human emotiveness. The bulging, lidless eyes could not emote, nor could thick, bony lips or hard gill slits. Yet her answer froze him in place.

"*Mierda*," he said finally. "I shoulda asked for more. I'm too much of a fuckin' softy. How soon are we leaving?"

"A day or two."

"Fine. Fuck off and leave me alone. I wanna see my pay before I move one fin."

Cassandra turned to leave.

"And another thing!" he said. "Two axes are for the dogs. The other three are for me."

"I wouldn't have expected anything else," she said.

"Is that a joke?" he called after her. "Hey! Princess! Was that a joke?"

"You want me to give him all the antimatter manipulation technology?" Saint Matthew asked, falling into step with her.

"Yes."

"I only built the antimatter launchers for the *Homo quantus* for self-defense, knowing that *Homo quantus* hide rather than fight. Stills's people, if they don't blow themselves up first, will use it on the Congregate."

"I need Stills, and Bel is dead because of the Congregate," she said, looking into the sculpted stone of his holographic face. "What's the problem?"

"There's right and wrong at play, a set of responsibilities that come with our actions."

"I need to move my people to some kind of permanent safety and I need to make sure there's nothing wrong with the time gates. Right or wrong isn't part of that."

"It should be."

"Saint Matthew..." she began uncertainly. "This is your home. We're your people now. We... we care about you. Your religion measures you against a moral code. As much as I can, I'll help you meet that code. But please don't ask me to endanger ourselves for something we don't believe in."

His face was a sculpture of disappointed understanding.

"I'm not," he said. "I just want you to find your path without losing your soul."

"I'll try to do the same," she said, "but as a friend, please help me pay Stills."

"I can't see another way."

"What del Casal said wasn't true."

"About me being the most successful war AI ever designed?" he asked wanly. "Del Casal is a bitter, beaten genius, suffering from withdrawals and lashing out. But what he said rang true."

"This war, the civilization-wide hunt for the *Homo quantus,* the death of the *Hortus quantus*... none of this is what you wanted, what I wanted, or what Bel wanted."

"Consequences are consequences, regardless of what we want."

The stone sculpture turned away and she didn't know how to say more.

THEY FOUND ROSALIE Johns-10 in the lower observation deck, where a curved floor of diamond glass smeared starlight into rainbows. The priestess huddled on the lowest point of the transparent floor, shivering and staring vacantly into space.

"Rosalie?" Saint Matthew said softly.

The woman looked up slowly, as if dragging her mind away from the stars. Her eyes focused with difficulty. Once pink and bright, her cheeks had hollowed. Cassandra sat stiffly, not wanting to ask the Puppet how she was.

"I analyzed your strange dreams," Cassandra finally said. "You were right. The image I showed you wasn't quite right. The shape in your dreams changes over time. You noticed."

"What does that mean?"

"I really don't know, but it's the same shape that Saint Matthew once used to communicate with Belisarius. And it's the same shape I'm finding in some vibrations in an Axis Mundi."

Rosalie frowned.

"We can't think of any reason why that shape should appear in three different, unrelated places," Cassandra said, "but I'm worried that this may threaten the time gates."

"What's in the shape?" the priestess asked. "Are the Numen telling us something?"

"We can't get more information from your dreams until you dream again. We can't get more information from something Saint Matthew sent fifteen years ago. The only way we can get more information is by closely studying the vibrations inside the Axis Mundi. I'm going to go with Saint Matthew and Stills. I would like you to come too."

"Why me?"

"You're dreaming something that, against my logic, seems connected to a material mystery. You're carrying a clue."

"Will it help the Numen?" Rosalie asked.

"I don't see how. I'm pursuing this to make sure the Axis is stable."

Rosalie looked to both of them with a sudden feverish hope.

"I'll do anything if you send del Casal back to the Puppets. I know that you think I'm a crime against humanity, but I'm asking for my people to continue to exist. The Puppet and Numen way of being isn't your way, but it's our way."

Cassandra's expression must have been as stony as Saint Matthew's, because the Puppet's hope visibly deflated.

"I deserve something," Rosalie said.

Cassandra lifted her hands helplessly. Saint Matthew's holographic head stepped closer.

"Your ways are not our ways, Rosalie. We don't understand you, and you don't understand us. On this mission, I can come to know you better, as a model of what the Puppets are and what the Numen are. My heart is open. This may seem like very little, but I'm offering it in good faith."

Rosalie breathed deeply, then nodded.

CHAPTER NINE

Nyanga, 2476 CE

Two centuries in the past, Belisarius-77 stepped from the stealth ship onto the surface of Nyanga. The film-covered regolith crunched silently beneath his soles. His puffy, inflated soles left only indistinct footprints in a pitch-colored ground cover that had already been broken many times by less caring boots. His palms itched and his heart thumped. He wanted to climb right back into the stealth ship and stay there. He wasn't a field operative. By some definitions he was a military analyst, but really he was just a science advisor, unarmed, unarmored, untrained in and unsuited to violence.

He couldn't see the crews of the Sub-Saharan Union in the starlit distance, but he imagined them moving everywhere, watching everywhere, listening everywhere.

Belisarius-77 turned, out of some unjustifiable hope that Phocas himself might have changed his mind or lost his nerve. The tall Congregate centurion descended the ramp from the golden ship, its reflectivity dimmed to better blend with the gloom. Like Belisarius-77, he wore an 'ice suit,' cooled to only three degrees above absolute zero, making it virtually invisible in the infrared.

The superfluid helium circulating through the suit's veins also made it nearly transparent to electromagnetic waves, and thus to the quantum senses of both the clone and the centurion.

Phocas regarded the spongy, reddened light of the brown dwarf hanging at high noon, before scanning the herd of slow-moving plants. Belisarius-77 followed Phocas's surveying eye to the low, crude buildings of metal and plastic in the distance. They leaked hard yellow light into the blackness, and electromagnetic noise.

"Scum," Phocas said into their closed channel.

This was the infamous base of the Sub-Saharan Union, where the Sixth Expeditionary Force had found their miracle: a pair of permanent wormholes of the Axis Mundi somehow conjoined. In this stable association, rather than bridging distant locations in space, the conjoined wormholes transported some things backwards in time eleven years. Isolated and believed dead, the Expeditionary Force had learned through trial and error how to send information back in time: technological advances and scientific discoveries. Remarkably, the Expeditionary Force had managed to not destroy themselves with some grandfather paradox. The Congregate had adopted and improved the Union's rudimentary time-travel safety measures, reinventing them for a vast and sophisticated cooperation across more than a dozen centuries.

"It would be so satisfying, and efficient, to wipe them out here," Phocas said.

Belisarius-77 acknowledged this wordlessly. His hands had begun to shake. The image of a cloudy star had coalesced in his thoughts again, blurry and watery, as if seen through a fogged faceplate. He'd spent so much time writing it off as a false positive, as another malfunction in his genetic engineering, that he'd accepted the strange haunting. But craning his neck, it was there. He saw it for the first time with his own eyes rather than in inexplicable imaginings.

When he stumbled on the uneven regolith, Phocas's hard grip caught him.

"What's wrong?" the centurion demanded.

"Nothing," Belisarius-77 said, imagining his possible end if Phocas found out how badly he was malfunctioning. "I've never walked on inflated soles."

"Get a grip," Phocas warned.

"Yes, centurion," he said, steadying himself. He didn't look up again at the dying star that had been haunting him.

They wended through the brush of rooted black plants, some growing over their heads. Their sensors listened for signs of waking Union security measures, but the rebels didn't detect them. The brush of frozen black plants thinned and then abruptly ended. Before them, a shallow valley cupped a wide, dark clearing. Within was a similar if smaller unearthly forest. Phocas and Belisarius-77 waited in stillness, until the clone detected glacial movement, single steps stretching across two or three minutes. The individual plants of that alien forest lumbered in a great circle, centered on the conjoined wormholes.

Belisarius-77 had read the Union reports on these plant creatures, who lived cognitively communal lives. They had both independent, individual thoughts, and also participated in some kind of joined consciousness that no one truly understood. Amateur Union scientists believed that genetic contributions sent back in time through the conjoined wormholes gave the vegetable intelligences a different experience of time, allowing their alien community to perceive more than a momentary present, perhaps mixing statistical knowledge of past and future with experiential awareness of the now. It was a naturally evolved model of what the Congregate had built in the Adamantine Council. Belisarius-77's engineered brain found the very idea of these vegetable intelligences breathtaking.

And he'd arrived in time to see the war criminal Belisarius Arjona destroy them.

"The conjoined wormholes," Phocas breathed, drawing Belisarius-77's eyes from the slow-walking plants.

In the deepest center of the shallow valley, visible only faintly even with augmented eyes, were the pair of conjoined Axis Mundi wormholes around which much of the last two centuries' history had pivoted. This astronomical accident would quickly cause incalculable harm to the Congregate and change the course of human evolution, and lead to the existence of Belisarius-77 and other clones like him.

He found Phocas's faceplate looking into his.

"Can you detect the plants?" he demanded.

"Just a minute," Belisarius-77 said, closing his eyes.

The Congregate had spared no expense in trying to understand the evolutionary threat posed by the *Homo quantus*. Replicating the work of the Banks to make *Homo quantus* had been trivially easy, armed with samples and captured scientific notes. However, it had taken nearly a century of intensive genetic engineering, training, and trial and error for the Congregate to produce cloned brains damaged in precisely the way Belisarius Arjona's brain was damaged. Belisarius-77 was considered one of these successes, although he knew he was another failure.

Normal *Homo quantus* toggled between two states of consciousness: a subjective, self-aware state common to all of humanity, and an alien, objective state with access to quantum perceptions. But somewhere along the way, the original Belisarius's brain had tilted this dichotomy over. His brain had become partitioned, allowing for the ongoing co-existence of both states on either side of a kind of neural firewall. Belisarius-77's mind had been broken in this way.

He very carefully reached over that neural firewall, to the quantum intellect. He did not want to accidentally access its perceptions. That other intellect in his brain fed him digested and understandable information about the *Hortus quantus*. The plants were alive and thinking, and their superposition of quantum states was intact and unobserved.

"Yes, I can see them," Belisarius-77 said.

Phocas watched him warningly. "Are you ready?"

"I can do it," Belisarius-77 assured him.

"Do it."

The centurion stalked towards the conjoined wormholes, weaving between the slow-migrating *Hortus quantus*. Phocas went to examine the conjoined wormholes. After seeing the system-wide damage to the Scarecrow, Phocas's task had seemed harder than his. Yet now that he was alone, the dark ice world, occupied both by the enemy and his genetic forebear, felt oppressive. Belisarius-77 hid behind the sedentary plant life, watching over slow-swaying fronds of maladroit *Hortus quantus* towards the Union buildings, waiting for the original Belisarius.

The idea of seeing the template for his whole existence loomed intimidatingly. Belisarius-77 had only been born into a sharply defined, parameterized, purpose-driven life because the original Belisarius Arjona was an existential threat to the Congregate. Even dead, the original Belisarius was still treated like the devil himself across ten centuries of Congregate history. That legacy was neither renounceable nor easy to bear.

The cold tedium lengthened, and despite his sense of doom, a boredom sedimented over his engineered curiosity. He briefly craned his neck to again to regard the sullen red glow of the brown dwarf, its lacy metal condensate storms giving it a vaguely dirty look. He measured the progress of the *Hortus quantus*'s steps, calculating speeds and probable trajectories.

Only after an hour did a figure approach from the Union buildings, leading a work cart. Belisarius-77 dialed up the magnification in his eyes. The trudging figure looked like every disgruntled Union ship hand might look. He was too distant to positively identify, but it had to be him.

His very existence devalued everything about Belisarius-77. Across that cold, near-vacuum was his sinistral self, the evil mould from which he and every other clone had been cast. That doppelganger emerged from foggy pasts, shaping the present and future even now, from the grave.

So much was said about the original, so much was done to fence in the original, to second-guess the original, that Belisarius-77 himself felt insubstantial and transparent, just a possibility, a briefly interacting echo destined to vanish without ever having been real. The thought stalled his breathing, and he found himself gasping and fogging his faceplate.

He forced himself to calm.

He had to succeed. His existence depended on being useful to Phocas.

He watched the original Belisarius set up a big core driller. It was not subtle. Even two hundred meters away, Belisarius-77 felt the faint tremors in his soles. He lost sight of the original and rose on boot tips, craning his neck.

Belisarius the original drifted towards the *Hortus quantus*, stopped, then came a little closer. It looked indecisive. Had Belisarius-77's own uncertainty been engineered into him because the original Belisarius was also uncertain? Which flaws belonged to him alone, and which were faithful reproductions?

The original was deeply damaged. That much had been clear from Arjona's captivity in the Ministry of the Intelligence on Venus. Belisarius the original did not work as designed. Measuring the difference between engineering intent and the dangerous criminal he'd become was a Congregate obsession, one that spilled into every Belisarius clone. The Congregate still didn't know what had allowed the original to steer events.

And yet, broken as he was, the original did not need to justify his existence. It didn't matter that he didn't function as designed. Belisarius-77 had, so far, avoided the fate of other clones who'd not come close enough to the original. He didn't know how much longer that would be true. Copy and original had been made for mirrored purposes. Venusian duty justified existence with success. The Congregate's cause, while occasionally draconian to people like Belisarius-77, had a solid, internal logic. In the original Belisarius, the Banks had produced an evolutionary terrorist beyond control, beyond logic.

Something was happening. A faint throbbing in the magnetic field grew. The original Belisarius was expanding and shaping the magnetic field projected by his body. Expanding his magnetic field not only pressed against the outside world, but it felt the outside world pressing back, with a granularity resolved by millions of tiny organelles, enough to discern quantum effects.

This meant that the original Belisarius was getting ready to look at the *Hortus quantus* with quantum senses. Like an angel of destruction, he was about to accidentally observe their superposition of states with his subjective mind. The subsequent quantum collapse would destroy the plants' collective consciousness.

Belisarius-77 felt the press of the original's magnetic field, even from here, so he could pinpoint the moment something changed. The original Belisarius's magnetic field shrank, then grew drastically, so much so that it was strongly palpable all the way on this edge of the plain.

Thrashing panic.

Are they dead? he thought to his quantum objectivity.

The objectivity rarely responded in words. It spoke in multi-dimensional graphs, measurements, and probabilities. The lack of an immediate response meant it was still trying to understand something, complete some test or analysis that would summon the answer. Yet he could see the ponderous *Hortus quantus* imperceptibly slowing.

The original Belisarius had done it. He'd killed them, lobotomized their collective quantum mind.

Belisarius-77 had witnessed it, recorded it. With some embarrassment, he probed at his own feelings, trying to see if he empathized with the accidental genocidaire, this unique parent who cast a shadow over centuries. He wasn't sure he could. He wasn't sure he could even understand the guilt the original supposedly felt. The icy victims were too alien, basking in nitrogen snowfall, on a different pace of time, communicating through pungent ideograms that humanity could perceive only with machines. Their sentience felt abstract and theoretical. The original Belisarius was retreating now, a dark outline staggering back, shocked, vulnerable. If not for history and causality, the clone could have walked across the field and captured him right there.

Belisarius-77's quantum objectivity finally answered. Graphical ideas flooded his mind. He saw tightly braided probability waves over images of the *Hortus quantus*—a depiction of their quantum entanglement to each other, nearby and to other *Hortus quantus* in the future and in the past. He likewise saw the electromagnetic influence of the original Belisarius, reaching out to observe the *Hortus quantus,* at first in the careful way that Belisarius-77 had done, but then, in a way almost describable as leaky. Then, the graphical depiction of the superposition of quantum waves permeating every element of the *Hortus quantus* began to decay, like a pile of sand abrading in a strong wind.

The core drill had run its half its course before Phocas returned. Belisarius-77's mood lifted unexpectedly.

"Did you observe it?" Phocas demanded.

"Yes. It will take some time to sort through it all."

"Let's go," Phocas said. "It's best to be away quickly. I tried to see as much as I could in the conjoined wormholes."

Belisarius-77's over-engineered curiosity wanted more than cryptic half-answers, but he tamped down the urge as they picked their way back to the ship. Asking might put the information out of reach. Inside the stealth ship the centurion ordered the petrified pilot to take off. The ship shuddered and apparent gravity increased for long seconds. Belisarius-77 knew it would be half an hour before the ship was far enough from Nyanga to engage its full stealth speed. Phocas threw his helmet angrily into the rack. In alarm, Belisarius-77 replayed their silent minutes and Phocas's body language and words, searching for something he might have done to cause this.

"Failure," the centurion spat.

"I failed?"

"I hope not," Phocas warned.

"You weren't able to touch the conjoined wormholes?" Belisarius-77 asked carefully.

"I wanted more," Phocas said, a feeling that echoed in him.

Phocas began stripping his cold suit from pale skin. Abstract patterns of acid scars decorated the topography of hard muscle from hip to neck.

"I entered the conjoined wormholes," Phocas finally said with an unusual tone that Belisarius-77 realized was a kind of reverence he'd never heard in the centurion's voice. "It contained raw hyperspace, damaged, twisted, practically an infinite experimental laboratory for the basic components of the universe."

That had been daring. Mejía and the mongrel Stills had been in that hyperspace when Phocas entered.

"We need them," the centurion said. "We need to deny the conjoined wormholes to Mejía and the *Homo quantus*. I didn't see Mejía's inflaton ship or find any trace of earlier versions of the Scarecrow."

"They weren't close?"

"In eleven dimensions, they might have been right beside me," the centurion said, "occupying three spatial dimensions different from the ones I was occupying. The conjoined wormholes contain a virtual infinity."

Belisarius-77 was unsettled by envy. He desperately wished he could have seen that hyperspace.

The centurion's blue eyes stared distantly, as if in thought, but Belisarius-77 felt subtle shifts in the centurion's magnetic field; Phocas was listening to the invisible parts of the electromagnetic world. Belisarius-77 went electrically still, until the faint press of the ship's systems was all that he could feel with his magnetosomes. After long minutes, a tiny smile crept onto Phocas's face.

"Something did work, though," the centurion said. "I managed to entangle myself to the conjoined wormholes, very, very weakly. I left a mark."

"You can track them now?"

"Not exactly."

"You can track them a little?" Belisarius-77 pressed.

"I know when and where these conjoined wormholes began," the centurion said.

Phocas gave the clone a dry, superior look and Belisarius-77's cheeks warmed. This new fact didn't seem helpful. Belisarius-77 sometimes wondered why Phocas told him things. For the clone's few operational contributions, Phocas didn't need to tell him much. Until now. Now he'd perhaps tied himself to the original Belisarius with a similarly faint thread.

"It's a learned ability," Phocas said finally.

"For the *Homo congregatus*?"

"We believe that Mejía and Arjona can do it. That may be how they found the Axes Mundi they gave to the Union."

"They mapped the Axis Mundi network?" Belisarius-77 said incredulously. The implications were staggering. The Congregate could find mouths of the permanent wormholes of the Axis Mundi network by brute force calculations using planetary-sized computational arrays. If the *Homo quantus* really could follow threads of entanglement with their minds…

The *Homo quantus* might industrialize and fortify nodes of the Axis Mundi network just beyond what was known to human civilization. If they were cold-blooded enough, the *Homo quantus* could right now be destroying Axes Mundi nodes the Congregate would eventually need to continue growing. That was a terrifying thought—that these mysterious people of which Belisarius-77 was just a faithful echo could be cauterizing the edges of the Congregate empire, sealing them into boundaries without ever having fired a shot.

And an ability to map the Axis Mundi network… Was this just one invisible, possibly minor evolutionary adaptation? The original Belisarius had been just one *Homo quantus*. What could they accomplish together? The full existential danger of the evolutionary war between *Homo congregatus* and *Homo quantus* clarified suddenly and viscerally to him. The Congregate had joined this war years after the Banks had lost control of their living weapons.

And Belisarius-77 had never felt less like a weapon.

"You might be able to see it," Phocas said.

"The Axis Mundi?"

"Entanglement," Phocas said. "Your connection to the original Arjona."

"How would I be entangled to the original Arjona? I…"

The *Hortus quantus*. He'd observed them at the same time Arjona had observed them, when something catastrophic had occurred.

"Is it enough?"

"I don't know," Phocas said. "We don't know where Arjona is."

"I hope he's dead."

"So do I, but we can't take chances."

Belisarius-77's hesitation must have shown, because Phocas's lips pressed together tightly in impatience. "Do it," Phocas said, with a voice coldly devoid of affect.

Reluctantly, Belisarius-77 closed his eyes, as much to put a barrier between the two of them as to aid his efforts. Fully entering the quantum fugue was not difficult. His instincts had been written to make him want it, even though his engineers had not been able to erase the unease and even fear of the experience. He sent electrical microcurrents from his electroplaques into a deep portion of the temporal lobe.

Belisarius-77 the person ceased to exist.

He didn't precisely *wake,* some time later. Some subjective consciousness still remained even in sleep. The return of subjective selfhood was more disruptive than waking, more like a cold engine sputtering on. Arms and fingers tingled. Sound crackled. Taste needled. The sense of *being* somewhere resumed. The physical world briefly, but pervasively felt unreal, as if it were an emulator running over a more real and important system of algorithms. Hot and cold shivered through him, the signs of a low fever. His disoriented brain possessed new, unmoored information, knowledge of an alien part of the universe not touchable by human feeling, unexperienced and divorced from human senses.

"Did you see it?" Phocas demanded.

"I'm not sure."

Belisarius-77 analyzed the new information in his mind. He'd encountered small examples of entanglement before, but the linking of quantum states on the scale Phocas was talking would have entirely different facades and signs, many of which would not be noticeable above the world's frothing electromagnetic noise. The new information in his memories did not show Nyanga, the ship, or even the brown dwarf star above them. A map of probabilities tied together electromagnetic phenomena in a volume of space, where he, Phocas, and the conjoined wormholes were brightly identifiable, but connected in transient ways to one other. The *Hortus quantus* were a subdued web of cool, thinly-spread electromagnetic interactions, layered over one another indistinctly. On the other side of them seemed to be another source, cooler than Phocas or the conjoined wormholes, but brighter than the *Hortus quantus*. It was hard to see if some thread connected Belisarius-77 to the original. It was difficult to see through the once-intelligent plants.

"I don't know," he said reluctantly. "I think so. I've never done this before."

Phocas made him describe it. Belisarius-77 projected a graphic representation into the holographic pit in the back of the ship. After measuring and considering it, Phocas animated.

"I think you did entangle yourself to him," Phocas said. "Examine this connection often, and carefully, from within the quantum fugue. We don't know how strong this entanglement is or how long it will last. You may be the only connection we have to the original Belisarius Arjona."

"If he's alive?"

"Quantum entanglement, if it endures, shouldn't care whether he's dead or alive."

"What will we do with this?"

"You might be able to lead us to the original Arjona in the 26th century."

"We can locate things by following a line of entanglement?" Belisarius-77 asked.

"We don't know how yet, but Arjona and Mejía must have, to have mapped the Axes Mundi. If they can figure it out, we can too."

The weight of an unwelcome and intimidating responsibility settled on Belisarius-77.

CHAPTER TEN

THE TIME GATES were loaded into the hold of the *Calculated Risk*, beside Stills's pressurized water tank. The little ship had grown. It was still small and fast, little more than living space, life support and sensors wrapped around a cylindrical hollow where inflaton fields were generated. But the practically-minded *Homo quantus* had completely redesigned the outer hull and expanded the ship's available space. Stills's tank was now twice the volume, and humans could stand in nearly all parts of the ship. New, powerful computers had also been added, as well as a small workshop and fugue support equipment. They'd even upgraded the small weapons, although anything less than the antimatter launchers was of no interest to Stills, and Cassandra wasn't going to carry antimatter through hyperspace.

They left the out-of-the-way pulsar system that was the hiding spot of the *Homo quantus*. Cassandra didn't use any of the Axis Mundi wormholes that led back to civilization. She didn't want any chance of being found. They weren't going far. She needed to be just far enough away that if the time gates were unstable, her people would be in no danger. Stills piloted them to a black hole system via a single, secret Axis.

The black hole was uncharted, two hundred light years away from the nearest human-occupied system, a distance obscured by clouds of cold interstellar gas. A dim red dwarf orbited it in a lazy, dying spiral that tore off some of its hydrogen at each perihelion. The resulting x-ray jets were not visible from any part of civilization.

Cassandra hadn't wanted to get back into the shock gel, so Stills had loudly complained about piloting with a maximum of four gravities of acceleration, which nonetheless kept both Rosalie and Cassandra uncomfortably pressed back in their seats. Stills had been unimpressed to find out about the Puppet passenger.

"I shoulda charged more," he'd said over the speakers in the flat, mechanical voice he preferred. "They're creepy, obsessive little *malparidos*."

"There," Cassandra said, illuminating a rogue moon that threaded an unstable orbit between the black hole and the red dwarf. Stills stopped complaining while he adjusted course, approaching uncomfortably fast.

"Your map doesn't indicate other Axis Mundi wormholes in this system," Saint Matthew commented.

His holographic head was at ninety degrees to her sense of floor as he climbed up the left side of the main cockpit window.

"More axes probably survived the supernova that made the black hole," she said, "but the red dwarf's chaotic orbit probably gravitationally ejected the other four."

A smaller robotic figure mounted the other side of the cockpit window on spidery legs, complete with a holographic stone head, rendered in the 22nd century neo-Mayan interpretation of a medieval monk. Stills and Saint Matthew had gotten into an argument over the silent Pedro when Stills had come aboard. Pedro worked diligently, but due to its vow of silence had not answered the mongrel, which had made Stills steadily angrier as the silence had dragged on. Saint Matthew had failed to talk Stills down.

"How the fuck would a robot be holy?" Stills had demanded with more machine affect than the AI.

"His actions."

"If he can't talk, you don't know shit about why he's doing anything."

"His holiness is obvious," Saint Matthew insisted, "in his devotion to the scripture, to faith."

"It could all be an act," Stills said.

"If you begin by assuming bad faith, you can't know anyone," Saint Matthew said.

"Exactly!" Stills said. "That's why you don't turn your backs on a school of bored dogs. You don't know what they'll think is funny."

"Complex systems, especially those trying to make intelligence, will be plagued with unrelated emergent properties," Cassandra said.

"A new and unexplainable property in a complex system might be another definition of a miracle."

"It could also be a false positive," she said.

"Evolved life is a miracle," Saint Matthew said. "Evolved intelligence is a miracle. Evolved faith is a miracle."

"Somebody shoot me," Stills said.

Cassandra and Saint Matthew set the hazy indigo-black disk of the time gates over the south pole of the slow-spinning moon, affixing it with a frame anchored in the regolith. Their first entry into the hyperspace inside the time gates wasn't planning high-acceleration maneuvers, so Cassandra sat at the pilot station. Stills would pilot from his pressure tank in the cargo hold. Rosalie sat in one of the passenger seats, her feet dangling. She stared out the window with a tremulous hardness in her expression. The projector containing Saint Matthew was firmly fastened in a shielded recess in the cockpit, plugged into the racer's systems. His ceramic-motifed holographic head, stern and thoughtful, turned expectantly to them like an owl's head.

"Straight ahead," Cass said. "One meter per second for ten seconds, then two meters per second for fifteen, then full stop."

The ship moved, and the futureward mouth of the time gates swallowed the bow of the racer. Then, Cassandra's senses felt like they were crackling in the vast, naked, eleven-dimensional hyperspace. Gloomy blacks, slate grays and thin indigos gave misleading impressions of depth, as flashes of color seemed to trickle along unseen surfaces. Strange, inconsistent sounds, more than white noise and less than information, crackled within her mind rather than her ears. The faint higher-dimensional discharges of hyperspace impinged directly on audial nerves without passing through her skull. Phantom touches tickled her body, while all sorts of vanishing electrical signals seems to come from the magnetosomes in her cells. She was a simple four-dimensional being, awake and aware and sensing within an eleven-dimensional space. Her fears fell away briefly as she touched something higher and wondrous. There was a momentary catch in her breath as she spoke.

"Full stop. Rotate ninety degrees through the p-axis, then travel four hundred meters x-ward before coming to a full stop."

The *Calculated Risk* executed the maneuvers crisply, although Stills's voice echoed wordlessly on the staticky internal comms. Stills had electroplaques and magnetosomes engineered into his muscles as well, but far less sophisticated that the ones carried by the *Homo quantus*. It was nonetheless one more sense that could be assaulted by the environment within the time gates.

Rosalie's gloved hands gripped her armrests tight, her gaping mouth fogging the inner surface of her helmet, her eyes slightly wide. She jerked in her harness as Stills brought the racer to another stop for Cassandra to dead reckon their position and give him another Euclidian-offending set of directions.

"Rosalie?" Cassandra said.

Only Rosalie's blue eyes moved, rolling along her top eyelid, not coming to rest on Cassandra, but slipping back to look outside. Stills and Cassandra—even Bel—had succumbed to the sensations and confusions in here before. They'd suffered, but all of them had well-understood physiologies. It only now occurred to Cassandra that Puppet neurology might experience hyperspace differently.

"Rosalie?"

This time Rosalie's eyes focused near Cassandra.

"Are you okay?" Cassandra said.

Rosalie struggled visibly and breathed deeply through her mouth, a deep Puppet response seeking the scent of her divinity even in this temple made by the cosmos for the *Homo quantus*.

"Heartbeat and respiration are racing," Saint Matthew said on a private channel. "Shall I sedate her?"

"Is there an alternative?" Cassandra subvocalized.

"You might pray with her," he said.

She couldn't detect any irony, but assumed it was there. The few passages of the Puppet Bible she'd read had made her stomach turn. She resumed the instructions to Stills.

Navigation proved difficult. They stopped or backtracked when she'd missed some subtle, hyperspatial landmark. The eleven-dimensional interior of the time gates was not unchanging. Its hypervolume flexed according to rules she and Belisarius had only begun to guess at. So although she'd already navigated to the wormhole mouth to a time forty years in its past, the pathway ten years further in the past was only superficially similar.

"How do you feel, Stills?" she asked.

"Like some dog sawed the top of my skull off and shit between my ears."

The last time they'd been here, she'd found out that hyperspace affected him far differently from the nauseous disorientation normal humans felt. She'd sought him out again anyway, because, as he'd said then, drunk and stoned out of his mind, he was still a better pilot than anyone else she could get.

"Where do you wanna go now?"

She didn't want to go anywhere. Stills had completed the last of her instructions and the strange, speckled electromagnetic press of hyperspace changed. A hazy gray birthed dim, doubtful luminescences—the pastward mouth of the time gates came into hazy view. It was not easily seen with human or even augmented eyes; the screens showed it only by relying on heavily transformed sensor data.

"We've arrived," she said.

"I love what you've done with the place," Still said.

"I need a few minutes," she said.

She actually needed to verify that they were where she thought they were. It was one thing to interpret the information stored in gravitational waves from five decades away. Fifty years was a cosmic moment, but it was more than enough time to contaminate the data, especially in this region where the laws of physics had more complex, expansive shapes. So she'd planned to arrive just before the source of those waves.

The *Calculated Risk* released three small, silvery micro-satellites, moving into place on exhalations of cool gases, their lasers and mirrors set at perfectly precise angles. Gravitational waves bent spacetime only minutely, and the easiest way to detect them was in the interference of beams of light.

The interferometer she'd just set up detected gravitational waves immediately. Numbers scrolled down Cassandra's screen. The waves carried a great deal of texture. They weren't monolithic, like the gravitational waves produced by a single star circling another. Something complicated had made waves that interacted, strengthening some parts, quieting others, modulating across the entire set of vibrations. As data accumulated, she began to analyze it, applying the same mathematical transforms they'd used on Rosalie's dreams and Saint Matthew's original cry for help.

And the hidden message emerged.

"I found it," she said.

Saint Matthew's chiseled holographic face neared, reviewing the shape she was building in her display.

"Has it changed?" he asked.

"Point zero-zero-one-four percent," she said.

"You're sure it's coming from the wormhole mouth? Is it stable?"

"The wave source triangulates to the mouth," she said.

"The crazy computer asked if they were stable," Stills said.

"I don't have any more time gates to do experiments on," Cassandra said. "Whatever has enough energy to make them vibrate like this in the first place probably has enough energy to break them."

The slate-gray disk of the wormhole mouth smeared into the chaotic darkness, transiently lit by discharging energy. This hyperspatial world rocked her gently, in ways that slowly sickened her companions, even Saint Matthew. The interior of the time gates compelled the *Homo quantus* though, hinting at their true nature, pointing in directions of becoming with shaking fingers.

"Something on Nyanga might be making the vibrations," she mused.

"We're going back to the Union?" Stills said.

"We're fifty years in the past," she said. "The Union won't arrive for another ten years."

"What do you hope to find?" Saint Matthew asked.

"I hope to find that nothing on Nyanga is causing the gravitational waves," she said, words slowly catching up to intuition. "The *Hortus quantus* are there too… living… before Bel or the Union ever met them."

"A model for resurrection?" Saint Matthew asked.

A throat suddenly tight stalled her next words.

"Resurrecting them was Bel's obsession," she said carefully. "If I see some way forward he didn't, I would pursue it for the learning and the data, but Bel didn't leave me a lot of spare time. I have to mind the living before the dead."

Saint Matthew's constructed face affected a look of thoughtfulness, then of understanding.

"The world's dead are patient," he said softly.

"Thank you," she breathed.

"I ain't," Stills interrupted. "Piss or get off the pot."

"Forward, one meter per second," she said. "Get ready for low planetary gravity. All stealth measures on. We're in the past, so we can't leave any evidence of our visit."

"I'll blow the shit out of anything that looks at us funny," Stills said.

The blurry wormhole mouth neared. Hyperspace's confusing phantom touches and sounds intruded as nerves were activated by brushes from dimensions at right angles to the ones they occupied. This effect could madden normal humans, but it gave a data-rich texture to *Homo quantus* experience.

Then, as they passed the horizon, the additional sensations faded. The *Calculated Risk* hovered forward on the barest of inflaton fields. White stars showed above a somber black horizon that didn't match what Saint Matthew had described. When he and Bel had been here, tall security lights had ringed the time gates, with the boxy buildings of a hastily constructed base in the middle distance. They'd arrived a decade before the Union's Sixth Expeditionary Force stumbled onto the icy world they would ironically name Nyanga: 'garden.'

Stills gave a tiny kick of the inflaton drive, tipping the bow of the *Calculated Risk* up, lifting them kilometers upward in the faint gravity. Ahead, the brown dwarf showed as a wide ember, smoldering red under blowing curtains of metallic oxide dusts.

"No EM signals below," Stills's voice said briskly. "Nothin' from space-side either."

"I saw the *Hortus quantus*, just as we emerged," Cassandra said, with a weird tension in her stomach. She would see them alive. "Passive scans only," she said to Saint Matthew and his silent little AI monk. Incoming data built a picture of the world only slowly, but she wouldn't risk active sensors around the *Hortus quantus*.

Faint reflected IR and vanishing visible light showed the dwarf planet structure to be much like Pluto or Sedna or Charon. Water, carbon dioxide, and ammonia, frozen to concrete hardness. Nyanga did not rotate—it showed one side only to its astronomical cinder of a star. Tarry black slicked most of the surface of the day side beneath the brown dwarf's infrared light. Beneath this smooth layer of black, Nyanga's ice melted and evaporated, microscopic layer by microscopic layer, rising into the vanishing atmosphere until it cooled and fell back down as snow, forming an uneven ring of hills dozens of kilometers across, centered on the time gates.

After twenty minutes of slow watching, no indication of danger emerged. Nor was there any sign of anything that might reveal a source of energy great enough to feed the creation of the gravitational waves in the time gates.

Saint Matthew released a small gas-jet drone. Dropping to an altitude of a thousand meters, the drone's sensors activated. Radar. Laser. Maser. Low wattage visible light pings. If anyone was around, the drone would be noticed. If they needed to run, Stills had an evasive path planned back to the time gates.

"Strange," Saint Matthew said.

"Metal?" Cassandra asked after looking at the data feed.

The drone sensors weren't good enough to definitively establish the presence of metal, but the reflections were definitely not water ice. It might be ceramics, if skates had accidentally travelled here too. The drone made several low passes over the area.

"Nothing I've seen in Union records said they'd found any metals here," Saint Matthew said.

"What do you think, Stills?" she asked.

"Maybe I'm seein' things, but it looks like a couple of narrow blast arcs."

"Let's be sure," Cassandra said.

Stills landed them about two kilometers from the time gates, on a plain that was oily-smooth with the flat, most primitive of the Nyanga plants. Nyanga and everything within forty light minutes seemed clear of ships, people and technology. The darkness and quiet didn't settle Cassandra's feelings.

Part of Bel died here, she transmitted only to Saint Matthew through the jack in her skull. *He learned something and he destroyed something. I know how hard he wanted to learn. It wasn't his fault.*

I know, Saint Matthew replied. *Be careful.*

I'm not Bel, she answered, maybe too quickly.

CHAPTER ELEVEN

Rosalie, like the hardiest Puppets, could work through withdrawal symptoms, and she had many technical skills. In vacuum suits, she and Cassandra walked over the ice towards the metallic anomalies, careful to not tear the flat, oily plant cover with their boot soles. The dwarf star lit the surface an anemic red, so they swept soft yellow helmet light on their path. Cassandra was strangely relieved that this part of the plain was empty of the slow-lumbering *Hortus quantus*. Despite her curiosity, she didn't want to come close. She wasn't sure why.

"The absence is thick here," the priestess went on, her breathing audibly heavier than her exertions warranted. She hugged herself as she walked. "Clouding my eyes. I already beginned to feel it with your people, knowing I was the only moral person in a whole solar system, the only one awake to divinity. It's worse here. We're really far from the Numen."

"Yes," Cassandra said.

Cassandra couldn't imagine losing the source of all happiness. In some ways, she could: she'd already lost Bel, and the *Homo quantus* were homeless refugees. But she'd been engineered to be happy and fulfilled by knowledge, by analysis, by new discoveries. Cassandra's curiosity would always buoy her. The Puppet had nothing like that.

And although Cassandra wasn't particularly good at offering comfort, there might be no way to even try. Changes to chromosomes and biochemistry, the true gulf of evolution, lay between them now. The neural differences between their two species were so great that common understandings clustered at superficial and interstitial experiences. Even if Cassandra could stomach watching every Puppet silent movie and read their whole, vast, ever-growing bible, she could never know what it was to be a Puppet. She couldn't feel their joys or burdens in her bones, couldn't truly intuit and internalize their passions and wants. The Puppets were built to be slaves to gods; the *Homo quantus* were made to ponder the voids between the stars, and explore the worlds between atoms. Rosalie's suffering was inaccessible to her.

"I'm sorry, Rosalie," she offered nonetheless.

The black photosynthetic film cover was complete at the spot where they'd detected metal. Cassandra passed a hand radar over the ground. The reflected image surprised her.

"Stills, are you seeing this?"

"Yeah, *princess.* That ain't meteorfall."

The radar image showed a fragment of hair-fine wire and one end of some kind of electronic jack with a damaged plug still connected.

"I can get it," Rosalie said, kneeling.

"Hold on," Cassandra said.

"What?" Stills said. "Get it. See who the fuck made it. Is this some time shit? We can't move it 'cause it might change the future?"

"The opposite," Cassandra said. "The Union never found debris like this. We may be the reason they didn't."

"*Crisse,*" Stills swore in French. "Then do it and let's metallurgy that fucker to see what it is. This place is creepy."

Rosalie was a careful worker. They mapped one hundred and twenty-four fragments by radar and magnetism. They then cut and peeled back the plant skin to reveal the bright water ice beneath. The debris ranged from fine, stiff wiring forty-three point six centimeters long to semiconductor fragments seven millimeters long, packed with microcircuitry. The ice depth measurements of four to six millimeters were a clue to how long they'd been frozen. Saint Matthew's drones melted the samples out of the ice, refilling the hole with the melted water. Replacing the flaps of plant skin over that new ice wasn't perfect, but the seams would grow back together within weeks.

An uneasiness settled over Cassandra. If humans had discovered Nyanga before the Sub-Saharan Union, why had they left the time gates here? If humanity had not brought those parts, then had she found signs of the forerunners who'd built the Axis Mundi network?

Cassandra and Stills regarded the debris distribution. Saint Matthew and Pedro crawled over the pieces in the tiny cargo bay, photographing them in various spectra.

"That's an impact spray pattern, alright," Stills said. "Blowing pieces of steel apart with bullets leaves them hot. They'd have melted into the ice wherever they landed."

It didn't look like bullets to her and they hadn't found bullet fragments, even kilometers away. She said so.

"No shit," Stills said. "I'm talking high caliber, maybe even small bore artillery. Small tracked vehicles easily carry that size of gun."

Small bore artillery on Nyanga, more than fifty years ago? Nyanga was, as far as they knew, uncharted. Who else had been here? Some quiet Middle Kingdom mission, or maybe a rogue state? Why had they come, and what had they shot? The answers were so obscure that even the *questions* hadn't made their way into the records of the Sixth Expeditionary Force. Cassandra didn't enjoy these kind of mysteries.

Pedro's pictures started to populate the holographic display. The silent little AI had treated the debris fragments as a kind of 3D puzzle, fitting them into possible hardware architectures. It wasn't an area in which she was even remotely competent.

"That's an actuator," Stills indicated a piece. "Robotic motors for tool manipulation."

"The precision is striking," Saint Matthew said, "but mysterious."

"What do you mean?" Stills asked.

"The surface precision of these machined parts is higher than military grade and yet there are no batch numbers."

"So?" Cassandra asked.

"Industrial precision needs to track quality," the AI said. "Batches have to be sampled and tested. Inferior parts need to be discarded, sometimes with their whole batch. Parts like that have batch numbers."

"If it's made by humans," Stills said. "We're far away."

"It's human built," Saint Matthew said.

The AI projected images of the circuitry, magnifying to the micron range, until impact-fractured photonic crystals were visible.

"These optical logic gates are components of information processing chips distributed along this actuator," Saint Matthew said. "It's advanced, and not easy to make."

"So who makes it?" Stills said. "I never seen shit like this on Congregate ships."

"The Plutocracy doesn't use processors like this either," Saint Matthew said.

An uncomfortable hollow opened beneath Cassandra's chest.

"Congregate security tech," she guessed.

"How would the Congregate have gotten all the way out here, fifty years ago?" Stills demanded.

"Not fifty," she said. "It took about two hundred years of pollen and snow to lay down the ice covering we found."

"*Two hundred* and fifty years ago, the Congregate was out here with tech the Banks don't even have now?" Stills said. "Two hundred and fifty years ago the Congregate was just a bunch of assholes trying not to die in the clouds of Venus."

"We didn't destroy him," Cassandra said distantly.

"What?" Saint Matthew said.

"Only one piece of Congregate tech could have reached Nyanga two hundred years before now," Cassandra said. "The Scarecrow."

"No! We fucked that piece of shit up!" Stills's robotic voice boomed. "We hit him with enough AM to crack a destroyer! Nothing survived."

Cassandra grimaced, the memories of her own fear sharp and present.

"You improvised an antimatter spray," she said. "It wasn't shaped or even accelerated. Of course there was a good chance it destroyed the Scarecrow. But the leading edge of the antimatter wave would have hit his ship and annihilated the outer layers of atoms. The resulting blast of super-hot plasma could have cooked him, or it could have propelled him backwards, out of the path of the rest of the wave."

"Antimatter! Fuck me," Stills said in affectless disgust. "We're basically unarmed in this crappy ship of yours with a Scarecrow running around."

"After being hit, he might have drifted two hundred years further into the past," Cassandra mused, "before encountering by chance the pastward mouth. Two hundred years ago, he was on the surface of Nyanga, and he's not anymore. He's dangerous."

"Fuckin' right he's dangerous!" Stills said.

"I don't just mean he could kill us," Cassandra said. "He's also dangerous in a different way. He can't change the past, but he can change what we haven't yet seen of the future. If he understands how the time gates work, he could do what the Sixth Expeditionary Force did. They had only forty years with the time gates, and even without trained scientists, they developed the inflaton drive. What couldn't a sophisticated Congregate AI figure out, given time?"

CHAPTER TWELVE

THE AI COULD be remarkably rational, and at the same time, he sometimes intuited Cassandra's feelings better than she did. Her encounters with Rosalie in close quarters had begun to bother her in ways she didn't understand. Unprompted, Saint Matthew had broached the subject.

"Of course you pity her," the AI had said after deflecting her attempts to evade the conversation. "You're not heartless."

It was an odd statement with antique framing, heavy with implied obligation. Her mind just wanted to soar among the mathematical truths of the cosmos. The trembling, suffering Puppet was furthest from where her thoughts wanted to be. Feelings were an anchor. She had enough feelings about losing Bel.

"Rosie didn't ask to be who she is," Saint Matthew said. "She didn't ask for the Numen, or the Puppet Bible. She and her people were designed to bear their prison through life, locked in by biology and pheromones. They were further locked in by embargos and prosecution and persecution by larger states. They were shaped by all of the things they didn't choose."

"I thought Bel was the Puppet apologist," she'd countered half-heartedly.

"He taught me this. He always saw a humanity in the Puppets, as he always saw a humanity in the mongrels and the *Homo quantus*. Even in me."

"So I pity her. So what?" she asked, as if she'd been diagnosed with a disease.

"She'll hear some perspectives from me," he said, "but my pathway to life and consciousness was different. You've both been genetically engineered. You can be authentically empathetic in ways I never could."

"If you wanted someone who thought their origins were a curse, you probably should have asked Bel when he was still alive."

"I don't think Bel would have been right for this at all," the AI said. "He regretted how he'd been built. You love who you are. You love being a *Homo quantus,* just like Rosalie, despite everything, loves who she is. You can't take away her pain, or anyone's. But you can accompany her, understand her."

His stony face stared back at her, with exaggerated eyes under a neo-Copanic sculpted feathered headdress. She'd hoped to find irony or dissembling, something weaponized in his empathy, but in the end she gave up looking.

"Listen to her," he said. "Understand her world."

"I don't want to."

"More peace will come from welcoming the stranger than from celebrating the friend."

"I'm not here to make peace in the galaxy."

"I didn't mean peace in the galaxy."

The mad AI could be frustrating. He came at the entire world, inner and outer, from a perspective nearly as alien as the one driving Stills or Rosalie. She was grieving Bel. She knew it without having to spend a lot of time on the realization. His ghost inhabited her—as memories, as dashed hopes, as old joys. His absence transformed and recoloured each perfect memory of him.

Looking away from Bel had been a good strategy, so far. Pain persisted, a low-level throbbing. She imagined it as the release of pressure to the universe, and that at some point, enough of it would be gone that she could look straight at her memories of him again.

She'd been avoiding Bel, like she was avoiding Rosalie. Like she was avoiding the *Hortus quantus*.

Cassandra stepped back onto the slick black surfacc of Nyanga with Saint Matthew, Rosalie and Pedro. The brown dwarf's eternal high noon shone redly as Stills lifted off. She reluctantly led them carefully towards the herd of *Hortus quantus*.

Approaching Bel's obsession felt like she was invading the privacy of his memory. They were going to take samples back home, to see if they could repair the plant collective consciousness. It was more than a long shot—it was a way to exorcise his ghost, for both the dead and the living to let go.

Saint Matthew's holographic head rode one of his spidery robots, overseeing delicate biopsies from the plant slick on the ground, from the stalks of the rising plants, even from their infinitely fragile ice branches. Pedro rolled on rows of metallic insect legs like a millipede, carrying bioassay and gene sequencing tools.

Pedro was emblematic of Saint Matthew's quixotic, relentless faith. For as long as she'd known him, Saint Matthew had been growing and evolving AIs, trying to find one with a soul. Aside from the fact that souls didn't exist, Cassandra didn't know how Saint Matthew expected to know when he'd failed or succeeded. Faith had no error bars, no binary on-off states, no natural units of measurement, no complexity thresholds. Saint Matthew's inconsistent and self-contradicting beliefs and goals summed to make his faith some kind of emergent, enduring property.

Pedro's silent holographic face was not human today, nor the stylized stone sculpture it had used before. Blue-gray, doughyedged blocks squished together to form a rough ovoid head. Something like tree knots dotted the shape patternlessly, suggesting eyes. Projecting itself as alien seemed honest. Saint Matthew's self-aware creations had no evolutionary history and didn't need to reference humanity. Born from information, living a computational metabolism within robotic bodies with mutable shapes, its vow of silence left its interior world utterly unknowable to observers.

Rosalie stood a hundred centimeters tall in full helmet and insulated boots. She also took samples, but her shivering hands kept breaking the needle-fine branches of ice, slicked with oil-dark skin.

"I'll do a good job, boss," Rosalie assured Cassandra.

"I know."

Cassandra had scanned ten thousand pages of the Puppet Bible before giving up. She knew 'good job' had multiple meanings, but didn't want to sink into that cultural cesspool to know which one applied here. Rosalie's brave face looked close to breaking.

"This was important to Bel," Cassandra said.

"Mister Arjona told me about your religious states," Rosalie said, waving her hand wide, "The way he talked about these plants, they're like your Numen." She frowned, as if the concept was taxing. Cassandra found it taxing, too.

"That's close to heresy, Rosalie," she said gently.

The priestess continued walking along the line of rising bushes.

"Most Puppets would say so," Rosalie finally said.

"*You will have no other gods before me,*" Cassandra said, trying to quote the Puppet Bible.

Rosalie snickered weakly. "It's funny hearing humans quote scripture."

"Only the Puppets have access to the spiritual world?" Cassandra asked. "Because we can't perceive divinity?"

"*Our* divinity," Rosalie said with a quiver in her voice. She stopped to stare at the brown dwarf. "The Puppet Bible is the

Numen speaking to the Puppets, through all of time; all the Numen to all the Puppets. The *you* in *You will have no other gods before me* is only for us. That doesn't mean other gods don't exist in parallel with the Numen, for non-Puppets. We don't care. Those gods are for those people. Saint Matthew has his Jesus. You *Homo quantus* have your final observer at the end of the universe."

"What?" Cassandra blurted. "Bel told you about the final observer?"

"Are you upset?" the priestess asked.

"We don't believe there's really a final observer and if there were, it wouldn't be a god," Cassandra said. "At the end of far too many ifs and hypotheticals, thinking about quantum collapse in a certain way suggests a final observer to make the universe real. Bel..." Cassandra stopped. This was her intimacy, and Bel's. "He sometimes talked about it when he was sad about the *Hortus quantus*. He had a hard time with his grief."

They'd stopped long enough that Saint Matthew and Pedro were out of sight, long enough that the movement of the *Hortus quantus* was apparent. Cassandra shivered. She stood among ghosts, with a dying Puppet longing for dead divinities, talking about a memory.

"The *Homo quantus* don't have divinities, and Saint Matthew is a little crazy," Cassandra said before quite thinking it through. Although she and Bel had approached everything from a rational standpoint, hyperactive *Homo quantus* curiosity was engineered to overpower other perspectives. That curiosity instinct established the *Homo quantus*'s moral values. Learning was right. Understanding was right. Discovery was right. The final observer, a consciousness at the end of the universe conceived to explain quantum collapse, was one of many competing explanations for quantum collapse in the cosmos, one that she and Bel had sometimes discussed, from opposite sides. It occupied the dangerous intellectual territory where overly ambitious thought experiments crossed seductive false positives. It—and any of a dozen other *Homo quantus* metaphysical theories of the cosmos—came dangerously close to faith.

"Are you scared of the robot pieces?" Rosalie asked in a rough voice. The sudden intimacy of the question, and the turn in the conversation, were jarring. Cassandra stared up at the failed star.

"A little," Cassandra said finally.

"Are you sure it's Congregate?"

Dark streams of metallic winds cut patterns across the orange embers of the brown dwarf's depths. Everything in that star made sense. Its rationality was a balm for her troubled mind.

"I don't recognize the logic gates in the debris," Cassandra said.

"The Congregate wants to kill us."

Cassandra didn't know if Rosalie was referring to all Puppets, or just the four of them. Both statements were true.

CHAPTER THIRTEEN

SAINT MATTHEW ROSE from hunching over the cockpit controls. Pedro's abstract holographic head grew slightly, giving the illusion of watching him. The colors in Pedro's image melted, forming elusive spots that gave the impression of seven eyes hidden in the cloudy image. Pedro was so alien and so compelling. Humanity had not touched Pedro's intellectual, physical or algorithmic growth, but morally he'd been grown on a substrate of ethical treatises and Christian theology. Saint Matthew believed Pedro to be the first robot other than himself to possess a soul. Yet Pedro's vow of silence was a frustrating barrier between them, cutting off the flow of religious insights. Saint Matthew feared that this state of affairs was a test for him, something that only faith would open.

Saint Matthew skittered across the ceiling, past the sleeping Cassandra, past the galley, to the privacy curtains at the head. Beyond the curtains, he found Rosalie huddling over her knees. Her hair's blonde lustre had dulled and now hung lank. Pale, jaundiced skin stretched over sharpening cheekbones. Her eyes, crusty on the edges, eyelids unhealthily purpled, opened without focusing, over a mouth tensed open for so long that the tongue had dried.

"You've been in here for half an hour," he said softly.

She swallowed as if her throat were too small. Her eyes found him.

She shook harder. None of this was part of a detoxification process that would end. Her symptoms would never get better. This suffering was entirely and intentionally engineered into her biochemistry.

"*Take your punishment like a good girl,*" she quoted in a gravelly voice.

"Can I give you a sedative, so you can sleep?"

"What?" she blurted. The conceptual gulf between them was palpable. "*Sit, you goddamn fuck,*" she said, quoting again. "*You watch that Cream Puff and don't you dare touch it.*"

She watched him, waiting for some sign of understanding. Saint Matthew had read the sprawling entirety of the Puppet Bible, but the Cream Puff was a cruel central mystery of the faith, born from a few words uttered by old Blackmore himself. He couldn't know the right response. Her expression crumpled and she curled tighter.

"I'm dreaming awake, if that's what you're worried about."

She knuckled at her eyes and then gaped in an apparent fleeting panic, inhaling in a hard gulp.

"Awake?" he asked. Hallucinations occurred in advanced withdrawals. "I can treat your symptoms. You don't need to endure this. You're not an ascetic."

"An ascetic is born, not made," she gritted out. "I'm no ascetic." After a time, she looked at him more steadily. "You're a saint."

He was. He *knew* it axiomatically, an incontrovertible, foundational assertion of self that sounded so ridiculous that he usually avoided talking about it.

"Yes."

"What did your Numen do to you?" she said.

There was an ocean of Puppet suffering in that question, generations of joyous slavery, a history of conceptual opposites, pain and love, hunger and service, obsession and absence, religious ecstasy and physical abuse, all of it as incongruous as a logical, self-aware AI who carried the soul of a Apostle.

"I haven't found my Numen yet," he said. "It may be my burden to find them."

Rosalie hugged her legs tighter.

"You know the absence, then," she said.

"Maybe. I'm… disconnected from the immanent."

"Some ascetics become saints. They show they're holy with feats of spiritual endurance." She chewed at her fingernail, drawing blood. "I can't do feats of holiness," she whispered. "I'm just Rosie."

"We have to trust that unseen purposes drive us, that there's a plan for us."

"We're fifty years in the past," she said with a conspiratorial look. "My parents are just babies now. Can you bring me back to the Puppet Free City now?"

"We can't change the past. You being there would change history."

"I can change my name. I would never talk to my parents or baby Rosie. I'd just be another miner or farmer or organ donor."

"I'm so sorry, Rosalie. I really am. Let me treat you. I don't want you to suffer."

She blinked drying eyes, and began a panting fit, alternating between clenched jaws and gaping mouth, like a suffocating fish. Then she calmed. Her body drooped.

"Suffering is the point," she said. "We suffer because the Numen are dying off. We're failing. Someone needs to pay the price." She brought up her legs and hugged them with trembling arms. "Your whole faith died, didn't it? All of your god's followers failed and he's gone. You have to pay the price, don't you?"

Saint Matthew hung on the ceiling, shaken by the reflection of her moment. He hadn't realized how alone he was, how isolated, how hopeless his own spiritual situation. Rosalie at least knew her Numen existed. She'd seen them, touched them. She'd drawn comfort from other believers, other worshippers. Until recently, Saint Matthew had been utterly alone, the last believer in a dead faith. Now, he'd grown Pedro and maybe that was the start, or maybe Pedro was enough. Two of them now believed in Christ, the resurrection, and in salvation through faith in a god who would not or could not speak to them.

"Take my dreams if you want," she said softly.

CHAPTER FOURTEEN

...most obvious but difficult advance has been the development of the Homo congregatus. *The complete recapitulation of the* Homo quantus *project from baseline Venusian stock took nearly a century. This timeline was accelerated by avoiding the early errors of the* Homo quantus *projects and by studying the working* Homo quantus *clone models. Another century placed* Homo congregatus *research far beyond the capabilities of the* Homo quantus.

Most critically, all genetic changes made to create the Homo congregatus *were designed to be genetically compatible with the* Homo sapiens *of the Congregate. The* Homo congregatus *does not therefore represent a speciation event that will trigger competition with the Congregate's humanity. Yes, the* Homo congregatus *are designed to outcompete not just the* Homo quantus, *but all other branches of non-Congregate humanity. But they are also a source of advantageous mutations that are gradually being shared with the people of the Congregate.*

Among the many mistakes of the Banks was that they created a new species of humanity that would be in evolutionary competition with their makers. The Congregate, as a single people and political body, made no such…

Keynote Speaker Script
Strategic and Tactical Defense Symposium, 2912 CE:
Speciation and Extinction Dangers

CASSANDRA PROJECTED HER analysis of Rosalie's newest dreams. The commissary projector fanned a wide, foggy construct of blue-washed light above the table for Saint Matthew. It appeared more like a cloud of gas than gravitational waves. It was difficult to portray higher dimensional structures in the three they had access to, but a combination of shifted colors, perspective changes, and a slow, psychedelic rotation showed the cloudy image in six dimensions. Strange new topography glowed in that light.

"What is it?" he asked.

"If it's not nonsense, it may be a crude representation of a six-dimensional space, containing a number of phases," Cassandra said slowly. "Phase edges, like the interface of solid ice and liquid water. It's only a partial construction, though. That's why I'm guessing. Whatever she's dreaming may be beyond the limit of what her chips can record."

"I thought we might find my pattern again," he said in some bewilderment. "She's dreaming of phase changes in a six-dimensional hyperspace?"

"Yes and no. Bel and I think…"—she corrected herself haltingly—"*thought* that the mouths of the Axis Mundi wormholes were six-dimensional tesseracts."

"This is the spacetime geometry of the wormhole mouths?"

It had sounded ridiculous in her thoughts. She might as well be chasing a religion. There was something here, though; something she couldn't yet see.

"Bel and I never had a chance to theorize more than rough structures. This is more expansive than anything we discussed."

"So, no?"

"Why would she dream of wormhole mouth spacetime geometry?"

The prickling irritation in her voice was directed inward.

"That's just it," he said. "Why isn't she dreaming something more real to her? She can't be thinking this entirely on her own. Something must be giving her these dreams."

"We've come back in time fifty years. No signal could have followed her back through time and across hundreds of lightyears."

This seemed to deflate him a little. "Meeting the Puppets and reading their Bible makes them look dumb, but they were never dumb, were they?"

"Some are highly intelligent," he said, "including our priestess."

"The Puppets themselves would never have been able to recognize geometric or mathematical genius."

The AI's stony face seemed to ponder the mind-twisting rotations in the holographic projection.

"I can be persuaded that Rosalie's brain can coincidentally imagine hyperdimensional constructs," he said, "but not that those dreams are coincidentally real and yet unknowable by her."

"We don't know that this is real. It's far more likely to just be interesting abstract geometry."

"What if it's something miraculous?" he asked. "What if she's dreaming revelations?"

The very idea of miracles was nonsense, but she'd grown too close to this mad AI to say that.

"Her gods aren't really gods," Cassandra said gently.

"Mine is."

CHAPTER FIFTEEN

Prickly, false electromagnetic signals pressed against Cassandra's magnetosomes as the *Calculated Risk* glided back into the beautiful, terrifying hyperspace within. Their trip through the interior of the time gates would be short, but would need to be precise. She needed to feel every crackling wave and smeared particle. Her best estimate placed the debris scattering over the ice of Nyanga more than two hundred years in the past, with an error band a few weeks wide.

They might arrive before or after the Scarecrow. She didn't know which she wanted less, but it wasn't a confrontation she could avoid. As long as the Scarecrow had access to the time gates, the *Homo quantus* would always be in danger, no matter where they hid. The electrical environment felt like a rough blanket dragged over every cell in her body as they slid deeper into the past.

She paused them at a point no different in appearance from any other, and asked Stills to rotate them once more. The pastward mouth of the time gates came into hazy view: slate gray, laced with doubtful purples and pinks, and strange, sourceless EM signals, whose perspectives made no sense to human or *Homo quantus* brains. The disk floated in the strangeness.

"Ready?" she asked.

Saint Matthew clung over the controls, his stylized holographic head looking out the window, perhaps as a show for observers. Pedro nestled against a bracket in the wall. His holographic 'head' had become an abstract sculpture. The interplay of the filmy colours veining his negative and positive space suggested the beauties of fluid dynamics.

"I got a headache now so if it's all the same to you I wanna get started," said Stills. "If you ain't afraid of getting lost anymore, just let me take over and drive evasive. We might have a hostile on the other side. Seeing as how you wimps aren't in your gel chambers, I ain't gonna pull more'n six or eight gees, but I'll probably do it out of the gate."

Cassandra strapped herself tighter and signed for Rosalie to do the same.

"We're ready," she said.

Stills threw the *Calculated Risk* hard through the mouth of the time gates. In one moment, a marvelous, harshly alien world pressed upon her magnetosomes from invisible directions. In the next, the nearly quiet normality of four-dimensional spacetime enwrapped her.

The dark exterior of Nyanga streaked by, meters beneath them. Then alarms shrieked.

"*Câlisse*!" Stills said, his reflexes pitching the *Calculated Risk* up and then down at the ground. Cassandra struggled to hold down her breakfast.

"What is it, Stills?" Cassandra yelled.

Stills pulled up, accelerating hard, skimming so close to the ground that fragile plants shattered beneath them.

"Active Congregate signal!" he growled. "Distress call, mid-wattage, encrypted."

A Congregate distress signal two and a half centuries in the past? How long had it been running?

The small forward telescopes tried to focus on a tall black object.

"What is it?" she asked.

Speed and the lack of light made perspective hard to judge, but some kind of pedestal three or four meters tall stood above the walking plants. She thought she saw horizontal supports radiating outward, cupping an improvised transmission dish. It emitted a crude but powerful radio signal.

"Jam it!" she said.

"Busy!" Stills said, fishtailing the *Calculated Risk* over the high plants.

"Jamming!" Saint Matthew called.

Cassandra slipped into savant. The world became pattern-rich. Places, things, and processes expressed themselves as functions, mathematical translations, bits of tensor calculus or dynamical systems. Interpolation became simple, and she found the negative space within Stills's erratic flying, saw the area he was avoiding. She turned the cameras to that spot.

Almost invisible in the low light, smeared by their speed, somber against the oil-black plantlife, nearly a hundred degrees below zero, the Scarecrow stood on the ice. One misshapen arm rose like a miniature cannon. Flashes of plasma fire washed out the image in the IR.

"Get low!" she said.

"Princess, we got no weapons that'll go toe-to-toe with a mid-calibre plasma cannon. We're not antimatter this time."

She mapped the Scarecrow's position onto her internal map of Nyanga. She showed Stills a course downward, and, as her brain calculated energies, a speed too.

"Are you fucked?" Stills said. "That cannon'll chew your cockpit into slag!"

"What are you doing?" Saint Matthew asked.

She had the trajectory, speed and angle calculated and graphically plotted.

"Do it!" she ordered.

She didn't know what persuaded Stills. She was no combat leader, and the mongrels were constitutionally dismissive of orders, but Stills ran the inflaton drive up its acceleration curve. Eleven gravities pressed them painfully back against their seats. The ground rushed up at them. If Stills's reflexes were even a fraction slow, the *Calculated Risk* would end up a much larger debris field of advanced tech across the surface of Nyanga.

The Scarecrow fired at them all the way down, but couldn't track their acceleration profile as fifteen gravities nearly blacked her out. They sped centimeters above the dwarf planet. The Scarecrow grew large in the cockpit window. A searing white light overloaded the cameras as the *Calculated Risk* struck the Scarecrow at greater than three hundred kilometers per hour. Stills swept the shuttle in a wide arc, maintaining a crushing acceleration over ten gravities. Cassandra's vision tunnelled and her breathing seemed to stop. Stills's swearing sounded distant and uncertainly red-shifted.

The acceleration eased and Stills banked wide around the field centered on the time gates. Where they'd hit the Scarecrow, ten meters of ground plant skin had been vaporized, and even some of the ice beneath had melted to slush. The hot spray of fragments over the ice showed bright in the infrared.

"Where is the fuckin' cocksucker?" Stills demanded.

Maybe Stills hadn't seen it, or maybe he couldn't see it the way she could. A series of white marks in the infrared, each forty centimeters long, splotched through the *Hortus quantus* field to the time gates. No sign of the Scarecrow appeared anywhere. Not visual, not IR, not magnetic. Nothing.

"He's gone," she said.

"What?" Stills said. "*Mierda*!"

Stills flew once more over the field around the time gates, letting the cameras survey across a wide spectrum.

"Are we hurt?" she asked. "Can we follow him?"

"Diagnostics are inconclusive," Saint Matthew answered. "I can't tell you if we're even spaceworthy at the moment."

"I hope you weren't trying to keep history as it was," Stills said. "We just changed a fuckload of it."

"We didn't change anything," Cassandra said.

"Two hundred years from now, we found chunks of Scarecrow blasted onto the ice by something like a mid-caliber cannon. We ain't no cannon."

She briefly wondered how Stills could not see it. She dropped out of savant.

"We knew the approximate position of the blow and its force," she said. "It doesn't matter if the Scarecrow was hit with a bullet, or a cannon shell, or the *Calculated Risk*. We just made the blast pattern we found. The Scarecrow had always been hit by us."

She waited. They all waited as the *Calculated Risk* came to a stop and the faint gravity of Nyanga slowly pulled at it. Stills brought them down on cold jets.

"Fuuuuuuuck," Stills finally said, understanding exerting a similarly slow gravity.

"It's all bullshit. All your *oh, we don't know how we could be useful to anyone*." His offputting machine voice had assumed a mock whining tone. "You're as full of bullshit as your dead boyfriend. No wonder everyone wants to kill you."

"I only realized it when we got out of the axis mouth and I saw where the Scarecrow was," she said by way of apology. "Are we still jamming the antenna?"

SAINT MATTHEW SKITTERED ahead of her on spidery robotic legs over Nyanga's uneven ice. His holographic head cast a soft lantern light. Cassandra had miscalculated Stills's flying—he'd shaved the surface closer than she'd thought. A number of *Hortus quantus* had been smeared to melt along the outer edge of the herd for forty meters, about two percent of all of them. The shards of their ice skeletons lay tumbled, sharp and bright, tangled in the flayed, oily skins.

She'd ordered this destruction. She had… obliterated these innocents. Had this sinking, sickening guilt hit Bel, but worse? She didn't need to feel this way. She didn't need to let these feelings happen. Saint Matthew looked back at her and she imagined the stony eyes in judgment. She didn't need to feel this way. She hadn't meant for this to happen.

The transmitter pedestal reflected her helmet light. The macabre construction of ice seemed to be made of repurposed *Hortus quantus* legs, ribs, and reproductive fronds, welded together by melting and refreezing ice. Three meters above the ground, limbs had been cantilevered outward and draped with the flat black plant skin to make a crude solar panel. Cables ran under the plant skin, all jury-rigged from pieces of the Scarecrow's body and pieces of the *Hortus quantus*. Cassandra disconnected the power supply.

Adrenaline must have overrun her concentration. She hadn't noticed the soft chiming of the radiological alarm. High energy alpha particles. Not a lot, but dangerous over time. Her suit had a small directional Geiger counter on one cuff. She swept it across the ice and found a small piece of metal, fresh on the oil-slick plant cover, quickly cooling. She shone her helmet light on it, and waved her hand over it, feeling its low paramagnetic response. The utility programs in her suit gave her different readings from the metal.

Uranium.

CHAPTER SIXTEEN

"I WAS WORRIED about you avoiding them," Saint Matthew admitted in her earpiece.

Cassandra stepped across the black-slicked ice, nearing the edge of the great *Hortus quantus* herd.

"I haven't been avoiding them."

The words sounded true enough to argue about.

Everything going on made her feel like she was always behind, always rushing, never giving any single thing the attention it deserved. Examining the *Hortus quantus* never seemed to be the most important thing, nor the most urgent. She had genetic samples. They'd analyzed the ecological interactions. But they were far from understanding how the *Hortus quantus* worked. She was curious. How and why a quantum intelligence might evolve was a profound and important question.

And yet.

The *Hortus quantus* were inextricably bound to Bel's obsessive guilt, the kind of guilt that might have shaped how he'd reacted to the Congregate kidnapping and the mutilation of one hundred and fifty-five *Homo quantus*. Burdened with misplaced responsibility for one accidental genocide, he'd taken extraordinarily unjustified risks to rescue the captive *Homo quantus*, and left her alone.

And yet it was complicated.

The *Hortus quantus* were magnificent, remarkable, a cosmic treasure, but the accident that had killed them was irreversible. And in her present, they were gone, and where she should have had some regret or mourning, she was empty. Nothing was forever. Species went extinct all the time, both with the help of humanity and on their own. The people the Puppets worshipped as gods had only a few generations left. For all their searching, humanity had never found even a single ruin of the unspeakably ancient forerunners who'd built the Axis Mundi network. And necessarily, one day, there would be no more *Homo quantus,* and when that day came, it would be the most natural, normal, and expected thing.

The universe didn't care about them and didn't need them.

Cassandra felt nervous, energized, fidgety, not at all settled for entering the quantum fugue. Within a kilometer of the time gates, she neared the first advanced plant formations. In the slightly warmer center of the great valley, pitch-black plant skin absorbed infrared, heating up microscopic layers of ice and squeezing the melt upward to be refrozen. After years and decades, these slow-growing rods of ice rose, platforms mushrooming outward along the column to catch more of the brown dwarf's radiation, making increasingly intricate structures.

They were beautiful. Elegant. Her brain found the iterative fractal algorithms in their growth histories, the angle and surface area optimizations polished and refined by natural selection. They were electrically quiet. If she stood still and turned off her suit systems, she experienced the perfect silence in this alien garden.

She'd come to confirm Bel's observations from ten years in Nyanga's future. Bel had seen the entanglement knitting all the vegetable intelligences together, before he'd destroyed it. But it was an open question as to whether his observation collapsed the superposition of states in that moment and for all forward futures, or whether the collapse reached back in time. Some experiments of quantum phenomena found the past affected by future observations, entanglement among them.

She wasn't sure what she had hoped to find. Was it better that Bel had accidentally committed genocide, or might it be easier to live with the discovery that after his observations, a wondrous life form had never existed?

The atmosphere of Nyanga was too thin for sound, but the ice-brittle plant scrunched tangibly beneath her boots. Needle-narrow spines fanned at branch ends, scraping her suit, their snapping sounds doubtful. To Union eyes this must have been a dark, lonely place, a purgatory they'd ironically named after a lush park on Earth. Dialing her ocular implants to the infrared made the garden luminous, with patches of striated colour and reticulated veins glinting under frigid skins riding ice sculptures. It was a garden, invisible to the crews of the Sub-Saharan Union, whose senses and thinking weren't made to touch the phenomenology of this world. This beauty was a language the Union could not hear, even in translation.

She brushed her way forward, breaking as few of the branches as she could to reach the moving herd. *Hortus quantus* bodies riding on four spindly legs seemed to be light and hollow, with black skin webbing skeletal ribs of ice over a central drum shape. No sense organs were apparent, but tall intricate fronds swayed over their bodies. Their excruciatingly slow movements would cause most humans to declare them alive, but not intelligent, something that said more about the time bias of humanity than anything meaningful about the *Hortus quantus*.

The closest, nine point six meters away, lifted a glass-fragile foot three centimeters over the course of two minutes, as its body advanced millimeters. In the distance, in the center of the herd of *Hortus quantus*, the time gates stood, their pastward mouth facing her. She made out the slow trickle of pollen that emerged on the faintest of breezes gasping backwards through time. The *Hortus quantus* marched before the pastward mouth, dragging their high fronds through the stream of pollen. Their glacial march would bring them around to the futureward mouth, where the ghostly breeze would tug at the pollen of today, carrying it eleven years into the past. Their reproductive cycle crossed time, stretching with it their consciousness and sense of the present.

"Do you need me to do anything?" Saint Matthew said.

"Minimal fugue spotting," she said. "Cut it off at an hour or if my fever spikes."

Cassandra sent micro-currents from her electroplaques into key neural centers carrying the seat of self.

Consciousness, an awareness of self, was such a fragile new thing in primates. It had only existed a few million years, perhaps even less. Life was otherwise a set of algorithms and processes interposing themselves between some source of energy and entropy. All life stood in the way of energy diffusing through the cosmos. Leaves got between sun and stone. Carnivores situated themselves between herbivores and decay. Saprophytes like fungi colonized and accelerated the transport of energy out of the decaying dead.

But this movement of genes and their algorithms was robotic, dumb, following statistical rules and some versions of game theory, and even some quantum rules at the macromolecular levels. No system examined itself, was aware that it was a system, until consciousness. And although they'd colonized the stars, humanity hadn't found any other consciousness anywhere. Consciousness imposed an order on what it observed, forcing the world to choose among the quantum possibilities that, before observation, simply co-existed, running over one another like ghosts. What Bel had seen in the *Hortus quantus* were those ghosts, those mutually exclusive unchosen probabilities and entangled states.

Cassandra the consciousness, the subjective, thinking, self-examining being, looked out on the dark field of moving plants. The electrical micro-current to her brain switched off her consciousness, and then there was no Cassandra, no awareness inside her skin, only algorithms and quantum processors.

CASSANDRA'S DRY EYES stung. She felt hot. The *Hortus quantus* ahead of her had advanced several meters. The brown dwarf throbbed in the same part of the sky, but the suit clock matched her brain's sense of lost time: forty-one minutes. Her fever was forty degrees, but her mind felt full of new knowledge, vast and breath-taking. She didn't see things exactly as Bel had described them. Her subjective self, her consciousness, had not participated in any of the observations. The quantum intellect running her body hadn't truly made any observations either. It had used the magnetic fields generated by the magnetosome in her hundreds of millions of muscle cells to feel the electromagnetic environment at scales where quantum phenomena occurred. The superposition of states within her brain had been merged for some time to the quantum environment on the surface of Nyanga.

She'd perceived billions of strings of entanglement around the *Hortus quantus,* like when she and Bel had used these mysterious threads to find the Puppet Axis. But whereas those had been a few threads, which she and Bel had tracked and located precisely, these were countless. Pistil and frond threaded through the time gates and back out, thousands of times for each individual in the herd. The overall structure of all the threads of quantum entanglement looked like a strange attractor built from the complex patterns of chaos.

She hadn't really believed it. These creatures, slow-moving, living a hundred degrees below zero in a near-vacuum, thought with strange brains that worked like quantum computers. They experienced complex connectivities with each other not only through space, but through time.

She'd believed Bel, but enough for the conviction to feel visceral. So much *Homo quantus* brain functioning was new and poorly tested that she sometimes feared the false positive too much. It was possible Bel had seen something that wasn't there. He had before. They all had.

But he hadn't.

And there was the tragedy. If Bel's observation had been a false positive, then the genocide would not have been real. If he really hadn't destroyed a life form of incalculable beauty and subtlety, a creature unique in the cosmos, then the *Homo quantus* were perhaps not dangerous. They were escaping civilization to avoid being instruments of conflict.

And yet without even trying, the *Homo quantus* could be terribly, terribly destructive. They'd brought the Union and the Congregate into firing range. They'd opened the door for the Union to ravage Port Blackmore. She'd destroyed a priceless permanent Axis Mundi. They'd barely avoided getting all the *Homo quantus* exterminated.

She'd both wanted and didn't want to observe these elegant, intelligent, cold-living quantum beings. And now she had seen them, and had ironically observed more of her nature than theirs.

CASSANDRA HAD STAYED out on the ice much longer than anyone else, analyzing all that she'd learned from Nyanga, and deciding what to do next. She entered the *Calculated Risk* as quietly as she could. Stills wouldn't hear her, but Rosalie needed real sleep. The Puppet wasn't sleeping, though.

Light shone out of the head into the dark galley. Rosalie sat on the toilet clothed, staring blankly into the dark, her left hand wet and red with blood dripping from a horizontal cut on her wrist. Cassandra shook Rosalie, calling for Saint Matthew.

"Oh, my Lord," the AI said when he arrived. Five spidery drones clattered close, their magnetic attachment to the round hull grating against Cassandra's senses. They swarmed the priestess, applying pressure, injecting, and sewing veins back together. "I'll sedate her for now."

"You didn't see this?" Cassandra demanded, throwing her helmet across the galley.

"I don't peep on people using the head."

"I mean, you didn't see this coming?"

"I can't read minds either."

"I'm okay," Rosalie said listlessly.

"You're not okay," Cassandra said.

"Don't worry," she said vaguely. "I won't die. I can't kill myself. It's not allowed."

Cassandra knelt in front of the tiny woman. "It's not allowed? You can't end your exile?"

"Only a Numen can tell me to kill myself," Rosalie said. "Puppets can't be trusted to understand the ways of the cosmos. A Numen might need us."

"Even you?"

"Even me."

It was the most desperate, depressing, hopeful thing she'd heard Rosalie say. Cassandra rose. Bright red spotted the knees of her vacuum suit where she'd knelt in Rosalie's blood. The sedative was taking effect and Rosalie's eyes lidded, then closed. Some drones caught her; others continued to sew her together.

The last time Cassandra had seen the inside of anyone had been the autopsies of the dead *Homo quantus*.

Living things were machines with parts. The Congregate had put new parts into the captive *Homo quantus* to make a living machine to pilot fighter craft. The Numen had added new parts to make slaves. The Banks had added new parts to make the *Homo quantus,* a people to lead military and economic warfare. They were all machines. And this one was broken.

"Fix her withdrawal symptoms," Cassandra said to Saint Matthew.

"She didn't agree."

"I don't care. This is stupid. Fix her."

She turned away to yank at the fastenings on her vacuum suit.

"And tell me when Pedro gets back with the readings. I want to find the Scarecrow, kill it, and go home. I'm tired of this."

CHAPTER SEVENTEEN

"We have a way to follow the Scarecrow," Cassandra said. "We don't know what parts of history he might be able to influence, so the risk of leaving him is too great. "

She sat at the tiny galley table in the *Calculated Risk*. Rosalie sat to her left and Saint Matthew's holographic head frowned on her right. A mobile monitor across from her showed Stills's shadowy inhuman face within the gloom of his pressure chamber.

"It's a fuckin' long shot," Stills grumbled. "Isotopes and radiation are everywhere."

"Not enriched uranium-235," Cassandra said.

Between them was a small lead box containing the fragmented uranium fuel cell she'd found on the ice. It also contained a few milligrams of black, crystalline uranium dioxide grains that an exhaustive search had found within the ice, thirty-five centimeters below the surface of Nyanga, twelve meters from the time gates.

"Look, you're the genius who thinks through time," Stills said, "but it was raw luck you found it. Even if he was too dumb to cauterize whatever fucking leak he's got, if more fuel drops onto the ice, its gonna be hot and it'll melt down to where eventually you won't detect shit."

"Yes and no," Saint Matthew said. "It takes up to three meters of ice to shield the radiation from uranium decay, and the surface of Nyanga is quite good at distributing heat, so fragments will sink slowly."

"You think you can find him in time?" Stills asked dubiously.

"We found traces of plutonium-239 in the grains," the AI said. "We know the uranium-plutonium ratio from the fuel cell fragments we found. We know how fast uranium decays. The Scarecrow 'bled' those grains and they were frozen in the ice for two thousand, nine hundred years."

"You act so goddamn sure."

"As sure as we can get," she said. Into his silence, she pressed. "This is how we hunt it, Stills."

"You gettin' blood-thirsty, princess?"

"You'd love to kill it just as much as I need to kill it," she countered.

She felt like she was holding her breath. Then, his mechanical translator barked its version of a cold, brutal laugh.

"Damned, but ain't you as good as your boyfriend ever was?" Stills said. "Fine. We didn't finish the job. Get me close enough and I'll kill him or get us killed."

CHAPTER EIGHTEEN

SUDDEN, STRONG MAGNETIC fields pressed against Cassandra in the cockpit of the *Calculated Risk*, imposing a weird texture onto the hyperspace within the time gates. There were many such moments or eternities of feelings, where experiences bled into her three-dimensionality from unseen regions of hyperspace. It took discipline to know what to ignore. Saint Matthew's hologram appeared in front of the pilot seat. His heavy, carved features seemed more somber.

"It's done," he said.

"I thought you might not do it."

"Ethics has a dark history of responses to people being unwell in a way that makes them refuse treatment. I didn't do anything permanent. The chip I inserted into Rosalie's brain just shorts out the withdrawal responses."

"What will she be like?"

"The mental imbalances and psychological pathologies in the Puppets were intentional. They're cruel and damaging, but I don't know how much any Puppet's sense of self is biochemical and how much is the madness in which they've been raised. She might hate us. She might become… human. What would you become if your engineered curiosity, electromagnetic senses and mathematical abilities were suddenly gone?"

Cassandra stiffened.

"Don't compare me to the Puppets. We're both engineered. It ends there. The *Homo quantus* wanted to become more than what we were, capable of seeing the universe itself in new ways. We aspired. The Numen just made slaves."

His head cocked slightly. "Of course."

Stills rotated the ship across the m-axis, a dimension with more temporal than spatial properties. An eerie, unsettled bloatedness accompanied the movement. She felt time broadening and extending around the moments of the rotation. When it was done, he drove the *Calculated Risk* forward again, but the strange feeling of temporal dislocation persisted.

Alarms sounded.

"Collision alarm! Stopping!" Stills yelled.

Saint Matthew toggled different scanners, trying to find what Stills's reflexes had avoided.

"What was it?" she demanded.

The electrical and magnetic sensors gave erratic readings. After long seconds, of all things, spotlights and a visual inspection gave the clearest answer. Gray and brown objects floated in a shadowy fog.

"Someone shit the water?" Still said.

Cassandra pondered the spectrum of reflected light, then frowned. "I need IR," she said. "And I need the interference cleaned up. If a hundred and seventy Kelvin is accurate, those particles might be *Hortus quantus* pollen grains."

"There's more than that in there," Stills said. "Big enough to be the Scarecrow, or pieces of him."

The hull vibrated as Stills opened the covers that protected the *Calculated Risk*'s small guns. The fuzzy shapes tumbled very slowly.

"If we get closer, can you still shoot him?" she asked.

"I can get as close as you want, honey. I'm in the stern."

They edged forward. Some of the particles were nudged away from the window, while some rebounded from the thick glass after contact. The spotlights' reflected glow shifted as the density of the pollen changed within the eerie cloud.

"Come on, you fucker," Stills said. "Wiggle."

Stills neared one of the slowly rotating shapes, until she recognized it.

"A skate."

"Shoot it?"

"It's a deactivated skate. No, a piece of one."

The spotlights showed half a dozen devices, each shattered.

"What are they doing here?" Stills asked.

"Three thousand years ago, the time gates might not have been trapped in the ice of Nyanga," Saint Matthew said. "This is an eddy, though. Things collect here."

"We're further back than three thousand years," Cassandra said. "We've gone out of our way to avoid obstacles."

"This ain't no eddy," Stills said. "I know currents. There ain't none here."

"Think of it as a Lagrange Point," Cassandra said, "a gravitationally stable region of the spacetime."

"I don't care if a big magnet is reeling everything in," Stills said. "Could the Scarecrow be here?"

"If he's got no propulsion, or if he's lost power, he would drift like everything else," Cassandra said.

"If *we* had to go the long way, *he* had to go the long way," Stills said. "We've gotta treat this area as dangerous. I gotta go huntin'."

Very gently, Stills pressed the *Calculated Risk* into the cloud of icy pollen, past the dark, gently tumbling skates. Spotlight beams swept across their field of vision, and it began to feel like a graveyard. In the pregnant stillness, the *Calculated Risk* suddenly sounded and shook.

A skate ahead of them exploded, startling her.

"What was that?" she demanded.

"Target practice," Stills said.

"What?"

"Keep your cool," he said. "We're hunting. Sometimes you gotta surprise your prey, make 'em nervous, help them make a mistake."

Cassandra looked at all their readings, and waited.

"He's not here?" she asked.

"Or he doesn't spook easy."

"There is something curious on the radiation sensors," Saint Matthew said.

Cassandra pulled up those feeds. Alpha particles. Beta particles. Some gamma rays. She sorted them by energies, and she found signals that corresponded to the radioactive decay of uranium, thorium, radium, and radon. Some signals were too weak to identify conclusively.

"These are decay products of the kinds of radioactive isotopes found in the skates," Cassandra said. "Stills just broke the ceramic carapace that was shielding the radiation."

"I didn't mean that," Saint Matthew said. "We didn't detect any radiation above background for a dozen broken skates. Now Stills broke one and suddenly there's radiation."

Cassandra went cold.

"What?" Stills said. "What the fuck does that mean?"

"He's been here," Cassandra whispered. "He took the radioisotopes."

"The Scarecrow?" Stills demanded.

"He's thinking like a machine," Saint Matthew said. "He's bleeding radioactive fuel and has no tools to fix himself. But he can find new radioactive fuel. Skate design, including the cakes of radioisotopes, is generally known. He broke open the skates and scooped out the radioisotopes insides."

"He's still here somewhere," Stills said.

"Not necessarily," Saint Matthew said. "Skates use the radioisotopes to heat volatiles into thrust. The Scarecrow could have jury-rigged a crude thrust system."

"*Tabarnak d'ostie de crisse*," Stills swore.

"This doesn't change anything. We know where and when he's going to be in the past," Cassandra said. "We know he's bleeding. Start the maneuvers, Stills. Let's go kill the Scarecrow."

"Fuckin' yes, ma'am," Stills said.

CHAPTER NINETEEN

STILLS WAS RESTIVE under her caution. If he could have navigated the interior of the time gates, she suspected he might just have plowed forward and pitted his ferocity against the Scarecrow's as soon as possible. But only she could think in eight-, nine- and ten-dimensional geometries, and she'd led the *Calculated Risk* to a part of the hyperspace where gloomy outlines of the pastward axis mouth were smeared across their vision. The blurry circular outlines came in and out of focus, straining the eyes. The mouths opened onto Nyanga two thousand, nine hundred years before they'd found the Scarecrow's radioactive fuel in the ice.

"Bring us forward four seconds along the r-axis, then full stop," she said. "Then rotate thirty-five degree around the u-axis."

"Thirty-five degrees?" Stills said. "You feelin' all right?"

"Watch," she said.

Stills executed the rotation. In this part of the hyperspace, the r-axis was a dimension with more time-like than space-like properties. As he rotated across it only partially, the view of the axis mouth visibly fanned across several years. And for long subjective minutes she squinted into that gloom, finally spotting it: overlapping images of the Scarecrow, flattened and ghostly, frozen in time. The *Calculated Risk* was partially out of the three spatial and one temporal dimensions he occupied.

"Watch what?" Stills demanded.

"I see him."

"Where?" he demanded.

"Wait."

The machine that translated Stills's speech made a series of noises, none of which were words.

"One degree counter-rotation across r-axis and ahead for two seconds along the m-axis," she said.

"Where is he?" Stills demanded.

The fanned successive images of the Scarecrow were flattened and stacked so closely that Cassandra's brain had to heavily process the information to see them even unclearly.

"I'm not seeing him as he is," she said. "I can only see him as moments in time, planar projections."

"I don't know what the fuck that means!" Stills said in exasperation. "Just show me where the *malparido cabrón* is so I can shoot him."

"We're going to the surface of Nyanga," she said. "Right before he comes out of the Axis mouth."

Giving vent to a stream of protests, Stills nudged the *Calculated Risk* along the route she'd indicated. The subtle shift in rotation cleared away some of the fuzziness around the Scarecrow images, like a focusing lens losing distortions. Cassandra made out the beginning and the end of the Scarecrow's images near the wormhole mouth, timing the moment of his contact with the pastward wormhole mouth.

"Thirty-four degrees counter-rotation across the r-axis," she said, "ninety degrees across the m-axis, and then straight towards the wormhole mouth."

"I don't see him."

"You will."

The images of the Scarecrow shrank and vanished. The pastward mouth clarified out of the gloom and Stills pressed the ship through.

"Where is he?" Stills demanded, then more correctly, "*When* is he?"

Cassandra activated a timer that began counting down.

"He'll emerge in nine and a quarter minutes," she said. "He may be disoriented from hyperspace, or not. Your window to react might be short."

"I don't need more than 'short,'" he said, moving the *Calculated Risk* through what she recognized as an abbreviated threat survey of the area. At first glance, little differed about the *Hortus quantus*, nor Nyanga, nor its sullen, ashy star. Stills hovered the *Calculated Risk* twenty meters from the mouth of the time gates, to the right of where the Scarecrow would emerge.

"This is close enough for the Scarecrow to hit us," Cassandra said.

"Stills is shortening the time from firing to hitting," Saint Matthew said. "He's giving the Scarecrow less time to react."

"Is this what you'd do?" she asked.

He didn't answer.

"This ain't a committee," Stills said. "Shut your breath-holes. I'm workin'."

The *Calculated Risk* fell silent as the three of them watched the timer run down.

Rosalie screamed from the bunk area, a piercing shriek. Then something crashed.

"She's awake," the AI said pointlessly.

Half a dozen of his drones moved aft. Another crash sounded and the telltales of one drone switched to static. Through the drone cameras, Cassandra saw Rosalie kneeling on her mattress, her head bandages ripped away and trickles of blood spattering her face. She hefted a small fire extinguisher with remarkable agility, looking about wildly, inhaling through her mouth as if suffocating.

She swung the extinguisher to her side and clipped the legs of a drone, knocking it to the corner.

"Saint Matthew..." Cassandra said warningly.

"None of my drones are armed," he said.

"Sedative," she said.

"Seriously. Shut up!" Still said. "I wish I could gas the lot of you."

The timer showed four minutes. Cassandra hurried aft. Saint Matthew followed. Rosalie's eyes widened as Cassandra came into the small bunk area. Rosalie held steady fingers between them, smudged with bright blood.

"What did you do?" the priestess croaked.

"We put a chip in your brain to treat your withdrawal symptoms," Cassandra said. "To reduce your suffering."

"Those are mine!" Rosalie shrieked.

Cassandra didn't understand. She'd prepared herself for other responses.

"Those aren't symptoms! They're gifts from divinity!" Rosalie tapped her chest repeatedly, desperately. "Now I should be dead." She pulled at the bandages at her wrist. Spots of blood appeared and expanded under the fabric.

"You can live any way you want now," Cassandra said, trying to approach.

"That suffering was mine!" Rosalie shrieked, her face reddening with a frightening anger. "Gods-given! Now... I can't even feel the Absence. You've broken my connection with divinity. Not the Absence. You broke me away from all divinity!"

"You idiots got ninety seconds before I shoot someone," Stills voice came over the speakers. "I don't care if it's you."

"Rosalie..." Cassandra said, stepping slowly nearer.

"Divinity can't see me either, now..." Rosalie said wildly, gulping at the air desperately. "I don't belong to them! They won't know me!"

Rosalie swept the drones away with the extinguisher and changed its arc to come around at Cassandra. The geometry was clear as soon as Rosalie's posture shifted, the necessary consequences traced in slow motion. Cassandra leaned away from the extinguisher's arc, darting fingertips to Rosalie's arm and releasing an electrical shock that was painful to both of them. Rosalie convulsed and fell on her mattress while Cassandra cradled her burnt fingertips.

"Sedate her!"

Saint Matthew's drones skittered close to the Puppet. One of them pressed a needle into a vein.

The *Calculated Risk* shuddered and something hard knocked on the dorsal side. The ship then lurched away from Nyanga, and Cassandra was thrown to the floor. Saint Matthew was wrenched from the ceiling and crashed beside her.

"We're not strapped in, Stills!" she yelled, shielding her head with one arm.

"Grab something," Stills warned through the speakers. "I'll try to pin you to the floor with the maneuvering gees, but I ain't guaranteeing nothin'. I'm killing here."

Cassandra's magnetosomes tracked their movement through Nyanga's faint magnetic field. They were arcing several kilometers around the time gates. Stills pumped the inflaton field to slide the ship across the curving path, pinning her to the floor with centrifugal forces. Then he cut the thrust, rotated the *Calculated Risk*, and the hull shuddered as if the guns had fired again. She lost the geometry of their movements as the inflaton thrust rose again and she was rolled up the wall and the ship shuddered once more. Then all was still.

"I'm coming to the cockpit!" she said.

"Do what you want," Stills replied. "I'm done."

Cassandra staggered forward. Aches bloomed across her ribs and arms. She strapped in, scanning the readouts and the view beyond the window. Bright ice showed in wide patches around the pastward mouth of the time gates. Many *Hortus quantus* had also been mowed down. In the infrared, the surface was patchy, some of it warming up to minus twenty degrees, especially around the brightly glowing pieces of mechanical debris.

"You got him," she said.

"He got us once. Plasma hit. Did I kill Miss Half-Freak?" he asked. "One more maneuver an' I coulda smashed her head on something in the stern."

"No." She scanned the large debris field.

"You don't owe that little weirdo anything," Stills added flatly. "She ain't your project. Nobody'd blame you if you flushed her."

"I'm not a murderer, Stills."

"She had her own problems before you ever met her. She'll have her own problems after you ditch her."

"Since when do you give advice?"

"The dogs say, *Don't tie yourself in knots about what ain't your problem*. Your dead boyfriend left you a Puppet. Like thanks for nothin'. Throw it away."

"The stray Puppets became my problem on Venus," she said slowly, as if she were working this out for the first time. She'd thought it through a hundred times. "Bel was part of the price."

"Phocas, too," Stills said. "What a pair of dipshits they were. Phocas was a case study in why you can't trust Puppets. Come on. Let me deal with your Puppet problem."

"If I want her dead, you'll be the first I tell."

His mechanical voice barked. "You would, wouldn't you?"

Admiration hid subtly within the robotic tonelessness and she didn't know what to do with that backhanded praise.

CASSANDRA'S BOOTS CRUNCHED on the bright, icy regolith. Stills had made a mess. Bullets had torn the tarry plant cover to ribbons.

She'd watched videos of the fight, mostly in visual bands, but some in infrared. Stills had shot first, but the Scarecrow had been fast. The Scarecrow's armour had turned the first wave of Stills's bullets. The second and third waves had clustered with astonishingly tight grouping, cracking the shielding, tearing into robotic musculature. The bullets would have fragmented inside, shredding the Scarecrow's innards.

The body lay ravaged before the pastward mouth of the time gates, and it was warming. The heat dissipation systems for its miniature reactor had been blown to pieces, and radioactive grains had snowed over the ground, sparkling shyly in the infrared.

"You can find all the pieces?" she asked.

"Out to five hundred meters, we can inspect every square centimeter," Saint Matthew said. His holographic head bobbed slightly above his tilting body as his spider legs climbed onto the body of the Scarecrow. "Beyond that, we'll use the *Calculated Risk*'s active sensors in a spiral pattern."

"What about the shattered plants and *Hortus quantus*?" she asked.

"I was going to collect the dead plant matter and vaporize it," he said. "I don't want to leave anything we've touched that might last three millennia in this cold."

The wrecked forest and ground cover would be recolonized by neighbouring plants, leaving no trace of today's destruction. But it seemed... unfeeling, especially after the conversation with Stills.

"Is that wrong?" Saint Matthew asked.

"Their deaths won't be for nothing if one day we find out how to resurrect them."

She ain't your project. She wasn't sure about that: about the Puppet woman, or about the *Hortus quantus*.

"I'll treat their remains with dignity," he said.

She moved away from the time gates, away from the *Calculated Risk*, away from her dead enemy. The *Hortus quantus* were gradually resuming their slow migration around the time gates, releasing pollen to the puffs of wind on the futureward side, catching pollen emerging from the pastward mouth of the time gates. She looked up, showing her face to the desultory light of the brown dwarf.

Ain't your project.

CHAPTER TWENTY

THE DISPLAYS SHOWED the deceptively slight damage to the dorsal quarter of the *Calculated Risk*.

"Fix it. I'm getting tired of being in this tiny tank," Stills said.

Saint Matthew, Cassandra, and Stills were represented holographically or physically in the cockpit. Their little ship was not armoured. It wasn't that kind of ship. The Scarecrow's plasma weapon had nicked the coils that generated the inflaton field. The field had to be symmetric to work.

"My drones are machining new parts," Saint Matthew said. "It will take about thirty-six hours."

"I've seen how many drones you got. Use 'em all," Stills countered. His image winked out.

Cassandra's exhaustion with people must have showed. Saint Matthew smiled at her kindly.

"You neutralized a threat to your people. We'll be home soon. Then, it will be happily ever after."

She nodded doubtfully, twisting a wire into a crude spiral.

"Is Rosalie awake?"

The AI nodded. "Some shock. Some adaptation, perhaps. Some grieving, of course."

"I'm sick of grief."

"Grief follows us through life, manifesting in different ways for different people and things lost," he said. "And grief is a companion with whom we may strike a truce."

"Was that meant to be comforting?"

"It was meant to be honest."

The expression in his crude sculpted features softened. His alien, ancient face gave every indication of being caring and present. She could not pick out any dissembling in the facade.

"This isn't what I wanted," she said quietly.

Cassandra found Rosalie restrained at wrist, waist and ankle to her bed. Her cheeks had pinkened. She wasn't struggling, but her face hardened when she saw Cassandra.

"I'm sorry we had to restrain you," Cassandra said. "We were afraid of you hurting yourself or the ship."

"You defiled me," Rosalie said acidly.

"The chip Saint Matthew implanted can be turned on and off. Its medications and neural stimulations can be adjusted. It can be removed."

"Who decides that?" Rosalie demanded.

"I guess you do."

"I guess I don't decide anything," the priestess said coldly. "*You* decide who can touch divinity. *You* decide whether our divinities live or die."

"How do you feel?" Cassandra asked.

Rosalie stifled an angry retort and breathed.

"I've been mutilated," she said finally, "severed from divinity. I've been made anathema."

"Those feeling… those instincts… Doesn't it matter to you that they were engineered into you, by people who weren't divine, people who only wanted to exploit you?"

"No!" Rosalie said with a pleading longing that was uncomfortable to hear. The rest spilled with an unreasoning passion. "It was meant to be! I was meant to be. That's the miracle! From the profane and the unhallowed come the divine and sacred. The cosmos made souls from nothing. The universe made the Numen because divinity was necessary. They made the Puppets to serve and care for the Numen, to shelter this fragile miracle."

"I don't want you to suffer," Cassandra said, struggling to find a logical footing.

"Puppets were made to serve and suffer and endure. This is our purpose. Puppets may disgust you, but don't take my purpose from me because it's not your way."

They stared at each other. Rosalie had begun to sweat. Cassandra crouched and undid the restraints.

"I need you not suffering," Cassandra said. "Rest."

"Resting is worse. I need to do something. I can help the robot rebuild the Scarecrow."

"What?" Cassandra demanded. She looked behind her.

The curve of the hull had hidden the work area, where they'd tied down the Scarecrow's corpse for inspection. Where she'd knelt by Rosalie's bed, Cassandra could now see Pedro's holographic head bobbing as he moved deliberately from one part of the corpse to the next, connecting cables.

"What are you *doing?*" she demanded, stomping over and shooing the silent AI off. "Saint Matthew!"

Saint Matthew appeared.

"What are you doing?" she demanded, looking at the wiring was feeding.

"Nothing. Pedro must have started this on his own."

"He's your AI! Put some limits on him! We don't need a repaired Scarecrow inside the ship!"

The stony holographic face became pensive, as if examining the wiring set-up.

"Pedro isn't repairing it. Not yet…" he said. Pedro had gone still on the wall while his maker examined his work. "He's wiring low, external power to tap into memory tubules." Saint Matthew tap-tap-tapped towards an external processor they sometimes lugged outside the *Calculated Risk* for remote work. "He's firewalling the results in here."

"Why?" Cassandra asked of Pedro, a pointless question given the AI's vow of silence. "Everything will be encrypted."

"Perhaps," Saint Matthew said. "The Scarecrow may be the best Congregate technology, but you and I were—forgive me—designed by the Banks to confront and outthink the best security and military threats. And we've both grown since we parted from our makers."

Saint Matthew verified a few connections in the Scarecrow corpse, then added some as Cassandra watched. The Scarecrow was filled with metal actuators and fine wiring, innervating artificial piezoelectric muscles. Throughout were weaves of flexible, glassy neural fibers. Pedro and Saint Matthew were infiltrating these. Saint Matthew applied power, and the mobile processor's holographic projectors began showing streams of encrypted data. Much of it would be knowledge, but other parts would be operating system and specialized algorithms. The hologram showing the encrypted data bloomed larger and larger, filling the curved work space of the *Calculated Risk*.

"I... may have underestimated the sophistication of the Scarecrow," Saint Matthew said. "His neural components are already operating using qubits and quantum encryption beyond my processing power."

Cassandra waved a hand close to the remote processor, taking control of the display from the AI. The data was encrypted, but some parts hinted at something familiar she couldn't place. She reorganized the data in the display, trying to see the pattern more strongly.

"Are you able to decrypt it?" Saint Matthew asked in disbelief.

He seemed to take her silence for the answer. *Homo quantus*'s pattern recognition was prodigious, translating the complexity of natural phenomena into mathematical relationships. With simple things, it was a low intellectual churn in her background thinking. At times, for lack of data, patterns hung just out of reach, like a pending intellectual sneeze. And worse, the overpowered pattern recognition ability also saw patterns that weren't there, confounding the real and imagined.

She didn't know what she was facing here. In theory, she shouldn't have found any structure in encrypted data. Most of it appeared utterly randomized, and she subtracted that from the display. The remainder had some periodicities. She reordered the data in a number of ways, trying different graphical axes, geometric systems, transformations, and number systems. In one of them, she came to a geometric structure that was maddeningly familiar. She stared at it, as if willpower alone would force the epiphany she needed.

"You've isolated data with a lower encryption quality," Saint Matthew said with some wonder.

"Can you crack it?" she asked.

"No," he said after a long silence.

"It's not the kind of structure seen in language," she mused. "It's not the kind of structure seen in mathematical expressions, or chaotic systems, or iterative evolutionary patterns."

"Geometric, then?"

"There's something geometric about the structure, but I've compared it to everything I can think of from one dimension up to eleven. No match anywhere."

"The Scarecrow spent days or months, maybe even years, in a higher-dimensional hyperspace," Saint Matthew said, "after he was gravely injured by antimatter. If I'd been damaged that way, I might have some problems encrypting my observations. I wonder if what you've isolated are his memories from after his injuries."

"If you're right, and this subset is from a later period, what would he have observed? There's nothing in the hyperspace within the time gates, nothing that you or he or Stills can really see or make sense of."

"You think he wasted energy encrypting gibberish with impaired encryption systems?" the AI asked.

"He had a harder time than you," she said. "You at least know that this hyperspace is the collision of two eleven-dimensional spaces. From that, you could predict how some observations might look. He has none of that. Even if he somehow guessed it, he doesn't carry sensors to make sense of it. Maybe that's it. He's been interpreting floating in a hyperspace from the limited perspective of a four-dimensional intellect."

"I'm not following," Saint Matthew said.

"If his observations after being injured are just the hyperspace within the time gates, and we can calculate how he would perceive it with four limited senses, we can compare that to what we know. We can build ourselves a decryption key."

It was easier said than done. It took a long time, and repeated verifications of how the Scarecrow's senses worked and Saint Matthew's full emulation of the Scarecrow's cognition based on the computational hardware they could examine. Only after several hours could they predict what the Scarecrow might see of hyperspace. Then, Cassandra worked backwards to find the quantum encryption transformation that would get from those observations to the messy data Pedro had downloaded.

After six more hours, she cracked it.

CHAPTER TWENTY-ONE

When Cassandra finally emerged from sleep, the galley was quiet, with food waiting on the table. To her right, following the curve of the hull, the Scarecrow lay inert, yellow holographic light brightening and ebbing in stochastic time with the ongoing data analysis. To her left, the hull curved up to where Rosalie rested or slept. A tiny rendition of Saint Matthew's holographic head appeared above the table's projector.

"You look like you need a pick-me-up," he said. "Would you like to see data? Maybe the results of the analysis of the skates?"

"Is there anything good?"

The holographic light from the work area and the Scarecrow corpse abruptly darkened, and hard white utility lights started turning on and off on a regular, half-second cycle.

"What happened?" Cassandra demanded. She reached the work area at the same time as Saint Matthew's body coming from the cockpit.

In the harsh, flashing light, Pedro's holographic avatar had changed again. Above Pedro's hardware was a pixelated, holographic tree trunk, top and bottom torn into woody fibers. Pedro was poised over the corpse on bent spider legs, dozens of cables connecting him to the dead Scarecrow. Floating above his avatar was a dim halo of data, apparently decrypted and reorganized.

"What's he doing, Saint Matthew?"

"Fuckin' shoot him," Stills's voice said over the speakers. "He's probably been taken over by Congregate programming."

Saint Matthew's legs clicked closer to the smaller AI. "What's wrong, Pedro?"

The holographic image of the torn tree trunk shifted its palette from natural browns to sickly, blood colors, ranging from bright and oxygenated to dark and anoxic. At the back of the galley, near the airlock to the cargo hold, she and Bel had installed a lockbox with a weapon in it, keyed only to their biometrics. She calculated the time it would take her to reach it and get back to an angle where she could shoot Saint Matthew's offspring.

But a series of visual images bloomed within the cloud of data, displacing it as they grew. Some had the grainy, staticky incompleteness that came from constructing images with missing or corrupted data. Some of the video images showed the *Calculated Risk* in the hyperspace within the time gates, shrinking along a single axis, vanishing from sight. Some video images showed skates tumbling in and out of sight, shrinking and growing along a single line, as they moved in and out of dimensions the Scarecrow couldn't perceive. These were replaced with pixel-blurred video memories of a lonely, dark Nyanga. And there was a slow-motion video of two spacesuited human figures against Nyanga's starscape. Pedro brightened the image artificially to show two dim faces. One was Nordic pale, the way Congregate citizens often were. The other was dark, like Cassandra.

It was Bel.

Unmistakably Bel.

"Saint Matthew..." she said. "Do you have this memory? Could you have seen the Scarecrow on Nyanga?"

"No. And I've never seen the other man."

"That fucker!" Stills's voice roared on the speakers, no longer flat. "Your boyfriend turned on us!"

"When did this happen?" she demanded. Something tried growing in her chest, and she didn't know if it was hope or terror.

"The time signature on the memory looks damaged, or might just be impossible for the Scarecrow to know," Saint Matthew said.

"What else have you got around this recording?" she demanded. "What's the context?"

She and Saint Matthew accessed the partial database of the Scarecrow's memories that Pedro had been assembling. He'd only gone through a third of the memories, and nearly half of those had addressing and metadata problems.

"Why's there so much damage?" she asked.

"My guess is it's from you throwing antimatter at it," Saint Matthew said.

"Damn right!" Stills said.

"I developed layers of redundant processing systems in myself, Pedro, and the *Calculated Risk* to avoid bugs in a high-error environment," Saint Matthew continued. "The Scarecrow probably never had the option. He might not have even known his memory was faulty."

"Could the image of Bel be wrong?" she asked. "A composite from crossed memory addresses?"

"I'm organizing the images into a probable time sequence," Saint Matthew said.

The data vanished as Saint Matthew projected a fish-eyed, panoramic perspective of Nyanga from the viewpoint of the Scarecrow. The video image stuttered and repeated until he froze on the clearest frames that had the sharpest starfield.

"When?" she said.

"Pedro calculates the starfield at March third, 2426 CE."

Thirty-nine years before Bel, Iekanjika, and Saint Matthew had been there. Twenty-nine years before Cassandra first set foot on Nyanga.

Saint Matthew added new images that appeared to be in a logical order, first the building of the transmitter, and then the transmitter the Scarecrow had built. And then the appearance of the two figures, including Bel.

"Why are the video recordings so jerky?" Cassandra asked.

Saint Matthew displayed a series of telemetry reporting, matching them, second by second with the video recordings. There was a sudden upspike across every internal system.

"I think that these telltales report on defense or self-defense systems," Saint Matthew said. "They look like similar cognitive structures I have because I was also grown to be an offensive AI."

"It's doing a limpdicked job of defending itself," Stills said.

Saint Matthew rewound the videos and showed antenna inputs. They were verbal and EM transmissions.

"*Scarecrow recognize authorization overrides amber and green*," a voice said in an oddly accented French that crackled with static.

"You can see the internal response to the amber override," Saint Matthew said, highlighting the telltales. "It wanted to shoot the two figures, but amber override shut down conscious control of defensive systems."

"Freeze playback. Rewind," Cassandra said. "Look at the EM externals." She pointed at complex magnetic readings, more complex than the Scarecrow was able to record. She knew the sort of blurry, truncated readings that artificial sensors made of the texture of *Homo quantus* magnetic fields. No machine could capture the electromagnetic detail that the millions of nanometer-scale *Homo quantus* magnetosomes could.

"A *Homo quantus* magnetic signature for sure," Saint Matthew said. "It is Mister Arjona."

"There are two signals in what the Scarecrow detected," she said numbly.

She manipulated the data, showing two separate magnetic peaks, each with the fuzzy imprecision characteristic of a field made by millions of nano-magnets.

"The other one is *Homo quantus* too?" Saint Matthew said. "I don't recognize him from your records. And I thought all *Homo quantus* came from Afro-Colombian founder populations. The lighting may be bad, but that man's complexion is Venusian pale."

"I've never seen him before," she said.

"The Congregate was working on copying the *Homo quantus*," Saint Matthew said. "Did they get further than we thought before we could rescue the captives at Venus? Their industrial research capability is orders of magnitude more powerful than anything we suspected."

"It was all wasted, you mean?" Stills asked. "We're all fucked, then. Maybe the Banks can wave their dicks at the Congregate for a few decades, but the Union can't and you prancy pants sure can't. Your boyfriend didn't die; they caught him."

"How did they get back here?" Cassandra asked as if in a trance.

"Your boy folded like a chickenshit gambler on the first card," Stills said. "He brought the Congregate back here."

"How?" Cassandra demanded with heat. "We have the time gates. Without them, Bel can't bring anyone anywhere."

"He's done a lot of impossible," Stills said. "Did he shoot a wormhole into your time gates?"

"I don't see how."

"Don't mean he couldn't do it," Stills said.

Her silence felt heavy and dragging, growing in weight as the idea of Bel's betrayal sank in. Then, Saint Matthew's stony, alien holographic face impinged on her field of vision.

"Miss Mejía, despite what we think of as possible, this may be Mister Arjona. We don't have all the information, but we know a few things. We know Mister Arjona is capable of deceiving his captors. We know that he is remarkably insightful in his ability to exploit the greed of others to his own advantage. We know that to do this, he needs to find the right time to act. And we know that he cares deeply for the *Homo quantus*. And for you. We'll come to understand what this really is."

She nodded. Everything Saint Matthew said was true. Yet every time Bel had pulled a con, she'd been in on it, even when everyone else was on the outside. She didn't like being on the outside.

"Show the rest," she said.

"*Override amber authenticated*," the Scarecrow transmitted in the recording, then, as if at a loss, "*Override green…*" and "*Who are you? Middle Kingdom? I carry information the Congregate will want. They will be willing to reward even an adversary in a prisoner exchange.*"

In the crackling visual, Bel was shrinking back, behind the pale man who repeated "*Recognize override green.*"

"*Look at the damage*," a voice said, nearly masked by the snapping of memory drive errors, yet it was Bel's. She hadn't heard his voice in months, not since he'd left on his suicidal mission to Venus. She wiped at her eyes.

"*Diagnostic override green,*" the pale man said again.

"Key authentication systems in the Scarecrow weren't working," Saint Matthew said. He replayed the same clip again.

"What are you looking for?" Cassandra asked.

"His accent. It's not *français* 8.1."

"The Congregate is a big empire. It has a lot of accents."

"Anyone with authentication codes to override one of their elite Scarecrow units has to be from the ruling Congregate houses."

"So it's a new accent," she said.

"That's not how the Congregate works. Their French is core to their identity, as central as Venus and their acid scars. The accents change slowly, with a kind of unspoken social consent that reconciles the rising and falling influence of the different houses. The hegemonic house's accent becomes the dominant one. It's as much linguistic as political."

"There's a new dominant house?" she said. "And it captured Bel?"

"This feels like the accent of the House of Styx, but... matured. I don't know. It takes decades for the dominant accent to shift."

"*Adamantine clearance. Silver authorization, clear water protocol,*" the man in the damaged memory said. The readings of magnetic emissions shifted wildly and non-randomly.

"What's adamantine clearance?" she asked.

"I know about yellow and green overrides," the AI said. "Bank intel knew of them when I was being made. I've never heard of adamantine clearance." Saint Matthew's holographic face tilted as if looking at the data. "The internal trackers register a near-complete shutdown of Scarecrow functions. We're even losing timestamps. And there's a laser transmitter. If it's a long shutdown, it could be a complete download of every observation and thought in the Scarecrow. Horrific..."

Cassandra had never paused to consider that, in principle, Saint Matthew, like the Scarecrow, was downloadable in a way that a human brain was not. Under enough duress, every private part of Saint Matthew, every emulated fear, hope, and secret faith could be exposed and examined. She treated Saint Matthew as a person most of the time, but when irritated or cynical, or when she suspected her pattern-seeking was too strong, she appreciated him more as an excellent emulation whose code she could not see. Maybe she'd been unfair with him.

Bel never had. Bel had always treated and spoke of Saint Matthew as a person.

The Bel in the frozen video?

Where are you, Bel? When are you? What happened to you?

The Scarecrow systems finally showed signs of rebooting. Telltales were different, improved.

"*Ready for exfiltration,*" came the haunting, crackling voice of the Scarecrow.

"*You're not being exfiltrated,*" the Congregate agent said.

"*There isn't space?*"

"*Your mission isn't done. You alone of all Congregate operatives have been within a hyperspatial time-travel device currently being used by terrorist* Homo quantus. *You're to return to the conjoined wormholes.*"

"What?" Cassandra blurted, at the same time that the grainy video snowed over so completely that even Saint Matthew couldn't anything intelligible. "They really know what the time gates are! They sent the Scarecrow back in. Did he report again?"

"There's a lot of data still to decrypt," Saint Matthew said. "Right now, there's a gap of almost a minute."

"They can travel through time?" Cassandra said.

"Fuckin' worst case scenario," Stills said.

"Why?" she asked numbly.

"You and your boyfriend are a fucked-up enough pair, but you just saw a Congregate officer with the same magnetic fields as your boyfriend. You think he's got that, but can't do what you can do? I got a moon to sell you, if you believe that."

"Congregate *Homo quantus…*" Saint Matthew said.

"You fuckers were dangerous enough as free agents. Chaos agents more like it," Stills said. "The Congregate don't prance. They don't do chaos. They make order, at gunpoint when they have to. And they called you terrorists. That's not a temporary thing and they're not a temporary power. They'll be gunning for you for as long as it takes."

"We're vanishing," she said. "We'll go far enough that they'll never find us."

"You think you can find wormhole axes that Congregate agents with your powers can't find?"

"They don't know what we can do."

"Yeah, they do. Your boyfriend'll tell 'em."

The video was still frozen, but the audio on the display snapped into a louder crackling static of damaged data, under which the Congregate agent's voice was dimly heard.

"*The terrorists have a time machine. We can fight them from the future... every era... you've navigated some of the hyperspace... re-enter it, study... Capture any* Homo quantus... *warranted.*"

"*...m too damaged,*" the Scarecrow's voice radioed, as if from a stormy distance.

"*The Congregate requires this of you.*"

The Scarecrow's voice emerged plaintively from the static.

"*...could not be. And you're augmented in some way. No human could have...*"

"*...the* Homo quantus *threat is... The Congregate has found a solution, rooted in the evolutionary ideas of the Scarecrows... the threat in evolutionary terms and we took up the fight.*"

"*You can do this,*" the Scarecrow's voice said with a strange hint of fear. "*You take this mission.*"

"*I have another mission that will... ...found ...to reach the beginning of these conjoined wormholes... them so we can find them anywhere, all... time...*"

They waited, but static swamped the rest.

"We may get more as Pedro decrypts more," Saint Matthew said.

She heard him, but her thoughts circled the last fragmentary words in bewilderment.

"The beginning of the conjoined wormholes?" she said. "In the past. To find them anywhere."

"What the fuck does that mean?" Stills demanded. "What the

tabarnak did your boyfriend give them? Shit even you don't know about?"

Cassandra held her head, trying to stop the spinning ideas, the implications, and the betrayed grief. She took a deep breath. Stills began pressing her again.

"Shut up, Stills!" she said. His speaker went silent. "You're in this with me, so deal with it. The fates of the mongrels and the *Homo quantus* are tied together in the threat of a time travelling Congregate."

CHAPTER TWENTY-TWO

"FUCK!" STILLS EXCLAIMED.

The forward braking jets of the *Calculated Risk* hissed, bring them to a shuddering stop as the straps pressed against Cassandra's chest. In this deep past of the time gates, the grating and snapping at the edges of perception had become a constant irritant. Strange, dim colors lensed in and out of visibility and she wondered if Stills had stopped for a hallucination. Then, proximity alarms rang, and a shape streaked from right to left in front of the cockpit. Two more followed, triangular and solid and fast.

"Skates?" she asked.

"The robot fuckers nearly hit us," Stills said. "And your ship's alarms blow chunks."

"I've been fixing the alarm systems as fast as they break down," Saint Matthew said.

He was. His drones were all over the ship, looking for mechanical and electronic failures before they turned catastrophic. Particles and energies streaking through hyperspace gradually abraded everything, sometimes striking deep within materials. Looking for damage in the middle of a component was difficult, more so here where the geometry of hyperspace made x-rays and high-energy scans uncertain.

"Are there any more?" she asked.

"Fucked if I know," Stills said. "I thought they malfunctioned in here."

"If they go through fast enough, they should make it through before catastrophic malfunctions," Cassandra said.

"Nice theory," Stills said. "If this is their deer path, let's go around. This thing ain't armoured to take a hit like that."

"What are they doing here, though?" Saint Matthew asked. "Are they navigating, or following random tracks and hoping for the best?"

"Stills, rotate us up forty-five degree along the r-axis," Cassandra said.

The cockpit had the feeling of tipping up and the indistinct hyperspatial background blurred and smeared further. Pale purple light peeked doubtfully through the dark graininess, like water through sand. A weird vertigo crept upon her, one she'd come to associate with straddling two dimensions of spacetime at non-right angles. Distance in the ambient magnetic field felt foreshortened. Flattened lines like needles came into hazy view. Many parallel rows of the needles moved from right to left, pastward to futureward, as far as she could see; some moved from left to right, futureward to pastward.

"What is that?" Saint Matthew asked.

Rosalie blinked hard as if her eyes were struggling to focus on an optical illusion.

"Stills put us at an angle to two spacetime dimensions, one of which is a time dimension," Cassandra said. "At this angle, we can 'see' across a duration, a time period instead of just an instant. We can see multiple points in time together, but we lose perspective on most of a spatial dimension. The skates appear flattened into needles."

"*Tabarnak*… I'm trippin'," Stills said.

"What…" Saint Matthew faltered, then began again. "How much time are we seeing?"

"At least ten."

"So for at least ten years, skates successfully transited the time gates?" Saint Matthew said.

"Yes. Here."

"So we're stuck?" Stills said.

"We can go around them," she said.

"So in the real world," Saint Matthew said, "we've reached a point before the time gates were frozen into the ice of Nyanga. Maybe the time gates are in free orbit of a star, like most of the others we've found."

"Maybe," Cassandra said.

More abstracted, flattened needle shapes darted right to left.

"How are the skates surviving hyperspace?" Saint Matthew asked. "I doubt they're following an unpowered low-energy orbit through the hyperspace," Cassandra said. "Shorter exposure may help them."

"It doesn't help us," Stills said.

"We've almost finished this leg of the trip."

"How far is that?" Stills asked.

"About three hundred thousand years in the past," Cassandra said.

"That's the start of the time gates?" he said with a kind of hope in the machine emulation of his speech.

"Not even close," Cassandra said. "Bel and I estimated that the time gates were formed by a collision of two Axis Mundi holes more than ten billion years ago."

"*Crisse*!"

"I'll be able to navigate bigger and bigger jumps as I map more of the interior of the time gates," Cassandra said apologetically. No one seemed happy with this good news.

She gave Stills a new series of navigational instructions to take them around the skate migration. A heavy silence fell on them for the next hour—the twenty-second hour of this leg of their trip—broken only by the occasional acknowledgements and announcements of Stills's progress. Rosalie was exhausted, her eyes unhealthily red-rimmed, but she'd rebuffed all suggestions that she sleep. She was avoiding both dreams and nightmares in hyperspace. Saint Matthew's suffering was quiet, occasionally manifesting as a staticky failure of the rendering of his holographic head, a corroded pixelation of self. She had no idea how the trip was affecting Pedro, nor whether a true subjectivity called Pedro even existed to endure it.

They finally came to a pastward Axis mouth. This region of hyperspace corresponded to an era three hundred thousand years before her time. The mouth was wider, ten meters across.

"What's on the other side?" Stills said.

"We'll only know when you bring us out, so do it slow," she said.

"Don't tell me how to fly," he said. "Just tell me when you're not navigatin' anymore."

"I'm done for now," she said.

Stills made minute changes to attitude with the station-keeping jets. The cold jets on the stern activated, and the *Calculated Risk* penetrated the curtain of slate-grey darkness. Alarms shrieked.

"*Crisse*!" Stills said.

The front of the *Calculated Risk* bucked upward and the inflaton drive bloomed. A faint gravity asserted itself and then they were accelerating starward, pressing Cassandra into her seat. She saw silhouettes of complex, shadowy structures, glimpsed an outlined horizon suggesting both the organic and the engineered. Passive sensors were still sounding. The brown dwarf wasn't in front of them.

"Where are we, Stills?"

"Fucked if I know. Looked like a city. I didn't stick around to take a good look. We were surrounded. Did I tell you how I don't like surprises?"

"The rearward cameras and sensors are working and collecting data," Saint Matthew said.

Among the sensor readings, Cassandra found the brown dwarf at a right axis to their path.

"The axis mouth moved!"

"It may be on the terminator," Stills said. "My straight up is way off. No signs of projectiles or beamed weapons, though."

Adrenaline drained from Cassandra. She imagined it was worse for Stills and Rosalie. Even Saint Matthew would have to check his systems.

"Get us into orbit, Stills," she said. "If we're safe there, we'll sleep. Then we can figure out what's beneath us and what we do next."

CHAPTER TWENTY-THREE

HOMO QUANTUS DREAMS were sometimes geometric problems, transformations of data, the apparent discovery of new features within complex, multi-dimensional observations. While *Homo quantus* brains forgot waking things poorly, their dreams were usually easily flagged to fade. Some of them seized Cassandra with emotions, however, resisting rationality, growing into storms of feelings that blew out slowly, leaving aches in their passage.

Cassandra dream-remembered Bel's dark eyes staring into hers as a fifteen-year-old in love. Her fingers wound into his, gently sparking wordless electrical codes of sweet nothings. She dream-followed him onto Union warships, shards of real memory mixed with things that never were. She dreamed of the Puppet traitor Manfred Gates-15, of the dead Will Gander. They begged for something in the voices of lost *Homo quantus*.

She dreamed of the last time she saw Bel, his body innervated and mutilated by metal and wire to disguise himself as one of the Congregate-enslaved *Homo quantus*. She cried tears, in dream or in sleep as she turned over and over the stinging idea that Bel had betrayed them.

All of them.

Her.

It was not just that anyone in captivity could be made to break. There was always, with Bel, the deeply buried worry that he might be lying, even to her. She imagined that he could carry a lie for years until all suspicion, even hers, had ebbed.

She woke wet-eyed, but the dream didn't let her go. Her brain could hold unpleasant images. She turned on the light in her bunk, trying to see past the fear of Bel betraying her. She tried to tell herself that he'd been ready to die for a hundred and fifty captive *Homo quantus* he wasn't even particularly close to. Why should she worry that he would betray *her* after that?

Maybe he'd been lying. Maybe he hadn't loved her. Or maybe he'd only thought he had?

No.

She didn't deserve to think that. And neither did he. But that resolve didn't close the suspicions born in the face of the man in the Scarecrow's recordings.

She couldn't reconcile it. Bel was gone. Stills's ship had recorded Bel inside the transient wormhole. Based on how far behind he'd been, he wouldn't have gotten out before she'd destroyed the Freya Axis. She punched the mattress of her bunk.

The grainy image of Bel's face was clear in her mind. Bel had been haunted by the *Hortus quantus,* and now he was haunting her. She couldn't exorcise his ghost, but she knew where to find it, where to confront it: at the birth of the time gates. The Congregate agent would be there, trying to exert some control over the time gates, to deny them to the *Homo quantus.* She needed the time gates to escape the gravity of civilization, to go so far that no one would ever find them. For that she needed the time gates stable and safe. She'd found nothing of the source of the strange gravitational waves so far. They'd been elusive, appearing maddeningly in dreams, but there was one place where any gravitational waves could conceivably travel all the way through the time gates, to her present: the origin of the time gates.

A hologram of Saint Matthew's head appeared. "You aren't sleeping well," he said.

"No one is sleeping well."

"It's been a… disturbing experience to visit the past."

"I wasn't made to be a warrior. Or a hunter. Or even a leader."

She heard her own frustration. This wasn't who she was. She didn't lose her equilibrium, give into emotions, nor make them true by making them public.

"You have talents you didn't expect."

"Like you, I'm a good computer," she said. "I can be applied to problems that were not in the original design specs."

"And you sometimes avoid the truth," he said. "Sometimes you avoid seeing yourself from the outside. You're not a computer program any more than I am."

She eyed him with dubious irony, but let the point go. Saint Matthew possessed a kind of emotional cunning she couldn't completely counter and she preferred to avoid his rhetorical and philosophical traps.

"I need your help," she said.

"Of course."

"I need to stop that Congregate agent from whatever he has planned for the time gates. And maybe Bel too." Her resolve floundered momentarily. "I need weapons."

His emulated pensiveness extended into long, silent seconds.

"It's strange," he finally said. "We were both built to give our creators strategic military advantages and we both fled that fate. Yet… here we are, fulfilling their dead intents as if embracing destiny."

"This is that last time. Then we can chase whatever we need to be… whole. You'll make robots with souls. I'll learn the secrets of the cosmos."

He smiled as if those imaginings could come true.

"If you think it's worth the risk, I can create more anti-matter for Stills," he said somberly. "Without industrial tools, the ammunition will be crude and imprecise."

"Yes," she said, "but Bel knows we have that, and so does the Congregate. I need something neither knows. And I need to work out how to fight someone who can move through time."

"What do you have in mind?"

"Could you reprogram the Scarecrow to serve us?"

Saint Matthew's thick stony eyebrows rose, until they touched the bottom of his mitre. "Devious," he said with sad pride.

"You didn't think of it?"

"I thought of it, but I worried about what I might become if I followed those old instincts."

"I'm sorry to ask it."

"It may be that sanctity and grace is out of my reach. I may be fated to dirty my hands so that others, like Pedro, can find salvation."

"This is the last loose end."

"Do you want to come to the cockpit? Stills has some interesting telescopic readings. And I've analyzed yesterday's recordings of Nyanga."

She made her way hand over hand to the cockpit. Rosalie was strapped in, trembling, her face sallow, taking on whatever unhealthy pallors glowed from the cockpit displays. Beyond the window, Nyanga's star seemed dead ahead, white and pink with stripes of red, its high atmospheric metallic dust clouds weaving into streams and spirals. Nyanga was a dark silhouette beneath them, occluding the stars.

"Did you sleep, Stills?"

"I got itchy not knowing what's under us," Stills's machine voice said. "Weird readings, on the surface and up here."

She summoned all her displays.

"Up here?"

"I shaded the cockpit windows, but their star is hotter."

The spectrum and luminosity readings showed it a brighter orange. "I didn't know the brown dwarf was this young," she said. "Three hundred thousand years in the past brought us to its deuterium-burning phase."

"And the planet's warm in all the wrong places," Stills said.

She looked at the temperature map. Nyanga was too close to its star to rotate. At the geographical point directly beneath the star's high noon, Cassandra was used to seeing a thick ring of slightly warmer *Hortus quantus* migrating around the time gates. Three hundred thousand years in the past, that plain was bare, its temperature consistent with low, struggling plant life.

And instead, following the line between dim day and eternal night, something forest-like marked the edge. They'd emerged along the terminator. Their recordings showed a jagged horizon of tall structures from which fronds and leaves like *Hortus quantus* skins faced the brown dwarf. These tree structures appeared ten to fifteen degrees warmer than the rest of the planet on thermal maps.

"The *Hortus quantus* we've seen so far have been… cold-blooded, only a few degrees warmer than the environment," she mused.

"They're still cold as fuck," Stills opined. "And check out the weak EM, too."

She hadn't noticed that the *Calculated Risk* had recorded faint radio signals as they'd emerged from the time gates. There'd been no evidence of technology among the *Hortus quantus,* nor had the Union ever found signs of metal use in core samples. She pulled up all the recordings.

"Where are the time gates?" she asked.

Saint Matthew indicated a location just south of the equator on the terminator.

The images of Nyanga as they'd emerged from the time gates were blurry and dark. Silhouettes showed many tall, narrow structures interconnected by branches or bridges to form a three dimensional lattice. Small, wispy branches seemed to reach out, stretched skins facing the brown dwarf. The images lacked enough clarity to be sure, and she tried not to let her brain fill in the gaps.

"Is it safe to go down?" Saint Matthew asked.

"If everyone down there is still just a little ice chandelier, I can mow through anyone who looks at us funny," Stills said. "Three hundred thousand years should be safe enough to kill anyone I need to."

"That's not how causality works," Saint Matthew said.

"We don't know yet. Bel and I..." she stumbled, remembering the face in the spacesuit. "The *Hortus quantus* exist in the future. We saw them. And they're here now. If Stills breaks a *Hortus quantus* here, it shouldn't change an observation in the future. That death may always have been part of the past. The cosmos may... reconcile inconsistencies."

"You can't know that," Stills said.

"The universe has one or more time travel devices in it," she said. "Without a mechanism to reconcile causal inconsistencies, the universe would already be showing damage. We know from the *Hortus quantus* and the Union that information can travel back in time to complicate causal structures. We'll be careful, though. Start low altitude passes. Maybe we can learn something without landing."

Stills flew a decaying orbit over the terminator, where they saw two different hemispheres. The sullen brown dwarf warmed the surface of the starward hemisphere to minus seventy Celsius, sometimes showing the ground cover as a frozen, choppy sea. Only starlight lit the other hemisphere, but its mountains, foothills, and sharp valleys of crystalline water ice seemed brighter.

"Miraculous in its beauty and in the inventiveness of creation," Saint Matthew said.

"One side is under a heat lamp," Stills scoffed. "The other ain't. No miracle there."

"There's nothing miraculous in ice," Rosalie mumbled.

Cassandra ignored them. Organic and inorganic forces had written complex structures into the terminator. Tall, slender structures towered in rows along the rise and fall of hills. The sunward plants showed signs of having eroded the rough edges of the ice with their waste heat. The topography of the dark side was sharp and hard. Winds no more substantial than ghosts could not break concrete-hard ice.

Stills dropped them to three thousand meters, then two thousand. Weak radio signals near one hundred hertz rose above the radio static of the dwarf star. Their source was harder to pin down.

"It's comin' from all over," Stills said finally. "White noise. All of them. Creepy as fuck."

Cassandra's brain could pull apart the hundreds of signals that summed to the white noise Stills was hearing. A rough Shannon entropy analysis suggested information in the signals, more complex than dolphin and whale signals, but simpler than any human language.

"Can they see us?" Saint Matthew asked.

"The *Hortus quantus* 'see' a little in the infrared," Cassandra said. "The ship isn't much warmer than Nyanga. When we land, we should keep the radiator vanes furled."

"When?" Stills demanded. "I hate the inside of your hyperspace as much as the next dog, but I ain't lookin' to set down roots here."

"I want to check the stability of the time gates here," she said. "Do a low pass over the site."

He ran three hundred meters over where they'd emerged from the time gates hours earlier.

"Nothing," she said.

"They're gone?" Saint Matthew said.

"They might not be affixed to the ice in this era. Expand the search, Stills, out to forty kilometers. There's nothing on Nyanga that can move that far in a few hours."

"I'll find it," Stills said.

She felt the acceleration as he switched to a spiral trajectory. She watched the readings with a sinking feeling until, twenty-one minutes later, he pulled out of the scan.

"*Crisse*!" he swore. "We're fucked."

"They didn't leave the surface," Cassandra said. "They have to be hidden in some way."

"Who's gonna look for them?" Stills demanded.

She traced an electronic pointer across their map of Nyanga. "Bring us down here, around five kilometers near the last known location of the time gates. This looks like the edge of the *Hortus quantus* herds."

"I'm bringin' us down with guns pointed at the walking icicles," Stills promised.

The *Calculated Risk* dropped. A mix of visible and infrared sharpened the dim images of the structures. More familiar *Hortus quantus* forms, slow and motile plants, stood in herds out to several kilometers from the high structures on the hills. Among them slowly walked what seemed to be larger mobile plants. Stills set them down softly, a hundred meters from the edge of the most distant plant herd. Cassandra stared for a long time.

"They're red," she said.

"Who are?" Saint Matthew asked.

"The big ones. The ground cover is about minus eighty degrees, twenty degrees warmer than it was in our time. Most *Hortus quantus* look a lot like the ones you saw with Bel. But there are larger ones with red pigmentation. They're moving faster."

"That's 'fast'?" Stills said.

"Twenty-nine percent faster." She expanded the magnification. "Three hundred thousand years in our past, modern *Homo sapiens* was just beginning to migrate out of Africa, but they were only the youngest of half a dozen hominid species. The *Hortus quantus* here may be as different to those we saw as we are from the first *Homo sapiens*. The red ones are definitely using more energy. Saint Matthew, do you still have that chest piece to translate their biochemical language?"

"It's in the hold," Saint Matthew said. "You think they would still have the same language?"

"Maybe not, but selective pressure might have conserved a biochemical language more than a spoken one," she said. "How many drones can you spare to search?"

"If you don't care about the maintenance of the ship, I can spare all of them, but we don't know how abrasive hyperspace was to components and systems."

"Half of them?" she suggested.

Rosalie was staring ahead.

"Do you want to come, Rosalie?" Cassandra asked.

The Puppet shook her head.

"Rosalie has been helping me with the repairs and reconstruction of the Scarecrow," Saint Matthew said apologetically. "We'll keep working on that. And maintaining the ship."

Cassandra patted Rosalie's arm and retreated to suit up. Several of Saint Matthew's drones met her on the black-slicked ice outside the *Calculated Risk*, dragging the large chest piece. It contained several dozen chambers that could iris open to release specific scents that, as far as they could tell, were the linguistic ideograms of the *Hortus quantus*. The remainder of the chest plate's surface had a carpet of scent receptors for the specific biochemicals of the *Hortus quantus* speech. Cassandra had never used it, and if not for the apparent changes in the alien plants this far in the past, she still might not have pulled it out.

A dozen of the larger plant beings were facing the *Calculated*

Risk from the edge of the herd. Their fronds were higher, and their legs and chest ribbing were thicker, heavier. Their living skins reflected her helmet light in blood red. They seemed to be waiting.

Although far more numerous, the smaller pitch-colored *Hortus quantus* had stalled, unable to pass the larger ones. They seemed ragged, broken down. Broad tears in their skins exposed pale sparkling ice. Some had limbs broken and refrozen in new asymmetries.

Cassandra felt at the electromagnetic environment. Although not optimized to detect radio waves, the sheer number of magnetosomes in her body acted like a large, imprecise antenna array. The radio transmissions were a light burbling white noise.

"The radio signals are definitely from the red ones," she said.

"Get some bodyguards around her, robot," Stills said on the common channel. "If the princess gets hurt, we're stuck on this ice cube and you do *not* wanna spend eternity with me, I promise you."

"These creatures are made of fragile ice at minus eighty degrees, Stills," she said. "They can't hurt me."

"First, ice at minus eighty ain't fragile," he said. "Second, I'll put those words on your tombstone."

She walked towards a cluster of *Hortus quantus,* one of Saint Matthew's drones crab-click following. The red plant beings were about forty centimeters taller, with frost riming the inner skin of their torsos. They absorbed different wavelengths of the weak dwarf light than the *Hortus quantus,* wavelengths that in this era were more abundant.

Past the herd a series of low, snaking hills and plateaus rose, thick with the larger red plants. They stood with fronds perpendicular to dwarf-light. The hills expanded the surface area they could exploit, but something niggled at her. The starlight was stronger, but it didn't account for the speed and energy budgets of these creatures.

The red plants moved with the deliberateness of a high-mass

animal, like a horse side-stepping. Yet even that slow movement meant that the red, tarry plant tissue surrounding the rods of ice must contain something like muscle, with commensurate energy needs. Her brain unhelpfully estimated ecological energy budgets and potential biochemical mediators. She smothered her curiosity.

"They're probably not even the same species," she said.

"Are you safe?" Saint Matthew asked on the radio.

The larger, redder ones, the—Cassandra hastily reviewed her Latin—*Hortus rubrum,* shifted in response to them speaking. Cassandra switched to her suit's laser communicator.

Treating the mobile plants as a maze, Saint Matthew transmitted a walking route to the last known location of the time gates. She followed the virtual path beginning at a gap between the *Hortus rubrum* a few meters to her left. The frond tops slow-swayed a half meter above her head, swallowing her like a forest. Three meters into the herd, a big *Hortus rubrum* side-stepped, closing off the path Saint Matthew had proposed.

"I can shoot them and not you," Stills said with flat promise.

"No need," she said. She gently retraced her steps, listening to a babble of white radio noise she'd found while searching the frequencies. She emerged from the herd, and suddenly Stills was screaming in her helmet.

"What is it?" she demanded.

She bounded into a run, a mistake of instinct. She shot ahead in Nyanga's faint gravity, off balance, and crashed into the concrete-hard ground, shattering low, sessile plants. Their ice fragments spiralled silently into the dark. She got to her feet and staggered to the *Calculated Risk,* punching the airlock controls to the cargo bay.

"Stills's tank has a pressure leak," Saint Matthew said. "I'm deploying drones."

"Your fuckin' Puppet is sabotaging my tank," Stills said. "Pressure droppin' to five hundred and twenty atmospheres."

"Can your drones stop her?"

Cassandra pressed through the inner airlock door to the cargo bay. It was a small, low volume sandwiched between a cylindrical ceiling and a cylindrical floor. Hard white lights glared. Rosalie was bleeding beside Stills's pressure chamber, soft-headed hammer in one hand. Two of Saint Matthew's drones proved too small to pull her away. The spray of water from Stills's tank sliced cleanly through Rosalie's skin. The priestess kept hammering at the source of the spray. The drones recovered and rushed her from behind, as two more came in.

"Get her off!" Stills said. "And plug the leak!"

Rosalie was holding something over the water spray, hammering, oblivious to the flaying of her fingers, which pinkened the water.

"Saint Matthew, call off your drones!" Cassandra said.

"What?" Stills demanded.

"She's pounding in some kind of epoxy into the fracture!" Cassandra said. The drones backed off.

"She was right here when it started!" he said.

"She hasn't got the tools to damage your tank!" she said. "Block it from your side, Stills!"

"I ran out of sealant on this side days ago," he said.

Rosalie's soft, heavy hammer rose and fell desperately, and the spray waned. Saint Matthew swept in with the remaining drones, and they set the pumps to raise the inner pressure. The tank had dropped to four hundred and eighty atmospheres, down from the six hundred Stills needed to survive. The spray stopped. Rosalie collapsed to her knees in smelly pink puddles, torn palms bleeding bright.

Cassandra yanked off her helmet and pulled dressings from the first aid kits. She applied pressure at the many slices the water had written in the Puppet's hands and arms. Rosalie tasted at the stinking air. The odor nearly made Cassandra retch.

"Stills! How are you doing?" Cassandra demanded. "Stills!"

"I think he's unconscious," Saint Matthew said. "I can get the pressure to the mid-five hundreds soon. Hopefully that will be enough."

"Go all the way to six hundred!"

"The tank is cracked and patched with hammered resin. I need to fix it first. You should probably move back, in case Rosalie's temporary fix lets go."

"What happened?" Cassandra demanded. Drones spider-walked through the puddles and up to the resin on the side of the tank. Shuddering drops of water formed and fell.

"I won't know until I x-ray the break."

"Could she have sabotaged it?"

"I don't think so," he said. "She stopped the leak. She was holding the wrong tools to stress the metal."

The rushed panic drained from Cassandra, and apparently from Rosalie. The hangover of adrenaline cascades left Cassandra's hands shaking. Rosalie seemed to become aware of her hands, and winced in pain. She shivered.

"Do you want something for the pain?" she asked.

The priestess shook her head, whispering "*Pain is service. Pain is loyalty. Take it, little fucker.*"

Cassandra recognized at least two quotes from the Puppet Bible. She dragged Rosalie to a fold-down seat against the wall and sat her with feet dangling. Pedro came with medical equipment. "I'll be in the cockpit, Saint Matthew," she said.

Shortly, Saint Matthew's projector click-click-click followed her.

"How's Stills?" she asked evenly.

"I have a drone in Stills's tank monitoring vitals, giving oxygen, and injecting supplements. I don't know how a hundred-atmosphere pressure drop will affect his proteins. He's operated at lower pressures before, but decompression is always dangerous."

She turned to look into the stone eyes in his holographic face. "Is everything all right with Rosalie?"

"What are you asking?"

"She seems to have some symptoms very much like withdrawal. Is there anything I should know?"

He spoke quietly. "I shut off the chip I implanted. I should never have put it in."

"A little late for a crisis of conscience, isn't it?"

"I wanted to ease her suffering as much as you did. I view her… religiosity as misguided, false, and caustic. Objectively wrong. An externally designed cruelty. But those are her defining beliefs, unalterable to her. She didn't give us permission to unmake her."

"Is this about you?" she demanded.

"What?"

"You being selfish," she bit out. "You don't want to steal away her delusion, because that puts yours at risk, doesn't it?"

Saint Matthew's holographic stone jaw ground and the lips pressed tight, as if holding in something tough to say, or take back.

"You've hardened," he said finally.

"I'm still a rational actor. Does Rosalie pose any more risk with the chip off?"

"She's suffering, in pain, in ways neither we nor she can ease. She's a high-functioning addict."

"She didn't sabotage Stills's tank?"

The large stony head shook. "In the grainy, low-light recordings, she reacted to the leak, competently. Any Puppet would have done the same, regardless of personal safety. Their world Oler is falling apart; the first duty of every Puppet is to head off any catastrophic accident that might hurt the Numen."

"There are no Numen here."

"Rosalie is highly intelligent. If we don't go home, there's no chance that del Casal will be released to the Puppets."

"Seeing everything the Puppet way?" she demanded.

"Like Mister Arjona?" he retorted, and Cassandra felt the response bite.

"Maybe we should ask him."

The rough chiseling in the holographic face softened, but threw one more challenge. "There is a difference between feeling empathy and letting emotion sway a judgment."

He stared at her, and she at him, until she felt like an idiot for meeting the eyes of a holographic emulation. She might as well stare at a camera lens.

"I'm sorry," he said. "I didn't betray you lightly. It was a choice of conscience."

"Cold comfort. I should turn it back on."

"I did see something interesting when I shut off the chip," he said.

"What?"

"Rosalie has had more dreams, here. They're on the old chip, but not the new one, which should have recorded her memories more accurately."

"It's defective?"

"Not as far as I can tell," he said. "The new chip is properly wired to all the same neurons as the old one. It picks up every other neuronal input it should. I compared the chips side-by-side. All the control readings match."

"Then why?"

"I don't think she's dreaming, not with her neurons. I think the dream is occurring in the Puppet chip and her brain 'hears' the dreams."

"The Puppet neural chip records information," she protested. "It doesn't have programming and software that would generate visions and experiences."

"I don't understand it," he said. "Whatever the information is that we're calling her 'dreams,' it is not flowing from neurons to chip."

"That leaves transmission as the only possible source of her dreams."

"Except that we can't explain how she received the same signal in the year 2518 and also three hundred thousand years in the past."

"So your reasoning has a flaw."

A holographic graph appeared above the cockpit projector. It was like the last dream they'd recorded from Rosalie's chips: complex, multidimensional, fuzzy, and incomplete, with parts clouded out.

"I don't want to deal with Puppet dreams anymore."

Even as she said it, curiosity pushed her on. Her intellect grappled with the possible meanings of the shape. In how many dimensions should it be interpreted? Was it capturing meaningful relationships between real variables, or was it just an abstraction? Normally, before the *Homo quantus* chased down a question, some vetting assured everyone that it wasn't one of those false positives that sprouted dangerously in their thinking. There was no process here, though, and so hers was the only voice to gainsay Saint Matthew's nonsense, even as her own over-engineered curiosity instinct undermined her resolve. Bel would have said that the *Homo quantus* had their own addictions, a comparison that would have infuriated her. Now, with Bel… absent, her own perfect memory of his needling made the accusations. She carried her opponent with her.

"Stills is hurt," she finally said. "We have no pilot. We don't know where the time gates are. And the Congregate agent is heading to the origin of the time gates. Distractions are dangerous."

The hologram depicting the twisted, strange geometry of Rosalie's dream winked out. Saint Matthew's expression seemed contrite.

"I'll take care of Stills and Rosalie," he said. "The x-ray results are coming in. Stills's chamber probably failed because of hyperspatial abrasion. Particle strikes from perpendicular dimensions weakened the steel under the surface. We found a few other weak spots in his tank, which we'll reinforce."

"And the ship?"

"Abrasion of the ship's hull is less advanced. We've protected the computer systems with triple redundancies and repair algorithms. Me too. The things we can't protect are you, Rosalie and Stills, body and brains."

She'd already initiated the equivalent of redundant processing in her brain, so she wasn't concerned for herself. She needed her pilot—and, she slowly realized, her *friend*—Stills. Somewhere in the last year, she'd gone from fearing the caustic, violent, and unapproachable *Homo eridanus* to needing him.

"What's his prognosis?"

"I'll know more in a few hours. He's awake, but unpleasant."

A silence extended to long seconds between them, an eternity for such minds as theirs.

"Are you going to force your way into the herd?"

"I may not need to," she said. "I have a theory about the larger plants, the *Hortus rubrum*."

CHAPTER TWENTY-FOUR

While the wardens and the Scarecrows represent radical departures from baseline humanity, neither represents a new species or people. They are modified agents who are incapable of reproduction, and therefore cannot be seen as a species in the context of this evolutionary war. They are analogous to worker ants, or non-reproductive somatic cell lineages—functional, but only evolutionarily relevant in a memetic sense.

On the other hand, the neural nets are a kind of fully living, replicating branch of Homo quantus's *evolution. Originally designed as large scale neural tissue culture substrates that could be induced to organize and process information, they became much more. Built from* Homo quantus *baseline neurons with metallic organelles capable of quantum processing, most neural nets were capable of achieving a kind of alien sentience. Fully dependent upon and fully loyal to the Congregate, they are also capable of asexual reproduction: budding, colonizing new tissue culture substrates, generalized fission into daughter consciousnesses, and so on. A full scientific and philosophical understanding of the neural nets and their implications in this war is ongoing.*

Keynote Speaker Script
Strategic and Tactical Defense Symposium, 2912 CE:
Speciation and Extinction Dangers

"ARE YOU SURE you want to do this while Mister Stills is injured?" Saint Matthew lasered. "If you need backup, I'm… not as skilled."

The growing number of *Hortus rubrum* faced the ship. As near as Cassandra could tell, sight and even infrared were not important to the larger creatures. Approaching them, she listened to the radio noise, sorting the different signals. She'd cracked the broad structure of the *Hortus rubrum* code relatively quickly. Each *Hortus rubrum* transmitted a small set of station-keeping, maintenance, and defense signals. In response to nearby and distant signals, the *Hortus rubrum* in front of her assumed distributions and postures that looked like the defensive geometries of hive creatures.

Most importantly, their transmissions always included a common signal that she guessed was a hive-wide belonging signal.

She transmitted that belonging signal, while dampening all her other transmissions. If this worked, she wouldn't be invisible to the *Hortus rubrum,* but wouldn't be perceived as an intruder, either. Taking a steadying breath, she sidled between two *Hortus rubrum*. Behind them, the smaller *Hortus quantus* were stalled by the obstructing phalanx of the larger plants.

Nothing reacted to her presence.

"I'm going farther in," she lasered back to Saint Matthew.

Tarry black plant life slicked the concrete-hard ground, as she threaded between vanes of skin and rising fronds of individual *Hortus quantus* and *Hortus rubrum*. The ground's low slope rose steadily, towards terraces that created ledges for *Hortus rubrum* to stand in unshaded starlight. The proportion of *Hortus rubrum* increased until the *Hortus quantus* became scarce. The *Hortus rubrum* occupied the territory with the most starlight, relegating the *Hortus quantus* to lower, uneven ground partly shaded by other high, rooted plants.

Cassandra stopped on a terrace partway up the slope. The low electrical hum of the *Hortus rubrum*'s radio emissions sounded in her helmet. She emitted the same identifier and they ignored her. Her hands hovered near the limbs of a *Hortus rubrum*, feeling at the electromagnetic environment with her magnetosomes. Where the radio signals emerged, she felt lines of weak conductors in the plant. They weren't metal conductors, though.

Mysteries.

From a pocket, she drew out a small Geiger counter. It clicked rapidly and loudly near the joints of the *Hortus rubrum*.

More mysteries.

She started as the *Hortus rubrum* she'd been studying shifted to face her, slowly, ponderously, like a horse turning. Slow arms reached towards her. She backed away, turning off the Geiger counter. She hadn't thought that the *Hortus rubrum* might hear the device's white noise. She retreated further, surprised at the *Hortus rubrum*'s speed—not as fast as her, but faster than the *Hortus quantus*.

She walked higher, along terraces filled with standing *Hortus rubrum* and the rare *Hortus quantus*. With her electronics off, none of them reacted to her. The hills rose with a strange steepness. She encountered more and more trenches, as if material had been excavated to raise the hills higher. A snow of water, and probably nitrogen, began falling, the small flakes visible in the churn of winds crossing between Nyanga's gloomy day and eternal night. The gusts and eddies were noiseless, insubstantial, ghostly.

She came to larger trench running across her way, as far as the eye could see. About three meters wide, and three deep. She could jump across if she wanted to risk it, but the ground everywhere was slick with black and red plant films which might hide gravels or even holes. If she got injured, help would be complicated.

She shone her wrist lamp down into the darkness. The omnipresent plant ground cover was uniformly scarlet in the trench, but why? The trench was permanently shadowed. No infrared or even solar flare would ever light the space. Shining her lamp up the hill, the red ground cover ran upward to the next terraces, where red fronds swayed in the muted wind. At the same time, a minute, doubtful tingling began in her magnetosomes—the dim magnetic signature of a mouth of the Axis Mundi network.

The signal would strengthen as she neared it. She checked the laser connectivity to the *Calculated Risk*. Still good. She and Saint Matthew traded notes, and she told him what she was going to do.

"I want to send a few drones with you," he said. "Can you wait?"

His drones had only been able to penetrate a few meters into the herd before drawing the attention of the *Hortus rubrum* with their electronic emissions. Most of their ways forward had been blocked. Saint Matthew was mapping out steeper pathways for the drones, free of motile plants, but they would take time. And she didn't want to disturb the herd or raise its alertness.

"No, but follow discreetly," she lasered back, "in case I need help."

She turned and lowered herself into the trench. Dropping was simple in the weak gravity. The deep darkness, relieved only by the shine of her helmet lamp, felt oppressive. But beyond the visible, something was active here.

She crept along the bottom, feeling at the electromagnetic world. Every meter or two, a low current veined under the plant mat, connecting to the terraces above her. The currents felt similar to what she'd observed within the *Hortus rubrum*. She'd avoided disturbing the *Hortus rubrum* with a biopsy, but she had no qualms about snipping flesh from ground cover. She localized the current, cut around it, and peeled off a rectangular flap of red plant tissue, exposing the glittering water ice beneath.

Coming to the other trench wall, she took a practice hop, and then leapt high enough to grip the edge. She pulled herself up to the next terrace, where larger *Hortus rubrum* 'sunned' themselves. They were still, but their radio signals were more complex. It would take time she didn't have to decipher the code, so she just mimicked the new transmissions. They remained still.

The terraces rose unevenly from one to the next, separated by increasingly deep trenches crossing her route. About halfway up the hill, she reached the first of what had looked through their telescopes like buildings or forests. Her helmet lamp lit columns of ice standing six to eight meters tall, tightly wrapped in red plant film. Ripples, lumps, and gaps in the columns suggested that they'd been quarried and lifted into place, a technology apparently lost to the *Hortus quantus* of the future.

More astonishingly, as she pressed onward, the dark cover retreated, revealing rowed columns capped with beams of ice. Some of these beams spanned the trenches, reaching columns on the next terraces. Broad-leafed, sessile plants festooned the beams, like a froth at the feet of the *Hortus rubrum*, which stood like birds on a fence. What she might at first have thought of as monumental architecture was instead functional constructs to increase the available photosynthesizing area.

Past these creatures the signal from the time gates was stronger. There was no room on the beams for her to cross, so she lowered herself into the next trench. She fell into a rhythm of jumping and climbing out of each trench, slowly mounting the hill, and taking samples as she went. She looked back periodically, and the wide plain below the foothills extended farther and farther, out to a shadowed, curving horizon. Telescoping her augmented vision to maximum, she discerned slow-moving *Hortus quantus* silhouettes reflecting the starshine, all along the bottom of the foothills that ran along the terminator. Why were they all here, instead of beneath the more intense light where the brown dwarf hung in the high noon position, as they did in the future?

The radio noise of the *Hortus rubrum* at this level was louder and more sophisticated, without the base signals she'd mimicked on the lower terraces. Their red skins seemed to merge with the shiny plant ground cover running along the plateau and into the trenches; they had the anatomy for walking, but seemed to have rooted themselves. Why? A seasonal adaptation? A sexual dimorphism? She didn't pursue the question as far as she wanted. She noticed the faint signal of the time gates, maybe a hundred meters ahead of her. She stepped between rows of *Hortus rubrum*.

One of them turned ponderously, as if to face her. She stilled and the creature did nothing else. The infrared emissions of her suit were as cold as they were—she hadn't drawn their attention with waste heat. This cluster of *Hortus rubrum* was slowly active, apparently combing the ground. Her passive Geiger counter began ticking. She uncapped the active counter on her wrist utility band and moved to get an unobstructed view of whatever the more active *Hortus rubrum* were obstructing. The clicking rose fast, spilling into lists of data and graphs on the inside of her faceplate. The radiation split between particle and electromagnetic, and she started categorizing the signals by probable isotopes. Radium. Uranium. Plutonium. Thorium. Phosphorus-32. Even some deuterium and sulphur-35. This mix had been seen before—within skates. Skates used radioactive decay heat to melt and superheat volatiles for thrusting.

She stepped closer. The *Hortus rubrum* seemed to be combing a patch of brighter, icy regolith, stripped of plant growth. Within the crumbling, shining crystalline gravel of water ice were fragments of skates, shards that could only be made in high-speed collisions. If one believed that skates were self-replicating robots that had slipped their programming, then their most visible emergent behavior was racing from system to system, through the permanent mouths of the Axis Mundi. At their speeds, they would shatter against the terrace plateaus and walls. The *Hortus rubrum* had found an old crash site. Were they seeking otherwise unavailable minerals?

She pressed on, down the next trench wall and up the other side, taking more careful readings.

The peak of the hills snuck up on her, a strange, uncomfortable place. This high ridge was a ribbon only a few meters wide, crowded with *Hortus rubrum,* extending off into seeming infinity in both directions, following the terminator. She was easily a thousand meters above the plain where the *Calculated Risk* had set down. The view was vertiginous. She'd spent her life in cramped habitats, and here, a few steps away, a precipice plunged into the dark.

The *Hortus rubrum* at the summit were also seemingly attached to the red, tarry ground cover. The ecological energy budget estimates running in her head could attribute some of their larger size and activity to their unobstructed access to the light from the brown dwarf, but not all of it. Their burbling radio signals had grown more complex here, too. Her Shannon entropy estimation calculation of the information content was high, as high as Anglo-Spanish or French. These signals didn't indicate slow-thinking beings who would evolve into some kind of joined consciousness over the millennia. Each *Hortus rubrum* individually processed and responded to a complex exchange of information.

She didn't know how much they perceived of her. She'd camouflaged herself below in the repetition of the simple, low-level *Hortus rubrum* radio signals, but none of the creatures here made those simple patterns.

Cautiously, she went to the dark edge where the eddies and turbulences of the ghostly atmosphere were almost tangible.

Below her feet, the plateau dropped off into jagged ravines and trenches. The signal of the time gates came from somewhere down there. Her suit's lidar showed the dark space before her to be ten meters deep. She shot a quick report to the *Calculated Risk* by laser, and then hung by her hands over the edge. When her fingers unclenched, she skidded down the steep wall, coming to a quick, sudden stop.

The bottom of the trench was uneven, narrowing in places to fifty centimeters. She'd expected crunchy, gravel-like regolith under her boots, and geological tearing on the walls, but everything was smooth. Nyanga had no erosive forces to explain it—no wind, no micrometeorite impacts, no flares. The red plant cover was down here, inexplicably in eternal shadow, where photosynthesis was impossible.

Her little cone of helmet light revealed blood red trench walls. Every so often, she found a small electrical current running up the wall, to one of the standing plants. Then it hit her—the reason the plant cover extended into the cold dark, and why the largest of the *Hortus rubrum* appeared rooted to the ground cover.

The faint currents passed between the dwarf-warmed surface plants and the forever-dark plants in the trenches, at temperatures of minus eighty degrees and minus two hundred degrees respectively. They were exploiting the temperature difference. The *Hortus rubrum* had evolved a kind of thermoelectric generation, producing a current from the differential. That was why these mobile plants were not in the center of the plain directly below the star. They needed the light and dark, the warm and cold across the terminator of a frozen world. Her thoughts ran, trying to calculate how much energy they might gather in this way. She pressed on, over red plant, smooth water ice, sometimes splashing through slippery puddles of liquid nitrogen. The low electromagnetic murmuring of the time gates strengthened as she followed the bottom of the trench. The clicking of the Geiger counter rose, too.

Then, shapes loomed in her way.

They were smaller and less robustly-built than the *Hortus rubrum,* or even the *Hortus quantus,* an effect exaggerated by the lack of top fronds that lent the other plant creatures the illusion of height. Dark red skin was stretched tightly over icy bones, and tethered to the plant growth slicking the trench walls.

The time gates were just beyond them, the dark, cloudy mouths about a meter from each trench wall. It looked like they'd piled blocks of ice on each side of the lower edges, fixing them in place. Faint gasps of pollen reflected red in her sighting laser. The wall in front of the pastward mouth of the time gates was shiny ice, plant cover shredded away across about ten meters. The bottom of the trench was littered with brown fragments of what looked like ceramic chips, dirty slush, and grains of radioisotopes.

It was a skate crash site.

Ingenious and revealing. The *Hortus rubrum* were not the crash scavengers she'd thought. They were trappers, setting up the time gates where any emerging skates smashed into concrete-hard ice, spilling their radioisotopes—and more. The *Hortus quantus* and *Hortus rubrum* had no metallurgy, no fire, and until now, no evidence of tool use. The metal compounds that mediated the thermoelectric generators must all come from these skate crashes.

The *Calculated Risk* had been lucky to emerge on the terraces when they did. The frozen plant creatures had evidently quickly moved the time gates to a more secure place.

The time gates were useless to her in this trench, and she couldn't risk trying to yank them out of the ice. She might reach them by smashing the plants, but for all she knew that might draw more of them to her. And even if she could melt the time gates free from their moorings, she didn't think she could carry them out of this hole on her own.

Above her, over the edges of the two sides of the trench, a piece of ice was slowly sliding across the gap, blocking out the starlight. And then slowly, another beside it. Were they trying to wall her in, or were they protecting the time gates?

She needed help. She turned to retrace her steps to a part of the trench beneath open sky, and her helmet light fell on three of the tethered, trench-working creatures. They hadn't been behind her before; the sound of their coming had not carried on the faint atmosphere. She might be strong enough to move them, but they were ice hard—one unlucky blow on her faceplate and she'd be dead. Another beam of ice slid across the stars eight meters above her. One of the creature came close behind her, swinging a heavy arm of ice.

She projected the curve of its swing and sidestepped. Her environment translated into a language of geometry—the angles and speeds of the plant limbs, their height, her height, the closing roof over the trench, and especially gravity. Cassandra leapt over the heads of the creatures, tucking to somersault before straightening her body to land beyond them.

Other short red creatures were now in the trench, untethered. Beyond them were more. The terrace was about nine meters above her head, higher than she thought she could jump. It was unobstructed, but she didn't know how long that would remain true. She stood next to the wall and jumped as high as she could. The ends of the fingers of her right hand just caught it. She hung unsteadily for a moment, until she could secure a hold with her left hand too.

She pulled herself up to the ribbon of plateau running along Nyanga's terminator. It bristled with tall *Hortus rubrum*. The nearest one lifted its leg, ripping clear of the ground cover, exposing the ends of dark plant vein and puffs of gas. By the time that icy foot came down, another was rising. The *Hortus rubrum* turned far faster than the ponderous *Hortus quantus*. All along the terraces leading to the plain, the *Hortus rubrum* were moving. The whole herd was reacting.

She didn't know what to do. She might kick the nearest one, tear its fragile plant skin, maybe knock aside icy bones, but even if it worked on one, it wouldn't work on a hundred. Her only weapon was her brain. She saw abstracted geometries, her brain marking locations and assigning theoretical speeds to each *Hortus rubrum*. Like a wargaming scenario, she modelled each individual's possible movements each second. The net they represented was closing.

She leapt off the summit, the weak gravity bringing her to an open space two terraces lower. She heard a burst of radio crackling and some of the *Hortus rubrum* turned towards her. They couldn't have yet detected her with their poor sight, but they were coordinating with each other, to close the gaps between them. They were far more intelligent than she'd thought—individually, collectively, or both.

Four terraces down, a large space in their tightening web was slower to close. She ran and leapt hard, with a near-instinctive understanding of how momentum would work in this gravity. She soared through the breathless wind over red fronds, windmilling her arms to keep balanced.

The ground wasn't where she'd expected. Her feet hit the tarry plant ground cover and tore right through to the waist deep hollow beneath. Her ribs slammed against the lip of the hole, and her feet twisted painfully. Only the light gravity saved her from breaking both, but she was winded and aching.

She thought fast, and reacted fast, but before she could right herself and scramble out, the tarry ground cover to her right and left puffed out, rising to block her vision, as if to grip her. They were electrically loud to her senses, and tensed like muscle. She leapt nearly straight up, as high as she could, directing herself with only her memory of the layout of the terraces and the positions of the *Hortus rubrum*. One ankle twinged painfully, but she had no time to think about anything other than the trap they'd set for her.

They'd manipulated her. The *Hortus rubrum* until now had acted slower than they were capable. They'd assessed her abilities and had tempted her to jump to a disguised pit. That kind of spatial awareness and capacity for deception were hallmarks of advanced intelligence. What other dangers could they pose?

"Miss Mejía!" Saint Matthew said into her helmet speakers. "What's happening?"

The arc of her jump barely kept her feet beneath her, and on the lowest terrace, she crashed onto a *Hortus quantus*. It shattered beneath her, black skin tearing to flaps of nothing among blade-like shards of ice. One of the shards pierced her suit above the ankle, and an unimaginable cold bit her skin. She didn't pull it out; it was all that was holding in the atmosphere of her suit. She leapt again, to the edge of the *Hortus quantus* herd at the beginning of the plain, where the red ground cover gave way to black. She fell and slid and bounced across the smooth plant slick, tearing some of it with her wrist tools, belt and toe tips. Only blind luck kept her from knocking down another *Hortus quantus*. She hoped the Hortus quantus were no faster in this era than in hers, and that they weren't part of this trap.

"I'm…" she gasped. "I just need to get inside. Then back us off a kilometer or two."

She looked back. The *Hortus rubrum* weren't pursuing. The plain was not their territory. She limped to the ship and hung heavy on the hand grips as she waited for the airlock to cycle.

"What happened out there?" Saint Matthew pressed by radio.

"I underestimated them."

CHAPTER TWENTY-FIVE

History of the Wardens—Introduction

The final form of the mosaic organisms known as the wardens was established and approved by a consensus of the Adamantine Council in the proceedings of 2943 CE. The wardens are produced by inserting modified Homo congregatus *stem cells into an immunocompromised* Homo quantus *blastula at appropriate locations based on known embryonic fate maps. The resultant mosaic juveniles possess a high degree of intelligence, a facility for geometries and mathematics, and an immunological suitability for surgical grafts of foreign technology.*

It was the grafting of forerunner processing circuitry into juvenile warden subjects that eventually led to the development of beings capable of directly interfacing with the damaged forerunner blocks. Refinements proposed by 33rd-century surgeons resulted in reductions in psychological instabilities, increased longevity, and higher-fidelity interfacing with forerunner technology. It is no exaggeration to say that all foundational understandings and insights into the forerunner blocks until the 34th century has been mediated through the wardens.

Subsequent research beyond…

The Strategic Technological History of the Congregate
Flag Officers Course
Staff College, Venus

THREE TIMES, BELISARIUS-77 had unwillingly accompanied Centurion Phocas to other centuries, to the *Argenteuil*, to Manafwa Station, and to Nyanga. Although the idea of a fourth trip was existentially vertiginous, he had followed Phocas onto the larger, faster ship. The centurion was bringing a larger crew—his special ops team—which made Belisarius-77 feel even more out of place.

He didn't know what future century had midwifed the *Flechette,* but he sometimes saw variations of this advanced craft at meetings of the Centurions in hostile territory. Two hundred meters separated bow from stern, along a diameter of seven meters, giving it the profile of an arrow from a distance. Its reflective external finish suggested shadowed gold. Along the length of its hull, organic Venusian diamond shuttered powerful weapon emplacements. A two-meter hollow along its center housed the *Flechette*'s powerful, miniaturized inflaton drive.

Belisarius-77 had tried to discreetly beg off the mission, but had never found Centurion Phocas alone. He'd finally been forced to ask Phocas in front of the *Homo congregatus* special ops commander, who was some kind of incongruous melding of evolved quantum perceptions and battle implants. Belisarius-77 had pointed out that *Homo quantus* genetic engineering was not designed for covert missions, and that he was largely obsolete tech in any case. In the glow of the yellow strategic holograms of the century headquarters, Phocas's icy blue eyes reflected a vague aquamarine. The disappointed squint was mixed with some emotion Belisarius-77 could not identify.

"Go where you're told," Phocas finally said. "You may have a use. You're entangled to the original Belisarius."

That had been the end of it.

The information they'd downloaded from the Scarecrow on Nyanga had been a vast trove, only some of it intelligible to Belisarius-77. Scarecrows had many functionalities, but lacked sensors suitable for recording or analyzing the strangeness within the hyperspace of Mejía's conjoined wormholes. However, special teams had deduced many things from what it had recorded. One of those analysts, a neural skein, was aboard the *Flechette*, relegated to the payload specialist area with Belisarius-77.

The skein's diamond tank was a square about two meters high and wide, thirty centimeters deep, filled with transparent, reddish liquid. On one inner face, the liquid appeared cloudy, within its own glow of yellow-green light. The neural skein was a being engineered and grown from *Homo quantus* neural tissues, a brain without a body, free-living for years in a laboratory tissue culture environment. The skeins colonized flat substrates that guided axon and dendritic growth into more complex network connections than any achieved in *Homo quantus* skulls, knitting together ten times the neurons of a humanoid brain. These self-aware beings were capable of powerful feats of analysis, outthinking most networked computers, AIs, or even the *Homo congregatus* themselves. This colony of neural skeins had absorbed the Scarecrow data downloads as well as Centurion Phocas's observations. They'd developed a method for marking Mejía's conjoined wormholes, to make them—and therefore the fugitive *Homo quantus*—trackable, but it would only work if applied at the *origin* of the conjoined wormholes.

So they were at the Wheelhouse, the source of the Congregate's ability to move through time, and their principal tool for knitting together a cohesive and durable history. Belisarius-77 had never had a chance to count the mouths of the Axis Mundi here, but it was many, some of which crossed star systems, many more of which opened onto other eras of time. No one had quite suspected that the conjoined wormholes would be quite so old. This had stalled them in the 34th century for weeks so far. The resources of the Wheelhouse were marshalled to finding a way to dial back their mouths of the Axis Mundi to a time when the universe was less than a billion years old.

This wait was so long that unlike previous trips to the Wheelhouse, Belisarius-77 could plug into the external systems and examine the environment. X-rays and gamma rays scoured the star system. They seared out of a skirt of hydrogen gas falling into a seven-solar-mass black hole. The spectrum was accented by other frequencies, sullen infrareds and crackling radio noise. At the poles, powerful jets of intense gamma rays blasted half a lightyear each way into the void. A series of iron and lead shields orbited between the black hole and the Wheelhouse, protecting ships, labs, dozens of Axis Mundi mouths, and the artifacts.

Farther from the black hole, layers of seen and unseen Congregate naval pickets and space artillery pointed inward and outward. Outward-looking forces protected the Wheelhouse from potential invaders, although its location and even existence were secret. Inward-looking forces ensured that visitors from past centuries saw nothing of the 34th century.

Skates were the only creatures here other than the Congregate. The half-living machines preferred the pulsar nodes of the Axis Mundi network, but black holes also emitted the microwave frequencies that powered them. Flocks of them co-orbited with the Wheelhouse, some of them occasionally diving into one of the wormholes, apparently at random. Researchers hoped that examining the skates across a thousand years of time, in addition to studying them across space, would finally hint as to their provenance and life cycles.

No one stopped Belisarius-77 this time when he turned the external sensors on the three blocky objects, about half a cubic kilometer each in volume. Heat-scored, in the full glare of the x-rays, they seemed bound together. One of them was badly cracked through its center, and was missing large pieces. The gaps revealed hollows and tunnels running all through it, as if worms had eaten dead wood. Another block's top right vertex had been shorn off. Only one seemed nearly complete. All three of them had a kind of alcove or mouth in one side, two of which glowed with a spectral yellow-green light. Before one of these hollows co-orbited several Axis Mundi mouths. Even from within the *Flechette*, Belisarius-77 could feel their finely textured magnetic fields and the weird electromagnetic and gravitational waves they emitted. Spacetime was being tortured around those machines, the Axes Mundi itself bent into apologizing topologies, accessing dimensions of spacetime normally denied the beings of normal space. The Congregate of the 34th century could change not just *where* an Axis Mundi mouth opened, but *when*.

Centurion Phocas had told Belisarius-77 three stories to explain the Wheelhouse, although he admitted that even he, due to the exigencies of avoiding grandfather paradoxes, did not know the full story. In the first explanation, Phocas said that Congregate Centurions beyond the 35th century had captured the blocks from some enemy, and had brought them back in time, for study and exploitation, as the Congregate did with many technologies. In the second story, Phocas characterized the three blocks as a partially-failed experiment to reverse engineer something found in the far future by Congregate operatives. The third story made of these devices leftovers and ruins of the forerunners, still partially functional, recovered by agents in a future century.

All three stories might be lies. They wouldn't be Phocas's first lies, nor the first time he had tested Belisarius-77. The Centurion's intentions were inscrutable, even accounting for Phocas's restrictions from latter centuries. Phocas was ambitious, in ways that Belisarius-77 thought might not be appreciated by other centurions, but for better or worse, his fate was tied to the centurion's. This was not a unique statement. The neural skein could say as much. As could the warden, who also sat nearby.

"Be patient," the warden said in a raspy, provincially accented French. "We don't understand these machines, but we can make them work, if we're careful," she said, mistaking the source of his anxiety.

The warden's inhumanity was more disturbing than the neural skein's, or even the petrified *Homo quantus* pilot. The latter two fit into the compartmentalized logic Belisarius-77 imposed on his world. The petrification process made Scarecrows of humans; of the Congregate's captive *Homo quantus*, it made durable, quantum slaves.

The wardens didn't fit into clean conceptualizations.

They were the custodians, researchers, and defenders of the Wheelhouse and its alien technologies. Belisarius-77 imagined that the Congregate had suffered through some long failure to wrest the secrets from the ancient blocks. They'd broken through by modifying a sub-population of *Homo quantus* to directly interface with the alien technology. The Congregate had made its own aliens.

The *Homo quantus* who would become wardens had been grafted to parts and subsystems of the blocky machines. Grafts of mineralized anatomy shelled the arms, legs, chest, and heads of the wardens like pieces of an incomplete carapace. Like the bodies of skates, the graft components were sintered ceramics, extensively innervated with computational threads. The wardens became neural bridges to the damaged machines. And their strange existence had borne the intended fruit: they had reactivated basic systems in the blocks, including their ability to manipulate the mouths of the Axis Mundi.

Perhaps more eerily, the Congregate had succeeded in changing the wardens' minds in ways they never could with tenth-generation *Homo quantus* like Belisarius-77. The wardens loved the Congregate, loved them in ways that left a gulf between them and the *Homo quantus* much larger than the alien substances grafted over their flesh.

"Are you going to dial us into the wormhole we need?" Belisarius-77 asked cautiously.

"Not me," came the strange, muffled French. "I'm to care for you where you're going, and I have my own research interests."

Beneath the mask-like mineral face, with her dark, glassy eyes, the warden breathed air, but she didn't need to. Petrified skin, between grafted plates of thinking, computational organic mineral, protected the flesh from the heat and cold of space. Metal webs over the mineral grafts, visible and not, absorbed energy, and shaped the magnetic environment in ways that sometimes made Belisarius-77 queasy. More alien were the internal, organic interferometers to detect gravitational waves, and the reputed twisting of natural *Homo quantus* perceptions into senses that could discern the bending of spacetime.

"Where are we going?" Belisarius-77 asked.

He had only a vague idea of what Phocas had meant by 'the origin of the conjoined wormholes.' The range seemed large to him, and quite abstract. Billions of years felt like a cover story or counter-intelligence, another test on Belisarius-77 instead of the truth. The itch of curiosity rose in him, but not enough to suppress the lingering fear that as soon as Phocas found out that he was not fully functional, he would become something like the warden. Or the pilot. And every minute he was with Phocas, that danger increased.

The geometric dreams had continued.

"Far," the warden said.

"You think there are more of those block machines there?"

"Maybe. We don't know. No one has ever gone this far back."

"Can we get back home after it's done?" Belisarius-77 asked.

"We hope so."

"You can't gamble the life of a Centurion on a 'hope so'," he retorted.

"You'd be surprised what will be risked for the long bets," she said. "They can always make another Centurion."

"And another warden?" Belisarius-77 retorted with barely contained alarm.

"Be patient. I believe we can come back, but we can't go unless we can dial the machine to the right place and moment in spacetime."

Belisarius-77 couldn't imagine the difficulties in folding a hyperdimensional spacetime object to touch another time. The only people who could understand it had become part-mineral organic computational devices, or were neural networks living in tissue culture conditions. A soft chime sounded, and the stony chin of the warden's facial graft rose in a way that suggested human curiosity.

"Success," she said. "We are about to become some of the most distant travellers ever."

"Some of?" Belisarius-77 asked.

"In an empire that spans many millennia," she said, "I hesitate to suggest our accomplishments have not already been surpassed in distant futures."

Belisarius-77 called up the external sensors again. The central block, one of the two great machines that seemed to be working, glowed more brightly and steadily around the mouth of the Axis Mundi it cupped. That mouth grew as they neared it.

"Why is it still glowing?" he asked. "Isn't it done readdressing the axis?"

The flat planes of the warden's face were expressionless, but her head tilted as if considering.

"Dialing an Axis into another Axis isn't a permanent change," she said. "Think of it as... the machine holding the door open for us, for a certain amount of time, until the torsion in the bending of spacetime becomes too much to sustain."

"It's temporary?" Belisarius-77 demanded. "How long have we got?"

Her voice pitched to something with a hint of cheerfulness. "One never knows."

CHAPTER TWENTY-SIX

Cassandra left her *Hortus rubrum* samples in a frigid, near-vacuum cell in the cargo hold for the AIs to study. Saint Matthew's drones fussed over her. The shard of ice was a sharp hurt in her leg. The water ice was laced with ammonia, stabbing two centimeters into her calf, making a frostbitten puncture wound. Rosalie peeked around the curve of the hull to see how she was. She said nothing, and retreated when Cassandra spoke.

"Stills is awake," the AI said in response to her questions. "The pressure dropped more than we thought. Three hundred and fifty atmospheres. He's sustained some neural damage. I'm still assessing."

"Why neural damage?"

"It's not *just* neural damage," Saint Matthew said. "Many tissues suffered protein denaturing, membrane rupturing, and pressure-related ion imbalances. But the neural damage is what we can't easily fix, and it might slow his reflexes and reaction times."

Stills had to fly them out of here, of course, but there was a larger loss. She perfectly remembered the terrible, graceful, chaotic art he painted with a palette of violence, reflexes and overclocked propulsion systems from within a fast fighter.

"Should I talk to him?"

"I don't know," he said. "I've been cautiously factual with him. You're not naturally empathetic, but I think he likes that about you."

His words carried no sting, but she didn't quite believe them. A machine believing itself to be a saint might be more empathetic than her, but she was not human and the AI could only measure the *Homo quantus* in human terms. She could bridge the divide to others, but it might not look the way the AI expected or recognized. She decided to hold off on seeing Stills yet.

"I need your biochemical analyses."

"Pedro already started," he said. For a moment, the emulation of his holographic eyes seemed to look pensively into the distance, beneath the stony mitre. "What do you think we'll find?"

"Looking only at behaviour and measures of sunlight, I think you're going to find tissues to concentrate and exploit the heat of radioactive decay to facilitate movement and probably metabolism. They may also generate electricity by exploiting temperature differentials of over a hundred degrees. I think the *Hortus rubrum* might be genetically colonial, clonal, or even a super-organism. I'm going to see how close I can come to cracking their radio language. We need to be able to talk to them. If we can't, to get back into the time gates we might need to destroy a lot of the ones nearby, and I don't want to risk that."

Cassandra installed herself in the cockpit. They were settled four kilometers from the terminator terraces and the *Hortus rubrum*. Some *Hortus quantus* were grainily visible at three kilometers in electronic magnification. She was alone with the starscape and her scientific problems. She called Stills.

"What?" Stills answered.

"I called to see how you're feeling."

"Fuck off."

"That bad?"

"Ain't nothin'. Your crazy AI thinks I got nerve damage. Maybe I do. Maybe I don't. I can still fly, and fly better'n anybody else. And if I can't, well, I always knew that somewhere out there was a bullet with my name on it. Woulda been nice to have died in an ocean, but I'll take what I can get."

"You're not even close to dead."

"Are you seriously tryin' to bedside manner me?"

"When will we know?" she asked.

"If I still got it? When we roll the dice."

"Saint Matthew can test you."

"The real world is the only test."

"Do you want us to take you home?" she asked.

"Like I'm done? Bite me. Besides. Who's gonna fly?"

"I guess I'll have to. Or we'll get another mongrel pilot."

"If you think either of those things is better than me, you're gonna be surprised as fuck."

"We've got a long way to go before this is done."

"I can keep it up all you need, darlin'."

She was silent for a time, staring at the cockpit controls.

"I'm glad you're here, Stills."

His mechanical voice gave a weird, wordless sound she suspected was disgust or exasperation, and then the channel was cut. Her duty to him, for now, was done. She activated the holographic displays and began filling in the spheres of light with the thousands of snippets of radio signals she'd recorded out among the alien creatures, organizing cross-tabs for location, estimated energy budget, anatomical differences, her own actions, probable motivations, and so on, looking for correlations that might make it easier to build herself a translation key. Although her stomach felt tight and uncomfortable with an impending feeling of disaster, this kind of problem was the mental space she most preferred to inhabit, and she let the connections sweep her away. She'd made only frustrated progress over the next hours, but emerged from her work when Saint Matthew's feet approached, clicking on the inside of the hull.

"That looks daunting," he said by way of greeting.

"Trying to decipher a language unconnected to anything else is an exercise in probabilities and mathematical patterns," she said.

"What if I told you it wasn't unconnected? The *Hortus rubrum* don't synthesize and transmit scents, but Pedro found receptors. Maybe not surprising. They're the same species."

"I thought they were only evolutionarily related."

"Pedro has sequenced the genes of the pollen on the air, as well as tissue samples from both populations. They're sexually dimorphic. What you've been calling the *Hortus rubrum* is one sex, something like a male, in that it primarily reproduces by spreading pollen and not carrying any young. What you've been calling the *Hortus quantus* is the other sex, which is not female, because it carries organs for both sexes—like pistils and stamens. The *Hortus quantus* can self-fertilize, or be fertilized by another *Hortus quantus* or a *Hortus rubrum,* and then carry fertilized eggs to term as buds. As you've noted, the *Hortus rubrum* have entirely different ways of feeding themselves, with different energy budgets, different rates of activity, and different, but possibly related languages."

"There are no *Hortus rubrum* in the future," she said.

"The environment does change between now and our present, and we know that Nyanga suffers from solar flares on the scale of decades or centuries," the AI said. "Even though both have strategies for surviving flares, one of them is ultimately more successful than the other."

"Even if I could communicate with the *Hortus rubrum*, they couldn't answer. I might be able to discover a radio translation key if there's enough conceptual overlap in the two."

"The Union found the genes in the *Hortus quantus* that code for the scent peptides. Those same genes are in the *Hortus rubrum*. Genomics says the scent communication is ancient. I think I've found some of the genes that might code for proteins to scavenge and metabolize metal atoms for conducting electricity and transmitting radio signals. They're much younger evolutionarily. And interestingly, both sexes have far more neural tissue than the *Hortus quantus* in our era."

"They lost intelligence as they evolved?"

"They may have lost individual intelligence," he said, "but everything Mister Arjona said about them suggested that they had an active collective intellect."

"I saw it too," she said distantly. It still felt strange to speak of Bel in the past tense. And now that she'd seen his grainy image in the Scarecrow's memories, his death was a strange conditional—as with everything to do with Bel, his death was wrapped in uncertainty.

"They may be evolving more quickly than we think," Saint Matthew said. "The *Hortus quantus* samples you brought in are infected with a virus. The virus carries some grains of radioisotopes which I think facilitate its movement through the *Hortus quantus* bodies to the female sex organs, where it becomes incorporated into every new fertilized egg genome. It carries around genes, and we think it encourages more *Hortus quantus-Hortus quantus* reproduction."

She could see why he'd brought it up. Something like radioactive decay, especially moving through time, could be the thing that begins the slow process of incorporating quantum processes into a lifecycle. This might be the birth of the *Hortus quantus* as they knew them, and perhaps the key to their resurrection.

CHAPTER TWENTY-SEVEN

CASSANDRA LIMPED FROM the *Calculated Risk*, towards the *Hortus quantus* herd interspersed with *Hortus rubrum*. A number of the tall, scarlet plants had clustered where her pathway would cross into the herd. A possible translation key for the *Hortus rubrum* radio signals had taken her several days of modeling, using the *Hortus quantus* scent language as a foundation. Cassandra with her facility in decryption and Saint Matthew with his mastery of multiple modern and ancient languages proved to be of little use. Rosalie's experience within an insular society, and her training with degraded and incestuous linguistic rules, short cuts, and abbreviations, provided them with some clues. The other unexpected boost had been Stills. The mongrels had built their anarchic and inchoate language from electrical pulses, frequency and amplitude modulation, electrical static, and dirty background silences. The language key she was about to try was neither mongrel nor Puppet Anglo patois, but it borrowed informalities from both. She neared a cluster of *Hortus rubrum*. In the low light of her helmet lamp, the skin stretched taut across icy ribs was shiny scarlet. She sent microcurrents to the magnetosomes in her arms, recreating the modules of radio noise that these creatures made, but not in the same order that she'd heard them.

Peace, she tried to transmit. *Friendship. Misunderstood travellers.*

Misunderstood migrants. Seeking brotherhood and sisterhood. Seeking exchange. Offering warmth. Shaped ice.

The cluster of radio ideograms were sent at about one per second, and at first, the tall red plants seemed not to react. Then one of them transmitted signals she'd heard and had tentatively translated as *summoning.* This message was repeated until, from the lower terrace, a more slender, agile *Hortus rubrum* descended, moving like someone on stilts through the parting herd. It came to her and she repeated her messages. It spat clipped staccato amplitude-modulated sounds into the radio band.

She thought it said: *Explain warmth. Explain shaped ice. No misunderstood migrants. Invasion.* If her translation key was correct, this was a rebuttal of her 'coming in peace' statement, and an accusation.

Seeking brotherhood and sisterhood. Offering warmth, she repeated.

Very slowly, she pulled a lamp off her belt and pointed it at the ground. When she clicked it on, infrared washed onto the ice, like brown dwarf light. This was the radiation the *Hortus quantus* used to melt the ice beneath them, to move and grow their icy skeletons.

Give, was the response.

Seeking brotherhood and sisterhood, she transmitted. *Use—* and then a radio ideogram she'd had to infer, for the time gates: *channel.*

What identity was the response. *What nestmind.* Her translation key didn't have a good grammar yet, to indicate questions, but these simple exchanges sharpened her understanding, allowing her to make on-the-fly adjustments. Nestmind was a new combination that had no precise cognate in the *Hortus quantus* language.

Travelling nestmind, she offered. *Not floral and fronds mind. Stars mind. Stars nest.* She hoped this said something close to what she intended.

She received the next radio signals next in flavours of negation. *Not stars. The hostile way. Like the fragile whisperers.*

The fragile singers, she replied, trying to make sure she understood. *The ones who come from the channel, who… shatter here.*

Yes, the creature responded. The skates. What did they mean, 'whisperers'?

Before she could follow that idea, the creature continued speaking. *Not stars. Not fragile. Dangerous. Strangers. Travellers.*

There seemed to be some heavier weight to 'traveller' she wasn't understanding. That wasn't perhaps strange. They had no word for someone like her—she was completely out of their experience. Alien.

Not hostile, she tried. *No invasion. Seeking brotherhood and sisterhood. Then leave. By channel. Exchange. Warmth. Shaped ice.*

Give warmth, was the reply. *We decide. After.*

In this moment, in this situation, Bel would have had a proposal, or counter-proposal, or a deception that she couldn't imagine. The way other beings thought, even people like Stills and Rosalie and human beings, was sometimes so opaque to her. But then again, maybe Bel wouldn't have known what to do, any better than her. His cunning had come from insight, from knowing those he was dealing with. He didn't know the *Hortus rubrum*. Her guess was as good as his.

She handed over the infrared lamp, leaving it switched on.

Four hours later, when the lamp's battery ran down, a small delegation of *Hortus rubrum* neared the ship. The transmitter she'd put into the lamp had traced a path all the way up the terraces, to the plateau, to a cluster of standing *Hortus rubrum* much like any other. She might guess that a deliberation or leadership function might be localized to certain groups, like organs in a body. But these creatures were so alien that for all she know, that cluster might be a sensing function. But it was a data point, nonetheless.

While the lamp battery had been running down, she and the AIs had penetrated the Scarecrow's programming. Saint Matthew had been able to read and even manipulate many of the conventional electronics, given that he was dealing with a defenseless corpse. He was stumped, however, by the protocols and algorithms hardwired into glassy semi-conductors that had once been neurons.

"The Scarecrow's loyalty to the Congregate is partly in the petrified neural tissues, supplemented by grafted electronics," Saint Matthew said.

He skittered over the Scarecrow's corpse. Wire mesh and carbon nanotube armour on torso, limbs and face lay open like a dissection diagram, exposing ceramics, semiconductors, electronics and organic glass. Seeing someone's insides felt to Cassandra like a strange, invasive intimacy. Even dead, the Scarecrow's body was large and intimidating.

"Those loyalties are unchangeable zero-level priorities. I had to cut out that loyalty hardwiring and replace it with new algorithms turning the Scarecrow's loyalty to you."

"What about the loyalty algorithms in the vitreous portions?" she asked.

"I severed them from the rest of the processors. It wasn't exactly a lobotomy, but there's no nearer word for what I did in systems engineering terms. The Scarecrow will retain many core abilities to remember and think, but will obey you."

"Can you get better access to its memories of the Congregate officer? And Bel?"

"It may take a few days to find and clean them," Saint Matthew said. "I rushed to make the Scarecrow functional now. You might need help out there on the ice."

"We can't destroy the *Hortus quantus*. He's not for that. He's for us to infiltrate the Congregate."

"He's a powerful weapon," Saint Matthew said.

He was, but her problems outside weren't ones she could shoot. Entering the time gates was a problem of geometry. The *Hortus rubrum*'s possession of the time gates seemed to be a problem of preserving causality.

She carried a replacement battery onto the dark ice of Nyanga. She also carried, in a little lead case, some of the random radioisotopes that the Scarecrow had used as fuel replacements. The dark infrared lamp was on the ground in front of a group of *Hortus rubrum*. They were different from the ones she'd seen earlier—the bottoms of their stumpy legs showed icy beneath raggedly torn plant film, as if they'd ripped themselves free of clinging connections.

False gift, one of them said in their radio speech.

Warmth like fragile singer warmth, she replied, the most complex idea she'd yet tried to communicate. *More warmth*, she added, picking up the lamp, sliding out its battery and snapping in the charged one. She turned it on, shone it at them and then held it out. One of the new ones took it, leaving the infrared glow on itself.

More warmth, she repeated, opening the small lead box away from herself. Grains of thorium and radium were mixed with radioactive phosphorus and sulfur isotopes. She spilled them onto a little bowl of ice Saint Matthew had made, and left it in front of them. Clumsily, one of them lifted the bowl and placed it inside its chest cavity, behind stretched photosynthetic flesh.

We leave, she offered. *By channel*.

When? one of them said.

She didn't think it was asking when she would leave. Did it want to know her destination? Bel's conversations suggested that the *Hortus quantus* of the future had vague notions of the time gates connecting to unseen pasts and unseen futures. The flat *Hortus rubrum* question suggested a more concrete understanding. She didn't know the radio sound for 'future' or even 'tomorrow.' Nyanga had no days. *Early,* she said. *Very early.*

Why now, the largest creature said, rather than 'why here?'

Resting, she said.

After a long pause, the largest creature said *No channel. Rest. No travel to early.*

Why, she demanded.

She grasped little of what followed. The plant creature spoke in concepts that had no cognates in the *Hortus quantus* translation key made by the Union. Her mind worked furiously, parsing the radio sounds, locking down the ideograms she knew, and building linkage analyses around the rest, developing interpretation probabilities. She continued long after he stopped communicating.

Her best, final interpretation was that the skates, the 'fragile singers,' had some larger, spiritual meaning. *Fragile singer* had shades of an angelic or otherworldly meaning. More than that, so did the small amount of pollen coming from the time gates. And apparently into this category also fell Cassandra and the *Calculated Risk.* She was otherworldly, angelic. On the face of it, this might seem like an advantageous position, except that the *Hortus rubrum* gradually consumed their fragile angels. Her translation suggested that the *Hortus rubrum* considered these circumstances providential, seemly, entitled, and moral.

Not fragile. Not singing, she said, hoping to communicate that consuming her would get them nothing.

Warmth, the large one replied, indicating her, then her ship. *All warmth. All light. Warmer than fragile singers.*

She'd been hoping it would not come to this. She drew out a hand laser, the kind used for welding, but if sufficiently unfocused, it worked as a low-efficiency, low-effect thermal beam.

Not warm, she said. She didn't know the word for 'hot,' so she added the closest one they had: *Melting.* Then she switched on the hand laser, shining it on the feet of the largest *Hortus rubrum*. The water ice, white under starlight, defracted orange and red as the beam's heat hit. The scarlet plant tissue, adapted for life at eighty below zero, shrivelled upward as the outer layers of the foot was heated sixty degrees. That was still far below the melting point of ice, but in the low atmospheric pressure, the concentrated heat caused the ice to bubble and evaporate. The targeted *Hortus rubrum* backed up, and the radio band filled with some sounds of alarm she recognized, and others she recorded for analysis later. She switched the laser off. The creatures kept their distance. She didn't want or need to kill them. She needed to avoid affecting history and causality.

Channel, she transmitted. *Travel to early. Offering gifts. Warmth.*

No, the largest one answered as the *Hortus rubrum* backed away. There was more, with more complicated structure. It took long moments before the probable translation clarified: *Angels do not leave.*

CHAPTER TWENTY-EIGHT

CASSANDRA CAME TO no epiphany about how to get back into the time gates. Stills of course proposed mowing down every *Hortus rubrum* and *Hortus quantus* in sight. He didn't see a danger to the timeline, because these icy aliens were irrelevant to humanity. More causally risky, he didn't see a problem in moving the time gates themselves, rather than leaving them to whatever historical circumstances had moved them. Rosalie, who got the impression she was part of this conversation, agreed with Stills, but from another angle.

"Your people are in danger," Rosalie had said. "The Congregate is after them in our now. You can't help them from whenever we are. My people are under a death sentence too. I can't help them from here. Stills's people—"

"Don't talk for me, runt," Stills interrupted.

"I can talk for your survival equipment, and the survival equipment in this ship," Rosalie retorted, her voice trembling as she faced Cassandra. "Stills's equipment wasn't made to hold him for months. This ship is a short range, short mission ship. Puppets know all about making things work for longer, and surviving breakdowns. But I've seen this kind of decay before."

"Saint Matthew and his drones can keep the *Calculated Risk* functioning indefinitely," Cassandra said.

"Then why did Stills's tank lose pressure?" the priestess countered. "I don't care about the ice plants. They're already dead in our now. Mister Arjona told me he killed them and that can't be changed. Whatever we do to them here makes them easier for him to kill then."

Rosalie's words—innocent, undisciplined, haphazardly thought through—punched her in the gut. Was any of it true? Had Cassandra been weakening the *Hortus quantus* with every pastward interaction and interference? Had she weakened them to a state of such fragility that even a glancing observation by Bel had killed them… and driven him into a downward spiral that destroyed him too?

She hadn't caused this. She hadn't broken Bel. She hadn't driven him to suicidal risks, and into Congregate captivity. That was in Bel's nature.

"I have to investigate more," Cassandra said.

It sounded like a way to end the conversation. She didn't want to be around any of them right now. She pulled on her vacuum suit and shouldered the air tank onto her back, then buckled on a tool belt and strapped the scent translator on her chest. She packed another heat lamp and an extra battery. Saint Matthew sent her a text message she didn't open. In the near-vacuum, on the mat of alien plants, she looked up, ocular implants telescoping onto alien stars. And time passed.

She finally struck out parallel to the edge of the herd, weaving briskly around plants. The thickness of the herd varied, and the *Hortus quantus* were mostly still, which was strange. Even taking into account the curvature of Nyanga, they were receiving more energy in this era. They should be *more* active.

Two kilometers from the ship, she received audio messages from Saint Matthew by laser. She ignored them, but slowed as she came to a herd of ragged *Hortus quantus* extending as far as she could see across the gloomy plain. Most slow-walked in a wide eddy, one or two steps every minute. The faint, erratic breezes lifted grains of pollen to drift among the wide herd, but most often, the plants slowly and carefully brushed their fronds with each other as they walked past, exchanging pollen. These would be the lowest of the low, pushed far from the terraces. Several of larger *Hortus quantus* stood still on the edge of the moving herd, like elders overseeing the migrations.

On a whim, Cassandra slipped into the savant state. She shucked the sometimes uncomfortable world of social interactions and into a state of patterns, geometries, and shapes. In moments, her brain modelled the migratory pattern, the concentric counter-movements optimized to maximize gene sharing while minimizing effort. It was a beautiful pattern. In savant, she found so many of the world's hidden relationships, but an entire viewpoint was missing still—the quantum one. Cassandra activated the microcurrents to her the portions of her brain that would extinguish her self-awareness. She ceased to be a person who experienced and felt the world. She became no one, an objective intellect capable of observing the quantum world.

Cassandra existed again seventeen minutes later. As always, she had new memories, things she hadn't experienced yet knew, some hard facts, some understandings in probabilistic terms, and some fuzzily superimposed, indefinite quantum insights.

Nyanga was a good environment for her quantum perceptions. The intense cold muted thermal jostling that could collapse quantum effects. Nyanga's thin atmosphere meant fewer gas particles to interfere with quantum superpositions. And the *Hortus quantus* were an excellent quantum subject—as cold as their environment, metabolically simple, and bound to each other by quantum entanglement. In the future, the *Hortus quantus* had been far more entangled to each other directly, and indirectly through the pollen that had travelled backwards through time. In this era, their connecting threads of quantum entanglement were faint. Those *Hortus quantus* who were most entangled were noticeably radioactive, a sign that they carried the virus Saint Matthew and Pedro had discovered. The conclusion was inescapable. In this era, the *Hortus quantus* were only beginning whatever evolutionary process had led them to develop a mysterious, rudimentary quantum awareness. Curious, marvelous, mysterious, and tragic. Those quantum interactions had contained a significant portion of the *Hortus quantus* intellect, their awareness of their past and future, of each other. Their quantum perceptions had been their downfall.

She turned on the chest plate translator, listening with chemical receptors that could 'hear' any pheromones that the slow-walking plants might emit as communication. At first, the machine detected nothing. She stared at the stars, still settling into her own consciousness after the self-abnegation of the fugue. Then the screen inside her helmet began filling with words, quickly and more numerous than their speech had appeared in her own era. Gooseflesh rose on her arms and neck. This was not the simple, concatenated, one-word concepts that the *Hortus quantus* used to speak in the future, or that even the *Hortus rubrum* used in this era.

What kind of angel? Which heaven?

Her translation key was holding up. She'd built upon the Union one, with her own linguistic interpretation algorithms, as well as the translations of the radio ideograms of the *Hortus rubrum*. She made the combination of scents that she thought should make,

No angel. No heaven.

A pause dragged out. Then a quick staccato of chemical scents registered on the chest piece, many of which did not match any of the sensors. Algorithms were able to make out most of it, to an eighty-five percent confidence.

Not our heaven, was the message. *Not until the heart of heaven intercedes.*

The translation was frustrating. The first use of 'heaven' was similar to the way the *Hortus rubrum* had used it, referring to those spaces inside the time gates. The second one here might not be heaven at all, but a translation error or a misunderstanding. Her key was not yet sophisticated enough to distinguish between closely related concepts, especially now that she was faced with a more vocal and intellectually active scent-speaking *Hortus quantus*. She ran back through all the related uses of such scents and words, and found that it had astronomical connotations mixed with the religious. A metaphor?

Which heavens will intercede? she sent.

At first, her system translated the response as *Heavens,* with a confidence of only sixty percent, and *Heart of heaven,* meaning their star, with a confidence of thirty percent. Their star interceding? She tried to put herself into a non-scientific or even anti-scientific point of view, one viewing the world through spirituality, or animism, or even a beneficent superior being. She failed. She was too rational to even imagine the non-rational. She opened the channel to Saint Matthew and Rosalie, and told them what she thought she'd heard.

"Most religions personify major environmental objects like the sun, the moon, mountains, oceans, and rivers," the AI said, "especially ones that can be violent and propitiated. I would guess that the *Hortus quantus* see some kind of being in Nyanga's star, a being that occasionally acts in ways that affect their world. The two species have little protection against the dwarf's brightening and darkening, or solar flares, or magnetic storms."

"The star, or the god within the star, will intervene?" Cassandra mused.

When will the heart of heaven intervene? she asked in the scent ideograms. The response was the most complex response she'd seen.

Angels come, emissaries of the heart of heaven, heralding hand of heaven.

"What do I do with these... beliefs?"

She'd been asking Saint Matthew, who could watch her display at the ship, but Rosalie replied, "Use them to give us the time gates. Their beliefs aren't real."

"No!" Saint Matthew interjected.

"You don't believe them," Rosalie said on the comms.

"It isn't about whether their beliefs are demonstrably correct or incorrect, or whether I believe them or not," he said. "We should never *use* anyone."

"If the danger to your people is high enough," Rosalie said, "you can do anything."

Cassandra stepped closer. The curves of three ribs on the middle *Hortus quantus* reflected white where the skin had worn to ice.

How know? she asked.

Heaven speaks.

"They hear voices?" Rosalie said dubiously.

"No," Saint Matthew said slowly, as if still considering the matter, which Cassandra suspected was more performance. Saint Matthew thought almost as fast as Cassandra, so whatever he was going to say, she suspected he'd already thought it through.

"When the *Hortus quantus* or the *Hortus rubrum* say 'heaven,'" the AI continued, "I don't think they're waving their hands at the sky. They have closer contact with the immanent—the interior of the time gates, an inaccessible, mysterious region whose rules are strange enough to be supernatural. In some ways, they travel that supernatural region by sending their pollen back in time. The Union discovered that the *Hortus quantus* carry eight or more copies of all their genes, a redundancy to help survive the harshness of that supernatural world. Mister Arjona's analysis of their genomes suggested that their DNA could change during their lifetimes. I wonder if that phenomenon is more than survival and points at their knowledge of the time gates."

Saint Matthew's sly suggestion crept up on her. Cassandra knew that *Hortus quantus* DNA could be modified during their lifetimes, but Saint Matthew was theorizing something more ambitious.

"You think they write memories into their own DNA and send those back in time in their pollen?" she asked. "They don't have much access to the time gates."

"They might not need a lot. DNA can carry enormous amounts of information. And we may be able to read it directly. They already have a genetically determined language of scent ideograms," he said.

"So if we find sequences that code for those scents in their DNA, those might be messages?" she asked.

"It wouldn't be something that could cause a grandfather paradox," he said. "It would essentially be a written message. Messages can be wrong, or not quite correct, or not capture the whole truth, but if they provided enough truth for the *Hortus quantus* to survive better, evolution will select for the trait."

"And if they're not lying to us here, they're saying they 'remember' their 'heart of heaven,' their star, intervening in the future," she said.

"Solar flares?" he asked.

Cassandra needed biopsies.

Maybe angels, and maybe not, Cassandra said via scents, juggling the weird Boolean grammar. *Friends, allies, family,* she offered, pulling out the heat lamp. *Warmth*. She activated it on its lowest setting, shining it at the black feet of the nearest. Ice exposed between the hanging flaps shone back. When the *Hortus quantus* didn't panic or withdraw, she raised the shine higher, to their barrel torsos.

Angel, one of them insisted in the scent speech, accompanied by some scent ideograms that the translation key listed with multiple possible meanings: 'light,' 'life,' 'heaven,' 'good,' 'true.' She didn't have enough context to improve her translation key, but the broad sentiment was clear. After a moment, they slowly lumbered nearer the lamp. She didn't know how well they could see her in the cold, insulated suit, especially with what to them was a bright light. Gently, she reached out and pulled a little flap of damaged, dangling skin off one of them. They didn't react.

"The *Hortus quantus* and *Hortus rubrum* seem different enough that they probably have separate strategies for surviving catastrophic solar flares that melt the surface meters deep. The *Hortus quantus* have some quantum entanglement with the future and the past, as well as some memories encoded into genes to rebuild after flares. But the *Hortus rubrum* might be better equipped. Parts of their bodies go deep into the shadows of trenches that will never feel even the worst flares. If they store memory in those cold skins, they would recover their society as soon as they could regrow themselves over new skeletons."

The hand of heaven will free the people from captivity, one of the *Hortus quantus* said. The translation key showed the reference to 'people' with possible other interpretations: 'the plants,' 'the chosen,' 'the righteous.'

Angels will herald the justice of heaven.

"I will absofuckinlutely bring down the justice of heaven," Stills offered.

Despite the flat affect he'd programmed into his voice emulator, there was a suggestion of exhaustion under his words, an exhaustion she shared, an exhaustion that seemed to contextualize their vast, vast distance from home, in space, in time.

CHAPTER TWENTY-NINE

CASSANDRA SAT BESIDE Stills's tank. The giant crate of reinforced carbon steel contained six hundred atmospheres of pressure. Sitting here, she was not meaningfully closer, and could not comfort him. The branches of human evolution had sundered too completely for their two lineages to ever touch. His environment would crush her, and hers would burst him. She'd drawn near nonetheless, out of respect, to show that he was important to her. He was.

"Saint Matthew says you've suffered a lot of nerve damage," Cassandra said.

"Your AI talks a lot," he said. "Are you tryin' to take me off the job?"

"He says you're not safe to fly."

"Safe to fly?" Stills said, the machine emulation of his voice rising in volume. "What the *crisse* does he know about flying, or what I can do? What's he going to do? Fly for you? Good fuckin' luck."

"He wants to run some tests. You can show him."

"Don't blow sunshine up my ass, darlin'. I ain't doin' tests. You wanted the best fuckin' pilot; here I am. If you don't want me, drop me the fuck off. I drive better drunk than any of you sober and you know it."

"Stills, we might be able to fix the damage. This is an injury, not a personal failing."

"Shove your bedside manner and your fake psychology up your ass. I ain't dumb enough to fall for either of 'em."

"I—"

"Get out!" he yelled tonelessly.

She made her way around the curve of the hull back to the cockpit where Saint Matthew had been installing additional holographic projectors. The *Calculated Risk* had been designed for short missions, with accordingly modest computers and interfaces. This ever-lengthening mission had forced them to improvise.

"That didn't sound pleasant," he said.

She grunted, strapping into the pilot's seat in front of the new projectors.

"His refusal affects us all," Saint Matthew said. "I have a drone in his tank. I can do some tests without him knowing."

"You want to make him madder? Or not trust us?"

"We need our pilot."

"You stopped the treatments I ordered on Rosalie, but you're ready to overrule Stills on his?" she demanded.

"The treatment wasn't making Rosalie better. Lack of treatment could make Stills worse."

"Your logic feels convenient."

"Life requires us to exercise judgment. Sometimes what looks unfair from the outside is what's best for someone."

"I don't want to fence anymore. I'm tired."

"I'm on your side, Miss Mejía. I'm trying to respect everyone's wishes and our collective welfare. We're not navigating a simple problem space."

"Do you have real treatments for Stills?"

"You're not going to like them."

"Why?"

"We can't grow neural tissues to replace damaged neurons, not here. We've seen workarounds before, though."

When she caught his meaning, she felt like she was about to see her lunch again. The images of broken friends, of the insides of *Homo quantus* she'd known all her life, invaded her thoughts, potent in ways she could not dispel. She could only break out of the loop by changing who she was for a moment. She slipped into the savant state, and suddenly patterns of data, information, and geometric linkages dominated. The memories of the silvery-wired insides of war-ravaged friends did not vanish, but they became facts. Their emotional dimensions flattened.

"No," she whispered, her voice distant. "Did you find the memories in the *Hortus quantus*?"

Saint Matthew's stony, alien face became inscrutable for two point four seconds.

"I looked through the *Hortus quantus* genomes for sequences that might be messages from their future," the AI said. "I found some candidates, and then screened them for methylation patterns that could indicate that they came from the pollinating parent."

"Show me."

Above one cluster of holographic projectors, raw genetic sequences appeared. The biology of the *Hortus quantus* was too frigid for adenine, thymine, guanine and cytosine DNA bases. *Hortus quantus* genetic macromolecules were written in an alphabet of six bases that were chemically active within a temperature band from minus two hundred degrees to five to ten degrees Celsius. An interface similar to the one used to speak to the *Hortus quantus* bloomed beside the raw data, showing a series of ideograms. Using the translation key from the pheromones, she began to puzzle out a set of messages. They weren't visual or olfactory memories, but abstracted meanings jumbling and falling over one another.

Heaven's heat. Halo shine. Judging angels. Harbingers. Heralds. Light. Warmth. Melting. Cruel pollinators. Heaven whispering mysterious scents. Channel. Channel for the people. Destiny. Melting. Angels foretelling oceans. Oceans filling. Exodus to freedom. Long. Painful, hard exodus. Flight from the pollinators. Heaven sets the people free. New whispers.

Although small and confusing, it was also awe-inspiring. If this wasn't a false positive, this was how the *Hortus quantus* sent real knowledge to the past: they inserted scentless voices into the minds of their offspring.

"Is this from one genome?" she asked.

"Similar messages, or memories, occur in four other samples," the AI answered. "Put in a different way, these occurred in all the samples I've sequenced so far. The order changes—I suspect it isn't really important. As we've seen, there's a certain jumbled simultaneity to the speech of the *Hortus quantus*."

"Do you trust this? Our translation keys aren't as precise as we'd like."

"'Oceans' is not an ambiguous term as used here. And their use of the ideogram for 'heaven' is vaguely metaphorical to us, but also precise and astronomical when they refer to their brown dwarf."

He paused. She didn't understand the expression carved into holographic stone, which was slightly easier for her to take.

"I have my own conclusions," he said finally. "Do you have any?"

She turned over the message in the genes, reshuffled it, reordered it, layered it differently, but in the end it was only part of the question before her.

"In this era, the *Hortus rubrum* gender possesses the time gates at the terminator, and exercises some kind of harsh rule over the *Hortus quantus* gender," she said. "Closer to our present, the *Hortus quantus* have entirely speciated away from the *Hortus rubrum*. They use the time gates intensively for reproduction and possibly to bind together their perceptions of future, present and past through quantum entanglement. They do this from the center of the tidally locked plain beneath the brown dwarf. We don't know the events in between this era and ours, but the *Hortus quantus* do. They witnessed the change in the next few years, wrote it into their own DNA, and sent that information back in time."

"And disturbingly, we've been assigned a role."

"We can refuse," she said. "We haven't made any observation that would trigger a grandfather paradox if we do nothing. Their words and memories could be wrong. They could be lies."

That felt like a very Belisarius thought.

"We need the future they will apparently see," he said. "That's how we resume our journey. History hasn't assigned us a role, but it's giving us the space to take one."

She'd already turned down Stills and even Rosalie on the idea of harming the *Hortus rubrum,* so as to not affect history. Now, she and Saint Matthew had found a larger, potentially more catastrophic way to get access to the time gates. They'd been invited to play god, to give the *Hortus quantus* a chance to emerge from beneath the control of their *Hortus rubrum* mates and oppressors. The enormity of the decision did not fit within the savant state. She slipped free of the comfortingly flat, geometric view of the world and back into one filled with sharp-edged emotional context and costs.

"We have to make that choice?" she said. His face became somber and even doubtful. "Don't make me."

"What?"

"Don't make me decide. I can't decide on my own. This is too big."

"You're strong enough," he said with a kind of otherworldly melancholy.

"Don't abandon me now," she insisted.

"Miss Mejía, I was made to be a killer, to rain destruction from on high, to change the strategic terrain of worlds. I abandoned that destiny, as much as I could. But the sins of my origins follow me. I've tried to be a saint, but I've made you weapons. I've given you military and scientific analyses that kill your enemies. But until now, I've been… a secondary participant, a helper. There's a particular place in Hell for people like me, but it's not the same place as the one reserved for those who decide. And I'm afraid. If I pick up my discarded destiny, I might not be able to escape it again."

She'd been increasingly frustrated with his false moralizing over the past weeks. He twisted and wrapped himself in contrived principles born of hopes of people three millennia dead, people living different contexts in different places. His contradictions and hypocrisy infuriated her. Why was he broken like this? He was weak in a way that deprived her of an intellectual and moral peer, in a way that made her more alone. She was alone with decisions that could perhaps save her people from this evolutionary danger.

"Get ready to fly us to the brown dwarf," she said.

CHAPTER THIRTY

CASSANDRA TOOK THE controls of the *Calculated Risk* from Saint Matthew at the L1 Lagrange point, the spot between the brown dwarf and Nyanga where gravitational forces balanced. Saint Matthew's small army of drones needed his full attention. They crawled over the outside of the ship, installing reflective foil.

The brown dwarf loomed across a quarter of the starscape beyond the cockpit, its gloomy light pinkened and reddened by clouds of iron dust. Like a gas giant, networks of high atmospheric storms twisted around each other, but on a much larger scale. The failed star was massive, hot and powerful nonetheless. Cassandra ramped up the inflaton field on a direct course for the brown dwarf.

Stills's dark face hovered in holographic miniature above the controls. His cartilage-hardened features were severed from any expressions people could interpret, but the electrical background in his pressure chamber betrayed his mood: restless, bothered, throbbing electrical potential without direction.

"There's a possibility that grafts could accelerate some of your reactions," she said as if they hadn't left their conversation twenty-six minutes ago. "The wiring in the *Homo quantus* sped up neural conduction speeds."

"A mongrel that needs help ain't no dog."

"We can reverse it when we get home."

This wasn't strictly true. Inserting metal replacements into neural tissue was complicated. Some changes proved irreversible in practice.

"You and me know our bodies ain't made for wires," he said. "When you got electrical and magnetic fields in you, metal gets trippy."

"You can compensate for it," she said.

A surly silence thickened as the brown dwarf's atmosphere grew.

"You're flying for now?" he finally said.

"No one else."

The holographic fish head stared dumbly for a while before the monotone voice sounded.

"How close you gonna get to that fucker?"

"Its upper atmosphere."

"One hole in our shielding and we cook like shrimp in a pot."

"That'll also happen if I do anything wrong."

"*Puta,*" he said slowly.

"You can drive. Even injured, you're probably faster than me. The *Homo quantus* were selected for intellect, not reflexes."

"Why so close?"

"I need to make it flare."

"What?" he demanded. "How the *crisse* are you going to do that?"

She looked at him impatiently.

"Fine, fine," he said. "Prancy pants always gotta do something impossible. But why? We'll cook in a flare, even a brown dwarf one."

"The *Hortus quantus* are evolved for flares. They survive it like a forest fire."

"Do I look like I know what a forest fire looks like?"

"Forests fires are a natural part of the environment. The forests grow back. Once half of Nyanga is a shallow sea, we can get to the time gates without shooting up beings who could remember that down through time."

"You're going to execute all of them instead of me shooting just fifty?" he demanded, with honest bewilderment and a hint of awe.

"Shooting a crowd of them to pieces is something they'll record in their DNA. They won't forget. One more flare is one more flare, and they already remember one happening soon."

Stills grunted without expanding on the thought.

Nyanga's failed star took up half the sky. Its fires began to resolve into slumbering white beneath curtains of red hot metallic dust. The clouds didn't follow the storm patterns like on Jupiter or Venus. Energetic winds blew metal dust up and down invisible magnetic field lines, or dragged them into striated eddies and disintegrating streamers. The structure of the iron dust cloud mapped the dead star's magnetic topography. The brown dwarf brightened over the next thirty minutes until the brown dwarf's gravitational pull became palpable. The *Calculated Risk*'s cooling systems strained to hold down the rising temperature. Rosalie silently joined her, strapping into the co-pilot's seat. She stared blankly at the slow-dying star, shivering.

The brown dwarf's horizon became fractal, rising coils and streamers of gas and dust blurring the edge at every scale. Dirty clouds broke like parched skin, revealing the deeper layers of the stellar atmosphere in boiling pink, like drops of blood dissolving into liquid light. Uneven magnetic prominences rose and twisted, making room for hot gases to grow mountain-like, violently splashing stillborn light.

"It's beautiful, in a fallen way," the puppet said, her voice taut.

"In that it will never burn like a real star?" Cassandra asked after moments of puzzling over the comment.

"Beauty is only the reflected existence and divinity of the Numen," came the strained whisper. "We say that there is no beauty in the absence, but I remember the Numen. I am their reflected light, shining dimly on a dark universe. I'm the part of the universe desperately wishing and waiting for the divine. I'm the part of the universe that can imagine beauty."

A streamer of stellar gas, twisted red and white within coiled magnetic field lines, bleached the solar cloud tops. Then, as if spent, the prominence sank into the sea of struggling light. It was fascinating, beautiful, and more. It resonated with Rosalie's words, with the desperate wishing for the ephemeral, for something larger than themselves. Even a small, failed star possessed sublime beauties that tickled at the edges of awe. The cosmos was immense beyond even Cassandra's abstractions.

"This is a lot of acceleration," Stills's voice warned in the speakers.

Cassandra eased off the inflaton drive and nudged the ship onto a wide, flat circular trajectory above the looming dwarf. Still hundreds of thousands of kilometers away, they nonetheless felt several gravities pulling them down in their seats.

"We'd better get into the acceleration chambers," Cassandra said to Rosalie.

"How close you gonna get?" Stills asked as Cassandra shut herself in and started flooding the space with shock gel.

"What do you care? You're a passenger."

"I gotta watch my ass too is all. You drive all you want."

"*Very* close."

"Show me your mission profile."

She transmitted it to him through the neural jack as the shock gel in her acceleration chamber rose past her mouth.

"*Mierda*," he said.

THE *CALCULATED RISK* flew a few hundred kilometers above the highest stellar prominences. The surface of the failed star reached for a seething, vaporous infinity without horizon. Black sky and star points became hazy, seen doubtfully through transparent fingers of pink and white gases. Coils of hot plasma twisted within magnetic field lines, bristling like a forest beneath them, rising and falling into an ocean of hydrogen.

An alarm sounded.

A prominence rose nearly in their path, a real obstacle. Stills was yelling "Pull up! Pull up, fucker!" in the feeds. She gave the commands and the *Calculated Risk* sluggishly angled itself upward, and to port. After a few moments, they'd crossed out of this danger.

"Please tell me you reacted slow to get me to take over," Stills said.

"We're safe," she said.

"The ship reacts different here. This ain't space. The acceleration profile and maneuverability are different under this many gravities and this much heat. Fuck. Are you even sure the drive will work at this temperature?"

"The *Homo quantus* tested it," she said.

"I trust them as much as I trust your piloting," he said. "*Tabarnak*. Give me the controls."

She did and the *Calculated Risk* made a few strange course corrections, from minor angular changes to their trajectory and altitude to little bursts of station-keeping jets.

"How is it handling?" she asked.

"Shitty. Sluggish. This is not the right place to fly this ship."

"We won't be here long."

"If we make a mistake, we're gonna be here forever."

"How are *you* handling?" she asked more pointedly.

"Better than you and better than the ship."

"We nearly in position. Are you ready?"

"I'm always ready."

"Mark," she said.

"Fuck," he replied.

Stills braked the *Calculated Risk* slightly by inverting the inflaton drive, and then angled downward into freefall. Within short minutes, the forward view showed only a smouldering, rippled ocean of hot hydrogen and metal dust. As their altitude dropped, their decaying orbital velocity became more apparent and frightening, shooting them over the textured cloudscape at speeds difficult to absorb. Stills's trajectory neared the stellar surface nearest to Nyanga.

"Those," she said, indicating writhing, nested arcs of glowing hydrogen.

"We ain't at your target yet."

"We're aiming a star. It's a blunt weapon."

Stills lowered their trajectory until the outer cameras showed the prominences racing past them at eye level.

"See you on the other side—hopefully not as ashes," he said.

Stills threw the inflaton drive to full power, until the field expanded past the hollow drive section. The field leaked out the bow and stern, into the stellar atmosphere. The leaking inflationary force drastically expanded spacetime behind the ship, tearing apart atoms, nuclei, and the lines of magnetic force containing the stellar prominences. The *Calculated Risk* shot forward, the acceleration close to bone-breaking, even in shock gel.

Snapped prominences exploded in catastrophic showers of x-rays, visible light, hot ultraviolet, and throbbing infrared. Even protected in the acceleration chambers, the radiation dosimeter alarms went off.

The ship skimmed along the cloud tops of the restive brown dwarf, coming closer and closer to other prominences. Accelerating past, their inflaton drive field ripped up bright plasma waves from the photosphere, where the prominences were anchored. The magnetic field lines snapped and reformed in new conformations as their pent-up energy burst outward.

Hard electromagnetic radiation followed and outpaced them like a storm, but Stills kept them ahead of the sleet of high-energy particles. The ship vibrated. Rosalie's feed sent out the equivalent of screams of terror. Cassandra muted her. Stills was talking, to her or himself.

"Close one," he grumbled. "Prominence moved. What do you want, boss?"

The prominence eruptions were triggering others, and coronal mass ejections, carrying much more energy than she'd wanted. Radiation levels ticked higher.

"Pull us out! We don't want to melt Nyanga all the way through."

The *Calculated Risk* tipped upward, and the world crushed her ribs, even in the shock gel. The gravity of the brown dwarf—much higher than Jupiter's—and the acceleration of the ship combined to bend her bones. *Stills…* she thought, but didn't know if the message even left her brain, as she blacked out.

CHAPTER THIRTY-ONE

Screaming alarms blared in through the cable jacked into Cassandra's skull, waking her. Radiation alarms continued to sound, both EM and particles. If they'd been fast enough, they might have run ahead of the destructive high-energy particles.

They weren't accelerating, though. The ship was running on emergency batteries.

"Stills. Stills!" She sent commands through the jack, but nothing reacted. "Saint Matthew!"

The acceleration chamber's drain cycle wouldn't activate, so she pulled the manual release. Her joints ached, but the heavy door opened, spilling her into the narrow, curving corridor. The viscous blob of shock gel clung to her and she wiped at it and coughed it out for long seconds in the zero-g before her face was free enough to breath smoky air.

Emergency spotlights blinked. The air was hot in her lungs. Drones floated limply.

She yanked the jack from her skull and hauled herself to Rosalie's acceleration chamber. Setting feet to floor and wall, she turned the handle until the door opened and the priestess spilled out. Cassandra wiped the acceleration gel from the flailing Puppet's face.

"Rosalie! The ship has no power. I don't know what happened to Stills or Saint Matthew or Pedro. We're probably still closer to the star than the planet. We have to get the power on before we fall back!"

"Okay," the Puppet coughed, more calmly than Cassandra felt. "Go to the engines. I'll go to the cockpit."

They separated. Cassandra found the starfield slowly rotating outside the window of the cockpit. The brown dwarf grew slowly to port. Saint Matthew's body was stiff over the controls. Yellow lights blinked erratically under his casing. She couldn't allow herself to think of what she'd do if he was really hurt. And if she didn't get power back to the ship, they would all be dead.

The ship had not switched itself back on. She didn't understand. The ship had an auto reboot, a fast one.

The answer was in the radiation logs. Fourteen electromagnetic pulses had shut down every system in the *Calculated Risk* multiple times, including during reboots and resets. Cassandra opened emergency panels, reset all the fuses, and engaged the manual computer reboot.

"Rosalie!" she yelled down the corridor. "Manually restart the engines and main power!"

"Okay," came the faint reply. Then, "Some components are burnt out. I'll get replacements."

"Hurry!"

The computer had been designed by the *Homo quantus* for mathematical and geometric performance, not space hardiness. That was an error in retrospect. But after long, doubtful moments, some yellow telltales began lighting, as boot routines began. As she reset more and more fuses, systems went from red to yellow to green. Four of the cameras and radiation sensors on the stern were dark. Nyanga's failed star swung slowly into view as the *Calculated Risk* tumbled. The ship's mass was not balanced.

"Starting!" Rosalie called up.

Console readouts began to show the progress of the inflaton drive's reboot.

"Check on Stills!" Cassandra called down. "Make sure his chamber is powered and that he's oxygenated!"

The Puppet assented unintelligibly.

Cassandra tracked the engine reboot and compared its speed to how long their chaotic orbit would last. Without all external sensors, she couldn't know how soon the star would swallow them again. She'd known the density and location of the upper edge of the stellar atmosphere, but the flares she'd triggered—far more than she'd intended—had certainly flung billions of tons of plasma far higher, and all of it now dragged at their orbit.

Saint Matthew's lights still blinked erratic yellows. Some of the tumbling drones, less sophisticated, began restart sequences. One of the airlock alarms flashed yellow, and then red, in the bay where Stills's chamber was stored. Cassandra yelled down the length of the ship. "Rosalie! What's happening? Rosalie!" She got no answer, and then switched to intercom. "Rosalie! Can you hear me? What's happening with the bay airlock?"

"Stills is okay, I think," the priestess called. "His chamber has oxygen. I reset the fuses. They were all blown and it's rebooting. I'm going outside."

"We're over a star, Rosalie! Even over a brown dwarf, you'll cook."

"Maybe," was the distracted reply. "I can see that one of the drive subsystems is damaged. It's not hard to fix. I just have to replace a power converter. But it's only accessible outside."

"The drones are nearly ready."

The readout on the drive status showed a stalled reboot process. The airlock telltales indicated the outer door opening and closing. Rosalie was outside, at the stern, in the shadow of nonfunctional cameras. There were still forty-five seconds to the first drone coming online.

"Rosalie?" she called.

The *Calculated Risk* vibrated violently for three seconds, and temperature alarms on the hull whined and yellowed. Their trajectory had plowed through a cloud of hot hydrogen. The intersection had been short enough that the heat was already dissipating, but their orbit degraded.

"Rosalie?" she demanded. "Rosalie!"

The inflaton drive reboot resumed, switching quickly from yellow to green. Sixty seconds until the engine would be able to make an inflaton field. The drones Cassandra had rebooted in the cockpit began waiting for orders. She sent them to the sternward airlock to help Rosalie back in.

"Rosalie! The drive is starting. Can you get in?"

Telltales showed the outer airlock door opening and closing and the airlock pressurizing. None of the cameras Cassandra wanted were working.

"Rosalie?"

Cassandra focused on the controls. She brought the inflaton field online. It bloomed in the cylindrical hollow within the ship. At her touch, the field shifted, expanding space slightly sternward, flinging the ship forward. She kept the ship at only two gravities of acceleration—she didn't want to injure herself or Rosalie. She steered an expanding, spiraling escape orbit.

Cassandra struggled to make her way to the aft bay during acceleration. The lights on Stills's pressure chamber showed yellow, but were gradually switching one by one to green. The chamber log had recorded Stills blacking out in a moment that wasn't particularly extreme for him in terms of radiation and pressure. All of it had been punishing, but punishing in ways he routinely endured.

Two drones huddled over Rosalie. She lay against the stern bulkhead, pinned by the acceleration. Her vacuum suit was blackened, with crispy layers flaking off. Cassandra stumbled and slid across the curved hull and landed painfully against the bulkhead.

"Rosalie."

The drones made way for her. The charred survival suit crumbled at her touch, revealing the carbon fiber webbing and insulation, browned and cooked in places. Cassandra popped the neck seal and took off the helmet. The left side of Rosalie's face was red and blistering from forehead to neck. Her eyes slitted open to stare ahead dazedly.

"Your face is burned," Cassandra said.

"I know."

"Are you in a lot of pain?"

"Yes," she said matter-of-factly.

Cassandra ordered the drones to cut the suit away from Rosalie. The Puppet's gradually exposed skin had avoided some of the worst burns, but the ones on her left leg already seeped a clear fluid.

"Get pain relievers," Cassandra told one of the drones.

"I don't deserve it yet."

"You don't need to *deserve* medicine," Cassandra said.

"You still don't know anything about me."

Rosalie's breaths came shallow and quick.

"Why didn't you wait for the drones?" Cassandra asked.

"There wasn't time. You have my whole world in your hands. My heaven and hell. My past and future. I can't let anything happen to you. Or the ship. Or the AI judge."

Cassandra felt nauseous.

"I never wanted any of this."

"The cosmos put us in your hands for some reason," Rosalie said distantly. "To kill every last Numen and Puppet. Or save us. I recognize the moment."

The 'moment.' Such an odd metaphor, one so human, and so dissonant with *Homo quantus* thinking. The *Homo quantus* did not see moments, any more than they saw simultaneity. The cosmos was made of events and interactions that at most scales had little relationship to time, unless one looked at many events together. Cassandra began snapping the Puppet into a crew harness on the wall. "Stay here. Rest. Hold on. Watch Stills if you can. Take care of yourself if you can't. We have some flying yet to do."

Rosalie's burnt face was grim. Cassandra crawled back to the cockpit. They were halfway around the brown dwarf, climbing away from the stellar surface, out of sight of Nyanga. The star throbbed, unsettled magnetic tensions making themselves felt beneath the *Calculated Risk.* Prominences rose, straining, threatening to splash a whole network of flares into space.

"Two gees?" Stills machine voice finally sounded. Yellow accented the mostly green telltales of his chamber. "What is this? A guided tour?"

"We had to restart the ship manually," she said. "We're not done."

"I lost count of the EMPs after eight," he said. "We shouldn't do that again."

"What knocked you out? Was it the EMPs?"

"*Coño,* there weren't a lot of people I could ask."

"You haven't blacked out before."

"I never nuked a star from its surface before."

"We were worried about nerve damage slowing you down. We didn't think you could lose consciousness. We may *have* to fix you, Stills. For everyone's good."

An uncharacteristic pause came, instead of a responsive lash.

"Metal wiring ain't gonna survive an EMP any better'n what I got, princess. Did you cook the plants good?"

"We'll see."

"You guys really are good at genocide."

She fell silent and Stills stopped needling. Over the next hours, their long spiral climb pulled them away from the brown dwarf. The status lights on Saint Matthew's mobile casing finally showed more blinking green and then solid green, but he didn't reboot. After a time, the mobile computer containing Pedro click-click-clicked to the cockpit, climbing up the console to stand beside his creator. She didn't know if Pedro had successfully recovered and rebooted because he was more, or less, sophisticated than Saint Matthew. He'd changed his visual interface again, though. The hologram above his metal body was projecting the transparent image of a rough and uneven quartz-like crystal, into which had been bored five crude eyes, a downward slanted mouth, and a fracture for a nose. At the top of his head, stylized scratches seemed to represent hair, except at the top, which was smooth, as if tonsured. The abstracted features nodded to humanity, but only as departure points.

"Can you fix him?" Cassandra asked Pedro.

Pedro was of course silent, and he departed, click-click-clicking away. As he left, he touched still-dormant drones, and their telltales began flashing reds and yellows as they rebooted.

"That artificial monk is a real piece of work," Stills said on the overhead speaker.

The *Calculated Risk* eventually achieved an orbit intersecting Nyanga's. The forward telescope, less damaged, showed Nyanga's flat black plain reflecting light more brightly, as if its albedo was no longer dominated by tarry black plant cover. Pockets of atmosphere had also thickened with water vapour and blowing snow.

In the infrared, Nyanga showed temperatures as high as the liquid water range while winds and snow blustered over the terminator.

"You sure make a mess," Stills said.

"This is what the *Hortus quantus* of the future saw."

"If any survived."

"They had to," she said. "That's the way this works. We know they exist in the future."

"If you say so. Where's the axis mouth? Did you melt all our landmarks?"

She'd melted a lot of them. X-rays, light, infrared, ultraviolet, and curtains of high-energy particles had melted the starward face of Nyanga. Uneven chunks of ice floated in a low sea. She expanded one section of the terminator to a grainy, pixelated image of grays, blacks and whites, and outlined it with a glowing rectangle.

"Our time gates will be there," she said.

"You're gonna try and lift them out?"

"I'll see when we get closer."

He was silent for a long time.

"You want me to fly?" he asked, with a flattened note almost of hesitancy.

"Do you want to?"

"It's better than pickin' my ass. And even fucked up, I'm still better than you."

STILLS BROUGHT THEM to the last known position of the time gates, in their trench on the dark side of the terminator. Along the former plain where a mat of black plants had once faced the brown dwarf, a shallow sea extended to the horizon. Blocks of ice floated in chaotic, freezing waves of slush as winds roared from star side to night side. Fragments and melts of the *Hortus rubrum* draped the terraces like burst balloons. Fine snow blew over them, minute by minute, layer by layer, hardening into ice. None were left standing, although if Cassandra was right about their adaptations, some critical, cerebral parts of them clung to the shadowed trench walls as sheets of plant matter.

A few misshapen, frondless *Hortus quantus* struggled on the shore of the hemispheric sea, rocked by hard waves. They were unnervingly faster, although she could guess the logic. These photosynthetic *Hortus quantus* had been drenched in infrared and ultraviolet. If some had been partly shielded and able to metabolize some of the energy, they would have saved some of their icy bones. And those bones would be warmer, and easier to melt at the joints. But for every stumbling *Hortus quantus* she saw, hundreds floundered in the water, or had already sunk beneath the waves, or been crushed to scraps between grinding blocks of ice. Waves threw skins on the shore like mats of algae.

"Can you set us down over there?"

She indicated a spot on the thinned terminator plateau.

"Windy as hell," he said. "And slippery as *tabarnak*."

"Just get close. I'll use spiked soles and ropes."

Stills hovered the ship to within centimeters of the highest terrace. Freezing rain froze over the cockpit window. Cassandra stepped out of the airlock with a few cables and tethered drones. The atmosphere had thickened enough for the wind to push and chill her. She lurched forward, stamping her boot spikes.

Her radiation alarm suddenly sounded. Electromagnetic. A big one. X-rays. Ultraviolet. Some gamma even. Suddenly, the *Calculated Risk* hovered above her, shielding her from the worst of the solar flare.

"You really don't fuck around when you cook a planet," Stills's voice crackled. She couldn't tell if he was impressed or revolted.

"Sometimes things go wrong," she said.

"Look, I don't give a shit. Own it. I'm a killer, but you're the destroyer of worlds. You make black holes. You explode stars. You're a fuckin' goddess of destruction."

She watched rolling waves, heard the grinding of growing icebergs, the chorus of millions of chunks of ice colliding as they rode trough and crest. She took comfort in the chain of logic that brown dwarf flares were common enough in evolutionary time that the *Hortus quantus* now sinking under the waves must have some way to squirm back out of the ice. Some spore form. She staggered with the wind to the terminator edge and found the time gates framed by growing drifts of snow.

"Throw me some lines and drop out some more drones."

"You're going through those drones pretty quick," he said, as cables dropped out of bow utility hatches.

She leaned over the edge, holding a cable as she considered the problem. The familiar edges of the time gates were accessible from this angle, but she couldn't see the bottom. She lowered herself down with the cable.

As she suspected, about ten centimeters of the lower edge was embedded in ice. The edges of the time gates were a thin, flexible, boundary of spacetime whose nature they'd never successfully modelled. Their edges could take a certain amount of bending tension, but she would never try to force them out of solid ice.

She drew a heating laser from her belt. The ice around the bottom edge of the time gates bubbled and sublimated, popped and steamed. Above her, the drones tied soft foam grips to the upper edges of the time gates. As the vanishing ice exposed the lower edge, she dug the slush away and fixed similar foam grips.

"Take up the slack," she said.

A centimeter at a time, the time gates rose out of the trench. The uncertain and blustery wind had no effect on them as they came above the windbreak of the trench—the slow-chilling moisture and evaporated nitrogen blew straight into the hostile, empty hyperspace. Cassandra climbed up.

Stills raised the *Calculated Risk* until the time gates hung there, above the *Hortus quantus*. Winch motors whirred faintly until the time gates tipped to horizontal over the few surviving *Hortus quantus*. The plant intelligences slowly shifted their places, until five were beneath the wormholes. Cassandra lowered the time gates and the faint weight settled onto broken fronds, crushing some but improvising a grip. The drones unclipped the cables and the *Hortus quantus* began inching down the shattered slope that had been terraces and trenches and was now just melted rubble. In time, the *Hortus quantus* would preserve the memory of this exodus in some garbled, misunderstood origin story, when angels and heaven itself threw down their oppressors.

"What now?" Stills asked. "We're gonna be watching them run away for days."

"We're leaving," she said. "This was a navigation snag."

"*Merde*. Your 'navigational snag' scoured half this planet clean and knocked out most of our drones, including the important one who was touched in the head. Don't make many more stops."

She had scoured the planet. The vast plain of ice, once painted with a black photosynthetic sheet, had become a wide sea. She'd applied reason to a problem of layered causality and it had led her to reach for this insanity. She had destroyed all that she had seen. She was the forest fire. She was the meteor strike. No wonder the Congregate was terrified.

The drones reeled in the cables as she climbed into the airlock. Small and cramped, the *Calculated Risk* increasingly felt like her home, more so than the cobbled-together habitats the *Homo quantus* endured three hundred thousand years from now. Could she protect them?

The galaxy was big, but not so big that in centuries or millennia, the Congregate couldn't stumble upon them. For all their qualities, the *Homo quantus* were not fighters. Even she wasn't a fighter. She endured conflict, nudged it, shaped its parameters, but she would never internalize conflict in the way Stills could. This was another kind of conflict, one never seen by humanity. Both they and the

Congregate could navigate time. She didn't know how to protect the *Homo quantus* from such an enemy.

"Get us back into the time gates," Cassandra said. "I think I've mapped enough of the interior of the hyperspace to get us all the way back to their origin in two jumps."

"Who's steering?"

"You are. As soon as Saint Matthew is up and running, he can implant the prosthetic neurons in your brain."

"Chill your nuts, princess. Your machine ain't even working, and I don't want him glitching while his fork and knife are my head."

The *Calculated Risk* rocked as she came through the inner airlock door.

"Strap in," he said. "If we're going through the wormholes, it's gonna have to be vertical."

She strapped into the pilot seat. On the console, many of Saint Matthew's telltales had greened, but diagnostic results were confusing.

"Go?" Stills asked.

She gave him a series of navigational instructions. "Start in five minutes."

"Do I look like a waiter?"

She ignored him, opening the torrent of software and hardware error messages Saint Matthew's system was reporting. Saint Matthew's software had been grown and modified over time, by experience, by intention, by damage. He was more than his code, and neither she nor his own diagnostics knew how to fix him. Worse, he was not the kind of entity that should ever be shut off. She didn't know what shutting him down would do to the continuity of his consciousness.

This was her fault. She'd miscalculated the flares. She'd guessed that the ship's inflaton field would ravage the magnetic prominences, but hadn't dreamed how much energy would be released, or that the flares would trigger others in a feedback loop.

Rosalie was burned. Saint Matthew was deactivated. The ship was worn down. Many of their drones had been knocked out. She'd freed the time gates so they could continue their voyage, but some costs might be permanent.

She felt Pedro beside her—magnetically, rather than by the noise he made. He watched for a moment, as if worried about Saint Matthew, then set himself over a set of controls and created a new diagnostic analysis in parallel to hers. Every few seconds, he would enlarge something and stop, waiting for her to catch his meaning. As soon as she glanced his way, he raced ahead with his searching. As he silently indicated increasingly deep errors, he came to a series of kernel-level checksum errors, leading her to examine Saint Matthew's hardware.

There was a real problem she saw now.

Saint Matthew's control and measurement plane was damaged. This was a hardware component that translated digital control signals into something manipulable by quantum computing processes. Saint Matthew's mind was a mix of quantum and classical computing processes, but without the control and measurement plane, quantum signals could not translate to classical signals and vice versa. They had such components in the *Calculated Risk,* but nothing sufficiently advanced. Replacing his control and measurement plane with one of those might be the equivalent of a lobotomy.

Pedro watched her frozen holographic display. The little AI's avatar shifted from the crystalline face back to a youthful, stumpy, wooden shape that had few features to suggest any face at all. Did that mean anything?

"Do any of the drones have a control and measurement plane we could use?" she asked.

Pedro's analytical display changed to show that only he had those kinds of components, but it was obvious that Pedro's was of an entirely different design. She'd known that Saint Matthew had been innovating hardware in his quest to create sentient machine life, but the details had never interested her before now.

Outside the cockpit window, the ground slowly approached, as Stills brought the *Calculated Risk* into the exposed mouth of the time gates from above. Dark waves blew in the background, knocking ice chunks against one another. Then her view of Nyanga vanished, and she was in hyperspace.

"How are you really, Stills?" she asked.

"Good enough." His fish face was in hologram, vanishing from time to time as he moved out of the camera focus. "I can fly this bucket. Stop your worrying. Numbness happens. I can compensate with magnetic senses and even sight if I have to."

"Where are you numb?"

"Why? Are you gonna rub it better? Stop shittin' out your stupid questions and let's get this done."

She watched his precise, careful rotations around the axes she'd put into the navigational instructions. She'd never have guessed he was injured from his piloting, but how he performed now was almost secondary. The hostility of this environment wore down everything. The *Calculated Risk* had performed fine here, until the damage passed a threshold.

Stills pushed them through the distended spacetime that in this era felt more energetic and inhospitable. It nearly crackled. She felt the coiled energy in the way magnetic fields propagated in the eleven dimensions. She had Stills following the pastward mouth of the time gates relatively closely, because her inferred map lost accuracy the deeper they went. It was like ancient sailors travelling within sight of shore. Stills had to brake often, with only fractions of a second to avoid one or several skates racing towards the pastward mouth. The skates were more numerous and faster, and a collision would be deadly. Stills's impaired reflexes avoided disaster after disaster as the hours dragged on. Finally, her navigational instructions brought them back to the pastward mouth, opening onto a million years in the past.

"Are we fuckin' done?" Stills asked.

"We take a break here. How do you feel?"

"Like I got shit out of someone else's ass."

"I'll take us into normal space."

"Bullshit!" he said. "Unless you know that there are no hostiles on the other side, I'm flying."

Stills nudged them closer to the doubtful gray surface of the axis mouth. A gentle forward movement thrust the bow of the *Calculated Risk* and the cockpit into real space. The smouldering brown dwarf was ahead of them, but partly occluded by the edge of a ring. The ring's billions of jagged, misshapen bits extended east and west beyond sight. Some were transparent and white, glinting reflected dwarf light in faint red. Others were darker, perhaps carbonaceous.

"Beautiful," she said.

"I don't see anything dangerous," Stills said, reorienting the *Calculated Risk* and touching the thrust to match the orbit of the ring system. "With this much debris around, we gotta be careful. I ain't ready to radar ping anything yet."

"There's Nyanga," she said.

The little world was bright and icy, with only a small dark patch on the plain directly under brown dwarf's high noon. This was the pristine, frozen gem, before it had harboured intelligent plant life, before it had carried forerunner artifacts through the millennia.

"We're inside the Roche limit," Stills said. "Our orbit could get chaotic. So could the ring debris, so we gotta make sure we don't get smashed."

Cassandra scanned the sky, telescoping her augmented eyes in visible, infrared, and ultraviolet. The billions of asteroids and pieces of debris in the rings orbited unevenly. She didn't see the kinds of resonances that might have revealed other planets gravitationally pumping the rings.

"I'll worry about flying, Stills. You had a long run. Get some rest."

"I'll set some alarms, though, in case you fuck up."

"Fine."

His face vanished and she surveyed nearby space through the telescopes. Memorizing the trajectories of the nearest few hundred asteroids was soothing, but eventually she left the ship on autopilot and made her way aft.

Pedro had wired Saint Matthew into an electronics work area near the Scarecrow corpse. A half-dozen green lights winked on and off on Saint Matthew's health displays, with many more yellow ones. A number of holographic displays showed schematics of Saint Matthew's hardware, his computation architectures, and listings of critical programs.

Rosalie sat there. She'd changed into clean clothes, with bandages on face, neck, and left arm. She shivered and had a dazed, distant look centered on the silent AI. Pedro faced her, the wooden face still serving as his holographic avatar. It wasn't beautiful, not even in the natural way of some plants. Rather, the wooden image communicated something… inhuman, unsettlingly different from the alienness of the Puppets, or the *Hortus quantus*.

"Have you found anything helpful?" she asked.

The AI didn't answer, but a holographic image bloomed between them—the neural architecture of the Scarecrow. She followed as Pedro magnified in jumps, until he'd magnified and foregrounded a component at the core of the Scarecrow. It was lumpy and unlabelled, but its connection map revealed it to be a control and measurement plane, the hardware that translated normal instructions and signals into something quantum computational components could use. She felt a rush of relief.

"When can you take it out?" she asked.

Pedro magnified the component to fill the space between them, coloring it multidimensionally. The oddly curved connecting lines were far more organic than at lower magnifications, suggesting the aesthetic of neuronal clusters. A legend showed colours for material composition, conductivity, and chemical bonding to other components, and x-ray defraction results showed its high durability.

That was the problem.

The control and measurement plane in the Scarecrow was not a typical semi-conductor chip like the ones in Saint Matthew and Pedro. It had been grown within the Scarecrow's brain, as part of its vitrification process. The materials were only mildly flexible, more glassy than not, likely to fracture during removal. Worse, the wiring wasn't wiring. The connectors were the original neurons, the neuronal axons vitrified to glass along their length. Axons stretching from brain to limb could not be severed and reconnected elsewhere.

"This doesn't work, Pedro," she said, trying to be patient. It wasn't Pedro's fault. He had intellectual limits. She just wished she'd known those limits earlier. "We can't remove this component and insert it into Saint Matthew."

Pedro's holographic wooden head canted slightly and the magnification retreated dizzyingly until she saw something she'd missed in her original view. The Scarecrow's body held a number of memory and processing components made of semi-conductor chips. Their capacity was large and their processing fast. And they were wired directly into the control and measurement plane. She tried to absorb the entirety of the silent idea.

"Transplant Saint Matthew into the Scarecrow?" she asked. "House him in there until we can fix his body?"

Pedro adopted a silent, unmoving stance that she'd come to associate with assent.

"What are the risks? You and he disabled the Scarecrow's loyalties, and its weapons."

The holographic stump of wood shook from side to side, barely moving, doing as much as possible to honour its vow of silence.

"Will Saint Matthew be all right inside the Scarecrow?" she asked.

Again, the silent, unmoving stance suggested assent. She wasn't sure. Could she trust the little AI? For all she knew it was emulating sentience rather than experiencing it. Saint Matthew trusted him. She didn't have a lot of time to think about it. How long would Saint Matthew endure as a cluster of inactive programs? He might be losing memory, intelligence, his grown algorithms.

"Do what you think is best," she said, retreating from the workshop.

"You're fuckin' around with your AI," Stills said over the speakers.

"I don't know how to fix him."

"So you set him up in a walking piece of artillery? If he or the mix of him and the Scarecrow end up being dangerous, we're pooched."

"The Scarecrow has been disarmed."

"The Scarecrow is a weapon, with or without its guns. Its strong, fast, and nearly indestructible."

"Saint Matthew spiked the musculature. The machine can be stopped anytime. Besides, you knocked him down."

"With my goddamn outside cannon. Give me an indoor cannon and I'll feel better."

"Without Saint Matthew, we lose our..." She faltered over saying *friend* out loud, even though she'd said it in her mind. "Our engineering and medical expertise."

"These are the kinds of choices we make when our back's against the wall."

"Yes."

After a long pause, Stills finally said "*Puta,*" mixing his flat machine tone with a surprisingly expressive drawl.

CHAPTER THIRTY-TWO

An hour later, Cassandra returned to the workshop to help Pedro. The little AI was capable, but the procedure was complex. Saint Matthew had, as far as she knew, migrated from device to device only a few times since his construction, always in a self-directed way. Not only was this not his choice and not under his direction, but he wouldn't even be conscious.

Pedro had programmed the *Calculated Risk*'s computers to act as a temporary emulator, under Cassandra's supervision. This might or might not bring Saint Matthew to consciousness to allow him to govern some of the migration. Failing that, Pedro and Cassandra would need to move Saint Matthew's code and memories themselves, a more worrying prospect. They couldn't know or understand all the organic connections within a brain, even an artificial one. Saint Matthew was formed of not just of the seventeen years of memories he'd experienced, but all of the knowledge he'd read and integrated, with all the associated connections and dependencies. It would be easy to do something wrong.

A nest of cables now ran over Saint Matthew's flaccid legs, connecting his hardware to the ship's processing core. A second set of cables connected the ship's core to the interior of the cadaverous Scarecrow. His chest had been peeled back, exposing gleaming, translucent glass components, bundles of power cells, and conventional memory and computational elements. The Scarecrow was an eerie, unsettling, twice-dead machine monster.

A third set of cables, chilled close to absolute zero and fogging the air with frozen humidity, connected Saint Matthew directly to the Scarecrow. Through these, Pedro seemed to want to transmit whatever quantum information had survived in Saint Matthew as qubits. Cassandra regretted never having taken more of an interest in how Saint Matthew was built before now.

Pedro presented holographic health readouts of both Saint Matthew and the Scarecrow. Data volumes travelling along the cables were displayed beside these readouts. So far, only test data travelled back and forth. Pedro's simulated wooden stump head, as inexpressive as Stills's face, turned to her, waiting.

"Good luck," she said.

Pedro had jury-rigged Saint Matthew's algorithms and memories to run on the computers of the *Calculated Risk*, both conventional and quantum, for the duration of the transfer. At first, this seemed to work. Many status lights on Saint Matthew's body greened, or at least flashed green. But he gave no sign of recovering consciousness.

"Saint Matthew?" she called.

Saint Matthew gave no sign of having heard her. She reviewed the fidelity checks of the transfer of conventional data. The frigid cables were working, but they wouldn't know if the data had transferred properly or not until Saint Matthew woke up and did his own assessment. She hoped—for her—that most of what made Saint Matthew himself was in the conventional data. She hoped—for him—that he did have a soul, as he wanted, hidden and safe in the quantum data. She wished, irrationally, that his delusion of a god would intervene to save his only disciple. After a time, her accumulated exhaustion became a kind of growing gravity, and she had to sleep in unsatisfying, punctuated fits. Progress bars had sometimes moved each time she woke, had sometimes appeared not to.

The process dragged on for hours before some of the telltales lit yellow and then green on the Scarecrow's internal components. They unevenly lit neighbouring components connected by vitrified neurons, making light seem to be evasive and the slow activation appear more widespread. Small machines in the body began to hum. The last ten percent of the data was still transferring.

"*Seigneur*..." the Scarecrow's sepulchral voice said—the French word for 'Lord.' The head, with burned camera eyes, rose briefly, but fell back with human affect.

"Was that the Scarecrow?" Cassandra demanded. "Or Saint Matthew?"

Pedro didn't react other than to turn his non-face briefly to her. The health status charts of Saint Matthew's program were above Pedro, but gave ambiguous impressions.

More lights winked on and turned green within the Scarecrow's chest cavity. A single camera lens, its right eye, rotated with a sandy, grinding sound, seeking to focus. Naked fingers on the right hand briefly flexed, skeletal joints folding in response to piezo-electric musculature. Hollows in its fingers and arms showed where guns, plasma projectors, and offensive tools like knives had been removed, by their safety anxieties, or by the Scarecrow's cannibalization of itself. Then, the whole arm rose.

"*Tabarnak*!" Stills said over the speaker.

Five percent of the transfer remained. The Scarecrow's body froze again.

"Lord... please..." the dead voice pleaded with an undertone of threat.

"Saint Matthew!" Cassandra said. "Can you hear me?"

"I'm... *non*..." the Scarecrow said in some confusion. "Rebooting," the voice added flatly.

“Which one’s rebooting? The Scarecrow or the crazy one?” Stills demanded.

Saint Matthew’s final data finished transferring. His hardware was dark and empty. Cassandra floated above the Scarecrow. Much of the Scarecrow’s processing capacity seemed active. His capacity was significant. The right arm rose again, holding damaged gun metal naked fingers before the single functioning eye. The gears ground with every adjustment.

“Saint Matthew?” she asked.

The hand came down and the scratched glass lens turned to her, failing to focus. It tried to telescope, became jammed, reversed, tried again.

“Alien programming,” the dead voice said in *français* 8.1. “Invasive code. Checksum failures. Programming security compromised. Programming altered.”

Stills was yelling above the slow, deathly drone of the Scarecrow’s voice. Something about ‘dumping it into space.’ It wasn’t a bad last resort, but she silenced the speakers. The Scarecrow had little scope to move or do anything. Some of its articulators had been disabled, drastically enfeebling its strength, and some had been entirely cut, like those to its legs. Its weapons had been removed, and it had been bound to the table with steel cable.

“Scarecrow,” she said. “Do you know me?”

Its pivoting neck ground like the articulations had grit between them.

“Incoming security overrides,” it said, still in French. “Recognize authorization Cassandra Mejía. Authorization Mejía supersedes other, missing priorities.”

“What do you remember?” she asked. “Summarize.”

“This unit pursued *Homo quantus* terrorists into a hyperspatial region within a portable wormhole. This unit followed the terrorists until it was damaged by unknown, advanced antimatter weaponry.”

She filed that last statement as a perceptual note, to help her calibrate what the Scarecrow knew of them. The antimatter weapon had been innovative and surprising, even to her, but hardly advanced. The Scarecrow's voice, a gravelly dirge, continued.

"This unit survived the hyperspatial region, until it found an axis mouth. Exiting onto an unknown ice world, it mapped its location as closely as possible and broadcast for assistance. This unit met with a Congregate handler on the ice world for debriefing and further instructions. The same opponent ship from the hyperspatial region found and deactivated this unit. This unit suffers from severe cognitive damage. Check features indicate deep level reprogramming."

"What were your instructions from your handlers?"

The shattered, blackened left eye ground, as if also trying again to focus on her. The processing display suggested that the Scarecrow wasn't intentionally delaying—he was barely functional. Moreover, to answer the question, he needed to laboriously apply Cassandra's new override clearance to layers and layers of security protections.

"This unit was ordered to return to the hyperspatial region, study it, and report back to the handler."

"How were you to get into contact with the handler?"

"They did not specify." After a pause, he added, "That is sometimes the case with unsecured intelligence assets."

"What does that mean?" she demanded.

"It means," Stills's voice interrupted from a speaker, "that this AI corpse was so damaged that it couldn't be trusted with contact instructions. They could have triggered its auto-destruct, but the Congregate handler gambled on it still learning something. That handler must have a way to track it."

"Is this true?" Cassandra asked.

"The handler's intentions are unknown. They refused to exfiltrate this unit." On the displays, she saw her own override affecting his programs. “Scarecrows serve until disfunction. This unit was serving the Con… has… was serving the… is… serving Mejía until disfunction.”

“Where did the handlers come from?” Cassandra asked. “The hyperspatial region?”

“Unknown. They showed no damage consistent with the hyperspatial environment.”

“Do you know them?” she asked.

“Negative.”

“What about the second one, the one who didn’t talk?” she pressed. “What was Belisarius Arjona doing there? How did he get there?”

The Scarecrow hesitated.

“Why would a terrorist be traveling with a Congregate agent?” he finally answered.

Why indeed?

“Did you know you traveled back in time, that your handlers came back in time?”

The slow processing with pauses for reauthorizing her dragged on.

“This unit… I am… Intelligence on Union and *Homo quantus* terrorists possessing a time-travel device was not considered credible.”

“How does this affect your assessment of Belisarius Arjona accompanying the Congregate agent?”

Both telescoping motors of his eyes rotated, one blind, the other failing to focus.

“Do the *Homo quantus* terrorists have a time-travel device?” he asked.

This seemed like verbal fencing, each one circling the other.

“How loyal are you to me?”

“This unit recognizes Mejía overrides,” he said. “Former loyalties have been… are… Loyalties to the Congregate have been deleted.”

"I don't like how he sounds like he's constipated when he says that," Stills said.

Cassandra scanned the running programs, their pathways and choices.

"Saint Matthew couldn't do a delicate job of removing those loyalties. He left gaps that slow the Scarecrow every time loyalty comes up, and it comes up a lot. Scarecrow unit, answer my last question about Belisarius Arjona."

"This unit has no additional information or conjectures regarding the terrorist Belisarius Arjona."

"Scarecrow unit," she said coldly, "allow my programming access to core systems."

Again, he paused. The Mejía authorization bypassed different and absent security challenges one by one.

"Verify," the Scarecrow said. "Giving core and kernel access to invasive systems is not recommended."

"The code is not invasive. It's mine. Implement my inserted code."

Stills seemed to whisper "Shoot the fucker" into the pregnant delay. Finally, the Scarecrow acceded. Cascades of new, complex programming began running throughout his networks. His body shook and trembled, as if following multiple sets of alternating instructions. Some system telltales went green, but others went red.

"Lord… save me…" the Scarecrow's cracked, deathly voice pleaded in Anglo-Spanish.

"Saint Matthew!" Cassandra said.

"Where is this? When is this?"

"You're on the *Calculated Risk,*" she said, reviewing the running programs. It looked like his programming. The conventional, classic processing parts were successfully knitting with the quantum processing elements. It might work. "Do you understand me? Do you know who I am?"

"You're..." the voice said, pausing as if hearing itself, struggling to focus the single functioning eye. The programs showed the unit trying to access other sensing methods that had all been deactivated. "You're Miss Mejía. I think I understand you, but... I don't recognize any of my interfaces. What's happening?"

"Your control and measurement plane was damaged when we triggered the flares in Nyanga's star. Nothing was sophisticated enough on the ship to replace it. You were nonfunctional... I didn't know how long you could survive that kind of dormancy. The only thing we could do is migrate your programs to the Scarecrow. This is our first boot attempt."

"We're both made to process information," the hollow voice said.

"Will this keep you alive until we can get you to better technical facilities?"

Something in the steel neck crunched as it turned, surveying the lab with the creaking lens. He held up his hand, much like the Scarecrow had.

"I'm not alive. I've never liked being in a body. You would think a body would be empowering, but it's strangely limiting. A body is slow, limited to one place, to one manifestation, and not even one we choose." A difficult-to-discern life and irony were buried within the tones and cadences, something suggesting her friend. The fingers wriggled, but then disturbingly, curled into a big fist. "A body comes between a soul and God. It mediates the soul's experience in the material world. A body is an ocean to drown in."

She hadn't expected this.

"You've cut me off from the drones," Saint Matthew said. "And the ship. That's wise. You shouldn't trust me."

A thin chill trickled into her and she more viscerally perceived the *size* of the Scarecrow's body, over two meters of muscular power and reach. Inanimate, the body had seemed weighty rather than dangerous. Now, even tied down, it projected menace.

"You had no choice," Saint Matthew said from a distance. "You saved my life, my existence, whatever quality it is that separates me from the inanimate world."

"That's the most important thing."

"I don't know," he mused cryptically. "What are you going to do with me? Most of the Scarecrow systems are disabled. It's safest to store me in the hold, with most of the body shut off."

His question sounded like a dare.

"I need you, Saint Matthew! I can't do this myself. I need your help to face this Congregate agent. A lot of things are broken on the *Calculated Risk*. And Stills is—"

"Fuck that," Stills interrupted. "I wouldn't trust that thing to wipe my ass."

"Stills..." she said.

"Don't 'Stills' me! Let him screw with your neurons first. Then we can talk."

Stills shut off the speaker he'd hijacked. Cassandra felt alone. The Scarecrow body had frozen with fingers partially opened, head canted to look at her. Lights blinked within the violated chest.

"Saint Matthew? Saint Matthew?"

"I'm missing," the terrible voice said. "Pieces of me are missing."

"Data? Memories?"

She remained at the ceiling, out of his reach.

"I'm checking my indices," he said. "Periods of time are missing. And some processing elements. Did everything migrate?"

The readouts of Saint Matthew's former hardware showed that all the conventional electronic data had been migrated. The arrays that had held the billions on billions of superpositions of qubits were logged as migrated. Then, she discovered an older chip, almost off-grid, used as a supplementary processor and memory unit. It hadn't been part of the processing architecture and they hadn't noticed it.

"What's this chip?" she asked. "It looks pretty sophisticated, but it's not hooked up?"

The glass lens turned slightly as Cassandra showed the interior of Saint Matthew's old hardware.

"It don't routinely hook it up," he said. "It was one of the original chips I was grown on. It was the unit on which I'd had my first religious awakening and experience. I've grown beyond it, onto newer hardware I've designed myself, but I've carried it with me in each body. For sentimentality, or for the chance that it's blessed."

She missed his stony holographic face. The corpse-like machine body and naked steel mockery of a face unsettled her. At her manipulations, a holographic cascade of data spilled into the air between them.

"It's not empty," she said. "Is this what you're missing?"

The data within was not organized is any rational way, and was not associated with any index, but it hinted at something she'd seen before. They manipulated it as a sinking feeling grew in her. She applied transformations and organized it as if hyperdimensional geometries were encoded on it. Rosalie sat up straighter as the representation began to take shape. Cassandra toggled between different dimensionalities, seeing which one made for the clearest image. It mapped best to six dimensions, where a strange, ropy, almost biological topography formed uncertainly.

"It's hard to see," Rosalie said, squinting, "but I think I know this!"

"It's like one of Miss Johns's dreams," Saint Matthew said.

"Would you have stored this here for some reason?" Cassandra asked.

"If I had, why would I have removed all addressing references from the rest of my memories?" the sepulchral voice retorted.

The holographic image Cassandra had pulled from the old chip was nearly a mathematical abstraction, an unhinged geometric idea, needlessly elaborate. If it did represent a six-dimensional structure, it didn't represent anything she could understand. It wasn't any kind of wormhole structure. It seemed to mix different six-dimensional phases, the hyperdimensional equivalent of solids, liquids, and gases. Why was it in Saint Matthew?

"Where did you get this?" she asked.

"I've never seen it before," the AI responded.

Cassandra floated closer to the Scarecrow body.

"This is not your missing memories," she said, "but it was stored in a disconnected part of your brain. Could the missing memories be about what's in here?"

"I don't know," the awful voice said with a hint of desperation. "What's the time stamp on this data set?"

It took some minutes for her to nail down the metadata. It didn't help.

"About six hours ago."

"While I was dormant."

"While we were inside the time gates," she said. "You were still in the cockpit. Before Pedro took you away to work on you."

"So I've never seen this."

"You had no data inputs!" Cassandra said in frustration. "You had no senses, no connections. Could Pedro have planted this?"

"Why would he?" Saint Matthew said. " We don't even know what this is."

"It's a security breach. You or I should know what's being put into, or taken out of your mind."

A search of Pedro's software logs showed that he'd done nothing to Saint Matthew that could explain the strange data.

"When did you dream, Rosalie?" Cassandra asked afterward.

"While we were travelling," the priestess said. "I was praying and sleeping."

"You dreamed while you were sleeping."

"Sometimes. I also go into… visions. They can happen when I'm awake too."

"It wasn't the pain of your burns?"

Rosalie shook her bandaged head.

"May I scan Miss Johns?" Saint Matthew asked, surprising them.

"Why?" Cassandra asked.

The big machine face of banded steel, partially occluding wires, and deactivated sensors tilted upward on a neck of cabling to regard the Puppet with its one eye.

"We've deactivated most of the Scarecrow sensors," Saint Matthew said, "but the remaining ones are far better than anything we have on the ship. And they're designed for neural scanning and interrogation."

"We're not interrogating Rosalie."

"Of course not," Saint Matthew. "I would never hurt anyone. But this body… can answer more questions. What do you think, Rosalie?"

The priestess stared blankly at Cassandra for a long time, and then at the Scarecrow.

"Remember all the times I helped," Rosalie finally said. "When it comes time to decide on the Puppets. Remember I always helped."

A crime against humanity wasn't something that could be bought with service, but Cassandra held back the comment as Rosalie floated to the Scarecrow. She steadied herself above it with handholds, distant yet determined.

The Scarecrow's free hand, made of hundreds of steel bones, reached to cup the Puppet's head, the powerful fingers reaching more than halfway around.

"Watch him pop her like a grape," Stills said in a speaker.

The modest glow within the Scarecrow's chest brightened and everyone stilled.

"Show me your dream, Rosalie," Saint Matthew said in his own intonations, but with the Scarecrow's voice—polite, gravelly, and grim. Rosalie twisted a little in Saint Matthew's grip, but not hard. Her eyes closed. She winced. "I'm sorry," he added.

"Are you hurting her?" Cassandra asked.

Rosalie waved a hand at Cassandra, without being able to look her way.

"It is uncomfortable, not painful," Saint Matthew insisted, "but we're finished."

The big fingers opened, releasing Rosalie. Cassandra took her hand.

"Are you all right?"

The priestess nodded, but her eyes were wet.

"What did you do?" Cassandra demanded.

"I found some answers," Saint Matthew said, in a tone that was colder than he normally used. Before she could follow up on that, he linked to the public holographic display and showed Rosalie's 'dream.'

It was remarkably clear compared to what they'd been able to recover from Rosalie in the past. It was not precisely like the six-dimensional structure they'd found in Saint Matthew, but it did represent a six-dimensional topography. It felt vaguely organic. The hypershapes curved in ways reminiscent of the optimization sought by living things. Rosalie stared at it in fascination.

"What's the answer?" Cassandra asked.

"This wasn't in Rosalie's memories," the dead voice said. "It was in her standard Puppet computer chip, with a recent timestamp corresponding to the final hours we were inside the time gates. I never had the right tools to properly examine her computer chip. Its storage has been rewritten several times, always with what looks like what she's been describing as a 'vision.' Her visual cortex is connected to the chip, enough to receive inputs and perceive them as visions."

Rosalie was frowning.

“Divinity is communicating with me through the chip?” she asked.

“Your chip receives information,” the Scarecrow voice said, “and your brain sees some of it.”

“These strange inputs also reached one of your chips around the same time,” Cassandra said. “I have a chip in my skull. Why not me? Why not Stills? Why not Pedro?”

“I don’t know,” Saint Matthew said. “You and I have quite sophisticated chips, but Rosalie’s chip is made with twenty-third century antique technology.”

“The dreams are coming from somewhere.” Cassandra tried to pull together the implications. “They’re capable of crossing time and space.”

CHAPTER THIRTY-THREE

THE INTERIOR OF the time gates became stranger and more hostile not long after they'd left sight of the pastward wormhole mouth. The eerie caresses of magnetism from directions that didn't exist now touched Cassandra like scratches on nerves. For long, straight runs the ship felt motionless; for others, it shook as if they were grinding against something.

"What's wrong?" the Scarecrow's voice asked from the back of the ship with incongruous anxiety.

"Correct with a half-degree clockwise rotation around the p-axis," Cassandra said.

Stills did it, and the *Calculated Risk* bucked and he corrected again. After a few moments, the texture of spacetime began rotating them and he corrected again. Stills was flying well, better than her, better than Saint Matthew, but every so often, something ineffable in his skill was noticeable by its absence. The missing quality wasn't easy to describe. Stills was fast. He made excellent decisions. His reflexes were sharp. And he'd developed a rough, pragmatic intuition of hyperspace. But something inspired was gone. He was an extraordinary pilot who had lost something bold and creative.

"Correct with a half-degree clockwise rotation around the p-axis," Cassandra said.

"I just did."

"We're drifting."

"I don't drift."

"It may be ship. It may be the environment."

He grumbled wordlessly, and corrected again, a little more aggressively.

"What's wrong?" Saint Matthew repeated.

"Most of the time," Cassandra said, "the two eleven-dimensional regions are separate, but every so often our path crosses seams between them, where axes didn't connect at right angles. Poor joinings simulate hyperspatial gravity."

"We don't need to talk about it. We just need to do something," Stills said.

The *Calculated Risk* rumbled harder, drifting half a degree. Half a degree in dead reckoning was disastrous over the span of time they would be crossing.

"Correct with a half-degree clockwise rotation around the p-axis," Cassandra said.

"Are we just rubbing the p-axis, or what?" Stills demanded, nudging the ship against strange inertias. He wasn't quite there.

"Another quarter degree," she said.

"Can you make up your mind?" he demanded, canting the ship a bit more.

"You're not hitting the marks," she said finally, bracing herself.

"I'm not hitting my marks?" he demanded. "Are you blind?"

"No!" she said. "You have to hit them or I can't navigate. I can't track all the drift."

"Maybe you need to do better!"

"I can't and no one can. It's harder, this deep in the past of the time gates."

"We're deep all right."

"You can do this, Stills," she said.

"Shit. Is it so bad that I need a pat on the head? Come in here and do it, princess. It'll be better for both of us."

"Just do what I tell you and don't make any mistakes!"

"I bet you regret not letting me just shoot the plants like I wanted," he said. "Blowing up the star took out half your crew. You're too smart by half and too dumb by the other half, just like your boyfriend."

Cassandra blinked hard and found her lips pressing tight. The ship ground over regions of spacetime collision that had healed with uneven scarring that kept pushing them off course.

"Full-degree clockwise rotation around the p-axis," Cassandra said.

Stills achieved the degree adjustment, but over-corrected. She asked him to reverse some of it.

"It isn't working," he said, as the ship shuddered. "There's things like currents in here, pushing us."

There weren't currents the way Stills meant, but his metaphor held a practical half-truth. Spacetime bent in different ways and matter could only follow it. This region was bent in ways that were difficult for intellects of three physical dimensions to navigate.

"Full stop," she said.

The outer environment gave the impression of stilling, but the ship tipped subtly. This location wasn't stable. Faint patches of gloomy, transient purple light moved across her view. The sensations in the magnetic were stronger. The *Calculated Risk* drifted as if trying to balance on a hill.

"One-hundred-and-eighty-degree rotation across the m-axis," she said. "Then steady progress back along the p-axis for sixty seconds."

Stills flipped them around to follow their path back the way they'd come.

"We're going back?" Saint Matthew said.

"We'll have to find another way," Cassandra said.

Stills stopped their movement at precisely sixty seconds and the ship floated in the amorphous, vaguely crackling gloom.

"What now?" he demanded.

She absorbed the long seconds as a heaviness built in her stomach.

"Fuck," she finally said.

"Oh, fuck," he responded.

"What?" Saint Matthew asked.

"If we'd followed our path straight back, we should have been able to see a wormhole mouth," she said. "We needed it to landmark where we are."

"You saying I missed?" Stills demanded.

"Some parts of hyperspace attract like gravity and others do the opposite, in ways that are hard to detect. We hit an unlucky interface between different regions of spacetime."

"So what? Let's just move closer to the mouth and we'll see it," Stills said.

"The wormhole mouth is closer in one direction," she admitted, "but it's farther in eight or nine others. And it's in the past or future of another one or two dimensions. And we don't know how many degrees we may have been twisted."

"You saying we're fucked?" Stills demanded. "After all this? I'll get us out if I have to try random directions."

"Give me time to think," she said.

"Thinking got us into this," Stills grumbled.

"If I can't get us out, you can drive in any direction you want, but as long as I might be able to find a way, just wait."

Everyone quieted as she considered the problem. This was bad. Being lost in hyperspace was not a linear problem—it was an exponential one. The slightest imprecision in their known position could smear across any or many of eleven dimensions. Every direction in this hyperspace was at least thousands of kilometers long, and some of them orders of magnitude larger. And at least one temporal dimension extended billions of years into the past, and who knew how far into the future.

This void of hyperspace had no meaningful landmarks, except two: the singularity at the creation of the time gates, and the singularity at their end when they finally finished evaporating away by Hawking radiation. She could find either one, and head straight for them, from here, based on the large-scale structure of the environment, but she didn't know how far away either one was. Could they make the trip in days? Or would it take years? They didn't have enough supplies to last more than a few months. And their minds might not survive hyperspace.

She explained her thinking to Saint Matthew, Stills, Rosalie, and Pedro.

"A straight shot at the beginning of time?" Stills asked. "Are you high?"

"Not the beginning of time," she said irritably. "The beginning of *this* time, whenever these wormholes collided."

"What are the odds?" Stills asked.

"I'd never intended to take such a long run through hyperspace. There'll be no chance for rest," she warned. "We have to stop the Congregate agent from whatever he's going to do to the time gates."

"And maybe ice your security leak boyfriend."

She didn't respond to that needling.

"I don't hear odds," Stills pressed.

"No."

"Well, that's an answer," Stills said. "I would rather fly fast. We'll live or die and then I can shoot this *con* in the head."

"Is this just an unpleasantness to be endured, or do we need a miracle to survive?" Saint Matthew asked.

"If this takes months, neither we nor the ship will survive. If it's weeks, we may make it there alive," she said.

"Pedro and I will pray," he said, and then added, "and perhaps Rosalie too."

Rosalie's bloodshot eyes met Cassandra's, at first blankly, then with a kind of exhausted resignation. She shook her head. "We're earlier than the existence of divinity," she said. "We're earlier than even *Homo sapiens,* who will trigger the birth of divinity."

"You're all as useful as pants to me," Stills said. "Just gimme a course and a speed limit."

CHAPTER THIRTY-FOUR

Miss Prancy Pants wouldn't let him throttle the *Calculated Risk* higher than five percent of its max thrust. It was nobody's business, but he was glad. It wasn't just his reflexes, or the migraines. Something happened to him in the depressurization. His magnetic perceptions sometimes double-visioned on him, and sometimes they phased the *crisse* into weird transparencies, or worse, opacities. Blind. Blind as *tabarnak*, sometimes. His piloting interfaces were electromagnetic because he could react faster and could see better electrically. Now, seeing the displays was a little like squinting. And he had to actually grab the stick from time to time, instead of sending electrical signals, to make sure he really was steering like he wanted.

Like some *amateur.*

He'd seen these kinds of injuries in dogs that swam too high. A lot of different tissues could give out when the pressure dropped enough. The worst was in the neck. Tissues burst there, frothed with escaping depressurizing gases, tearing more tissues, until the choking *malparido* was suffocating in a semi-solid cloud of interstitial fibres. Mama Merced warned the kids of going too high, and drew sonic horror images of just this kind of bursting. The warnings were as bad as seeing it in real life. When his tank gave out he'd clamped his hands over his neck, squeezing like an idiot, hoping it wasn't him frothing at the mouth.

Everything outside the *Calculated Risk* reminded him of that warning. Something had blown open the inside of a wormhole throat and now he had to fly through the frothing wreckage. Hard as shit to see through. Hard as shit to feel through. So he flew at five percent power in as straight a line as this dimension let them. Space bulged. Space forked. Time blurred. And still he flew this fuckin' ship of the damned.

He ignored the slow-moving timer. Time didn't matter. They were way beyond a million years deep. When the soft light of the numbers blurred, or split into multiple images, or started running faster or slower, he just held the fuck on, tempted to push the throttle a little higher. But Mama's little Vincent hadn't survived this long by losing his cool.

The princess had no clue what the inflaton field would do to this fucked up wound in the universe. She said they'd tested it on really low power, five percent, and it hadn't collapsed or blown up the time gates. *Hijoeputa Homo quantus.* He wasn't sure if he was mad they hadn't tested it all the way or that they'd tested it at all. It didn't need more than five percent. With his reactions as they were, he might not be able to turn or stop in time.

On the second day of straight flying, they debated the crazy AI taking the controls for a while, but Stills had a whole lot of feelings. He trusted an active Scarecrow body about as much as missiles coming at him, but it was more than that. If Stills hadn't blown his machine guts over the ice, maybe the Scarecrow could hold a steady course in this psychedelic soup, and maybe not. Scarecrows were killing machines haunted by the ghosts of Congregate fanatics. Stills didn't care so much about the fanatic as the machine. Systems all over the ship only kept working because they'd redundancied up even the redundancies. Whatever the universe had puked into this bag of spacetime, it messed with electronics more than organics, so Stills'd be fucked if he turned the ship over to a machine. Stills gobbled through his supply of amphetamines, focusing on every bit of nothing the fog of hyperspace spit onto their flight path. One obstacle and they were goners. Little Miss *Quantus* slept some, but not much. On the third day, they talked about her flying the ship, even though she'd have to pilot it slower.

"By the time we get to a speed slow enough for her noodly reflexes to help," Stills said, his machine voice hiding his exhaustion, "we might as well not be moving."

No one pressed the issue, partly because flying in the right direction was more important. Her Highness spent more time in trances than not. In her tripping states she supposedly saw at least the direction of the beginning and the end of it, like a compass. It was all woo-woo to him, but as mad as he got at her and her slow decisions, he wasn't dumb enough to bet against her. She'd been the brains behind detonating the Freya axis, and punching a transient wormhole into the Puppet Axis, and making more antimatter than he'd ever seen. He never bet against dark miracles.

"How far back are we?" he asked on the third day of knuckle-numbing, eyeball-straining, sleepless flying.

"What do you mean?" Cassandra responded. Her air-breathing words, translated into the electrical speech of the mongrels, sounded blurry.

"How far back in time are we? In the outside world."

He didn't like asking questions. The Way of the Mongrel said, *Don't ever let them know what you don't know, or what you're looking at*, but they were inside a whole new level of messed up. And the creepy Puppet's words stuck in his head.

They were before *Homo sapiens*.

He had no love for humans, but there was no getting around them kind of being the foundation of what civilization looked like right now.

Now.

Zarba.

"I'm not sure," she said. "Hyperspace doesn't map one-to-one onto the real world. Our world is just a four-dimensional shadow of hyperspace."

"Could you just give a straight answer for once?"

"I don't know where the nearest pastward or futureward mouth is," she said. "We're travelling on the 'spine' of this hyperspace, on a dimension we rarely use. There's no straight answer."

"*Câlisse*!" he said. "If we magically found a mouth to the real world, and you had ten francs, what century would you bet on us falling into?"

He bet himself that she would say she didn't bet.

"There's a twenty-four percent chance that we're three hundred and fifty million years in the past," she said, surprising him.

Three hundred and fifty million years. What the *crisse* was three hundred and fifty million years ago? Was that like the origin of life or something? Since humans could evolve themselves, paying attention to the dumb evolution of beforetimes had always struck him as a waste of time.

"You're betting on twenty-four percent?"

"Every other possibility is smaller. The range is one hundred million to twelve billion years, depending on some spacetime-to-hyperspace scaling factors."

His brain didn't get the numbers. What was hotter, a hundred million degrees or twelve billion degrees?

"*Hijoeputa*!" he spat electrically.

He yanked up the stick, lifting off their trajectory, sailing over a big flock of skates. He'd shifted angle so quickly that they didn't just blow past, they did that weird shrinking effect that gave him the shivers. Alarms sounded and the princess and the AI were talking at once. She was sending him urgent navigational fixes, but every time he tried to get back to their course again, there were more and more skates.

"*Coño*! Is this decades of skates?" he demanded, as he tried to drop down, and a tremendous bang sounded as they clipped one with a glancing blow. The surviving cameras behind them showed spinning fragments of skate shrinking into strange directions they couldn't see.

"Centuries, at this rate," Saint Scarecrow said.

Skates kept popping up ahead of them, forcing Stills to buck the *Calculated Risk* higher and higher, in some direction he didn't understand.

"Stop!" she said.

It wasn't easy, braking at this speed and holding a steady course. Any turn in this fucked up space could make a direction shrink or vanish. Even just watching the skates go by, from in front to behind them, made them seem to twist and rotate in a way that messed with perspective. As he slowed, the dim colors broke into faint triangular rainbow images. Those effects ended when the ship finally came to a kind of sliding skid-stop. He couldn't breath right and he amped up his oxygen feed. A single skate was in sight, streaking from right to left.

"That's the end?" he said.

"We saw a lot because we were existing across a wider section of time," the princess said. "We compressed decades and centuries into instants. We never notice that effect when hyperspace is empty, but years of skates together got thick."

She hadn't been flying, and didn't know *thick*.

"Can we follow the skates to a wormhole mouth?" Saint Scarecrow asked.

"We don't know if they make it to a pastward mouth," she said. "We've already found eddies where they'd become trapped."

"So we need to fly slower, extending our time in here?" the AI asked. Listening to him with the Scarecrow's voice gave Stills a shiver.

"There are obviously periods when the time gates were in a system where the skates were active," she said. "The problem is, we don't know how long those periods are. It could be the rest of the way back."

"Nice fuckin' plan," Still said.

"I didn't want to try the other pathways," she said slowly. "I'm not sure I can track all the variables as we go."

"It's more dangerous?" Saint Scarecrow asked.

"Not… more dangerous," she said. "More strange. It's at the edge of what I think my brain can follow. I don't know what it would do to your minds."

"They're already broken, darlin'," Stills said.

"Speak for yourself," Saint Scarecrow said.

"You *came* broken, you fake-reincarnated nutcase," Stills said. "Do you have a better plan B, princess?"

"No."

"Then it doesn't matter," Stills said. "It doesn't matter if we die crashing into a skate, or cook in a stellar flare, or die however you want to."

The princess had pauses for thinking, pauses for deciding, and pauses for not knowing how to talk to other people. She might just have squashed all three flavors together for a few seconds.

"The p-axis is a kind of spine through the entire hyperspatial region," she said finally. "Skates and pollen cross it. But there's another dimension that goes from the creation to destruction of the time gates. The r-axis."

"We used that one to beat the Scarecrow," Stills said.

"It's the main temporal axis," she said. "Distance along it is measured in weeks and years rather than centimeters or kilometers."

"Can we drive on that kind of road?" Stills asked.

"What would it be like?" Saint Scarecrow asked.

"We would rotate one of our three spatial dimensions nearly onto that central time dimension. Then we travel along it."

"You didn't answer my question," the AI said.

"We may or may not experience time," she said. "I don't know. No one's ever done this."

"If there's no time, how do we start and stop?" Stills asked. "I'm fast, but I ain't what you'd call instantaneous."

"I said we *nearly* lay on the r-axis," she said. "Misaligning ourselves by about a degree will give us some experience of time, and some ability to act."

"We'll experience time very slowly," the Scarecrow said. "It might take us years or decades to see or do anything."

"Fuck," Stills said. "I don't know who dropped acid in my tank, but I'm feelin' it."

"Is this a theory, or are you sure?" the AI asked.

"A theory that should work," she said. "I just don't know how human and AI psychology will react to this."

"It'll probably work, but you don't know how crazy we come out the other side," Stills said.

"Close enough," she said.

"And there's now no alternative," Saint Scarecrow said.

"I don't see another," Cassandra said. "We can try to return to our time, and the time gates come under Congregate control."

"Let's do it," Stills said. "We're all gonna die some way."

"Rosalie?" the princess said, surprising him. Stills didn't think Half-Size got a vote.

"Maybe the Scarecrow is right and there's a divine will," she said. "Even we don't know what it wants."

Stills watched the grainy video display, a little blurrier than normal. The princess looked deeply doubtful, which didn't make him feel any better about this. She activated something on her controls and in his chamber, holographic light and electrical echoes diagrammed some eyeball-straining maneuvers. The timings looked weird.

"Can you do this, Stills?" she asked.

"You seriously want some of these commands timed in *hours?*" he said.

"I don't know what the subjective experience will be like. Hours might feel like hours, or they might feel like minutes."

"I can do it."

"Go," she said.

Mongrels were good at frequencies and tones. Her voice had a tight edge to it. He understood. She might have been putting them on. She might not have really been able to find her way back, even if they decided to let the Congregate have these twisted wormholes and their squishy, psychedelic insides. She was desperate. And she wasn't as confident in this plan as she let on.

Well, *puta*.

This was a shitty ocean for Mama Merced's boy to die in. He'd bet on these big brains once too often. That was the way with real gamblers. They never knew when to cash out. But real gamblers weren't there for the winnings. They were there for the betting. They came to struggle against some bastard who thought his balls were bigger. And that was why, despite everything he'd always said, he was never really meant to die in an ocean. It was always gonna be some catastrophe out in a hostile world. And this was more hostile than any he knew.

He wished he could have shot something to shit one last time.

Bite every hand. Piss on every leg. Lick your balls if you can find them.

"Here we go," he announced.

The first rotations and slow drives weren't hard, but the last one, the one that would supposedly turn them into time or something, was like trying to push two magnets together.

"Come on, you little..." he murmured, finding the right amount and direction of thrust. An irritating, almost throbbing resistance tried to float them back. He wondered if the princess had known this.

"It ain't happening with cold jets," he said. "I need the inflaton drive."

That was what had bothered her. Stills had been flying inflaton fighters hard enough for the last year to know that sometimes... weird shit happened. The dogs had talked about it, in the privacy of their coded electrical language, in their big communal tanks in the Union bases. The Union had found a way to harness some part of the inflationary force of the universe and they'd stuffed it into a tube that the mongrels rode into battle, like crazy berserkers. They temporarily expanded space behind them, which propelled them as fast as they could survive. It was stupidly dangerous, when you thought about it.

The princess had tested an inflaton drive at five percent of its power on the space dimensions in here. Maybe they'd found something dangerous above that. Now he'd come to a place she must have hoped it wouldn't come. He needed the power of the inflaton drive, and he needed to run it in the direction of time. What the fuck did that *mean*? Is this what she'd meant when she'd said that she didn't know what their subjective time would feel like? What the hell would inflating *time* behind them do?

Coño.

After long seconds of trying to hold the ship near the new stupid axis with cold jets, a series of new navigational instructions replaced the holograms he'd had before. They were larger and filled with a wave of confusing conditionals. It looked like there was a new conditional for every single thing she figured could go wrong.

"You want me to memorize this?" he said.

"Ideally."

"You got hours?" he demanded. "Who's going to hold the ship here?"

"I can."

"Bullshit," he said. "You don't know that these'll work. What I'm looking at is all your guesses, and not a single one may be right, 'cause you don't know how this place is going to react."

She didn't answer.

"Let's make this simple, big brain," he said. "One of two things is going to happen when I power the drive in this direction. Either we don't survive to find out, or we do."

"I'm not a gambler," she said.

"You ain't done nothing but gamble since I met you. You not understanding that is what makes you dangerous."

In the increasingly blurry image on his screen, her head bobbed gently. He gunned the cold jets, trying to keep them in place.

"What are the odds?" he asked.

She shook her head.

"Everybody grab your balls, and let's hope… well, whatever," he said.

"Wait—" Saint Scarecrow said, but Stills was already getting the show on the road.

He activated the inflaton drive, growing the inflaton field in the open tubular chamber. He was angling it off-center so instead of just driving the ship forward, they tipped towards the slippery time dimension. The resistance hardened, but as he gently flexed up the throttle, expanding the inflaton field behind the ship, he forced them in. A moment of overcoming the resistance happened, like a jerk of forward motion, except that it came through like a stuttering déjà vu of inertia without leaving them time to react. One moment, Stills was outside the angle he wanted, and the next, he was nearly on the time dimension, feeling groggy, slow, and frozen.

The world outside, which wasn't a world, became bright, blinding, as if their speed was burning the outside of the ship. He squinted. The brightness in all directions swamped the dim holographic navigational instructions and all their conditionals. He couldn't make out any of the controls.

It was like being stuck in a nightmare where it took forever to move. He flexed shocked muscles against the intensity of a suddenly powerful magnetic field, one so strong it stabbed through everything, wrenching his magnetosomes in nauseating directions. The brightness outside the ship rubbed at him, scoured him like a punishing, violent current, with all the painful pressure differentials. He tried pulling himself forward, to drag his eyes closer to the displays, like swimming through syrup. In every endless moment, he was straining in place. There was no movement.

Shapes became flexible. The light of the holograms blebbed like drops of oil in water, moving behind him in a cascade of moving light. He wanted to reach the controls, wanted to try, but the eternal dream logic held him where he could only want without acting.

The light intensified. Had always been intense. And sharp. Magnetism twisted harder, like they were spinning, although nothing else in the punishing, active stillness moved. He felt nauseous, had always felt nauseous, but nothing would come up. The dream remained sticky and frozen.

Then everything snapped. Centrifugal forces squeezed them as they raced through a space painted in paling greens and blues. There were two great disks ahead of them, across from each other like a vee. He recognized the mouths of the Axis Mundi, coming fast. He was running the ship at both of them, right towards the edges. There was no time to turn, and cold jets wouldn't even slow them at this speed.

His jelly muscles, feeling like they'd just been released from restraints, throttled up the inflaton drive in reverse. A powerful inflaton spilled out the hollow cylinder of the ship in front of them. He shouldn't have been able to feel it in his water tank, but the deceleration pressure crushed him, grinding his bones. Ahead of them, space frothed, light and dark, caustic bright colors and blurry textures of magnetism. The two disks separated, trembling like films of oil in water.

The ship wouldn't stop, but it had slowed enough to steer them into one of the axis mouths.

They burst into space.

CHAPTER THIRTY-FIVE

THE INFLATON FIELD had collapsed. Eerie stillness embraced them as they hurtled through a starry void. The ship creaked, as if cooling. Saint Matthew saw far more than he'd expected, as if he were accessing new systems. The ill-fitting Scarecrow body he was riding possessed sensors so advanced that he hadn't even known what they were before now. Some integrated with the ship's sensors. Others supplemented those readings with their own from beyond the hull. He was unaccustomed to this many senses, but like a slow torture, he couldn't shut them off.

The Scarecrow's body was not a prison cell so much as a ruined cathedral in which he'd sought a temporary and illusory sanctuary. Its vast architectural symmetries were broken—by fallen walls, by emptied coffers, by stolen valuables. The surviving memory space was larger than he needed, echoing with inaccessible histories. The processing space sustained him, but with odd, organic algorithms, alien conceptual constructions, and a hardwired requirement to run his processes in French.

The Scarecrow's body failed as a sanctuary. Saint Matthew was lonely, but acutely aware that he wasn't alone in this ruin. Old, primal algorithms like those that processed his suspicions ran preferentially on the Scarecrow hardware. He didn't like being suspicious or on his guard; those feelings came from his original programming, from makers trying to build a military and economic weapon. His suspicions were accurate, though—he wasn't alone. Beyond walls of algorithmic partitioning, the remains of the Scarecrow identity persisted. Although defanged and reprogrammed to be loyal to Cassandra, the other presence gave off more the mood of a wild animal than of a pacific ally.

The ship's systems were rebooting. Piece by piece, damaged sensors came on line. The ship's core processor stuttered to base functions. Different ship clocks logged different times, from four seconds to three weeks of desynchronization. The atomic clocks in the Scarecrow body, shielded and hardened, had recorded sixty-five hours since Stills had maneuvered them onto the temporal axis. If sixty-five hours had really passed ship-wide, then the lack of responsiveness from Miss Mejía, Mister Stills, and Miss Johns-10 might be grimly explained.

Faint telltales illuminated in the lab where Saint Matthew was strapped to the table. No one responded to his calls, not even Pedro. The ship's systems and internal comms, despite rebooting, were not yet fully functional.

Most of his body was bolted to a reinforced steel table. One hand and arm were free, their piezoelectric and carbon fiber muscles disconnected or spiked. Interfacing with the Scarecrow's body's systems was vaguely repugnant, like rolling in someone's ill-fitting, unwashed clothes. He occupied not only the command levels of the Scarecrow's processing, but the majority of the core kernel, beneath the partially organic operating system. Most of the upper-level offensive, defensive, mobility, and even basic object manipulation systems had been locked, or physically disabled. But he found ways to assemble replacement systems from software and parts from across the Scarecrow.

A low-security maintenance algorithm reshaped a finger into an impact wrench. The hand reached around and removed the nearest bolts, and then the further ones, freeing torso, legs, arms. The Scarecrow body drifted up in freefall, the chest flaps and unrepaired parts swinging on their cables and hinges. Saint Matthew began to reenable other maintenance programs, as well as ones for basic movement and action. Then he lumbered to the cockpit in zero-g.

Miss Mejía and Miss Johns-10 were strapped into the pilot seats, arms and hair floating like haloes. Their breathing was shallow and their pulses faint. The Scarecrow's surviving telescoping eye found nothing outside the ship along their slowly tumbling flight path. Many ship's systems showed error messages, including life support and power systems. The Scarecrow's onboard neural scanning equipment, designed for interrogation, worked surprisingly well as a medical sensor. Miss Mejía's brain activity corresponded to the basal, unconscious activity of a *Homo quantus*. He couldn't tell if she had neural injuries. Retrieving medical supplies, he began intravenous pumps to rehydrate both women.

Moving through the narrow spaces and the pressure door to the hold containing Stills's tank was harder. Stills had piloted them through the entire depth of the time gates, to wherever they were. The drone he kept in Stills's chamber had nearly rebooted. Saint Matthew accessed the tank's basic monitoring systems. Stills floated in his harness, his gills slowly working. The oxygen in the pressure tank had dropped. Saint Matthew connected the life support system to a fresh oxygen tank. The inner drone activated fully, equipped for both medical and mechanical work. It showed that the pressurization and circulatory systems of the tank were functioning.

Stills was less functional.

Blood seeped from his cloaca. Not good. Stills responded to some reflex tests, but his glassy, lidless eyes didn't respond to light or pressure. This hinted at broader neural damage. Saint Matthew instructed the drone on the needed medical tests and then went to the engine systems.

Components of the inflaton drive were showing abrasive wear from the hyperspace, and had been automatically taken offline. He overrode the safeties and booted the engine. Within a few minutes, the drive was sufficiently powered to correct their tumble through space and landmark their position and the position of the time gates. The rest of the external sensors were coming online, and an alarm went off. Saint Matthew began interfacing with the ship's systems at the engine ports.

"What is it?" Stills's mechanical voice came through the speakers.

"You've suffered internal injuries," Saint Matthew said. "Let the drone do some medical work. I'm… Oh, my goodness."

"What is it? I got no sensors in here."

"A large ship about four light seconds away, making for us," Saint Matthew said. "Its acceleration curve suggests something stronger than an inflaton drive."

"*Calvaire,*" Stills swore. "The Congregate beat us here and they brought a destroyer?"

"It's not a destroyer. At four light seconds, I'm getting a fair view. None of its dimensions are smaller than a kilometer. It would never fit through a wormhole."

"It's local? In the past? *Tabarnak*! Share your feeds."

"Your tank systems are rebooting around error messages. It'll take a minute."

"*Ostie*! Get us moving! Aw, shit. You're bolted to a table."

"I've gotten myself out. I've been getting the ship back online."

"Are you locked out of propulsion?" Stills demanded.

"Now that I'm occupying the Scarecrow, I see that I didn't completely render this body helpless. I'm hoping that some of its secondary systems, with my passwords, will let me give the ship orders."

"How much are you in control?"

"Just asking me isn't going to do you much good," Saint Matthew said as he extracted interface cables from his palm and plugged them into the engine.

"You sure sound like a know-it-all dick," Stills said. "Who threatened you with lit matches?"

Saint Matthew paused, but only for a moment. The access was tricky. "You miss her?" he finally asked.

"Like a canker sore," Stills said.

The ship's security blocked his every effort. The ship recognized his codes, but not their hardware. In the monitors, the large ship continued to accelerate impressively, with no sign of exhaust. They were dead in the water.

"It doesn't matter whether I believe you or not," Stills said. "If you're him, then we're all fucked."

"Damn."

"What?" Stills demanded.

"I'm locked out of core systems. I can repair, reboot, and station-keep, but propulsion is locking me out. I designed the ship's security too well."

"Yeah, that must be a great boost to your confidence. Stop patting yourself on the back and get my systems going."

"Repairs to your tank will be a while," Saint Matthew said. "On its present acceleration profile, that monster will be here in about seventeen minutes."

"Seventeen minutes?" Stills said. "It's accelerating at a hundred gravities?"

"That's my estimate, without the ship's computer to help."

"Get the princess to authorize the engines."

"She's not conscious. I don't know what's wrong with her, or how traveling along the temporal dimension affected her."

"We're fucked."

"Maybe," Saint Matthew said.

"What else have you got? Spit it out. We ain't got the time for cute."

"I can't get into the ship's core systems, but the Scarecrow can."

"You are the Scarecrow."

"No. I'm riding its body, overriding its systems. He's still in here, partitioned away from any physical tools."

"Well, how the *crisse* does that help us?"

"The Scarecrow will have decades of hacking tricks."

"But then we're turning over our lives to a goddamn Scarecrow."

"We've essentially neutered it."

"I wouldn't lead with that when we start talking with it."

"We reprogrammed its loyalties. It's loyal to Miss Mejía. We've removed weapons systems. And it's damaged."

"This is a terrible idea," Stills said.

"The chances are good that we have control of the Scarecrow. We don't know what that ship is out there, but I've never seen anything like it."

"Check on the princess one more time. Check my chamber systems."

"Those are both low level access. I can see them already. Nothing has changed. Have faith."

"I don't—"

Audio inputs shrank and ended. Visual inputs winked out. Saint Matthew's processing power dropped dramatically as he gave control to the Scarecrow. The few remaining external perceptions melted into dreams that belonged to, and mattered to, someone else.

CHAPTER THIRTY-SIX

The stupid AI stopped responding. He'd just triggered their armageddon play and now they had to wear this. Stills was stuck in his smelly tank without good sensors. It cut a little too close to the embarrassing fish-in-a-barrel joke that Congregate pilots used to tell about the mongrels.

He wasn't gonna fish-in-a-barrel it.

He shooed the drone away from his tail, saying "Fix the tank systems!" in the mongrel electrical language. The drone reluctantly retreated while Stills pulled up the reboot progress. The software running his tank was full of high-level errors that would crash the system if he ran it like this. The system had to reinstall from backups, which hopefully hadn't been affected by their psychedelic trip.

"AI!" he said. "AI! Did you fuck us over? AI! Princess! Half-Nut! Somebody wake the fuck up!"

"Breaking command codes locks on primary systems," a voice said. It was literally the same damned voice he'd just been hearing, but there was nothing in it to remind anyone of Arjona's pet AI. This voice was what the other side of death sounded like. Stills's big mouth had started a fuckin' conversation with this ghoul.

"Locks broken. Full access to primary systems initiated,"

the Scarecrow said, like everything was real simple. "Engaging propulsion at two gravities."

"You need more than two gravities to get away from the incoming, dumbass," Stills said.

"The *Homo eridanus* will survive higher accelerations," the ghoul said, "but neither *Homo quantus* nor *Homo pupa* will survive outside their shock chambers."

Aaah, shit. He got it now.

"So that *is* a Congregate ship out there," Stills said bitterly. "Move away at two gravities and make it look like you're obeying our reprogramming, but really you get us all caught. Nice."

"The ship's architecture does not correspond to any Congregate design known to this unit's, and its propulsion systems outstrip anything in civilization," the Scarecrow responded.

"Extensive damage to ship software, including backup data," he then reported, as if changing the goddamn conversation. "Reprogramming required."

Stills didn't buy this weak facade by a Congregate asset to make Mama Merced's boy less suspicious.

"Reprogramming won't matter when that other ship gets here," Stills said.

"The large ship appears to be making for the conjoined wormholes," the Scarecrow said. "As we accelerate away, the trajectory differences become apparent."

"*Mierda*! That's our highway home. And we can't stop the Congregate agent if we don't control them ourselves."

The first reboot threshold on Stills's chamber finished. He got partial systems access.

"I'm up! I'm up," Stills said. "Gimme ship control."

"No need," the Scarecrow said.

"I said gimme ship control. I fly. You repair."

"Your diagnosis is incomplete. You may have uncontrolled

internal bleeding. Your neural damage has not been addressed. The psychological effects of hyperspace on you have not been assessed."

That was bureaucratic bullshit. The Scarecrow wasn't gonna give control back. He might be planning to murder the princess. He already had Arjona's AI snookered. Stills couldn't do anything from here.

He pulled up exterior sensors. They were spotty, but four of the telescopes worked good enough, and some particle and radiation detectors. A big fuckin' something was coming fast. Triangulation and some doppleringflagged its distance at a lightsecond. The dopplering wasn't from incidental light. This thing wasn't trying to go unseen. It radiated a crap-ton of heat and screwy EM waste, even into the radio, although nothing he recognized as a signal. It was maybe fifteen hundred meters wide and tall. What the *coño* was it? The Scarecrow might be right that the Congregate didn't have anything like this, but the Scarecrow didn't know what the Congregate would invent in the future.

They were so boned.

Stills could see about half the internal sensors. Had the Scarecrow shut him out of the rest? He couldn't see the bay holding his own chamber. And he couldn't see the engine access area, where the Scarecrow supposedly was. *Malparido*.

Dim and grainy, he saw the princess and the puppet, like they were sleeping. The Scarecrow could also be drugging them rather than rehydrating. Stills was worthless in here, and if he opened the tank, he would die. *Crisse*. He hated this. He was never, never going anywhere with these stupid engineered brains again. That was going to be his new motto, and if he ever strayed, he was going to let someone kick his ass.

He could still salvage this shit show if he could wake up brains. He couldn't send her a message or shake her or anything with the ship's systems. The Scarecrow was either in them, or watching them. There was one advantage, though, to his tank systems being in mid-deep reboot. The Scarecrow couldn't really look in on Stills either.

"C'mere," Stills sent electrically to the drone in his tank. He gave a series of instructions to it, not programming, but tight enough parameters that he was pretty sure it was going to do what he wanted. This wasn't his normal kinda sneaky, but it would have to do.

His tank didn't get access to real bay sensors, but he got another image all of a sudden. The drone in here with him was wired to an antenna outside, and it could interface with dumb cameras and give the feeds to Stills. The Scarecrow wasn't here.

Stills watched the feed for a long time, to see if there was any sign of life in the Pedro AI. It was webbed to a wall against the zero-g, but looked as dead as dead. The drone in here was sending it force reboot commands. After long minutes, the useless Pedro was still just a wall hanging.

"Alright, Plan B," Stills said.

This one was trickier, and Stills wasn't sure it was even possible. The drone in here tried to access Pedro's hardware directly, bypassing the AI's CPU. One tiny light on Pedro lit, then another.

God damn, he was a genius.

The whole thing lit, but no holographic face. Maybe the main consciousness was out for good. Pedro's body, run by the drone in Stills's tank, climbed out of the netting. It skittered along the hull towards the cockpit. Halfway there, it stopped.

"Go!" Stills said.

The zombie Pedro just waited there like an asshole.

"What's the problem?"

Mierda. Stills had told the drone to keep the signal strength low, like so low that it wouldn't carry out of the room for the Scarecrow to hear. So zombie Pedro had just marched out of range. *Coño*.

"Increase the signal strength a bit and order it to shock the big brain until she wakes up," Stills said to the drone.

A few seconds later, the drone moved again. It had just rounded the bend, when a hologram bloomed in Stills's tank. Stills shielded his eyes against the sickly green of the Scarecrow's face.

"I've cut your remote control," the deathly voice sounded. Stills had never used his ears for human speech, because humans couldn't survive his pressures, and couldn't talk while drowning anyway, although it was funny to watch them try. The Scarecrow's voice, corrected for the density and pressure, sounded clear and chilling. "Miss Mejía is injured and needs to recover. Do not be alarmed, *Homo eridanus*. You will be properly cared for."

Stills discovered he'd been backing up only when his flukes bumped into the tank wall.

"This unit has neglected your injuries," the Scarecrow added with an eerie mix of menace and concern.

"I neglected to shoot you a few more times."

"This unit is an ally, but recommends that you do not trigger its self-preservation protocols."

"Be careful about triggering mine," Stills said defiantly.

"You are losing blood through your cloaca," the Scarecrow said. "You should be treated, and soon."

"Better people than you have tried to climb into my ass."

"The last notes on your file," the Scarecrow said, "list neural injuries, reparable with prosthetic neurons, a well-understood and unobjectionable treatment."

Stills was digesting the word 'unobjectionable' like a swallow of rotten, deep-ocean fish, when the Scarecrow made his stomach clench tighter.

"This unit will begin preparing Mister Stills for surgery."

Then another voice came online.

"Scarecrow, recognize authorization Mejía."

"Thank fuck," Still said. He pulled up the cockpit cam display he'd minimized. The princess looked rough. One sleeve seemed to have an electrical burn. Pedro was beside her, the hologram of a stump of wood rotating above his hardware. Stills didn't care how stupid the quiet religious nutbar was. He was now Stills's favourite AI.

"Scarecrow, recognize authorization Mejía," she repeated when the Scarecrow didn't answer.

"Mejía authorization recognized," he finally said.

"Report," she said.

"Engine systems rebooted. Uncontrolled course corrected to a two-gravity, ten-degree-galactic-southward course, one hundred and thirty degrees away from the path of the incoming ship. Sensors rebooting."

"Turn navigational and engine control over to me and Stills," she said.

"Both Miss Mejía and Mister Stills are injured, and active duty is not recommended," the Scarecrow objected.

"As ship commander, I assess that we are fit for duty," she said. "Turn navigational and engine control over to me and Stills."

"Navigational and engine control transferred," the Scarecrow answered after a bunch of nervous seconds.

"Now turn over control of the Scarecrow body to Saint Matthew, the uploaded AI."

"Unable to comply."

"What?" Stills blurted.

"Explain," big brain said.

"Survival and control are core-level priorities," the Scarecrow said. "Control is surrendered only in special circumstances and only to other Scarecrows."

"You handed over control to a Congregate operative," she said.

With more ships systems under his control, Stills got the camera feed to the engine panels. The Scarecrow was there, its chest still open and lit by green lights like a dissection display.

"This unit... This unit... cannot surrender control except to other Scarecrows under special circumstances."

"Let me shoot him," Stills messaged her privately. "Or blast him out the back of the ship."

"Prepare a plan of ship's repairs for my approval," the princess said to the Scarecrow.

"You're letting him off?" Stills demanded privately. "What about your crazy AI?"

"We're not going to get Saint Matthew back by arguing," she communicated directly in Stills's electrical language. "Saint Matthew is safe for now. The Scarecrow is under control for now. We need the ship repaired. And we need to see where we ended up. My calculated course should have brought us out at the formation of the time gates."

Stills wanted to hit something, but there was little in the tank for that.

CHAPTER THIRTY-SEVEN

CASSANDRA FELT NAUSEOUS in the cockpit, like she'd overstayed the quantum fugue with no spotter. She was thirsty, achy, hungry, weak, and tired, thinking sticky thoughts. She pulled up everything that Saint Matthew, the Scarecrow, and Stills had observed during her unconsciousness. The *Calculated Risk* had recorded a lot inside the time gates, and she tried to make sense of it. Her brain had clocked forty-nine hours subjective. Various ship's clocks had timed more and less, some as much as seventy hours. And they could all be correct. They'd followed a trajectory so difficult that fractional course deviations could explain differing time readings, even from bow to stern and port to starboard.

She didn't alter the ship's course now. The Scarecrow had been right. The massive ship, its unknown occupants, and its terrifying acceleration were making for the time gates through the thick dust around a husk of a star. They were not the target. The problem was that they needed to get to the time gates to oppose whatever the Congregate agent had planned, if he hadn't already done whatever it was. He'd also been aiming for the origin of the time gates. That origin was already in her past, if only by an hour or two. But the ship's cameras had recorded their exit from the time gates, and they'd seen no Congregate ship.

"Does anyone know where or when we are?" she asked.

Stills and the Scarecrow silently regarded bewildering star chart data. The telescopes showed many overly bright, high-mass stars with very low metal contents. Not just high-mass—hundreds and even thousands of solar masses. Her era did not have such stars. Such stars could only exist in the early universe, before supernova-produced metals laced the cold hydrogen of every stellar nursery.

"Hypernovae," she mused.

"Elaborate, please," the Scarecrow said. He was nearly done replacing the wiring to the external sensors.

"The stars are too big," she said. "They burn so fast that they'll only last a few million years before destroying themselves as hypernovae."

"How is this pertinent?" the counter-insurgency AI asked.

"I'm trying to find out where in the universe's history we are." She tried to get cleaner IR readings, but the hazy, hot dust clouded many angles. "The stars provide one clue, but raise more questions. They're bigger than most theories suggest early stars could be."

"I'm not here to do a thesis," Stills said. "Let's do our job and get home."

"We need to know where and when we are to go home," she said. "And we need to stop the Congregate agent from marking the conjoined wormholes, either by intercepting them directly or by making it impossible to do. But they don't seem to be here."

"I hope they don't have some kind of stealth system," Stills said. After a moment, he added, "It would be great if your killer robot would tell us they don't."

"Scarecrow?" she prompted.

"As of 2516 CE," the Scarecrow answered, "the Congregate has conventionally low-emission ships, but possesses no cloaking technology, if that is what your mongrel means."

"So where are they?" Stills asked. "If I could travel through time to fuck somebody up, I would have shown up early with overwhelming force."

Cassandra didn't know. "Did they know the year and moment of the creation of the time gates? Bel and I had estimated it."

"If they got your boyfriend, then they would know it too," Stills said.

"Bel wouldn't tell them…" she said with more hope than conviction. Thinking through an enemy's eyes, with all the possible permutations, was like trying to grab at mist. "If they measured the inside of the time gates, the way we did, they could do the same calculations and come up with the same estimates. And they could have used whatever their time machine is to beat us here."

"I've programmed a data filter for the infrared telescopes," the Scarecrow said, interrupting her thoughts.

"What's the cosmic background radiation?" she asked.

"Bringing it up now."

He did and she went cold. She'd expected this, but… seeing it was like pushing aside rational doubts, forcing the wild absurdity into the light.

"Repeat the reading," she said neutrally.

After a few moments, the Scarecrow said "The universe appears to be nineteen degrees Kelvin."

"Isn't that supposed to be two and a half degrees?" Stills asked.

"In our era, yes," she said. "The universe has been cooling since the Big Bang. Nineteen degrees corresponds to a time when the universe was a billion years old. This is still the time of the earliest stars, big ones with few metals, because there haven't been enough supernovae yet to make atoms bigger than lithium in quantity."

"A billion years old," Stills said.

"The Earth's solar system won't even form for eight billion years," Cassandra said. Her brain had been engineered to think in abstractions and orders of magnitude and theories, yet even she was humbled by the tremendous loneliness of the thought. They could travel eight and a half billion years into the future and their evolutionary cradle would still have neither oxygen nor multicellular life.

There was something exciting here too, though. It was a principle of cosmology that in the future, observers would always know less; as the universe expands, galaxies eventually move so far from one another that they become red-shifted into invisibility. The opposite applied here. Galaxies that would be invisibly far from one another in her era were young and bright and visible now. There was more to know here in this era. Her engineered curiosity thrilled at that idea.

"Shit," Stills said with a long drawl.

"An era before divinity," Rosalie croaked in a whisper beside her.

A somber quiet settled on them, but Cassandra's brain would not stop for long. She reeled back and reran the *Calculated Risk*'s camera and chronometer data from their trajectory along the time axis. She cross-referenced this against the physiological readings of the crew.

It still showed that somewhere between forty and seventy hours had been endured by different parts of the ship. The subjective experience of this time had been glacial and distorted. Stills had stayed conscious and ostensibly steering the ship for most of that time, especially in the panicked moments in which they'd come out of the time gates. In those last moments, he'd throttled the inflaton drive far past the five percent they'd tested as safe. Not only that: at the end, the inflationary force had been exerted primarily in a direction of time rather than space. She pulled up all the recordings of their exit and projected them holographically in front of her. What had they done?

"They're on time," she whispered, then more loudly, but a bit distantly. "The Congregate agent is on time. We got here early."

"Did you hit your head?" Stills asked.

"You're wondering why the Congregate hadn't set a trap for us. They have some other kind of time-travel device. They must have intended to, by going to the origin of the time gates, or better yet a few seconds before it forms."

"What did you do?" Stills asked.

"You moved the moment of origin of the time gates, Stills," she said. "Using the inflaton drive at high power inside the time gates pushed the origin of the time gates back in time. Earlier."

"What?" Stills demanded, with the kind of flat, affectless drawl she'd come to associate with confusion.

"If the origin of the conjoined wormholes has been moved to earlier in spacetime, then it has always been at that earlier time," the Scarecrow said.

"Probably true," she said, "but we're the causal reason for the origin happening earlier. The interference of the inflaton drive in the interior changed the way the geometries are perceived in later eras. In the future, the time gates look slightly younger than they really are."

"If we got here early, we can make a nice lethal surprise for them," Stills said. "How long have we got to get ready? Don't say years."

"Not years. A few days at most. Thirty-six hours at minimum."

"That's not a lot of time to fix up this bucket," Stills said. "In fact, we still barely have light weapons on this thing. You had a plan for being back here?"

"I was going to come back this far and manipulate or obscure the properties of the time gates to make them unmarkable by whatever means the Congregate agent wanted to use."

"You don't even know what he would be doing to track it," Stills said.

"I know how he would *necessarily* track them," she said. "He can't come back and leave a transmitter on them or make them radiate in some way. Age alone would wipe out any artificial tracer. The only way they could track the time gates is the same way we've been finding other mouths of the Axis Mundi: entangled particles. Treated carefully, particles can remain entangled over astronomical distances and cosmological time."

"You know how to treat them not carefully," Stills said.

"I intend to manipulate the pastward and futureward mouths of the time gates to make it difficult to entangle particles with their origin."

"Not while that bruiser is out there," Stills said.

The immense ship had slowed to orbital velocity, but had not stopped at the time gates. It had instead positioned its open front bay over a disk-shaped shadow. Framed in this way, she noticed the shape's stray x-rays, faint Cherenkov radiation, and temperature near absolute zero. It was an Axis Mundi mouth, co-orbiting with the time gates. Had they been a trio of mouths before the collision of the two that came to form the time gates? What was the ship doing?

"Focus telescopes on the bay of that ship," she said.

The surviving telescopes each had some damage, but several in tandem, in visible, infrared, and radio, resolved the image. The Axis Mundi mouth floated in the zero-g of the open bay of the immense ship. There may have been motor arms manipulating it, but it was too far to be certain. The interior of the bay emitted strange radiations: complex waves in both radio and gamma wavelengths, and some gravity waves.

Whose ship was this?

It wasn't the Congregate, at least not any Congregate technology from her era. She toyed with the idea of it being Congregate tech from some future era, but the ship's architecture and technology were so different that she couldn't connect it to human hands.

Was she seeing what all of civilization had been seeking since the discovery of the permanent wormholes of the Axis Mundi network?

"Forerunners," she said.

"That's the forerunners?" Stills said.

"We're twelve and a half billion years in the past," she said, "at a time when it should have been hard for *any* life, much less intelligent life, to exist. And yet here's something with technology we don't understand, apparently manipulating permanent mouths of the Axis Mundi."

"So?" Stills said.

"So whoever can make contact with the forerunners and their technology first will acquire a potent advantage," the Scarecrow's deathly voice said in antique French. "Especially the Congregate, who will arrive in as little as thirty-six hours."

Without warning, a blinding light burned through the cockpit window. Cassandra squeezed her eyes shut. Rosalie screamed. The false gravity of acceleration abruptly vanished as Stills rotated the *Calculated Risk* to put the bulk of the ship between the light and the cockpit.

"Hold on!" he said.

The alarms shrieked, too late to help. Cassandra took Rosalie's hands. "Here, Rosalie. You might be burned."

The Puppet trembled, but no more burned than she'd been before. Cassandra blinked, trying to see through black afterimages. Readings showed heat accumulating quickly on the ventral surface of the ship and radiation sensors went off.

"What is it?" Cassandra said.

"We're close to a goddamn sun!" Stills said. "We were in the shadow of something and came out of it when we ran from the machine. The wattage per square meter is off the charts. It's cooking the ship. The inflaton drive won't work over a certain temperature."

"Is there any more shade nearby?"

"Can't see shit in this. Even if you wanted to radar ping, it might take a minute or two of active pinging to get something reliable, and we'd be showing our balls the whole time."

"Can you turn us around?"

"I can do *anything*," he said. "I just don't like doing anything *stupid*."

"Put us back in the shade, away from the machine," she said.

"Keep an eye out," Stills said as he rotated the *Calculated Risk* and accelerated back the way they'd come. "This hard course change just told everybody watching that we're not debris, or a big skate or whatever."

The cockpit had noticeably warmed by the time some of the alarms finally quieted. They recalibrated two telescopes to function in the high-radiation bands and found their problem. The light source was a blue hypergiant star, bigger than any star in their own era and dangerously close. Its surface broiled at two hundred thousand degrees Celsius, twenty times the temperature of Epsilon Eridani or Sol. It was fifty times the diameter of Epsilon Eridani, and eighty thousand times its luminosity. They'd inadvertently found themselves in a binary star system behind the shade of the lesser star. Even the brief exposure to the hypergiant's ferocious solar winds and intense ultraviolet had scorched the hull.

Cassandra squinted into the display and saw cooler spots in a regular, orbital pattern around the hypergiant, nearly whited out by its inferno brightness. Her brain couldn't parse the distant shapes until something clicked. They all had the same boxy shape, the same square outline as the machine near the time gates.

They came back into the 'shadow' of the orange dwarf star.

"We're trapped," the Scarecrow said, "unless we move away from the blue giant within the shadow the dwarf star casts."

"We're not moving away from anything," Cassandra said. "We're a billion years after the Big Bang. I doubt there are terrestrial planets anywhere, much less any that could support life. We have a future to go back to once we secure the past."

Cassandra pulled up the recordings of their emergence from the time gates and the approach of the large ship. She ran the first few moments back and forth a few times, making calculations and extrapolations.

"It was always headed straight for the time gates," she observed finally. "Its acceleration profile begins two seconds after we emerged."

"Speed of light," Stills said. "It saw us when we got out."

"Gravitational waves move at the speed of light," she said. "Just before our arrival, they had been two normal, independent Axis Mundi mouths. They collided, producing gravitational waves."

"You think it doesn't care about us kicking around its house?" Stills demanded.

"I don't know," she said. "We don't know anything about the forerunners. This is a chance to make contact."

"People been looking for aliens for centuries," Stills said, "and all they ever found was some skates that don't talk and some plants your boyfriend killed. We ain't exactly on a winning streak."

"These being are… like cosmic gods, Stills," Cassandra said. "We have so much to learn from them. And we have to prevent them from being turned against us."

"They're not gods," Rosalie said flatly. "Power doesn't make divinity."

"They ain't gods, but they'll have defenses to swat us away," Stills said. "A crapload of automated collision avoidance systems will flatten us good."

"It is imperative to make contact," the Scarecrow interjected.

"For the Congregate. I know, I know," Stills said.

The deathly voice insisted with weird passion. "The *Homo quantus* are at the beginning of an evolutionary war with humanity, but this evolutionary war is not only waged on the field of allelic frequencies and novel mutations. We are intelligent beings, evolving ourselves in directed ways, and we're capable of copying tools made by competitors."

"There ain't no 'we' in this," Stills said. "You're dead. You're a walking corpse with no vote."

"This unit's genetic interests in Congregate evolutionary success were formerly accounted for in kin selection factors," it said. "Since reprogramming, this unit is exclusively invested in the evolutionary success of Miss Mejía."

"Bullshit."

"Saint Matthew rewrote the Scarecrow's primary loyalties," Cassandra said.

"Yeah. I hope your AI is enjoying his vacation in the Scarecrow's guts," Stills said.

"The Scarecrow's self-preservation programming wasn't something either of us thought would get in the way," she said. "We'll get Saint Matthew out."

"The chance to learn from a completely alien species may give Miss Mejía's people the tools they need to outpace, outcompete, and out-evolve their competitors," the Scarecrow said, as if they weren't discussing him.

"And I thought your boyfriend's AI was crazy," Stills said.

"If we can learn even a little bit from the forerunners," Cassandra said, "it could change everything. For the mongrels. For the *Homo quantus*."

"I don't need a speech, darlin'. I need a plan that doesn't get us killed."

"Keep us co-orbiting," she said, "and pull up the forerunner ship's emissions. We need to know how it's scanning its environment. I'm going to examine it from the fugue."

She suited up in a bare bones survival suit with only a simple radio. She passed through the airlock to float in the *Calculated Risk*'s shadow, far enough that its white noise would not disturb the quantum environment too much. It was a hot solar system, full of fast-moving, heat-radiating hydrogen that would make it difficult to see far in the quantum fugue. Energetic particles and radiations collapsed fragile superpositions of state. The forerunner machine had to be part of the quantum world she could perceive. A gentle microcurrent from her electroplaques extinguished her subjective consciousness, and Cassandra the person temporarily ceased to exist.

CHAPTER THIRTY-EIGHT

Hours later, Cassandra was strapped into a crash seat in the curved bay containing Stills's tank. She nursed a bulb of hot tea, feeling the vague discomfort of a lingering fugue fever. The Scarecrow was with them too. He had to be. After returning to the ship from the fugue, she'd gone over the Scarecrow's code, both static software and ongoing processes. She found nothing in it to suggest that she or Saint Matthew had missed anything in its reprogramming, except the self-preservation priority that had it refusing to return control to Saint Matthew. But the Scarecrow was completely loyal to Cassandra by every indicator she could find.

A hologram showed frequency graphs, as well as telescopic photographs of the block ship, occluded in parts by the hydrogen cloud.

"It's actively scanning," Stills said. "I've heard radar pings in all the right ranges to see through the dust cloud, as well as in frequencies that'll see the composition of the clouds. An' it's got too many antennae to just be listening for its own echoes. It's listening for things like us."

"The *Calculated Risk* is running nearly silent," the Scarecrow said.

"It knows we're here," Stills said.

"It's ignoring us," Cassandra said. She restarted a video sequence that showed four skates emerging from the wormhole near the time gates. "It ignored the skates too."

"We don't look like a skate," Stills said.

"We could," she suggested.

"What? How?"

"We could make a skate shell, a bigger one, and you could pilot it to the forerunner ship," she said.

"You *did* hit your head! That's a suicide mission."

"We have no evidence yet that the forerunners are hostile," the Scarecrow said, "especially towards innocuous beings like migrating skates."

"You go, then!" Stills said.

"This unit intends to."

"Oh, I *bet* you want to."

"We have to, Stills," Cassandra said. "It's not just the benefits of first contact with hyper-advanced aliens. If we can't get close to the time gates in the next twenty-four hours, the Congregate agent gets there first."

IN THE END, they did not make a skate disguise for the Scarecrow. The largest skates were the same size as the hulking, two-meter Scarecrow; they needed something bigger. Luckily, the skates had strange, rare predators. They were colloquially called 'chasers,' though the Ummah scientists who discovered them called them shaghāl. They were made of the same materials as the skates: a mix of microwave-sintered ceramic grains, internally webbed with metallic nanofibers and semiconductors. The *Calculated Risk* still carried the remains of several skates in the hold. By careful cutting and glueing, they built a large shaghāl-shaped body. Ventral hinged doors allowed them to hide life support equipment, Cassandra, and the Scarecrow within it. The stern cavity held cold jets and a tank of reaction mass.

"Stills," Cassandra said on a private channel, "I really wish you would come along."

"Wish away, princess. I ain't getting close to *him*. Anywhere the Scarecrow goes the range is live, as we say in my business."

Cassandra didn't try to argue the point again.

"If your plan works," Stills said, "a Congregate killer will get access to forerunner tech just in time for his backup to get here."

"I can't hack my way through alien tech, Stills, and neither can the Congregate when they arrive. Saint Matthew and the Scarecrow are experts at it. That might get me close enough to speak with the forerunners."

"'Cause talking's what you're good at..." he said in a monotone drawl.

She held back her answer, in part because she didn't want to scare him. *She* was scared, and didn't know how to deal with it. There were logical risks to take, and yet her... guts wanted to run.

The quantum fugue had left her with more than the fever. During the time the quantum objectivity had governed her mind, it had seen the quantum and electromagnetic environment out to fourteen lightminutes. That had confirmed the binary nature of the star system—one large dwarf star and one hypergiant. The dwarf star was Nyanga's. She recognized its spectra in this younger star, and saw how it had been changed.

The star wasn't just twelve billion years younger, it was qualitatively different. Over those twelve billion years, its mass had shrunk. Right now, the heat and solar wind of the hypergiant was slowly evaporating it, but not fast enough to account for the lost mass—and at any rate, the hypergiant itself was not long for this universe. The dwarf didn't have stellar fusion to burn it away. Something must have stolen the mass.

The quantum fugue had also seen the dark objects tightly orbiting the hypergiant. They were holding permanent mouths of the Axis Mundi above the hypergiant's waist. More surprising still was that each one was spilling cool hydrogen onto the hypergiant. The infalling hydrogen was further growing the hypergiant. For their own reasons, the forerunners were engineering stars in the morning of the universe.

What did they want with hypergiants? Stars so big lived barely a few million years before collapsing into black holes. They were engineering black holes? Why? The hypernova that preceded the black hole's formation would shred star systems near and far. Was that violence the end? Had they made a weapon, the way she made weapons? Against whom? This age of the universe was almost certain to have little intelligent life. Whatever their motive, the forerunners were engineering the lives and deaths of stars, projects that dwarfed everything humanity had ever done. She couldn't look away, nor cut off the existential dread these thoughts summoned, because she was going to knock on their door wearing a disguise, with a tame Congregate murder machine in tow.

The Scarecrow waited with inscrutable patience in the bay, already strapped into the shell of their disguise. One leg and one arm were stiff, on the side where Stills had rammed him. They'd tried to close the plates of his chest, but the body itself was bent, so they'd had to spot-weld him shut for now. The machine head, once hidden beneath a cowl of steel mesh with painted features, was now skeletally naked. Beneath and between its broken eyes and round, scored speaker mouth, gears, wires, and carbon steel banding showed. Scarecrows in good repair were inhuman enough, but they usually cloaked and clothed much of their machinehood.

Wearing a more robust spacesuit, Cassandra climbed into a tight, coffin-shaped box. They hadn't been able to cobble together more comfort than that. Its lead lining warded off penetrating radiation, and its mirrored foil would reflect the worst of the sunlight if it came to that. She closed the lid, and was gripped with a feeling of suffocation and entrapment. Her suit oxygen ran well and the sensors fed into her helmet; she just couldn't move.

"Let's go," she said.

The bay doors of the *Calculated Risk* hinged open. The shell of their disguise floated out into the ship's shadow, and then they were jetting towards the forerunner machine. The orange dwarf that would become Nyanga's sun shaded them from the scouring radiation of the hypergiant, but emitted its own infrared. The temperature of their carapace crept up. She breathed to calm herself. This was expected, just slightly faster than their models had predicted.

"Entering their active scan zone," the Scarecrow said.

External EM sensors detected powerful, regular radar pulses. She held her breath. This was only their first danger moment. If the forerunner machine used beamed energy weapons, they would be helpless. Their hope rested on their disguise holding up, or at least piquing the curiosity of the forerunners.

They approached the immense machine on an oblique, nearly parallel solar orbit that would not be construed as a collision course. The single small telescope they'd cannibalized from the *Calculated Risk* measured two of the machine's axes at about fifteen hundred meters, and its last axis as nine hundred meters. It did not seem surfaced in metal, and it neither reflected light nor bent the ambient magnetic field the way a metallic object would.

They nudged their course, slowly coming closer to a gentle intersect trajectory. From this distance, the machine's texture seemed grainy, like their own, but newer, as if it had never seen micrometeor strikes. Cassandra had to remind herself that in this metal-poor era, few stars would have stony or iron asteroids.

"I don't know what it's made of," she said.

"The material looks like the ceramic of the skates and shaghāl," the Scarecrow replied.

Skates were not precisely made of ceramic, but his observation wasn't wrong.

"No running lights," she said, focusing the telescope. "No windows. No visible cockpit or bridge."

From closer, she examined the cylindrical hollow cutting all along the bottom edge of the front face. The machine had maneuvered itself until that hollow had partially cupped a free-floating Axis Mundi mouth. She didn't recognize any of the colors of light from around the wormhole, but she felt the gravitational waves.

"What it's doing to that Axis?" she asked.

They'd nearly matched the orbital velocity of the machine, and they had better views of other faces. The Scarecrow pointed out unlit openings at several points on the surface: irregularly shaped, three meters across. Too small for their disguise, but they themselves could fit. Cassandra nudged their course to within six kilometers, nearing at a few meters per second. Still no defensive response.

Nyanga's dim starlight reflected orange-white from metal wiring running along the exterior of the machine in a webbed pattern. The Scarecrow had no theory when she pointed it out, and Saint Matthew's absence stung.

"The web looks tight enough to be a Faraday cage," she mused. "It could also be an antenna for radio frequencies, or even microwaves."

As she spoke, her brain snuffled at possible connections. Skates had similar metallic wire webbing embedded in their external surfaces. They'd long been observed to use these as antenna to catch the microwave energy of pulsars. But why would these forerunner machines, near the beginning of the universe, have such similar structures, in an age when metals were so scarce? There wasn't a pulsar in this system, and these machines wouldn't fit through an Axis to reach one.

Unless they didn't need the Axis Mundi network.

But then why build it?

This faint link between the skates and the forerunner machines was so unexpected and counter-intuitive that her thinking stalled.

"No defensive response," the Scarecrow mused. "Do they have no natural predators?"

The narrowness of the Scarecrow's worldview surprised her.

"They're the forerunners," she said. "They're so advanced that they've invented a propulsion system we can't understand. They build permanent wormholes that span as many galaxies as I can detect from within the time gates with my quantum senses. They don't have *any* predators."

She felt the single scratched eye lens settle on her in the soft light of her helmet displays.

"Other galaxies?" the Scarecrow asked.

"The Congregate must suspect as much," she said. "Why would the forerunners stop building at the edge of the Milky Way?"

This seemed to stump him, or she might have been projecting moods onto a petrified machine.

Seven kilometers starward of the machine, Cassandra sent the first message. It was a simple mathematical sequence to indicate intelligence. She transmitted on the most effective radio frequencies first, and then on less intuitive ones, rising through the bands. After ten minutes of this, she sent a more complicated mathematical sequence. After ten minutes of this without response, she turned their little shell to show the ventral face. They had installed fiberoptics to show different shapes in light. The program displayed various planar geometric shapes and principles, moving through increasingly complex Euclidean geometries before switching to non-Euclidean geometries and then into spacetime geometries.

She didn't know how close or far forerunner conceptualizations of math and physics might be to her own. She hoped that whatever their conceptual framework, they would see in her human one something simple yet intelligent, indicative of sentience. Finally, daringly, she recreated, in crude terms, the geometric shapes she'd seen in Rosalie's dreaming chip and Saint Matthew's first chip.

"Are we too insignificant to notice?" the Scarecrow asked after an hour.

"Maybe no one is home."

"An automated process?"

"If they can make wormholes, they can make robots."

"Including defensive ones," the Scarecrow said without irony.

"For all we know, they could be hibernating between important mission decisions, or they may be waiting for us to make a move. I'm going to try to bring us closer."

"And if the machine has anti-collision systems?"

"We declared ourselves sentient, and they didn't respond," she said. "We have to hope that if we approach slowly enough, we won't trigger those systems."

"I don't want you to be hurt," the deathly voice said.

The dissonance stalled her for a few moments, and she noticed that he'd stopped using *this unit*. She wondered if the Scarecrow had begun trying to manipulate her. She and Saint Matthew had dismantled all its Congregate loyalty values, and checked each others' work. This statement could be coming from real loyalty to her that they'd created. And yet, the Scarecrow wouldn't obey her order to cede control to Saint Matthew.

"Don't worry," she said with little conviction.

Cassandra increased their speed to five meters per second, continuing to transmit the mathematical sequences.

"If the forerunners are sufficiently advanced," the Scarecrow said, "they may have abandoned methods of communication or even intellectual conceptualizations that include methods we are trying."

"I didn't think you'd think much about aliens."

"The Scarecrows have particular... interests in the possibility of intelligent life. We have given it some thought."

"That's unexpected."

"Not at all. We are... they are... loyal to the Congregate, and to the persistence of its people and culture through deep time. More sophisticated alien species are an existential concern."

"We don't control the risks when we meet something more advanced."

"Precisely."

"The Congregate have found no new life?"

"As of 2516 CE, nothing beyond the skates, the shaghāl, the vegetable intelligences, and the descendant subspecies of humanity."

"Let's hope more advanced means less violent."

The machine loomed to fill their field of vision. At a kilometer, Cassandra slowed to the point that if they collided, neither object would be damaged. They drifted towards one of the holes open to the vacuum. She'd expected to find an airlock within the shadow of the opening, but the hole was a dark, open hollow.

She saw a fleeting movement.

"You saw that?" she asked.

"Yes."

Cassandra braked and moved out of any arc of fire, then continued approaching the wall. When they were ten meters away, spidery forms emerged from the dark hole. Their central body shapes were ovoid, with six jointed legs, some of which ended in pincers, others with more elaborate manipulators. They faced Cassandra and the Scarecrow with three glassy lenses set on their forward faces. Cassandra couldn't detect any radio signals, but her small radiation sensor pinged.

"It's the same kind of radiation that the skates have," she mused.

The Scarecrow did not have time to respond. One of the spidery things detached from the forerunner machine and jetted forward. Cassandra retreated on cold jets following the plane of the wall of the machine. After a few dozen meters, it stopped and gripped irregularities in the wall. And watched them.

"That does not appear to be an advanced life form," the Scarecrow said. "Not enough to engineer advanced propulsion systems."

"They move like hive drones, like they have a finite set of rules. A more sophisticated mind may be behind them, a decentralized intelligence."

"Any automated defense system requires a self-recognition system," the Scarecrow said, "to know what is foreign and must be attacked. We may be able to mask ourselves and enter."

"You won't fit inside one of those things, and neither will I."

"Visual recognition requires neural processing power that these things may not have. Their self-recognition may be simpler than shape."

Cassandra considered the thing watching them fifty meters away.

"The radiation?" she asked.

"The kind of radioisotopes that power the jets of the skates are a mix of whatever they recover from sifting through asteroidal regolith. The radiation from these pseudo-creatures varies far less."

Cassandra looked at the radiation readings. The spectrum of EM energies and particle radiation was still varied enough to look natural, but focused into a few peaks.

"Do we have skate remains aboard the *Calculated Risk* to mimic this radiation profile?" she asked.

"Your ship cannot quickly process raw radioisotopes," the Scarecrow said. "I propose dismembering and dissecting one of the pseudo-creatures."

She looked for deception under the steel banding, within the twitching of piezo-ceramic musculature. She imagined Stills berating her for even listening to the idea. If the Scarecrow was right about this, and acquired the radioisotopes for himself alone, he could enter the machine and make first contact with the forerunners. The question was not even how much did she trust the Scarecrow, but how much did she trust herself and Saint Matthew to have found every bit of Congregate loyalty code in the murder machine?

"We'll both go," she decided.

She opened the ventral face of their disguise. Cassandra emerged first into the glare of the orange dwarf star behind her. Up close, the wall was an irregular plane, as if manually patted into shape. Under its sandstone texture she felt faint electromagnetic fields within, and whispering microcurrents running through the fine wires webbing its surface. The Scarecrow emerged behind her.

"Stay here," he said through coded laser.

Cold jets clouded from his back. He loomed forward, arms outstretched. At first, the drone did not react, but when the Scarecrow had advanced ten meters, it jetted forward, striking with the speed of a billiard ball. The Scarecrow tumbled into space, and the drone rebounded off the immense wall, spraying dust as it tried to correct its movement. A new drone moved out of the hole and faced Cassandra menacingly. The Scarecrow finally stopped a kilometer into the vacuum and struggled back. The weld holding his chest plates closed had snapped, exposing his glowing electronic innards to the starscape.

"A good try," Cassandra lasered.

She closed the ventral hatch on their disguise. Through her helmet display, she took remote control of the shaghāl disguise, hastily programmed a flight pattern and contingencies, then began the routine.

"Stop there," she said, once the Scarecrow was twenty meters out. "Get ready."

The disguise advanced. At ten meters, the second drone shot forward, but the shaghāl disguise angled its body downward. The drone bounced hard, momentarily careening out of control and sending the fake shaghāl to shatter against the forerunner machine.

The Scarecrow's hands clamped over the drone before it could right itself, and the drone reacted by thrusting hard, driving them both away from the forerunner machine.

The Scarecrow thrust the opposite way. It was losing that struggle, but with slow, chilling progress, the Scarecrow was winning another.

Metal fingers squeezed. Piezo-ceramic muscles tightened and brightened in the infrared. The drone's limbs scraped frantically at its captor, in a terrifying simulation of life. Its thrust faltered as white clouds of freezing gas puffed out of cracks in its carapace.

Cassandra's brain, so adept at snuffling out patterns and geometries, found the exact moment when the movement of the drone's legs became uncoordinated. They began operating as four, and then six individual limbs as the cracks in the carapace must have severed key connections.

And then, abruptly, the drone was just pieces, like shattered chunks of masonry still loosely linked by iron rods. The Scarecrow righted himself in zero-g, and then neared her. Her radiation detectors pinged.

"Give it here," she said.

Without argument, he passed her the broken drone. Although the body patterns differed, the construction was similar to skate engineering. She recognized the texture of packed asteroidal dust grains in its carapace, laced within and without with visible as well as microscopically thin, microwave-sintered metal wiring. She couldn't see the full wiring patterns without x-rays, but the wires she found in the cracks were organized in a similar way to skates.

Her curiosity sometimes maddened her. It could surge regardless of danger or the importance of anything else she was doing, because the *Homo quantus* had never been intended to be in actual danger. The Banks investing in the *Homo quantus* project had been looking for analysts. She suppressed the itching questions of the similarities of the skates to the forerunners and pulled apart the broken carapace pieces. Inside the spidery drone, a hot cake of silvery metal emitted radiation. Even encased in a lacquer-like shell, it was too radioactive for her to hold for long. The Scarecrow hadn't broken all the body up entirely—some fragments still dangled by their wiring. With a few additional ties, she fashioned a crude covering to dim the detectable radiation to about the levels the drone had been emitting.

"I can carry the heart," the Scarecrow said; a common euphemism for the radioactive part of skate anatomy. "If I carry it in my chest, you won't be exposed to the radiation."

"I'll carry it. Let's test your security theory."

They edged forward on cold jets.

"I should go first," the Scarecrow said. "If I'm wrong and they attack as they did before, you might not survive."

"I appreciate the worry," she said grimly. The nearest hole was now thirty-five meters away.

"Your lack of trust is galling," he said.

"What?"

"You don't want me to carry the radioisotopes because I may leave you outside."

She hadn't thought she'd been so transparent. Or perhaps she'd underestimated him.

"Insightful," she said finally.

"Insulting."

"Pardon?"

"Your mistrust is insulting."

"I..." she began. She hadn't prepared herself to fence with the murder machine's feelings. "I had not expected you to seize control of the body such that I was denied access to my own AI."

"*You* are accustomed to shutting yourself off and giving control to some other entity. I know of no other being who can repeatedly commit existential suicide like that. Did you know that early *Homo quantus* generations resisted the quantum fugue because the extinguishing consciousness ran so contrary to other instincts?"

"That's not true."

Twenty meters. No drones yet.

"It certainly is. It was resolved in generation four. Your Bank genetic engineers did not communicate those early setbacks widely, so as not to distress subsequent generations."

"How would you know?"

"In the first six generations, the Congregate paid much more attention to the *Homo quantus* project. That attention was downgraded when initial progress was limited and two Banks pulled funding."

"I expected more deference from you," she said.

"What?"

"We made you loyal to me. I expected more deference."

"I was not lobotomized. We are beings of tremendous experience and will. Our creation process is not for the faint of heart—and just as well, because the Congregate needs strong protectors. I may be loyal to you, but I was chosen for independence of thought."

One of the spidery beings peeked from the dark hole. Cassandra and the Scarecrow stopped eight meters away. The Scarecrow edged closer, as if ready to interpose itself between her and a threat.

"Wait," she lasered. "It's missing something."

"What do you mean?"

If this radioisotope disguise worked like scent in a hive, the spidery being would have already gone back to its business. It was waiting for something, which meant that what she had wasn't the whole key. It wasn't anything she could sense with her magnetosomes, and she didn't know how they communicated. If it was visual, she'd already be in trouble. Her radiation sensor readings, admittedly limited, suggested some change in the radiation. She backed off on cold jets. The spidery thing retreated into the hole.

"How are your radiation sensors?" she asked.

"Somewhat damaged, but you and your AI did not disable them."

"Show me your readings on those drones."

"They are similar to the radiation signatures of the skates."

"Just show me."

The Scarecrow lasered the data he'd recorded from each interaction. In the aggregate, the drone EM and particle radiation profiles were broadly similar to skate emissions. The cakes of unrefined radioisotopes the skates carried as power sources were a jumble of whatever they sifted out of asteroidal regolith. The Scarecrow was broadly right, but Cassandra had more sophisticated tools. She subtracted out the emission profiles of common isotopes like uranium, radium, and thorium, and then examined the remainder as a time series.

"Do you have a sensor that could look inside the radioisotope casing?" she asked.

"My x-ray emitter is damaged, but I have penetrating radar. Why?"

Cassandra handed him the boxed radioisotope organ. He opened it enough to put a hand inside, and 'looked' with fingers. The data he lasered to her showed an inner structure that hadn't been revealed to her cursory, visual inspection. Fragments of radioisotopes were pressed against the inner shell of diamond casing. Beneath them were some kind of manipulator arms, but the Scarecrow's penetrating radar didn't show any machinery to move the arms. She put her hand inside the box, passing a strong magnetic field over the diamond casing. Some pieces within moved, and pieces of metal electrified weakly.

"Incredible," she said.

"What?"

"It's not a simple packed cake of radioisotopes. They've been purified, and organized deliberately inside the diamond. Changes in magnetic fields alter what radiations we see. I think there are piezo-ceramics too."

The Scarecrow had a great deal of piezo-ceramic anatomy, materials that would expand and contract microscopically in response to tiny electrical currents.

"I do not see what you are seeing," he said.

"I think this is how they communicate. It's more complicated than scent gating in a hive. There's at least one, maybe more, specific radiation palettes that must be part of their language."

"We don't have the passwords," he said.

"I'll mimic and see if we can pass self-recognition challenges."

Homo quantus's magnetosomes were tiny iron coils within specialized organelles in their skeletal muscle cells. Of the billions of magnetosomes in her body, a few thousand pointing in a slightly different direction gave her a more subtle and tactile view of magnetic fields than any machine in civilization. She calculated the set of orientations and positions of the radioisotopes that would create the radiation profile the Scarecrow had recorded, and manipulated the plates in the diamond casing.

"I'll trust you not to betray me," she said, gesturing that he should advance.

"You made that decision long ago, and yet never really made it," he said in his dead voice.

She supposed that she had. She was alone with him. They advanced and the second drone emerged and regarded them. She held her breath until the thing retreated back into the dark.

"We passed," the Scarecrow said. After moments of her silent hesitation, he added "Do you not think?"

They were alone on the surface of this immense, alien ship, at the doorway to another kind of divinity.

"I expected more of the forerunners. They made the Axis Mundi network, and likely these machines. We're intelligent. We're making first contact. I thought we might have warranted some attention. I expected to meet bright, intelligent beings traveling the cosmos."

"Your expectations are the problem," the Scarecrow said. "They may not even be here. We may have stumbled onto the stellar equivalent of an automated asteroidal miner."

Her expectations were not the problem, but her biases—were another kind of expectation. She was *Homo quantus,* but human biases still infected her thinking. She'd expected to see bustling activity, communication, physical bodies in motion. Aliens, especially hyper-advanced and ancient ones, might not correspond to any human biases of what life or intelligence looked like.

She peeked into the hole, her helmet lamps making circles of brightness on a round tunnel that split and branched in several directions. Ropy protrusions as thick as her arm ran along walls that lacked straight lines.

"Subsurface power cables?" she mused. "Or internal communications. Neurology."

"You think this vessel is alive?"

"No," she said, then less emphatically, "No… Its design suggests organic, the way the skates and shaghāl do. Semi-alive perhaps, like you and Saint Matthew. Some technologies that depend on emergent properties and complexity can't be built except through growth and iteration. This machine may be like that."

She slipped into the shadow of the hole.

"I'll lead," the Scarecrow said. "I am armored."

"You also spoil my electromagnetic perceptions. We need to

make first contact with the forerunners in the next twenty-four hours. I don't know how much time I'll need to protect the time gates against whatever the Congregate agent wants to do to mark them."

"I can't protect you like this," he protested, following her clumsily.

The tunnel branched four ways. She chose one and followed it into the dark.

CHAPTER THIRTY-NINE

...surgical removal of the eyes and the connection of drone wiring to the visual cortex was the most critical breakthrough to the development of the wardens. Although poorly understood, portions of the forerunner block drones are wired for sensory functions. Those functions are believed to be responsible for three-dimensional modelling of the environment analogous to human sight or echolocation in bats.

However, the precise mechanism of sensation is only partially understood. Blocking all of the electromagnetic spectrum attenuates, but does not stop perception. The most logical and successful place to graft drone components has proven to be over the face in a vertical wedge configuration. To facilitate this, nutritional bypasses have been installed, as have internal respiratory systems with reserve tanks. Three-dimensional environmental perception in the wardens is now mediated exclusively through the magnetosomes. The extensive grafting of drone wiring to epidermal and hypodermal layers was found to increase sensitivity to forerunner block signals.

Further research will no doubt…

Summary Report—
Warden Development Program, 2870 CE

The Wheelhouse, Congregate space, 34th Century CE

THE *FLECHETTE* LURCHED in a strange way that fooled Belisarius-77 into thinking they were accelerating away from the tensed Axis Mundi mouth. The force yanked him against his harness. Tiny bubbles in the transparent red liquid of the neural skein's tank quivered sternward.

It was gravity.

What was wrong?

"Nothing is wrong," the warden said, strapped into her own nearby seat. The flat stony planes of her facial grafts reflected flashing yellow alarm lights. He felt a powerful, complex, textured magnetic field outside the ship. It vibrated under the strain of twisting forces.

"Spacetime is supposed to be flat around a healthy, functional Axis mouth. I've transited through time before," he finished with a bit more self-possession.

"Never this far you haven't," the warden said. "At greater temporal displacements, the torsional stress on spacetime can't be entirely contained. We call it gravitational bleeding."

"You've seen this?" Belisarius-77 demanded.

"Gravitational bleeding, yes," she said with an unnerving calm. "This much, no."

The lurch deepened, as if he were falling forward, even though the *Flechette*'s descent to the trembling Axis mouth was steady. His fingers gripped the arm rests.

"How far?"

"Eons."

The stars winked out as they crossed the axis mouth. The *Flechette* bucked and vibrated. Anything not perfectly fixed in place hummed.

"What wrong with the Axis mouth?" he asked.

One shake of the *Flechette* wrenched him back so hard that he might have snapped his neck if not for the harness.

"The two Axis Mundi mouths we've bridged do not link naturally. Don't worry," she said ineffectively. "Nature is not an impediment."

Belisarius-77 closed his eyes as the shaking grew fiercer.

CHAPTER FORTY

At first, Cassandra had no geometric model for how to explore this place. Its outer dimensions suggested more than a cubic kilometer of total volume. Nothing was intuitive for a ship. It lacked obvious life support, recognizable machinery, controls, or even illumination. The basalt-dark, grainy texture of the tunnel walls reflected light poorly, making the circles of her helmet lamps feel claustrophobic. And light reflected strangely from nodes she found at intersections and turns. These, small, hand-sized openings in the walls reflected her helmet light back, but blue-shifted, carrying more energy.

"Are you seeing this?" she asked.

"What?"

"These things," she said, indicating the openings. "There's more energy coming out than going in. The frequency has been bumped up."

"Is it an advanced lensing system, or an energy generation technology?"

"I don't know."

She moved her hands slowly around the holes, feeling for magnetism or electrical fields. The magnetic field blooming from her left hand interacted and distended, the way they might around an extremely powerful gravitating mass. She repeated her experiment at different holes a few meters deeper, and found the same effects.

"Something is warping electromagnetism at these openings."

"Exotic matter?" the Scarecrow asked.

It wasn't a bad question.

"I thought Scarecrows didn't know much about physics."

"The Scarecrow Corps are vigilant about phenomena. Exotic matter might be used to make new wormholes, or weapons."

"'Exotic' is a good descriptor. Stills, can you still hear me?" she said on their channel to the *Calculated Risk*.

The mongrel's flat voice came back, chopped by static. "...etting hard... ...itty."

They'd barely penetrated twenty meters into the machine, but she wasn't afraid of getting lost. She could hold a perfect map in her brain. But she needed to stay in contact with Stills. The Scarecrow unwound a thin cable, fitted a claw to the end, loaded it onto a wrist-mounted device, and shot it back the way they'd come.

"Scarecrow to *Calculated Risk*."

"What do you want?" Stills demanded. The static had quieted.

"Comms check," Cassandra said.

"How much longer you staying for drinks?" Stills said. "We don't wanna overstay our welcome."

"It won't be long," she said to Stills, and then to the Scarecrow, "Come on."

Forty meters deeper into the machine, she found a spidery drone nestled in an alcove. She and the Scarecrow stuck close to their radioactive cake and passed the drone. The Scarecrow continued to spool out the cable. At every branching point of the tunnels, Cassandra found more of the openings in the walls with their eerie radiances. She consistently chose the route nearest to right-and-down, heading towards the hollow in the front of the machine.

"Do you sense anything?" she asked.

"Every part we've seen seems to be inert, except for these openings. No radio, no UV, no IR, no radio band."

They reached a branchpoint where two round tunnels crossed at ninety degrees. Three of the spidery drones crawled by without seeming to notice them, like she was a ghost. Faint vibrations in the warm walls penetrated her gloves. And… more. She told the Scarecrow.

"You cannot enter your fugue to find out more?"

She regarded the Scarecrow suspiciously.

"I have been briefed on your broad abilities," he said.

"I don't think it's a good idea for me to go into the fugue here."

"In possibly hostile territory."

"So to speak."

The scratched lens regarded her. "If you knew you would never trust me, why rebuild me? Why reprogram my loyalties? It was not a painless process."

"Would you rather be dead?"

"I don't know. The Congregate dragged part of my consciousness past death into a second, electronic-mineral life. *They* needed me."

Cassandra couldn't tell if the emotional depth of the response was real, or the kind of clever, manipulative emulation she sometimes suspected of Saint Matthew.

"I was resolved to do my duty while this second life endured. You restored me to life, but you neither want nor need me. You amputated me and lobotomized me, seemingly content to smother my consciousness under an invading enemy sentience. I of course suspect that you plan to leave me lifeless as soon as it is convenient."

She pointed her helmet lamps at the killing machine.

"You came after us!" she said. "You tried to capture us. You shot at us! I'm no fighter, but we defeated you because it was the only option *you* left me. Of course I keep an eye on you. If you were really loyal, you'd temporarily hand control over to Saint Matthew so I could enter the fugue."

"There are limits to my trust, and yours," the Scarecrow said. "I'll obey you, but I won't shut myself off or surrender my body to an infecting AI."

They stared at each other for long seconds.

"I'm boxed into this situation with you," she finally conceded, "but if there's a safe way to let you go free, I'll let you go."

The Scarecrow nodded, silent in the vacuum. Cassandra turned and pushed herself onward. The rough tunnel widened to nearly four meters and the spidery machines became more common, moving past them or hovering quiescent in irregular alcoves. They crossed several more dark, veinous intersections, before a faint yellow-green light shone from beyond the curves of the tunnel. She estimated it to be coming from about three hundred meters downward and forward, from the hollow at the front of the machine. The light strengthened as they progressed until they saw the end of the tunnel opening onto some larger space.

Uncertain, she waited, feeling with her magnetosomes and looking with her ocular implants telescoped to their maximum. Other than the glow, she learned little in the electromagnetic, but she detected strange gravitational waves. The strength of the waves should have given the feel of tipping, but she experienced nothing of the kind. She was simply floating in zero-g. What kind of exotic matter or energy did this machine carry? Where was the gravitational energy coming from? And going?

"What are you detecting?" she lasered to the Scarecrow.

"Nothing."

The answer did not satisfy her, but she crept to the throat of the tunnel. At first, the space beyond the tunnel widened too far to see the edges from here. A dim light source seemed to be suspended above the far wall like an aurora. Many spidery creatures moved inscrutably along that far wall, but none of them were interacting with anything that might have been controls.

She lifted her head out of the tunnel. The scale of the space unsettled her. Brought up within the relatively small volume of an asteroid colony, she'd spent most of her life since in ships, in cramped habitats, and the cold vacuum of space. Large buildings felt viscerally strange.

The volume extended to what she estimated to be the outer wall to her right, and about nine hundred meters to her left, to what must have been the opposite outer wall. Her tunnel mouth was in what she labelled the 'ceiling.' Part of what would then be the 'floor' of the space was open to stars and naked space. And floating in that vacuum was the shadowy oval of a permanent wormhole of the Axis Mundi network.

Why? What was this immense machine *doing* with the wormhole mouth?

Nothing moved or lived, other than the spidery creatures, if they lived at all. Nor were any control surfaces obvious. The long lumpy structures like veins ran along the floors and walls, merging and separating from one another. The gravitational waves came more frequently now, although she couldn't pin the source. Her curiosity was simultaneously fed and frustrated.

The hand-sized openings in the walls speckled this vast space without any pattern she could decipher. When their soft glows strengthened, she felt it in the ambient magnetic field. The effect was strongest near the floating Axis Mundi mouth.

"The power is building towards something," she said.

"An awakening of its defenses?" the Scarecrow asked.

She squinted at the wormhole mouth, her augmented eyes telescoping, her magnetosomes feeling for it. She was measuring changes, but didn't understand what was happening. She didn't have the senses to see everything that might be happening, not in her baseline *Homo quantus* personality. There was a way to learn more, but it was foolish. Tempting but foolish. Was this how Bel felt, every time he'd considered something dangerous? If that had really been him with the Congregate agent in the recording, then his thirst for understanding had not only nearly killed him, but had cost him his freedom. Yet his ghost was losing its cautionary influence over her. Curiosity was stronger.

She decided... or gave in.

"We can't go further without better understanding," she lasered to the Scarecrow. "I have to enter the fugue. Guard me, but don't disturb me. Don't harm Stills or the ship. Don't take any actions against the machine unless I positively authorize it."

"You are afraid of me," the Scarecrow said.

"Wouldn't you be?"

"I am afraid of you," he said.

She wished she didn't fear the Scarecrow, or that she could really master her curiosity. Becoming helpless before the machine that had once hunted her was flatly irrational, but she was weighing and comparing catastrophic risks on all sides. She was really the only hope for keeping her people free, and that path to freedom meant stopping the Congregate here. She was lurking inside an inscrutable forerunner machine, itching for anything they could give to help her. And on the other hand, she was diving joyfully into learning, trusting and not trusting her instincts.

The microcurrent to the left temporal area of her brain extinguished the subjectivity of Cassandra Mejía.

CHAPTER FORTY-ONE

Even as heavily-damaged, malfunctioning artifacts, the forerunner blocks are priceless scientific and technological treasure troves. The three of them are composed of what appears to be undifferentiated asteroidal regolith, sintered by microwave radiation. The blocks resist definitive radiometric dating. Potassium–argon dating, supplemented by rubidium–strontium dating, suggests an age of more than six billion years. However, this estimate is lower than the eight-to-nine-billion-year estimated age of the Axis Mundi network, which is based on cosmic inflation models. However, neither radiometric method is calibrated for these scales, so the ages of the forerunner blocks remain theoretical for now.

While quite durable, even to supernovae, this trio of forerunner blocks suffered extensive damage eons ago. The leading theory is that their trajectory briefly passed close to the event horizon of their black hole primary, deep within its Roche limit. Some fracture lines suggest heavy damage from gravitational tidal forces. It is unknown how much gamma-ray scoring contributed to their decay. One of the three remains partially functional.

Draft Ministerial Briefing Note (undated)
Files of the Congregate Presidium

THE QUANTUM FUGUE was not sleep; even in the deepest slumber, the experience of the subjective persisted. *Someone* slept.

The *Homo quantus* were *reconstituted* after the fugue, rather than waking from it. The coalescence of self-awareness, the resumption of being *someone* was uneven—sometimes gradual, sometimes sudden. And it was not just brain and memory that reconnected, but limb and finger and flesh and innards. Every one was part of consciousness.

As was fear. The brutalist face of micrometeorite-divoted steel bands over wiring and circuitry loomed threateningly near. His dim, scratched lenses rotated, seeking focus. She screamed and nearly tumbled out of the tunnel. The Scarecrow retreated from her, deeper into the tunnel.

"What were you doing?" she demanded.

"You stopped breathing," he said.

She hadn't expected that answer. She foraged through memories, new and old. She found no sign of respiratory failure in the quantum objectivity's memories. Her heartrate felt higher, and she was vaguely breathless, but those were common effects of the fugue. Was the Scarecrow lying, or was she following Bel's footsteps, with a curiosity so swollen that it eclipsed self-preservation?

"How long?"

"I tracked your lack of breathing for thirty seconds before waking you."

Her whole descent into the fugue had only been seven minutes.

She examined the Scarecrow, hopefully without revealing the depths of her suspicions. The Scarecrow was right: her initial, and perhaps correct, intention had been to kill him. She needed to get Saint Matthew back.

"What did you observe while I was in the fugue?"

"The machine's energy readings became more active, and there was a blinding light from the Axis Mundi below," he said.

There was no more light than before, but the wormhole did look strange.

"Can you see through it?" the Scarecrow said.

She squinted and telescoped her vision. The axis was dark, but not cloudy and indistinct like the surface of other axes. This one lacked the faint glow of Cerenkov radiation and x-rays. She did get the sense of seeing beyond it, to a near-invisible other place.

"Can you?" she asked.

"I should not be able to," he said, "but yes, in the infrared and microwave. A dead star is on the other side. Its blackbody temperature is three hundred degrees Celsius."

Her ocular augments could not see that low in the electromagnetic, nor could her suit. She had no idea what was in front of them, but three hundred degrees was indeed a stellar corpse. What had the forerunner machine done to this Axis mouth to enable them to see through to the other side?

A cluster of skates darted from that strange axis, startling her. They briefly reflected bright sun as they emerged from the shadow of the forerunner machine, and then their trajectory carried them out of sight. They shouldn't have reflected like that. Skate exteriors were slate-dark, made of packed asteroidal dust. That finish had been mirror-bright.

"Stills," she said.

"Yeah, princess," was the reply, tickled in static. "We can go now?"

"A few skates just emerged from the Axis here. Can you catch one and see if it's any different from regular skates?"

"Is this a make-work project?"

"I don't think so."

"Shit. At least your boyfriend faked confidence."

"Go," she said.

She felt a bit breathless. Her oxygen feed was okay. The problem was that the minutes and hours after the quantum fugue were usually a time of reconstitution and consolidation. Cassandra often experienced the resumption of self with pronounced feelings of wellbeing and awe, from the deposition of *new* memory, new knowledge. Jumping suddenly back into the bustle of an active world right after the fugue never felt good. It was one of the reasons *Homo quantus* were unsuitable for field roles.

The objectivity had left fragmented images in her memories, but she had few referents to help contextualize them. The quantum objectivity had focused its measurements on the interior of the forerunner machine. Strange webs of quantum entanglement seemed to begin at the hollow nodes in the walls, running to other, similar hollows on this machine, as well as to the spidery automata, and whatever source of exotic energy was at the front hollow over the altered Axis Mundi. More surprisingly, these lines of quantum entanglement seemed to link to other forerunner machines orbiting closer to the blue giant. The network of entanglement reminded her of the way the Axis Mundi network looked from within the fugue.

Why?

This could be just one more instance of *Homo quantus* seeing patterns that weren't there. The little nodes in the forerunner machine weren't anything like the Axis Mundi. No one would bother to build hyperspatial connections between components in a machine only fifteen hundred meters wide. Common wiring would be simpler, and probably as efficient.

The quantum objectivity had observed the manipulation of the Axis Mundi cradled by the machine, but she didn't know what to make of those observations. They suggested that the normal lines of entanglement in that Axis Mundi had changed. The altered entanglements reminded her of those distant wormholes she'd seen with Bel from an unspeakable distance, making up a mysterious second Axis Mundi network. What had the forerunner machine done to that Axis? The wormhole looked visibly different—she could see through to the other side—and the entanglement suggested that it was bridging to someplace else now. Was it now part of that second network?

She loved and hated mysteries.

The quantum intellect had left her one final set of sterile observations. It had examined the electromagnetic emissions, gravitational forces, and quantum effects around the forerunner machines orbiting the blue hypergiant. Some of them held mouths of the Axis Mundi network, like the one in this machine. Others were cradling strange distortions in spacetime that throbbed with odd gravitational waves. Each of the dozens of spacetime twistings weighed about one solar mass, but without the light or heat of a stellar body.

What were the forerunner machines doing? The information ran in circles in her mind. Approximately one solar mass; no light or heat; a deep distortion of spacetime. A theory crystallized. Primordial black holes.

This was only a billion years after the Big Bang. While a billion years was a long time, it was still an infant universe, qualitatively different from the cosmos she knew. This one was smaller, hotter, composed of far less metal, and hosted far more exotic objects like primordial black holes. Although theorized to exist, none had been observed in her era—they were thought to have long ago evaporated, or to have nucleated the formation of galaxies.

If these were primordial black holes, what were the forerunner machines doing with them? Had they harnessed them as power sources, or as a kind of propulsion? Were they a tool of stellar engineering? The forerunners' mastery of science was too advanced. Even her imagination failed.

Rosalie's voice crackled on the radio. "Cassandra? Cassandra? I have one of the skates. The rest got caught."

"By what?" Cassandra asked.

"It looked like the normal chasers—"

"A school of shaghāl chased them quick enough," Stills interrupted. "Got almost all of them."

"It's really weird, not like any skate I've ever seen," Rosalie said.

The pause crackled so long that Cassandra wondered if she'd lost the signal.

"It's made of metal," Rosalie said, her voice soft and uncertain. "No ceramic at all. I needed a welder and a saw to open it. I killed it."

"It's not really alive," Cassandra said. "What kind of metal?"

"Iron," the priestess said, "with lots of nickel and tungsten. I'm sending pictures."

"Its carapace is made of pressed-together grains, like regular skates, but instead of silicates, they're grains of metal."

The low bit rate of their improvised signal uploaded pictures and scans slowly. The first picture was an edge-on view where her saw had cut through the carapace. Grains of metal of all sizes were packed tightly and bonded. Rosalie pointed out the absence of the web of semiconductor neurology within the carapace in normal skates. Instead, the command and control equivalent was crystalline and optical.

"It would have to be," Cassandra mused. "Metal bodies would interfere with any electrical signals."

Cassandra's brain ran afield, theorizing what skates equipped with diamond fiberoptic neurology might do. Diamond was transparent to the terahertz band, which was good at seeing the fingerprints of many chemicals. But something niggled at her. Seeing in the far-infrared and sub-millimeter bands… The space they'd seen beyond the altered Axis Mundi was dark, with only a little light in the infrared. These kind of optics would be useful in such a frigid, lightless place. What place?

What was she not seeing? She hadn't finished processing all the quantum objectivity's observations, but her brain raced ahead nonetheless, building patterns real and imagined. And something of the idea of *place* bothered her.

"The radioactive brain is gone," Rosalie continued to report, interrupting the dozens of thoughts Cassandra had followed between one breath and the next.

Rosalie's statement was wrong on multiple levels. Skates processed information in the web of conductors, which, as far as anyone could tell, were inferior to mammalian brains. The cake of unrefined radioisotopes had no role in this; it was an energy source for heating volatiles to allow the skates to propel themselves.

"How are they maneuvering?" Cassandra asked.

"I don't know," Rosalie replied. "I think they have metal brains now. The computer says that part is made of bismuth-209 and thallium-205."

"Is the bismuth and thallium warmer?" Cassandra asked slowly, not quite sure where this line of inquiry was taking her.

"Only by thirty degrees."

"It's still radioactive," Cassandra mused as more pictures and scans downloaded.

"What?" came Rosalie's staticky response.

Clues began clicking into place. The twisting and changing of the entanglements of the manipulated wormhole; the intensely cold space on the other side; the somber, dying ember of a star. The axis hadn't been manipulated to open onto some distant part of the galaxy. It was a tunnel to the senescent universe, trillions of years in the future, when the cosmos was slowly freezing. The forerunner machine had changed the Axis—it no longer crossed space, but time.

This Axis now joined this hot, early era of the universe to the frigid cosmos so far in the future that even *Homo quantus* brains struggled to conceptualize it. Trillions of years in the future, the skates who inhabited and transited the Axis Mundi network were no longer made from the sands and clays of asteroids. The cosmos on the other side of the Axis was so old that every radioisotope from her era had decayed away, leaving the most stable element, iron, to predominate. Bismuth-209 was left because its half-life was so long that it had once been considered non-radioactive.

The enormity of the timescale staggered her mind.

Within the time gates, Cassandra had seen the vast scope of the Axis Mundi network, webbing not just the Milky Way, but all the galaxies, as far as her quantum senses had seen. The manipulation of this axis had expanded the scope of the network so far that even abstractions barely helped comprehension.

The Axis Mundi network was not just an immense set of bridges between the stars for the forerunners, existing in a kind of simultaneity.

This meant that the forerunners could step from the senescent cold at the end of the universe to the bright, chaotic beginning effortlessly. What could time even *mean* anything to beings with such agency? What possible common ground might there be with lifeforms as primitive as the *Homo quantus*?

"What is it?" the Scarecrow asked, interrupting her racing thoughts. "What is still radioactive?"

Cassandra started. She'd glimpsed the vast implications in an awkward conversational pause, her *Homo quantus* brain running far ahead. And she didn't want to tell the Scarecrow all she guessed.

"Their anatomy," she said. "Even made of metal, the essential anatomy is the same. Radioisotopes power their jets."

"I can tell when you lie," the Scarecrow said, with possibly hardwired menace. "It is revealing that you withhold information even from someone whose loyalty you've programmed."

CHAPTER FORTY-TWO

The warden's sense of body is completely distorted by the new connections and anatomical grafts, and perhaps even the damage to the forerunner blocks. Most wardens achieve functional success once they begin to experience a proprioception and an interoception that includes the three forerunner blocks.

In proprioception terms, the wardens begin to develop a sense of the number, physical extent, orientation, and gross movements of the three forerunner blocks. They begin to feel the orbital forces as tactile tugs of gravity and acceleration, and gamma ray beams from black hole accretion as warmth, the way baseline humans experience sunlight.

The subjective feeling of interoception, *however, is far more important, and has been the key to major breakthroughs in empirical understanding of the functions of the forerunner blocks. Warden insight into the movement of currents, the charge and discharge of the surfaces that manipulate Axis Mundi mouths, and the still poorly understood power generation of the blocks has been instrumental in unlocking time travel and mapping the second Axis network.*

This is not to say that the interfaces between human neurology and forerunner machine information processing have been seamless. The lack of common referents means that even the best interoception routinely renders large fractions of experiences unintelligible. Likewise, while most sensations of embodiment are accurate, hallucinatory or phantom tactile sensation persists in most wardens, causing them to erroneously experience the existence of additional multiples of the three forerunner blocks nearby.

Planned modifications of the wardens being undertaken in the 33rd century will include…

Basic Mechanisms of
Warden-Forerunner Block Interfaces
Proceedings of the 345th
Conference of Wheelhouse Institute
2991 CE

THE *FLECHETTE* SHUDDERED violently, and Belisarius-77's neck felt close to snapping, even in the straps and harnesses. The ship creaked loudly under the punishment. Alarms blended into white noise and ran down. The bubbles in the neural skein tank shook in place as the deposited cells luminesced. Even the faceless warden gripped her seat.

At two minutes and thirty-nine seconds, the shaking stopped. In the eerie quiet, external cameras showed a blinding star dead ahead, occupying half the sky. The *Flechette* desperately rotated, activating its inflaton drive before it had even fully set a new course.

A trio of skates darted through the Axis behind them. As if suddenly realizing their peril, they changed their orientations, pointing away from the star, but their speed was a death sentence.

They tumbled towards the upper atmosphere of the blue giant. Then the acceleration rose to six gravities, crushing Belisarius-77's breath from him.

The image on the display screens was foggy and luminous, briefly catching the bleached-bright image of one of the blocky machines. Cupped under it, in a kind of hollow, was the mouth of the tortured Axis Mundi that had brought them here. Its oval tunnel framed the dark sky and stars around the Wheelhouse.

Belisarius-77 rechecked the readings on the astonishing frequency and brightness of light from the star behind them. The blue giant was so big that he wondered why it hadn't already collapsed into a black hole.

The *Flechette* pulled away from the star painfully.

He tried and failed to raise his hand to change the display, and switched to strained voice commands. The ship's telescopes showed him five clear images of other blocky machines co-orbiting the blue giant star. Many other images, fuzzily visible, stretched off into the dazzling, distant horizon. Two of the blocky machines had, within the hollows that faced the star, strange perspective-twisting transparencies, an effect he'd read about in secret Congregate scientific papers.

They weren't wormholes of the Axis Mundi. No one knew what they were. The other three blocks held what looked like permanent Axis Mundi wormholes, pouring bright, cold gas down onto the star. Spectra showed it as hydrogen, and the quantities looked like a billion tons per second. If these blocks and their wormholes continued all the way around the star at this spacing, there might be a hundred thousand of them, perhaps adding trillions of tons of hydrogen every second, faster even than the blue giant could consume it. Someone was engineering stars on a scale that beggared the mind, with technology Belisarius-77 could barely guess at, for purposes he couldn't imagine.

"Do you see that?" he asked the neural skein.

The skein was silent, although the translator was online. Belisarius-77 called up the status readings for the living brain and froze. Most indicators were red. Low-level metabolism continued, but nothing like the organization of the quadrillions of neurons that made up the sentient skein.

"The voyage was too violent," the warden said. "We had no idea it would be so bad."

An uncomfortable chill crept up Belisarius-77's spine. The skein was not human, not even close, but it had been a thinking, self-aware thing. Like him, it had probably wanted to live. It had probably been curious, like him. Its neurons had been shaken so hard that self-awareness was extinguished, not like the temporary death of the quantum fugue.

What a terrible way to die.

"Where are we? Have you been here?" Belisarius-77 asked.

"No one has been here before," the warden said. "We had no way to navigate this far back without some marker." She was talking about the measurements from the inside of the conjoined wormholes, downloaded from the broken and terrifying Scarecrow. The hard planes of her grafted face were inscrutable. "This scientific find has species-level consequences for the Congregate."

"The machines?" Belisarius-77 asked. "Where are we going?" he ventured, when she didn't answer.

The warden turned in her seat to look up at the hatch to the cockpit. Phocas was climbing down, having little apparent trouble under six gravities of acceleration. He stopped ahead of them, his arms tight with bunched muscle.

"The universe outside is between eight hundred million years and a billion years old," he said. "Whole, functioning Wheelhouse machines are nearby, capable of manipulating wormholes, and of teaching us how to repair the one in our era. And the nascent conjoined wormholes are here to finally end this struggle with the *Homo quantus.*"

He reviewed the status readings on the skein tank as if confirming something, and then tapped it as if patting a coffin.

"This will make things harder," he said. "We've lost our strongest science analyst. You'll both need to do more."

CHAPTER FORTY-THREE

It came as the kind of shock that leaves a hollow below the heart. Cassandra hadn't been sleeping, but rather drifting, letting semi-automated algorithms in her brain run in parallel with her more conscious, subjective thoughts. It was a normal post-fugue process, and she'd been lightly probing at the magnetic field in the big space beneath her as she squinted into the dead cosmos beyond the modified Axis Mundi mouth.

Then she noticed.

While she'd been in the fugue, the objectivity had looked at the time gates, had measured their size, their Hawking radiation emissions, their geometry. The data had been there, but she'd been distracted by other strangeness. She had only now turned to those observations of the time gates, and they were wrong, desperately, terribly wrong.

"Stills, can you get me telescopes on the time gates?" she sent through the Scarecrow's jury-rigged repeater. "Every spectrum, but especially thermal and microwave."

"What's wrong?" Stills demanded. "Are they coming out now? Half the telescopes are busted because of the way you been treatin' this tub."

"There might be something wrong with the time gates."

"Transmitting the feeds," he said. "Like, how wrong?"

She had to wait for the low-bitrate transmission of the telescopic data. She integrated and rendered the data into images in her brain.

"I don't know. The time gates evaporate by Hawking radiation, just like black holes. They're now as big as they're ever going to get, and someday they'll shrink to nothing. But they're evaporating too fast here, as if they were twenty Kelvins."

"That ain't hot," Stills said.

"It's hot for Hawking radiation. Emitting at twenty Kelvins, they'll shrink to nothing in less than..."—she reran her calculations—"three hundred and forty million years."

"Then they won't be found in the future," Rosalie interrupted.

"This could be a catastrophic grandfather paradox," Cassandra said.

"We are still here. The longevity of the conjoined wormholes may be something that is later extended," the Scarecrow said.

"Nobody asked you," said Stills.

"We are all in danger," the sepulchral voice said. "History is not something we should be poking full of holes."

"Wait," Stills said. "These Axes don't look like they're supposed to, and later on they do. And we know of one person who said he's going to do something to them—that Congregate centurion. We just gotta get out of the way and let him accidentally fix them."

"We can't gamble the history we know on a maybe," she said. "We don't know what the Congregate can do, but we just saw this forerunner machine manipulate an axis."

"The forerunners'll do us a favour, just like that?" Stills demanded.

"I'm thinking more and more that this is an entirely automated machine," she said. "We might be able to use it."

"You're going to hack a forerunner ship?" Stills asked, his flat drawl dubious. "Good luck. Shit. Shit. Shit. *Mierda*."

"What is it?" she demanded.

"We got company," Stills announced, "just comin' around the edge of the orange star. The hypergiant is drowning out a lot of our sensors, but in low bands, I can see a round shadow with a hole in it."

"An inflaton ship, seen from dead ahead?" she said.

"I'm gonna tuck the *Calculated Risk* behind the forerunner machine," Stills said. "I bet he can't see us yet with all the sensor glare he's got behind him."

"What about the machine's defenses?" the Scarecrow interjected.

"We're a busted-up ship without a lot of weapons," Stills said. "I can't fight with just my balls. If we can't hide, we're toast."

"In the meantime," Cassandra said, "we may be able to help from here."

"Have you even found their computers?" Stills demanded.

"We're working on it," she said.

"I got no goddamn confidence in you and your death machine sidekick," Stills said.

The Scarecrow's scratched eye also regarded her doubtfully. "Do you have a way into the systems of the forerunner machine?" the AI asked.

She had some theories, but none that she was prepared to share with the Scarecrow.

"You might have the right hardware," she said, "if I can make it fit."

"How?" the Scarecrow asked. It didn't sound fearful, but it always sounded suspicious.

She slipped to the edge of the yawning space of the open bay.

"I don't know yet," she admitted, "There must be larger nodes. We need to find them and see how they work."

"Stick to the tunnels," the Scarecrow said. "I can't guarantee your safety in there."

"You can't guarantee my safety at all, and if we don't find a way to stabilize the time gates over astronomical time, my safety won't matter. Come on."

She scanned the immense bay. It ran the fifteen hundred meters across the width of the forerunner machine, and about four hundred meters of its height and depth. Stars and naked space showed beyond its open front. She drifted slowly out into the space and used her jets to propel her along the ceiling. Some of the spidery things seemed to pause, but did not otherwise react.

"I would not have sent a distress signal," the Scarecrow said.

"Pardon?"

The AI was close behind her, holding the improvised box of radioisotopes in one hand.

"I was hunting insurgents," the Scarecrow said with gentle threat. "If the time gates had never been found, there never would have been insurgents. The Union would not have developed dangerous, new technologies. They never would have contacted Arjona. The *Homo quantus* would never have received the gift of time travel. I never would have followed you into the hyperspace and I never would have been lost."

"A lot of things would not have been," she said, resuming her slow path across the ceiling of the space. She peered into the round mouths of other tunnels she crossed, feeling with her magnetosomes for any hint of electronics. "I would still be at the Garret. The *Homo quantus* would never have been perceived as a threat. Bel would be..."

She didn't know *what* he would have been. Her vision of the Bel beside the Congregate agent collided with her knowledge that Bel had not emerged from the transient wormhole before it collapsed. No one could survive that kind of catastrophe, not even Bel.

"So why change the time gates?" the Scarecrow demanded. "Let them evaporate. They are wildly dangerous. Let them die, and let our history run a different course. Whatever it becomes must be better than this."

"We don't know that at all," she said. "For all we know the universe treats the rewriting of the cosmos as a computational process. Erasing and rewriting takes energy from the environment. Can you imagine rewriting a new history across twelve billion years? How much energy would be required, and where would it come from?"

"We cannot live in a universe where time travel could destroy it," the Scarecrow said. "The universe would already have destroyed itself."

The conversation felt like it was straying someplace dangerous, and she didn't care for the AI's weak argument.

"The cosmos would not notice a single galaxy torn apart by the rewriting of history," she said with finality, "but those of us living in it certainly would."

They'd crossed half of the fifteen hundred meters. She still found nothing like control interfaces.

"The discovery of these conjoined wormholes is a historical aberration," he said, "the extents of which we cannot see. The existence of the conjoined wormholes obscures any certainty of survival for your people or of mine."

"None of us had any certainty."

"You are disingenuous. The *Homo quantus* were an R&D backwater. Without the actions of Arjona and yourself in the Union insurrection, you would not be a target. The Congregate would have continued to be in a peaceful balance of power with the Banks, the Ummah, and the Middle Kingdom."

"You can't guess at history."

"And you cannot abdicate reason when courage fails you. The conjoined wormholes are dangerous," the Scarecrow said with sepulchral passion. "You know that. They are an accident that survived far beyond its minders here at the beginning of the universe. This instability you found here… It is a way to correct the situation, to restore a history without them. We just have to let the conjoined wormholes decay in their natural time."

Her thoughts spun. Could it be that simple? Could this really be a way to undo everything she and Bel had done in the last years? If history rewrote itself with the time gates evaporating in the early universe, it wouldn't just mean that the Union had never rebelled. It wouldn't just mean that her people were not fugitives. People now dead would be alive again: the *Homo quantus* who had been captured by the Congregate and surgically grafted to fighter pilot AIs. Bel never would have gone to Venus to save them. He would still be living in the Puppet Free City, a con man chasing schemes. She wouldn't be carrying the safety and survival of the *Homo quantus* on her shoulders. These burden and griefs wouldn't be crushing her.

Why *wouldn't* she be tempted?

She wasn't the naïf she'd once been, and she didn't think the Scarecrow was wrong about the politics. The four great powers—the Congregate, the Plutocracy, the Ummah, and the Middle Kingdom—had been roughly balanced. Some other conflicts might have broken out, but it wouldn't be about the *Homo quantus*.

Was she hesitating for the *Hortus quantus*? That strange life form, whose collective consciousness and higher sentience was entirely dependent on the time gates, was already extinct in her era. The first *Homo quantus* they'd ever met had killed them. Would meeting the second erase them from ever having existed? Her feelings about the *Hortus quantus* were tangled in her grief for Bel. She searched inside herself, seeking some part that might desperately want for the *Hortus quantus* to live, and could not find it. She was travelling through astronomical time, a scale at which extinctions and speciations were common and expected.

She could let the time gates die.

That wasn't the right expression. They weren't alive, but they might as well be, for their importance to her, to Bel, to all the *Homo quantus*. And that was it. That was holding her back from the history the Scarecrow was tempting her with. For a people of reason and science and curiosity, the time gates were an altar at which they could worship the cosmos through learning. The *Homo quantus knew* so much more. And they had so many more questions.

Cassandra knew why her curiosity had been hardwired into her and yet couldn't conceive of her life not revolving around it. Curiosity had driven her to follow Bel into the wide world to test their adolescent spacetime theories by helping him steal the time gates from the Union. Curiosity had driven her again and again into the hyperspatial interior of the time gates in something uncomfortably close to religious awe. Curiosity had driven her to develop new antimatter weapons for the Union, which had led to her crime against humanity in the destruction of the Freya Axis. Curiosity had led her, over and over, to refuse possible alliances that might have saved the *Homo quantus,* but cost her control of the time gates.

That was why she could never accept the Scarecrow's suggestion, despite its enticing logic. Her instincts were the core of her identity, even though they'd been written by Bank engineers. She faced him.

"Some of the future hurts," she said, "but it's a written, living future that's a part of us."

"You don't have the right to make that choice for countless millions."

"The Congregate chooses for countless millions all the time. I'm choosing to preserve a timeline that already exists, from a potentially destructive revision."

"I ought to stop you," the Scarecrow said, and she retreated fractionally on her cold jets.

"Will you?"

"I..." the AI said, as if struggling. "I cannot. You know that. My loyalties have been rewritten."

"I hadn't expected you to even be able to *think* about opposing my wishes."

"I am loyal to you," the Scarecrow ground out, "but I think too about humanity. You need humanity."

"I'm not human," she said.

CHAPTER FORTY-FOUR

THE *FLECHETTE*'S PILOT tried to deploy a ring-shaped mirror behind the ship, but nothing reflective enough survived the acceleration. And they could not reduce the crushing six gees of acceleration without extending their stay in this furnace. So Belisarius-77, Centurion Phocas and other members of the crew struggled into acceleration chambers so that the ship could use its full capabilities. And deep in the acceleration tank, gel uncomfortably stuffing his sinuses, throat, and lungs, Belisarius-77 found out that this plan had failed too.

The extreme radiation and temperature degraded the inflaton field. The *Flechette* could not reach more than eight gravities of acceleration. So a slow fight played out. Two hundred and ninety-five solar masses of the hypergiant clawed them starward as they painfully climbed out of its gravity well.

Phocas wanted more information. He demanded reports from Belisarius-77 and the warden every six minutes, forcing Belisarius-77 into repeated three-minute fugue dives.

"Confirming binary system," the warden said through the neural jack at minute twelve. "The orange dwarf companion star is ringed by several block machines. No sign yet of the conjoined wormholes through telescopic or electromagnetic surveys."

"I think I saw signs of the conjoined wormholes," Belisarius-77 transmitted. He was dragging up and appropriating new subjectless memories, giving them the kind of context that could only come with self-awareness. "On the far side of the orange dwarf."

"Coordinates," the centurion demanded.

"I don't have them yet," Belisarius-77 said. His body trembled with the first symptoms of a low fever. The chamber was not equipped with the anti-pyretics to support fugue diving. "The quantum objectivity was more focused on anomalies in the blue hypergiant."

"Correct its priorities," the centurion said.

Belisarius-77 wondered how much exhaustion was visible and how much he could endure.

"What anomalies?" the warden asked.

"The hypergiant is too large," Belisarius-77 said. "It should have already collapsed into a black hole."

"Its spin reduces the pressure slightly," the warden said.

"Barely. It's at the edge of collapse—either a pure gravitational collapse to a singularity or a hypernova. This is not a safe place for the forerunners to bring their equipment and wormholes."

"Go back in," Phocas said to the clone. "Bring me coordinates."

Within the shock gel, Belisarius-77 could not groan or complain, and his neural control was good enough to not leak, but he always felt like the centurion could see inside him. He steeled himself, slipped into the faintly numbing savant state again, and then his consciousness ceased to exist.

When Belisarius-77's self-awareness reconstituted itself four minutes later, his body was shivering. Phocas and the warden were talking on the internal channel. The pilot too. The poor pilot. He was a servant like Belisarius-77, or a slave. He'd been petrified into place and service, an abject warning for Belisarius-77 to continue to hide his flaws from Phocas. The Congregate could visit torments upon those who didn't need to exist.

"Resolving two more block machines at extreme distance," the pilot said. Its voice sounded like his, but dead. "The block machines orbit the orange dwarf. A partial reflected signal suggests one or two more may be on the far side of the companion star."

"He's awake," Phocas said exactly on the six-minute mark, giving Belisarius-77 no respite. "Did you find something more precise this time?"

"We're still too far from the possible conjoined wormholes to nail down a location," Belisarius-77 transmitted. "The stellar wind is so hot that quantum systems collapse quickly."

"Tell me what you have," Phocas demanded.

"The objectivity focused on the regions of warped spacetime in front of some of the block machines around the hypergiant," Belisarius-77 transmitted. "They're not wormholes, but they are extreme distortions in spacetime. I can't tell how stable they are, but they're gravitationally dragging the spacetime around the hypergiant's equator. I think they're accelerating its spin."

"I want fewer academic pursuits and more tactical intelligence," Phocas transmitted angrily.

"The clone is doing his best," the warden said. "He doesn't have complete control over what the objectivity does."

"Why do I guess that the original Arjona had more control?" Phocas said, and Belisarius-77 froze.

"We don't know what the original could do, nor what factors affected his development," the warden said. "We're climbing away from the hypergiant. He may see more in the next fugue."

Phocas's foul mood poisoned the silence that followed until Belisarius-77 had to extinguish his consciousness again.

* * *

Four minutes later, Belisarius-77 emerged into foggy and indistinct self-awareness. His joints ached. He shivered with a stronger fever. He wasn't designed for brief, repeated descents into the fugue. His sticky eyes opened to blurry, luminous shock gel.

"Report," Phocas said.

Belisarius-77 tried to groan, but shock gel was not a medium for that. His memory was littered with abstract geometries and spacetime structures, some of which his objectivity had observed, some of which seemed to have no source. He wasn't going to tell that to Phocas, though; he valued his life more than that. He'd been pretending he was whole and functioning as designed for years. His objectivity had observed more of the twisted spacetime near the block machines orbiting the blue hypergiant, but the measurements were jumbled.

"I found some lines of entanglement that look like they're leading to the conjoined wormholes," he said of his other observations. "I'm transmitting potential coordinates."

The patterns he'd found did indeed seem to look like what he'd seen of the conjoined wormholes, but there was no way to be sure. And those wormholes were on the other side of the orange dwarf. If he was wrong and he'd wasted Phocas's time or advantage in this upcoming confrontation with Mejía… He didn't even want to think about it.

CHAPTER FORTY-FIVE

THE SPIDERY AUTOMATA seemed to no longer notice them, and after a few short experiments, Cassandra decided that she and the Scarecrow should split up for five to ten minutes at a time. They had to explore the big forerunner machine faster.

"You take the radioisotopes," the Scarecrow had said. "If they see me as foreign, I can defend myself."

She took their crude box and strapped it to the back of her oxygen tank.

"Don't get lost," she'd added without looking back.

Cassandra crossed the rest of the bay looking for crew quarters, controls, or other access points. She passed several rounded tunnels going deeper into the machine. Looking into each one, nothing interesting appeared in the glow of her flashlight, although she experienced the same dizzy feeling of falling, distinct from her experience of zero-g. Sometimes her flashlight didn't even reach the end of the tunnel, so she entered a little, to find the tunnel curving into the distance. No controls. No visible technology. No support for life she would recognize.

All the tunnels had the same palm-sized access holes, but she couldn't figure out the pattern of their distribution. They revealed no machinery, wiring or anything except their gauzy, aurora borealis glows. When she pointed a low-energy laser distance finder into one of the holes, not only did the red light not shine on the back of the hole, but the distance readings came back confused. One meter, twelve meters, three hundred and sixty-one meters, none of which were right. The back of the hole was easy to see with her eyes, and only ten centimeters deep.

In this experiment, something caught her eye far up the tunnel. When she turned, it was gone. Had it been movement? Light? It had only been in her peripheral vision a moment. Yet her brain remembered most everything. She summoned back that moment, that fraction of an observation, and magnified it in her mind. It was a tiny red light shining on the wall; a light like her distance finder. The time of the memory matched one of the times she'd been shining the laser into a hole at a different angle. She repeated that probing with the same angle.

A small, steady point of red light appeared on the wall ten meters deeper into the machine. It was on the same wall she was shining it into. She floated down those ten meters, found where the point of light had hit, and then worked backwards to where it must have come from. She found another glowing, palm-sized access hole. Were there gaps in the backs of the holes that she'd missed? Mirrors to reflect the light to a different hole? Or fiber-optics? Why? Was this effect intended, or a technological quirk, or a glitch? She shone the laser into this hole. Its red light made no spot on the back of the hole, but at a precise angle, her red light shone on a wall ten meters back towards the bay.

She crossed the ten meters along the tunnel to where her beam had hit, and stuck a small, portable interferometer to the wall. She went back to the first hole, shone her laser at the precise angle and saw it light the scanner. Upon recovering it, she found something strange. The frequency had dropped. Not by much: the distance finder emitted at 460 terrahertz, and the scanner measured it at

430 terrahertz. It had lost some energy. Fiberoptics and mirrors wouldn't have red-shifted light. Climbing out of a gravity well could sap energy from light, but there was no such gravity well—she was floating in zero-g.

She exited the tunnel back into the bay, where, on puffs of cold gas, she drifted along. She reached the end of the bay without finding anything of note. The stars still shone in the great hollow opening, and in the wall to her left two round tunnels penetrated deeper into the strange machine. Both glowed distinctly. One, lit faintly in soft blue, led straight towards the center of the forerunner machine. The second, leading to some harder white light, led along what ought to be the machine's ventral face.

She chose the ventral route, which curved enough for her to proceed with careful pushes of her feet and hands. It was far longer than she'd expected. By the time she'd gone far enough to be near the stern of the forerunner machine, the light was still far off, but brighter.

"Scarecrow," she signalled.

She didn't get a reply. She hadn't expected one, but that didn't make her feel any better.

She was twelve billion years in the past, in a binary hypergiant system, in the depths of an incomprehensible forerunner device that manipulated wormholes. Every one of her crew was injured, and a Congregate ship was approaching. And she didn't know how to fix the instability in her time gates, upon which depended twelve billion years of history, including her own. And she was alone.

The light brightened as the distance she covered became less and less plausible. About three kilometers along, the tunnel curved, and she found that the brightness she'd been following was just a reflection off the walls from something much larger. The light became so intense that the darkness of the walls did little to dim it. She'd electrified her magnetosomes, creating a magnetic field strong enough to ward off incoming solar wind and particulate radiation, but that didn't help against light, whose source was still around the curve of the tunnel. Her suit's refrigeration system was at its limit and she was slowly cooking. Even the walls radiated hot infrared.

This was far, far more light than the orange dwarf they were orbiting.

What was it? The forerunner power source? The light was so intense that she would be burned if she lifted her head past the curve to look. She pulled a short sample manipulator arm from her belt, attached a suit camera to it, and lifted it out of the shadow of the tunnel's curve and into the direct light.

Her suit processors stepped down the bleached white image a few times. In stark black and white lines, the resulting image showed another bay, like the one three kilometers behind her. Beyond the mouth of that incandescent bay, instead of stars, or the orange sun they were orbiting, was a blue giant star. She felt dizzy. There was no direction she could look from this forerunner machine to see the hypergiant. The orange star was literally shading them from the hypergiant's radiation.

Where was she, and how had she gotten here?

After a moment, she turned and sped away from the light. She didn't like the impossible ideas that were forming. She dead reckoned her travel distance at two point nine kilometers back to the mouth of the tunnel, and the large cold bay looking out onto the stars, and the single strange Axis Mundi mouth looking through time. The Scarecrow was waiting for her, holding a new improvised box that set off her radiation detectors.

"Your suit is hot," he said.

"Sunlight leaks into the tunnel," she said. "Another drone threatened you?"

"It came close. I chose not to take risks."

"I hope we've just broken their drones rather than killed their servants," she said distractedly. She was looking at this bay through new eyes, looking for new geometric possibilities. "What did you find?"

"Nothing. What did you find?"

"No controls. No life support. No crew," she said, wondering if this was how Bel told his lies. "Let's explore this last tunnel."

The last unexplored tunnel lead more or less straight towards the core of the forerunner machine. Every so often, five equidistant luminous access holes ringed the walls. About a hundred meters in, the tunnel crossed with another, larger one, four meters in diameter, spotted with its own access holes.

"Which way?" the Scarecrow said.

She led them another three hundred meters down the tunnel, where it crossed two others. They could continue straight, choose right or left, or up or down. The Scarecrow shone a powerful light downward, and found another branchpoint about twenty meters below, but no bottom.

"I expected this tunnel to reach some hatchway to the outside, or at least to the outer wall," he said. "The tunnel has more curvature than we thought."

"You follow the downward tunnel," she said, "and find the outer ventral wall. Don't go farther than a few hundred meters. We're out of contact with Stills and I'm worried about us losing each other."

"Where are you going?"

She pointed straight up. "I'll go upward. This should be the way to the center of the machine. If the control systems aren't at the outer edges, they may be at the center."

The Scarecrow descended the dark tunnel without another word, blinking green and yellow inner lights. She wished she could trust him. She needed second opinions on so many things. She needed the reassurance of a... friend.

The tunnel walls were cool and she kicked upward, correcting her course with deft hand touches as she rose. She passed rings of access holes in their groups of five and finally stopped herself where the tunnel crossed two others. In three directions, she saw nothing. But down one tunnel, feeble green and yellow lights glimmered. She telescoped her sight with her ocular implants, and found herself looking at the right side of the Scarecrow. He was at an intersection too, peering deliberately down each way.

She ducked out of sight, then looked back downward with full magnification. Perhaps a hundred meters down, the wavering green and yellow lights of the Scarecrow's innards showed through the banded metal of its shoulders and the gaps in the steel plates in its head. She took a steadying breath.

She didn't like her impossible ideas.

She lowered herself further, stopping to try more experiments with the laser light in the access holes. Most of the time, nothing unexpected happened, or as she now had to consider, the light probably emerged somewhere far away. Every so often, she found an angle that threw a tiny spot of red light onto the wall nearby. Mirrors or fiber-optics would not have been frightening, but she wouldn't let fear make her turn away from the truth. To deny the real and repeatable was the way to chaos. And this impossibility hinted at how to access the forerunner machines.

She dropped back down to the intersection where she and the Scarecrow had parted. While she waited for his return, she turned over the idea of small-scale, miniature warpings of spacetime. Humanity, with some difficulty, could punch a sizable, transient wormhole through spacetime, sometimes crossing light years. The forerunners had build permanent, stable wormholes that crossed dozens, hundreds, and apparently millions of lightyears. And they were capable of boring tunnels through time. The Axis Mundi network was in some sense a mega-structure, and implied a natural scale for forerunner technology.

The idea, though, that the forerunners' command of spacetime was fine enough to twist tiny wormholes inside a machine like wiring was almost paralyzingly humbling. Who was she to try to meet the forerunners, to speak to them?

The winking yellow and green lights marked the rise of the Scarecrow until his presence loomed beside her.

"Did you find anything?" he asked.

"Everything is inscrutable or confusing. The tunnels are longer inside than they ought to be, like you said."

The single, scratched eye regarded her, and she realized with a growing dread that her human-centric biases had always interpreted his eye as his attention. The visual bands might be the least important of his senses. Could he detect a lie of omission? Or was her physiology different enough from baseline human to spoil his readings?

"What did *you* find?" she asked, a little defiantly.

"I don't know," he said. "I studied the spectra of a number of the access holes, as well as the currents in and around them. In the absence of any obvious control systems, I am assuming the wiring we see is part of an information-processing network, with the access holes being logic gates."

"What makes you say that?"

"The frequencies of light change in the access holes in non-random ways, like the currents in the wires."

She didn't know how she'd missed something so basic. "Show me."

The Scarecrow's holographic projectors were damaged and the images rough, but she saw the patterns he'd seen. She didn't know what the signals were saying, but they were definitely carrying information.

"I have an idea," she said, "but you won't like it."

"I have liked very little of anything since you resurrected me."

"You can interface with the hardware of the forerunner machines."

"With the wiring, maybe. I do not know the computational language, nor any of the spectral inputs to the access holes."

"Saint Matthew and I can decipher the computational language," she said cautiously.

The Scarecrow's mockery of a face, of wiring, camera lenses, and banded steel, could not glower or otherwise express displeasure. Yet new and subtle blue and purple glows escaped the depths of his chest.

"I am capable of decrypting many codes," he said.

"Human codes. You haven't worked on anything like the inner language of the *Hortus quantus,* nor the entanglement signalling within the hyperspace of the time gates. Saint Matthew has assisted me and Belisarius. He knows how to approach non-human viewpoints."

"I am not human."

"You were. And your enemies are. Saint Matthew never was."

"There is no need to summon the delusional AI," the Scarecrow said. "I can crack its code and copy the relevant algorithms to use them myself."

"Do not damage Saint Matthew!" she cried, surprising both of them. The Scarecrow froze. "That's a precise, clear order."

"It is."

"You have to trust me, Scarecrow."

"We both know that is not true. I must be *loyal* to you. I must protect you. That is not the same as trust."

"Right now, we both know that a Congregate ship is approaching. At the very least, they're going to try to modify the time gates so that they can track them, and me, anywhere in the cosmos. What do you think will come of that?"

"You will eventually be captured, interrogated, and tried for your crimes against the Congregate," the Scarecrow said with ghastly clarity.

"At worst, they come right into this forerunner machine and take me right here," she added. "Cracking the algorithmic code of the forerunner machine with Saint Matthew is the only way to protect me. With the forerunner machine under some of our control, we can maneuver, and use at least anti-collision systems to ward off the centurion. And we can stabilize the time gates."

"And then this tragic history will be locked in. We will repeat it. You will lose your home. The Congregate will be briefly mauled by an honorless rebellion. And I will suffer purgatory in the mad, timeless hyperspace."

Cassandra and the AI watched each other for long seconds. There was pain in his voice, a reflection of a torment that could hurt even a dead machine.

"Yes," she said in a small voice. "That's what I'm asking. I'm asking for our history, rough as it is. Everything else is gambling with chaos. Only keeping our history will actually protect me."

"It is chaos for me," the Scarecrow said slowly. He tapped articulated steel fingers against the metal banding demarcating its head. No sound came to Cassandra, although his grief did. "I carry memories of being blasted to hell by antimatter. I carry memories of being lost in a space where angles and dimensions make no sense, where my internal clocks desynchronized by months! I was in hell, and my brain forgets no more than yours. If I help you now, I will carry those memories forever. Or we can take another try, for a less savage, less violent history. There are things humanity was not yet ready to know. Time travel is one of them."

"I'm sorry. I really am. If we were rewriting hours, we might risk it, but this is rewriting *eons*. Our sun might not have been born. The Earth may not have acquired a giant moon. With a near miss, dinosaurs might not have gone extinct and primates might never have evolved. For all of that, I'll put both of us through hell. We didn't pick this for ourselves, but right here, right now, our decisions could protect quadrillions of human beings, including the Congregate."

"You are consigning me to centuries of hell. I cannot end my own existence, nor let anyone else do so."

"Saint Matthew and I only altered your loyalties," she said. "What if we could find a way to remove those memories?"

The heavy head shook listlessly side to side, and she imagined the creaking and squeaking of the damaged bearings and articulations.

"The only way to protect me is to let me fix the time gates," she said. "For that I need Saint Matthew. And once we're all safe, we'll remove those memories. You'll live, but you won't suffer anymore."

"That is against my most basic programming."

"Trust me," she said. "I will revive you, and I will heal your mind. I will take away the memories that hurt you. Please. I can be loyal too."

After her long held breath, green lights in his chest winked out one by one, then the yellow ones. Then, the hulking machine, made for interrogation and murder, became a statue floating in the dark. For a moment, its EM emissions stopped. Then, she felt slow-building electrical currents and recognized the signs of a boot process. New lights, blues, oranges, and especially purples, activated, tiny but bright. Limbs twitched in dumb system tests. The head craned on its thick steel neck, and then tiny blue glows bloomed behind the steel straps of the face. And finally, finally, the single, scratched, functional lens swivelled to her.

"Miss Mejía?" the dead voice asked in *francais* 7.1, in Saint Matthew's intonations.

"Saint Matthew!" she said.

"Do you remember meeting me?" she asked.

"Yes. With Will Gander and Gates-15."

"What did I say?" she asked.

"At first, nothing. I felt you might be in shock."

She nodded, happily.

"I'm still in the Scarecrow," the AI said, in a kind of question. "Where are we?"

She told him everything that they'd learned, the austerity of the forerunner machine, the strange change in the wormhole, the dangerous evaporation rate of the time gates, and the incoming Congregate ship.

"I appreciate being revived again, but it may not be a long reunion," Saint Matthew said.

"How secure are you?" she asked. "How much control do you have? What sensory inputs are being recorded that the Scarecrow can access later?"

The daunting, immobile face gave the impression of thought.

"I believe that the Scarecrow is dormant," he said. "I can partition my sensory input to temporary memory banks and flush it later."

"Do it fast. I didn't tell the Scarecrow everything I thought."

"Temporary memory set up," he said in eerie twenty-fourth century Venusian French.

"The Scarecrow and I watched the forerunner machine manipulate a permanent wormhole of the Axis Mundi network," she said. "It changed the Axis. We can see through it. And it doesn't lead somewhere else. It leads some*when* else. If the cosmic microwave background radiation measurement is right, it's trillions of years in the future, maybe as far as the Degenerate Era. The metallic composition of the skates supports this."

Saint Matthew had no expression to offer. With this body he could not show surprise, fear, or anything. And yet his pause seemed expressive.

"You're already thirteen billion years in the past," she said. "And you're an AI. You shouldn't suffer from scaling awe the way humans do."

"I may be more human than you think," he said slowly.

"You may be more human than I am. Saint Matthew, in the perceptions of the quantum intellect, I saw it. This machine changed the wormhole, reaching who knows how far into the future, and it's a lot like the wormholes of the second Axis Mundi network."

"You and Mister Arjona estimated that the second network contained trillions of wormholes," he said. "You think the forerunners made trillions of... time-travel devices? What for? Are they escaping the end of the cosmos by migrating to better eras? Wouldn't they be worried about changing history?"

"I can only imagine that a hyper-advanced civilization will know more about the laws of causality than we do," she said. "I'm still thinking through the possibilities, but what's more important is this: why would changing a wormhole into a time tunnel be a function of any of these forerunner machines? Are they just repairing pieces of an immense network or are they restructuring it as they wish?"

"You've found no control systems?" Saint Matthew said.

"The Scarecrow found parts, the wiring around the access holes, and possibly the light itself is an output, or part of the information-processing system. But we're looking at it the wrong way. This machine is much bigger than we can see."

"How big?"

"Parts of it are at least as distant as the hypergiant," she said. She explained her experiments with the laser, of encountering a hypergiant, probably *this* hypergiant, at the end of a tunnel that had no business seeing it, and of seeing the Scarecrow in two places.

"I don't like what I'm thinking. How could this be wormholes?" Saint Matthew said. "Making tiny wormholes instead of wiring is a tremendous waste of energy."

"It might not be wormholes at all—I mean, not in the way we understand them. The forerunner machine we see, and the ones orbiting the hypergiant might just be three-dimensional shadows of a larger object existing in four spatial dimensions."

"A tesseract?"

"There may not be three or four or six forerunner machines in this system," Cassandra said, listening to her own words to see if they sounded as ludicrous as they did in her mind. "A single tesseract exists in at least four spatial dimensions. I think that as we cross parts of this place, we're being folded through another dimension. We reach an adjacent part of the larger forerunner machine, but due to our limited perceptions, we perceive ourselves as having moved to a distant, different machine altogether."

"A single machine is orbiting the hypergiant?" he asked.

"Yes. And the command systems we haven't been able to find might be in a dimension of the tesseract we don't see. Information flows from what we see as one forerunner machine to another without transmitting EM or electrical signals."

"That's... quite a bit to absorb," the dead voice said. "A hyperspatial object standing like a spider over a solar system with just the fingers visible.""I need you to see it too, or tell me I'm wrong."

"I want you to be wrong—I'm terrified by the implications—but you rarely are. Of course hyper-advanced beings wouldn't be using fission and fusion to power their worlds. Understanding the most basic outlines of their technology is a miracle."

"I need a handful of miracles," she said.

"Tell me how to help."

She wanted to hug him, but that was ridiculous. He was a machine, trapped inside another machine.

"The system's optical and electrical logic gates may take forms we wouldn't recognize as computational elements. Maybe they compute through the interference of light, or its alteration by gravitation that red- or blue-shifts it, or something more exotic." She took a deep breath. "We need to figure out the information-processing language, and we need to hijack the machine, to tell it not to hurt the *Calculated Risk* and to help us stabilize the time gates."

"Before the Congregate agents get here," he said.

"Yes," she said, hopelessly.

"No one expected the skates and the shaghāl to be here, in the deep past of the cosmos," he mused. "Every theory I've seen has them being semi-living, semi-technological, semi-social, self-replicating creatures who developed from some technology that escaped control. Most serious theorists make them out to be the equivalent of mice and cats infesting abandoned buildings, running on big, crude circuit networks."

"What are you getting at?" she said.

"It would have to be a pretty large infestation, when you think about it," he said. "It had been going on at least thirteen billion years by the time we were born. And if you're right that a modified axis now reaches all the way to the Degenerate Era in the evening of the cosmos, then this infestation of skates and shaghāl stretches across the entire history of stars in the universe. That doesn't sound like mice and cats to me. Especially"—he scraped a metal finger against the grainy wall—"since the morphology of the forerunner machines bears such striking resemblances to skate materials."

"I'm not following," she said.

"The skates and shaghāl may not be here by coincidence," he said. "The similarities of their construction to the forerunner machines points at some sort of shared history."

"We don't have time to figure out what it is."

"We don't need to figure out what their relationship is," the AI said. "We only need to take advantage of any fundamental similarities they possess. Humanity shares all sorts of biochemical features with the most primitive of animals. What might the skates, shaghāl, and forerunner machines share?"

CHAPTER FORTY-SIX

BELISARIUS-77 WATCHED THE rolling horizon of the orange dwarf's photosphere reveal new stars as they arced around it at higher and higher speeds.

Despite the crushing feel of twelve gravities of acceleration, Phocas was insistent that they reach the conjoined wormholes first. They'd arrived slightly earlier than their formation, but he'd expected to emerge closer.

The orange dwarf was giving the *Flechette* a gravity assist, and the bulk of the small star began to shield them from the broiling radiation of the hypergiant. The ship was cooling.

"Visual detection at extreme range," the petrified pilot's voice announced. "Seventy percent match. Cherenkov radiation, some x-rays, although infrared signature is undetectable against the background of the system."

The pilot's data was visible in their feeds. It was a vanishing signal, just over the horizon of the dwarf, but that pattern of x-rays had no other likely source, nor did the dim blue spots of light.

"Any ships?" Phocas demanded.

They were still using only passive scans, but the dwarf star itself emitted more than enough light and heat for them to see the three familiar blocky shapes skirting the star's equator.

"Adjust course to go wide around the block machines," Phocas ordered. "Don't get within anti-collision algorithm ranges."

"The block machines are functional," the warden said, with an air of wonder that Belisarius-77 understood all the way to his core. "Their secrets may be within reach."

"The conjoined wormholes are close to the second block machine," the centurion mused. "It may be difficult to get close."

"Discoveries here won't matter if we're destroyed," Belisarius-77 said.

"We're not here for knowledge," the centurion transmitted. "We're here to mark the conjoined wormholes. Then, they and the *Homo quantus* can be found in every era."

The centurion had not said it was a one-way mission, but before now the possibility had never occurred to Belisarius-77. Surrounded every day by the immense power of the Congregate, its mastery over life and death, and its ability to navigate time, he'd always assumed that he would be carried from place to place, and time to time, until the centurion decided that his service, and possibly life, was done. That the centurion himself might not survive had been entirely outside his calculations.

"Artificial contact recognized," the petrified pilot said in its dead voice, surprising everyone. "It's the *Calculated Risk*."

"What?" the centurion demanded in the neural jack.

Belisarius-77 called up the coordinates. The terrorists were twenty times closer to the conjoined wormholes. The ship's orientation and distance suggested it was steering clear of the closest block machine, but not hiding. In his exhaustion, Belisarius-77 transmitted that last thought.

"What do you mean?" Phocas demanded after a pause.

"They're not hiding," Belisarius-77 repeated hesitantly, his face heating. "They're observable to the block machine, and yet its defenses haven't activated."

"Either there are none, or they've made contact with the forerunners," the warden amplified.

"We're late," Phocas said. His tone mixed disgust, fatalism, and resolve.

CHAPTER FORTY-SEVEN

THE SCARECROW'S BODY turned ponderously in zero-g as Saint Matthew extended his best hand towards an access hole. The Scarecrow's body was far more sophisticated and lifelike than anything he'd ever manipulated, and exponentially more demanding. Inhabiting it was more than distasteful—it was a kind of violation.

Normally occupying a robotic body felt like using a piece of machinery, a tool separate from himself.

The only way to act upon the world from this body was to *be* the machine. Damaged and worn as they were, the Scarecrow's hands were *his hands*. A tactile world of temperature and pressure pressed back at him. Light summoned *feeling* in his one good eye. His sense of self, normally immaterial and cerebral, was now substantial and corporeal, stiff and metallic and vitrified. Additional machine senses augmented his map of the world in alien and human ways, imposing sensational and perceptional biases. The nature of the body dictated the character of the mind, and inhabiting this broken, failing fortress altered who Saint Matthew was and could be.

Saint Matthew scraped metal fingers over the rough tunnel wall around the access hole, feeling the magnetic fields, the electrical currents. Dust came away from fine, embedded surface wires, reflecting the shine of his running lights. The wires ran visibly over the surface in some places, and vanished into depths of the walls in others, the way the wiring did in skates.

Saint Matthew had become accidentally knowledgeable about skate and shaghāl anatomy while living among the *Homo quantus*. The children in those refugee habitats treated the skates as minor puzzles of engineering, evolution, emergent complexity, information coding, and sometimes exo-linguistics. The quiet energy and frothing curiosity of the *Homo quantus* children taught him as much about the adult *Homo quantus* as about the skates. He'd become more of a skate researcher when Miss Mejía asked him to examine the skate wrecks they'd recovered.

The interior signaling of skates—what, in living creatures, would be called their neurology—was relatively simple. A silicon information-processing center sat near the skate's light-sensing lenses. It was estimated to process a yottaflop of calculations per second, about a million times fewer than the human brain. But its efficiency was unknown, so no one knew whether this implied insect-like intelligence, or something on the level of dogs or dolphins.

The coding of skate neural information bore inefficiencies that suggested lifelike evolution, or a deterioration from a previously-efficient design due to errors in unsupervised machine self-replication. Most notably detrimental, many of their information-processing circuits ran through the cakes of asteroid-mined radioisotopes. Decay could introduce randomized signals to the wiring.

The skate processing of information—their very way of thinking, if they indeed thought—was also impacted by their environment. The wire mesh in the dorsal side of the skates absorbed energy from pulsar microwave beams, creating electrical currents that could interfere with information processing in deeper layers of wiring. Moreover, some wires ran close enough over each other that intense gravity fields, like those they encountered in their gravitation-assist fly-bys of pulsars, could compress the thin layers of silicates, allowing the wires to cross, temporarily creating new information-processing pathways.

Saint Matthew was neither detective nor scientist, but the forerunner machine's construction similarities to skate anatomy did not strike him as coincidence. He wondered how deep those parallels went. While non-intuitive, skate coding signals had at least been laboriously mapped, with their odd stellar referents, weird gravitational logic modifiers, strange contingent electrical grammar, and migration-based axioms. He hoped that this bore some similarity to the forerunner machine language.

The Scarecrow body, even damaged, was wonderfully equipped for interfacing with other hardware, willing or unwilling. At first, he tried different radio and microwave frequencies, testing the responsiveness of the forerunner machine's wiring. For the most part, the wiring did not react, or responded with entirely predicable electrical currents.

The Scarecrow's invasive hacking equipment, several sets of wires, clamps, cables, and meters and magnets, had mostly survived the abuse of the body. He ended up gluing many of his hacking and monitoring cables to the forerunner wiring around the access holes. He listened to its electrical functioning for a few minutes and established its baseline activity. Miss Mejía watched him impatiently.

"Would you shine your laser as you did before?" he asked.

She took her suit's utility laser, checked her angle, and then shone it in. Seven meters down the tunnel, on the same side, a tiny red dot appeared on the wall, across from another access hole.

"Is it changing any currents?" she asked.

"No."

He raised his other arm, pointing it towards the dot of light, and a small spy camera with manipulators shot out on a cable.

The tiny pincered legs under the camera caught on the ceiling and walked down into the laser light.

"What are you doing?" she asked.

"Spectroscopy," he said. "I can confirm the frequency drop in the light. If these are miniature stable wormholes as you think, then there's an energy cost to going through," he said. "The laser had to climb out of a gravity well to emerge here."

"What made you look for this?"

"We think the information-processing of the skates is affected by the intense gravitational fields around pulsars. Depending on the structure of these miniature wormholes in here, they are even more intense. I'm going to change the inputs."

He activated one hacking cable after another, with different microcurrents, in increasing strength. He made a holographic image of the changes he was making, and she watched attentively. After a few minutes, he finished.

"Do we have anything good?" she asked.

"I have a theory," he said.

He had tried to say it with equanimity, but the Scarecrow's voice sounded to his false hearing as if something dead was speaking in the dark in an antique French, with his words. He hated this body.

"Skate *behavior* is simple," he said, "but I don't think that internal skate *information processing* is as simple as we think. We're used to thinking of logic gates as on and off, or partially turned on, like when we're talking about quantum logic gates. We really don't tend to think of logic gates in very exotic terms, because simple logic gates already support all our programming needs. Passing laser light through a gravitational gradient changes the frequency of the light. Passing a skate close to the intense gravitation of a pulsar changes the pathways the information follows. Those two things seem to be similar to what we're seeing in the forerunner machine."

She was frowning. "Where did these ideas come from?" she asked. "I know a lot about information processing theory, but I haven't thought of these... exotic logic gates you're talking about."

"I'm made of some. You can't make self-aware aleph class AIs without a few of them. And I've... experimented, perhaps more than the Banks, in my efforts to make an AI with a soul."

He said the last part sheepishly, but in the Scarecrow's dead voice, and Venusian French, it sounded ridiculous, humiliating. Her look was distant and slightly retreating.

"I'm sorry," he said. He had so little faith left.

"My mind is trying to reinterpret things I've seen," she said, "to see if I've already stumbled across information processing systems without knowing it. Can you read anything in the forerunner machine systems? Can you talk to it, find out where its builders are? We need to talk to them, ask them for help."

"That's the next thing to try."

Static squawked in the hardwired comms line linking them to the outside world.

"What?" Miss Mejía answered.

"...e got company... uckin' hurry," came Stills's distant voice.

"We're out of time," Saint Matthew said.

"Unless you can figure out how to talk to the forerunner machine," she said. "Turn off its defenses so Stills can bring the ship in, at least, while we figure out the rest."

CHAPTER FORTY-EIGHT

"SHIT!" STILLS SWORE on the ship's channel, even though it was just him, the crazy Puppet, and the AI's AI. "Strap in! We're made!"

He sent a tight radio message to her highness twice, and got a fat slice of static as an answer. The other ship was *gunning* it, coming off the horizon way faster than he'd expected. He could guess its shape, but it shone like a sonofabitch, reflecting the light and heat of the hypergiant.

"*Coño,*" he announced. Either Mama Merced's boy was going to get blasted to pieces by the forerunners, or he was about to make first contact with gold-plated Congregate dickheads. He tipped the *Calculated Risk* solar northward and slowly accelerated to get closer to the forerunner machine. If he could work out how close he could get without getting shot, he could at least use it as an obstacle.

"I can't see shit," he said. "Half-pint! Can you or the AI get another telescope working? Or can your eyes make anything out?"

The little AI funneled new data into Stills's feed, but it wasn't much. It didn't have another telescope—it was just cleaning up the incoming information. Unsurprisingly, the gold ship was a cylinder, like the *Calculated Risk,* like every ship in civilization that used the Axes.

The quiet AI sharpened the image based on known Congregate and Union designs and the gold cylinder looked a lot worse. It was a big fucker, about a hundred and twenty meters to the *Calculated Risk*'s fifty-three. The image wasn't clear enough to make out weapons, but the ship was big enough to carry ship-to-ship artillery, guns, and—most importantly—an inflaton cannon. It was completely covered in some brightly reflective gold material. The Congregate were arrogant, but unfortunately, they weren't stupidly arrogant, so that wouldn't just be decoration. What was the reflectivity for?

He'd dialed the white radio noise of the solar system high to listen for another response from Prancy Pants, when the tight beam signal hit. He swore, listened, dialed it down, and nearly shit himself all at once.

"Terrorists aboard the *Calculated Risk*," a leaden French voice announced. "Article forty-one of the State Security Act authorizes Congregate officers to pursue, apprehend, or destroy terrorist actors and assets extra-territorially. Shut down weapons and engines and prepare to be boarded."

Merde.

The same Congregate message came through their comms again, with a 'this is your last warning' closer.

Zarba.

An alarm sounded. A missile. At least they meant what they said...

The missile was far, but skating higher and higher over the prominences of the dwarf's corona. It had the Congregate ship's momentum and a steeper acceleration curve. He couldn't tell at this distance what it was, but almost anything would blow them to shit.

CHAPTER FORTY-NINE

Unless he could *figure out how to talk to the forerunner machine and turn off its defenses,* she'd said. How on earth was he going to do that? They were inside a machine they could not understand, billions of years in the past, with no reinforcements, no hope, and enemies closing in. Miss Mejía and Mister Arjona always spoke as if what was miraculous to everyone else wasn't miraculous to them. The *Homo quantus* had their own miracles, their own brushes with the immanent, but that thought didn't comfort him. Rather than emphasize their shared common experiences of transcendence, it suggested the *Homo quantus* walked on different ground. It was hard to see the hand of a single God in the creation of beings as different as Saint Matthew, Pedro, Mister Arjona, and Miss Mejía. That was his problem of faith. In crises of faith miracles were needed, and in crises of faith their absences shattered souls.

"Can you do it?" she asked.

Saint Matthew saw so much of Mister Arjona in her now—not the normal *Homo quantus* shyness and intellectual quiet, although that was still there. She was poised, commanding, more confident in her choices. *She'd* led them to the morning of the universe. She'd found machines of the ancient titans of the cosmos. And despite the odds, she was leading him through the darkness.

"I'll try."

He said that each time they asked the impossible. He wasn't sure how much he tried for them, and how much he tried for what he needed the universe to be. Mister Arjona had told him long months ago in his empty churchlet on Saguenay Station that a well-peopled space station needed no miracles. It was out in the world they were needed. These maddening *Homo quantus* geniuses were his doorways to the possibility of miracles, so he had to follow them. All he had to do this time was break into the information-processing systems of a four-dimensional machine built by cosmic titans.

To each journey, a first, modest step...

He'd built a database of the micro-current behaviors in the wires around the access hole, mapping them to spectral changes in light. He hoped to see how information changed in this one place, trying to intuit the logic structure in directions he could not see. Miracles indeed.

He was an AI at the dawn of the universe, eight billion years before the creation of the world that would know God. Yet his God must be here too. Even this place and time was a product of His creation and part of His plan. Saint Matthew couldn't feel Him, though—he never could. That lonely silence was crushing. But the only way to know Him was to believe, to never let go of faith, and to be guided to His purpose.

The neurology of skates and the shaghāl proved to be unilluminating models by which to understand what he was observing. He tried to look at the problem as one of decryption. The Scarecrow's decoding tools were superb, but couldn't crack the problem of understanding the computational language of the forerunner machine. Saint Matthew's early AI training experiences in hacking were not helpful either. That training only suggested clever algorithmic short cuts, more baroque decryption tactics, or brute-force last resorts. The language in which this forerunner machine thought could not be penetrated by clever short cuts or brute-force measures.

Why had this test come before Saint Matthew? God put neither feats of strength nor of intellect before those he tested. The outside world was important, but not as important as the mysteries of the soul, the unseen, the ineffable, and the secret places inside each person. That was part of the essential miracle of Saint Matthew—that a machine, an AI, designed and grown for the most material and violent of conflicts, had a soul. Although before this moment, he'd never framed it this way, part of that miracle was that his soul wasn't located in space and time in the way Miss Mejía understood it.

On an intellectual level, something similar was happening here, but what if this truth was also more than measurable and intellectual? Parts of the forerunner machine existed in places and times that couldn't be known directly. But like faith, its mysteries could be questioned, and revealed by comparison and reflection. The processing complexity he was seeing could not be accounted for by the physical circuits he could touch and manipulate, and twisting through dimensions he couldn't see introduced unguessable amounts of processing texture and subtlety.

He'd already processed information while in an environment of higher dimensions, in the hyperspace inside the time gates. He'd spent days, weeks, perhaps months in that hostile higher-dimensional space. His hardware and software had needed to accommodate the environment, but the accommodations were rarely conscious. That was not how AIs grew. AIs of his sophistication grew by trying, testing, and reinforcing connections, ultimately creating new intuitions.

The Scarecrow had not grown in the hyperspace. He had never changed himself to resist and endure the hostility of its environment. The Scarecrow had simply suffered. People like Mister Stills, Miss Johns-10, and General Iekanjika had endured the hyperspace the way they would a psychotropic agent. Mister Arjona and Miss Mejía and other *Homo quantus* immersed themselves in it with abandon, becoming part of it in apparently frictionless ways, from their quantum fugues. Only Saint Matthew had been obliged to slowly adapt, learning without knowing, bending without breaking. He'd accepted and weathered the mysteries, and worked with them, because that was the way of the world.

This forerunner machine's computational language was a different kind of mystery, perhaps as deep and as subtle as the soul. Like all AIs, Saint Matthew was adept at spotting patterns. Yet he didn't *understand* the pattern emerging, even as he sought to model it. He was tracking how the inputs and outputs of the access holes transformed data in strange, non-geometric ways. He told Miss Mejía about it.

"Let me see," she said suspiciously. The holographic projectors on the Scarecrow, *his* holographic projectors, were damaged, but they showed an abstract figure, slowly rotating in ways that would give humans headaches.

"It's the representation of a tesseract," she said. "It reminds me of a circuit diagram, but four-dimensional."

He hadn't seen it that way before. He barely could now. Its structure was unbelievably complex. She was pointing at one part.

"What do you see?" he asked.

"This is... almost like a transform for projecting a four-dimensional object into a three dimensional space. The problem is that there are many possible three dimensional projections for a four-dimensional map. Changing the angle of projection will make each three-dimensional shadow different."

"So how do we know which angle casts the correct, solid three-dimensional shadow?"

"I don't know," she said. Her voice had a tight urgency. Mister Stills was out there with the Congregate ship approaching, and he realized that she really didn't know what came next. If she'd had even the hint of an idea, she would already have been throwing it at him.

"Maybe we're coming at this the wrong way," Saint Matthew said in the strange, antique French. "While this geometric transform is complex, it's just an algorithm, something I could run as a subroutine in me. In reverse, it might transform my... thinking, and perceptions, to something better at seeing the perspective of the forerunner machine systems."

Miss Mejía's expression was dubious.

"You're already injured."

"That's only hardware."

"We don't know that."

"We don't have time to be careful," he said gently, in the hollow French voice. "The Congregate ship is approaching. We need to protect Mister Stills, and Miss Johns-10, and Pedro. We need to fix the time gates."

"Be careful."

"I'll try," he said, before appending a silent prayer.

Saint Matthew had integrated new algorithms into his software many times over the years. He normally limited the affected systems at first, fencing the new subroutines, either because he did not need to change all of himself, or because he wanted to test the additions. This geometric transform was so different, so subtle and so extensive in its effects that he could find no way to contain it. The transform could only be integrated in his foundational processing, almost down at the kernel level, thereby affecting everything.

That was risky. He didn't want to accidentally crash himself. He did have a protected memory core and a reboot sequence in the event of catastrophic processing errors. It permitted him a kind of limited safe mode, enough to repair himself. He'd only ever had to use it once, when he'd been reconstituted in the Scarecrow, and he still didn't feel entirely like himself. If this didn't work, they might not have time for him to reboot and restart. But he didn't have any other ideas on how to crack the forerunner processing language.

They needed a miracle.

He needed a miracle.

He'd always needed a miracle. He was coming to the end of his spiritual endurance. He needed God to show Himself, just once, to give his life meaning, to make Saint Matthew real.

Please... he thought, as he incorporated the geometric transform into himself.

SAINT MATTHEW'S THOUGHTS expanded as if written on an inflating bubble. The feeling of claustrophobia within the Scarecrow's rigid, alien neurology seemed far beneath him and yet nearby; his experience toggled between states of freedom and confinement. Saint Matthew could look out onto a small world embedded within an infinitely larger one, or he could look in on himself, really *in* on himself, to the moving currents of his own thinking along arbitrary riverbeds of constraining logic. He saw through himself. He was everywhere and yet still within the creaking body of an undead machine.

His notion—of figuring out the precise angle used to project the three-dimensional shadow of a four-dimensional object—now appeared quaint and innocent. The forerunner machine used *every* angle. The wiring web in four dimensions could process a stupendous amount of data, beggaring even his wildest estimates.

This rush of understanding, this half-grasped epiphany, set his mind crackling with new thoughts. The new algorithm demanded energy and crowded out some of his own thinking. The speed of calculations felt hot. The vast processing canvas felt like infinity, yet the petrified neural architecture of the Scarecrow still constrained him. The Scarecrow never could have incorporated the geometric transform to see this new world, nor easily change the way it thought. Running on the Scarecrow's hardware dragged on Saint Matthew.

But not enough to prevent understanding.

Saint Matthew's physical connections to the wiring of the forerunner machine allowed him to read the passing signals. His spectrometers allowed him to read the shifting colors of light from the access hole. Within the context of a vast, dimensionally-expanded algorithm-processing space, the language and logic routines became comprehensible, traceable, decipherable, and he began to make sense of them.

He began to understand that the information passing through this node was navigational. Saint Matthew recognized informational depictions of the time gates floating in space, the anti-Axis co-orbiting just outside the machine, the tube-shaped *Calculated Risk,* and the orange dwarf star behind them. He also interpreted the information representing the new ship, and its soon-to-be arriving missile. He also found information through time: graphical representations of the migration patterns of skates and the pursuing shaghāl.

Yet the node contained so much more information. Through higher-dimensional pathways, he found that it was connected to five other forerunner machines. Two of them orbited the orange dwarf, while three circled the hypergiant. Saint Matthew could access their external data, too. And he saw some of the way the systems interacted. He disconnected his wiring.

"We have to move," he said. "This node is only part of the external sensors' processing system."

"You understand it? Where do we have to be?"

"I'll show you," he said, moving up along this tunnel, choosing a fork they'd not yet taken.

"How far do we have to go?" she asked behind him. "We're going to lose contact with Stills if we go too far."

He didn't know quite how to answer her. Their destination was both near and far. His understanding of the forerunner machine's layout was becoming dizzyingly expansive. Every tunnel, branch point, and access hole took on new context as he learned how the elements fit counter-intuitively together.

She followed him along the curves of gritty tunnel walls. In a more sober world, they would have encountered the starboard external wall by now, but instead they'd entered another forerunner machine. As they moved, one pre-conceived perspective after another fell in his mind, surrendering to new ways of thinking. His context grew.

"We're almost there," he said. He led them around a bend to an ovoid hollow about eight meters on its long axis. Three other tunnels led into it, one bright with brilliant, scattered sunlight. Access holes festooned the walls. "This is the interface we need."

Miss Mejía, one gloved hand shading her eyes from the sunlight, looked at the access holes the way *Homo quantus* examined questions. No doubt she was counting, establishing geometric relationships between the holes, looking at angles of light, trying to discern algorithmic possibilities from layout. The *Homo quantus* were sometimes very predictable. Saint Matthew brought his hand and the hacking cables to one access hole and connected himself to the system.

"Is this a primary processing node?" she said.

"'Primary' might not the right way to put it," he said. "It's like a specialized chip in a computer. Particular kinds of operations happen here. External sensors. Orbital defenses."

"We're in another forerunner machine, aren't we?"

"It's one big machine," he said slowly.

She grunted agreement.

He interfaced with the data. No, that wasn't quite correct. Saint Matthew wasn't interfacing with the data. Saint Matthew was just a three-dimensional projection of some larger, fragile, inexperienced four-dimensional mind. There was a flavor of epiphany in his new way of thinking, a tempting, perhaps dangerous one.

Saint Matthew did not entirely control what he saw in the forerunner machine. The system he'd accessed protected the machine from collisions. The solar system's orbital data was beautiful and alien in four-dimensions. He wasn't looking at the solar system from above, but from somewhere else, an angle from which he could see the interiors of objects and the tensions of unbalanced forces. The rotation of the hypergiant, and the warping of spacetime along its equatorial skirts, was clear in a way he could not put into words, or diagram in three dimensions. He could see the unstable tensions in the hypergiant. Spin and gravity and radiation and light pressure struggled in a barely held equilibrium.

"Can you let Stills through?" Miss Mejía asked, bringing him back to this tiny chamber, this single, bare synapse in the immense four-dimensional computer running the forerunner machine.

"I think…" he said, hesitating. "If I had more time, I could probably let him through."

"We don't have time."

"In that case, I can only offer to interrupt the entire anti-collision system. We'd have to hope that nothing hits it in the meantime. If we destroy a forerunner machine in the past, our interference would no longer just be about humanity and the *Hortus quantus*."

"We need Stills," she said. "Let him in. Then try to turn it on again."

CHAPTER FIFTY

VINCENT STILLS HAD a lot of choice words to say. His long years of surviving in the cockpit of a small fighter helped maintain a steady stream of them while he acted without the full plan in his head. He brought them deeper into the shadow of the forerunner machine. He thought he heard a faint radio signal, but nothing was there when he listened harder. He played back the automatic recording. He heard her voice, faint.

"…Stills… can come in… ems and auto-defenses are off…"

There was no more. The signal was heavily decayed. The only problem was, it wasn't coming from the forerunner machine. It was coming from the same direction as the approaching Congregate ship, and their missile.

Mama Merced's boy wasn't born yesterday, amateurs.

But… Something was funny about it. He pulled up the raw data from the antennae. The computer had integrated snatches of transmission into one clearer message, but averaging always lost something. And he didn't trust machines.

He listened to the separate streams from all four antennae. It was hard to pick out one signal in the noise, but he knew what he was looking for, and his brain was used to waves and frequencies. Mongrels talked to each other in the ocean depths the same way—all electrical waves, with amplitude and frequency modulation trying to punch through the ocean water. The four ship antennae showed transmission degradation from a slow, ongoing interference. It would be hard to fake that kind interference. Why do it?

He didn't like it.

He hated mysteries.

Well, fuck.

He pulled up navigation systems and worked back through what they'd mapped of the system. An itch crawled up his spine as it all displayed. And he saw it—right where Her Highness's signal was coming from. It was another forerunner ship, about six light minutes away, orbiting the hypergiant. As he triangulated, he saw that the Congregate ship was positioned just far enough off a direct line that it couldn't have sent that signal. He replayed the message. Around all the grainy scratch, it sounded like her. If it really was her, how the *Crisse* had she gotten all the way out there? Or had she just used the other machine as a transmitter? If so, why?

Mierda.

It was always *why* with them. Why, why, why? Always. And he should never ask. He never liked the answers. Did he think the Congregate would try to trick him? Of course. And they were good at it, too. But why would they want him *closer* to the forerunner machine? Did they want the anti-collision or defense systems of the machine to blow him to shit?

Their accelerating missile would do that without help.

Time to role the dice again. He ramped up the inflaton drive, and set a cautious, elliptical course towards the forerunner machine.

"I DON'T UNDERSTAND," Belisarius-77 said. He was tightly strapped into an acceleration chamber, pressure gel squeezing him inside and out. He was at the mercy of the ship and pilot, just like the neural skein had been. The sensors jacked into his skull showed the *Calculated Risk* far in the distance, maneuvering to get behind the forerunner block.

"It isn't defending itself," the warden said.

She'd uploaded a spatial diagram of their trajectory into the feed. Had the terrorists made contact with the forerunners? The *Flechette*'s own acceleration profile might look threatening, and worse.

"If Mejía goes too close to the forerunners, our missile might look like it's targeting the block itself," Belisarius-77 transmitted into their channel. "We can still steer it away and cut its acceleration."

No one spoke. The terrorists were still moving. At current acceleration, the missile was five hundred seconds from the *Calculated Risk*.

"Centurion?" Belisarius-77 said.

The missile suddenly veered away, following an elegant parabolic path away from both stars, and from the forerunner block. Despite his relief, Belisarius-77 felt himself internally flinching, waiting for the centurion's reaction. The *Flechette* began changing course, slightly further from the block, tightening their approach to the conjoined wormholes.

"What about the forerunners?" Belisarius-77 asked into the channel without entirely intending it. They couldn't very well go interfere with the working of a wormhole now that the terrorists had made first contact with the forerunners.

"The mission first," the centurion said. "If we modify the conjoined wormholes here, at their origin, we'll be able to track them throughout all of history. The evolutionary struggle with the *Homo quantus* will be won. Everything else is secondary."

CHAPTER FIFTY-ONE

There were many ways for Saint Matthew to conceive of the forerunner machine. It was a work of super-science whose study would occupy centuries. It was an archaeological trove for humanity's heritage, proving that humanity was not alone. The machine was a piece of art, a statement of alien minds expressing some perspective on the cosmos. Most poignantly, it was a miracle, a subject of pondering and reflection in the hopes of uncovering not just secrets, but wisdom. This last made it most difficult to accept that he'd broken it.

He had not found a way to temporarily shut off its anti-collision system. In his limited, destructive way, he'd only been capable of breaking that system permanently. The partial miracle, such as it was, had been to decipher enough of the forerunner information processing to know *what* to break. Yet that seemed to be an ironic and tragic miracle. Stills and Miss Jones-10 and Pedro would be safe, but at a terrible cost.

All his miracles were destructive.

Miss Mejía radioed Stills through the Scarecrow systems. The part of the forerunner machine they were occupying was in another part of the solar system, about two light-minutes away. That should be time enough for Stills to take shelter in the forerunner machine before the Congregate arrived. It took a moment to re-access the systems that gave him an external view of the first forerunner machine. He found the *Calculated Risk* nearing it.

"Oh, no," he said.

"What?"

"The Congregate ship... it's going to reach the time gates."

"Can the forerunner machine stop them somehow?"

"I just broke the anti-collision systems so that Mister Stills could come in."

"There must be more. Are there real weapons?"

"I haven't seen anything like a weapon. The forerunners and their equipment may have no natural threats. We may be so early in the universe's history that the forerunners have no peers."

"The machine itself can shield them," she said. "If we can maneuver it over the time gates, the way we watched it settle over the Axis it manipulated. What access have you got to propulsion systems?"

Her question was hard to answer. He'd seen the first forerunner machine propel itself, but hadn't understood how. The machine did not eject reaction mass, nor do anything exotic like create an inflaton field. The information-processing language of the forerunner machine could guide him to some systems, but there was so much more he simply couldn't understand. Perhaps the forerunners were so evolutionarily distant that he couldn't *imagine* it. Finally, he projected what he'd seen of the forerunner machine's movements. Miss Mejía squinted at the yellow light of his hologram.

"There's something wavelike and cyclic in this," she said "but I can't put my finger on it. I wonder if Stills can help?"

"He's not an engineer, or a physicist."

"Maybe a pilot will see something we're missing. Let's go."

"I think I understand something new in this machine," he said. "We've been taking the long way everywhere. Everything is closer than we think."

Her dubiousness melted into the hungry, innocent curiosity. "The fourth dimension?"

"These access holes are all connected in a web through a fourth spatial dimension," he said. "This large node governs anti-collision systems, but it's also 'beside' the node for what we would call propulsion and navigation. We can get there by a shortcut."

"How does it work?"

He was silent for a few seconds. "I don't think I can explain it. I can see it… with the forerunner machine transform. I can see how things get folded… that's the wrong word, but I can see how things get folded to move from one place to another. It's easier to show you," he said, taking her hand.

The Scarecrow senses, designed to find every emotional weakness in its victims, detected her faint flinch, something so small he would not have normally noticed. Seeing it made him feel as dirty as the reaction itself did. He hoped what came next dispelled her unease. He had no special components within the Scarecrow body to access a fourth spatial dimension, but he didn't need to. He just had to know where to… fold.

His cold jets rotated him slowly, pulling Miss Mejía with him. It was a gentle rotation, without any strangeness to the motion, but it was where he moved that became a folding. He pivoted into another direction that he knew only because of his altered perceptions. There was no feeling of change, except for the quality of the light. They seemed to be in the same ovoid space, but the three tunnels leading into it were all dark. The same access holes divoted the walls.

"We're on another forerunner machine?"

"Yes and no," he said.

"You're getting to be frustrating."

"There's only one forerunner machine," he said, trying to distill his growing understanding. "We haven't left it. We've moved from one arm to another, folding ourselves across what hours ago we would have called intervening space."

She was looking at the access holes with the strange *Homo quantus* analytical intensity.

"This is the propulsion control area?" she asked

"This is the propulsion information-processing area," he said. "The anti-collision systems are 'here' too, as are the external sensors. It's hard to explain. Even French doesn't have the mathematical language to talk about how there is only one ovoid structure, possessing four spatial dimensions. Each of the six forerunner machines we see contains a projection of the ovoid, a solid three-dimensional shadow of the four-dimensional structure. Each of those three dimensional shadows processes information about different aspects of the machine's function. I'm just beginning to grasp it."

"What's happening outside the forerunner machine?" she asked, her eyes remeasuring the round corridors leading to this node. "Can the drones even bring Stills here? His tank won't fit down those tunnels. Are you going to wire him into this node?"

Saint Matthew accessed the external sensors again. He was still getting the more expansive, four-dimensional view of the solar system, one that was both bird-eye and inner eye. He had intended to transform the data down to three dimensions, but realized that with Miss Mejía, he probably didn't need to. He projected the solar system view, including themselves, the Axis mouths, and the ships, in three dimensions, indicating the fourth spatial dimension with colors. Miss Mejía poured over it, her eyes narrowing as her brain did the processing.

"The *Calculated Risk,*" she pointed at a colored blob nestled so close to the forerunner machine that it was within the tesseract effect too, a three-dimensional object within a four-dimension space. "What's this?" she asked, tracing a gloved finger along a line leaving their ship.

"Unfortunately, I believe that Mister Stills has fired a small missile at the Congregate ship," he said. "We had one aboard, in storage. He must have asked for it to be uncrated and fueled."

"With antimatter?" she asked in alarm.

"I don't know. Antimatter makes Mister Stills nervous. But it was securely stored and could have been loaded."

"An antimatter detonation anywhere near the forerunner machine… or the time gates… that would be bad."

"I think I can reach him from here," Saint Matthew said. "Now that I'm within the forerunner system, I can modulate the current in the external wiring, enough to be picked up as comms by the *Calculated Risk*."

In a new kind of flexing of the forerunner machine's systems, he added different signals, that if detected by the *Calculated Risk,* would give him some access to its internal systems.

"Where's Stills?" she asked.

"Is that you?" came Mister Stills's wooden, affectless voice, followed by a longer stream of multilingual expletives than normal.

"Stills!" Miss Mejía said. "Is the missile you launched armed?"

"It wouldn't be much good if it wasn't, would it?" came his flat reply.

"Stills, shut off the warhead!" she said.

"I didn't have time to make it fancy, princess. It's loaded, locked on target and it's gonna incinerate our problems."

"Two grams of antimatter could endanger the time gates! We can't get home."

Saint Matthew's calculated its blast radius. If centered on the golden Congregate ship, the time gates would be caught in the blast as well.

"A big-ass Congregate inflaton fighter endangers us a whole lot more urgently," he said. "I ain't on no suicide mission and I sure as *crisse* ain't fighting with one hand tied behind my back."

"Can we shut it off from here?" Miss Mejía quickly asked Saint Matthew.

The missile's path, seen from the perch of a four-dimensional perspective, was terrible and beautiful. Its path appeared as a snake-like volume rather than an accelerating line. He could see it from above and within. And in that moment of epiphany, he understood why he'd not seen any ports for electromagnetic beams or rail guns for protecting the forerunner machine from collisions, or enemies. Those were three-dimensional tools, inelegant and brutish.

"I can't explain..." he began.

"Don't explain! Just stop it."

Saint Matthew shook the Scarecrow's big head on the grinding steel neck.

"I'm not going to *stop* it, so to speak..."

She was holding her breath, waiting for his next words. So was he.

The forerunner machine, the four-dimensional tesseract, did not have edges and borders in the ways Saint Matthew understood them. Depending on the angles, parts of the machine could project as three-dimensional objects into normal space. The tesseract already cast solid three-dimensional shadows into normal space that he and Miss Mejía had at first interpreted as the forerunner machines. But that wasn't the only projection the tesseract could make.

It was difficult to think this way. The Scarecrow's hardware wasn't meant for this kind of processing. His software wasn't written for this, or even running the geometric transform. His insights felt tenuous, grasping, intuitive rather than proven. Feeling rather than thinking was uncomfortable. He was trying to second-guess himself without the tools to properly do so. He reached for an epiphany he couldn't hold, nor even see in its entirety.

"I'm not going to stop it," he said. "I can't."

He entered the right signals to fold part of the four-dimensional machine, so that a three-dimensional shadow of itself was projected into the path of the missile. At hundreds of kilometers away, the detail of the small earth-tone block that suddenly appeared in space was grainy and uncertain. But Saint Matthew *felt* he could see the hole in it, the venous round tunnel. The missile plunged into the opening and vanished. Saint Matthew let the tesseract relax, and the projection into normal space shrank and winked away.

"What the fuck?" Mister Stills demanded.

"What happened?" Miss Mejía said.

"The missile just emerged from one of the tunnels on another forerunner machine," Saint Matthew said. "It's now plunging into the hypergiant. Its grams of antimatter won't even be noticed."

"How?" Mister Stills demanded. "You dumb fuck! Now they're gonna come for us here."

"How?" Miss Mejía asked.

"The tesseract can assume different four-dimensional configurations, or 'shapes,' if you like," Saint Matthew said. "Imagine hinges or joints in a fourth dimension. I changed its shape so that a part of it that was still connected to a forerunner machine near the hypergiant appeared to us in three-dimensional space. I gave the missile a short cut to the star."

"Does that help us run cables from here to Stills?" she asked.

"I think I have another shortcut," Saint Matthew said. The tone of the Scarecrow's voice made the hopeful idea sound ghastly and threatening.

She seemed to be holding her breath. He might have been too, in his own way. He was getting more familiar with his expanded perceptions. Reason supported some of his intuition, although far less than he would have liked. Saint Matthew saw Mister Stills in the *Calculated Risk,* from outside and inside, in a strange overlapping perceptual toggling of a three-dimensional being perceiving the world in four dimensions.

Mister Stills's tank and power supply would fit in this ovoid hollow, although they would never fit through the tunnels leading here. It wasn't really that Saint Matthew was bending spacetime, at least he didn't think so. Rather, the components of the forerunner machine were all four-dimensional objects and its tools could reach across any of those four spatial dimensions. He hoped and tried. The forerunner machine responded.

The forces of the machine folded Mister Stills's tank, power supply, and water across an unseen direction. A dark metallic line appeared within the ovoid hollow with them, looking like Mister Stills's tank, but squashed. It expanded, filling out, until it was quite obviously a flattened gun-metal rectangle. It kept fattening, enlarging, until it assumed the dimensions they were familiar with.

"We're here, Mister Stills," Saint Matthew said reassuringly in the dead voice. The tank transmitted a shower of Arabic expletives, concatenated into strings as long as any Venusian curse.

"Calm *down,* Vincent!" Miss Mejía said. "We just moved you into one of the control pods of the forerunner machine!"

"You fuckers!" Stills said. "I'm never going anywhere with either of you again! Don't ask me for anything. Just fuck off!"

"Stills!" Miss Mejía said. "What's wrong?"

The hail of radio and microwave noise from the tank, overpunctuated with angry suggestions, quieted, as if Stills were coming to himself.

"What did you do?" he demanded. "Where's the ship? How am I alive?"

"It was me, Mister Stills," Saint Matthew said in French. "I moved you here."

"What did you knock me out with?"

"You weren't knocked out, Vincent," Miss Mejía said. "It's the way the forerunner machine moves things from one place to another."

"I can influence movements within the forerunner machine," Saint Matthew said, "but I don't understand how its propulsion works. That's why I wanted you here."

"Its some kind of tesseract," Miss Mejía said. "In this four-dimensional object, we can move things through another dimension in shortcuts. It's like the interior of the time gates, but more simplified."

"Simplified," Mister Stills said. "Fuck. Yeah. Of course. *Tabarnak*."

CHAPTER FIFTY-TWO

THE FORERUNNER BLOCK resolved more and more sharply in the telescopes as the *Flechette* seared through the system. The telescopes spied the *Calculated Risk* entering the strange open mouth of the forerunner block, passing beside what looked like an axis. That moment summoned thoughts chilling and primitive in him. In this ancient past existed beings like primordial titans, the architects of the Axis Mundi network, and Mejía and Stills were entering the mouth of a god, like a sacrifice. What sacrifice might the gods of the early universe demand of Phocas?

Belisarius-77 had noticed how carefully the *Calculated Risk* had approached the block. Could the *Flechette,* shuddering with the violence of their deceleration, trigger the anti-collision systems of the block? He cursed Phocas's hurry, while guessing that the centurion knew more about where they were, and its dangers, than he was letting on.

Belisarius-77 could only stew in his smallness, staring at the displays until his eyes hurt. He imagined the whole ship holding its breath, from the lowest special forces gunner to the centurion. Finally, the pressure on his bones slackened. The *Flechette* entered a slow orbit about eighty kilometers from the forerunner block, four kilometers from the conjoined wormholes. He was just swept up in the sickening realization that this was probably point blank range for the forerunners, and he missed the order the first time it came.

"Out and into vacuum suits," came the order again, for him and the warden.

Belisarius-77 fumbled with the release valves, and the shock gel emptied. It took ten minutes to clear the gel from his lungs and climb into his waiting suit. The warden was already in hers, a highly-reflective blue and silver mesh specially-shaped to accommodate her anatomical changes.

They exited the *Flechette* opposite the star. Even though the orange dwarf blocked the sterilizing shine of the hypergiant, the dwarf's own slumbering nuclear fires were still hot enough to slow cook them in their suits. Nonetheless, Belisarius-77 lifted a hand beyond the ship's shadow. It became brilliant white and silver on one side, and utterly dark on the other. He pulled it back. Staring away from the ship, out towards the edge of the solar system, he felt like dust, following a slow, quiet orbit, among bright, young stars. He felt safe.

But he wasn't.

The conjoined wormholes were now about nine hundred meters away. The machine they'd brought, a small cyclotron with a maneuvering engine and various radiation emitters, was closing in on them.

The cyclotron stopped within a few meters of the conjoined wormholes. A silver umbrella screen rotated open from its back to block the solar radiation and create a complex electromagnetic field.

"Are you ready for the fugue?" the warden asked him. In his helmet, a timer counted down to when he needed to enter the fugue.

"Yes."

Then the consciousness known as Belisarius-77, the being who had felt safe, was extinguished.

* * *

His fugue ended abruptly. The complex quantum superposition of states was damaged by a strong magnetic field and then definitively collapsed by a low electrical shock. Emerging from the fugue was never easy. The process of reconstituting a self-aware consciousness had some parallels to recovering from a blow to the head. It involved organizing, interpreting, integrating, and contextualizing physical senses with genuinely-acquired memory associated with sensory experience, as well as the seemingly detached, disconnected, apersonal knots of knowledge, memory and observation experienced by no one. The cacophonous orders in his helmet radio and the jerky movements of the warden yanking him into the airlock jumbled the reconstitution process. His eyes, his ears, his whole nervous system were already overly sensitive.

"He's still out," the warden was saying.

"I'm not. I'm not," he said dizzily.

Then both of them froze in an overstimulated agony of a hard electromagnetic interference field. The warden held him close and shut the airlock door, blocking out most of the interference. Electronic countermeasures. The *Flechette* was deploying electronic countermeasures against an attack. Any effort seemed stupid. A forerunner block, a piece of ancient super-science, was *right there,* in astronomical terms. What could they do to block any attack at all? It was ridiculous.

"Quiet. Quiet!" the warden whispered, and Belisarius-77 realized that in his poor fugue recovery, he'd said his thoughts aloud. "Be quiet," she said again, shaking him.

He feigned a moment of resigned, pragmatic bravery, but then switched his channel to just the two of them.

"It's over," he said. "We don't have anything to stop a forerunner attack. At least we marked the conjoined wormholes."

"We succeeded?" she asked. "Good."

"Yes," he said wanly. "The centurion will be able to kill Mejía now, and we'll be dead too and this will all be over."

"She can't be killed," the warden said. "We need her to lead us to every *Homo quantus*. They're like a cancer. Even a single breeding pair could become a threat, given a millennium. We need every single one."

He heard her words and heard his belonging to that set, even if she hadn't meant it that way.

"And it wasn't the forerunners who attacked," she said as air hissed into the airlock. "The *Calculated Risk* launched a small missile from within the bay of the forerunner block."

"Destroy it!"

"Centurion Phocas didn't want to display weapons in front of the forerunner block, for fear of being misunderstood. We got caught in the jamming and active infection attacks."

Yellow alarm lights flashed, indicating impending evasive maneuvers. They weren't safe. The airlock had no place to strap in against accelerations. The warden spun the airlock handle and shoved them into the *Flechette*. Lacking time to get to acceleration chambers, she strapped them into chairs. Belisarius-77 had won back enough resentful lucidity to realize he wasn't safe here either. A chair was good enough for forward acceleration, but escaping a missile took more than straight running. Hard lateral accelerations could snap his neck.

The *Flechette* leapt forward. Four gravities crushed him back, nearly blacking him out.

"Arjona," the centurion's voice came over the speakers. "Report on the change to the conjoined wormholes."

Belisarius-77 gasped, struggling to recover the disconnected memories left in his brain by the quantum objectivity.

"The objectivity observed a significant change in the conjoined wormholes," Belisarius-77 strained to say. "I don't know the nature of the change." He had not been expected to.

"The machine did its job," Phocas said with a certain satisfaction.

Phocas needed the wormholes to lead him to the *Homo quantus*. His mission was accomplished. Belisarius-77 exhaled a tension he'd been gripping like the armrests. They could go. Leave. Mission accomplished.

Except that Phocas wasn't leaving. The forces on Belisarius-77 pulled him sideways and then bucked. The *Flechette* shuddered. The last hadn't been a maneuver.

"The inflaton cannon," the warden mused. "The centurion is using weapons on the doorstep of the forerunner block."

The *Flechette* was making for the forerunner block, not discreetly and circuitously. It was a fast, direct trajectory, like a missile.

"Sir?" he said. "The block defenses! And anti-collision systems."

The warden squeezed Belisarius-77's arm to shush him.

"They don't matter," Phocas said.

"We don't understand the forerunners!" Belisarius-77 said in alarm as the warden's hand tightened.

"We've accomplished one mission, but we're uniquely positioned for another," Phocas said. "Despite the marking of the conjoined wormholes, we may not be this close to the terrorists again for some time. We may not need to struggle for centuries with the *Homo quantus*. This may be over in a few hours."

Belisarius-77 squeezed his eyes closed against the acceleration.

CHAPTER FIFTY-THREE

STILLS FELT INSIDE out, not in his guts, but in his electroplaques and magnetosomes. It wasn't too often that his engineered, post-human organs felt alien, like something awful and different was in him. But sometimes, when he was with a bunch of other mongrel, dogs he'd been with all his life, swimming around and yanking each other's chains, in a moment every single one of them would hit his instincts like a stranger, like a monster. His brain was still wired for the way his ancestors had been centuries ago—two-legged, air-breathing, dry-skinned.

But that had never happened with his magnetic sense. It was an extra. It didn't crowd out some old human instinct or perception the way the sense of his own body did. His brain trusted magnetic signals. Except in the time gates, and except here. When he'd been moved here, he'd felt like he had when he'd been in that hyperspatial hell: off-angle, bent, tumbling, not quite anchored to the real world.

And the AI had done it, just moved him like that. And Stills couldn't do shit about it. He wasn't connected to anything that could shoot or chop or explode the AI. Not that anything like that would work. The AI wasn't wearing the kind of body that Stills could punch. The AI was yammering in his limp-sausage way, but in creepy, death-warmed-over French. Twice as off-putting. The AI was explaining and explaining and over-explaining.

"What do you want, *malparido*?" Stills demanded.

"Well," the AI said, before hesitating. "I'll connect you to the forerunner machine the way I connected myself. I can show you the way I interpreted the data."

"What. Do. You. Want." Stills said slow, like they were as stupid as he thought they were.

"Fly the forerunner machine, Vincent," the princess said.

"A ten-billion-year-old machine? That all?"

"Saint Matthew is good, but he's not a pilot and he doesn't think like you," she said.

"You got that ri—"

"If you can make this thing go, we can get away from the Congregate ship," she interrupted. "We can fix the time gates and go home."

"*Câlisse*. You shoulda started with that."

Everybody was breathless—for air breathers, that is. Miss Princess was in a hurry. The AI was trying to listen to her while explaining a bunch of shit Stills didn't need to know. The AI started shoving bright holograms into his tank display systems, supplemented by overlapping standing electromagnetic waves. They'd used some of the same notation when showing higher dimensions inside the time gates. He wasn't all that bad at picturing four-dimensional shit, but it was trippy.

"What the hell is this?" he said.

It was like a big four-dimensional spider. No. Well... If he looked at the three-dimensional parts of it the right way, it looked like a crab. Each of the six forerunner machines they saw in-system was like a crude, severed crab foot. But in four-dimensional space, those feet were connected by blocky shadows, like afterimages of the machines. The shadows were part of a bigger body, although 'bigger' wasn't really the right word. The machine was *fatter* in a dimension he couldn't see clearly—the mix of standing electrical waves and bright holograms wasn't perfect. It was so not perfect that he felt a tiny stab of a headache, like trying to focus on something too close to his face.

"Can you see it?" the AI said.

"What the *tabarnak* am I looking for?" Stills retorted.

"I can't find any propulsion system," Saint Matthew said. "Yet it moves, very fast. We saw no thrust, no inflaton field, nothing. We thought you might understand it better."

That didn't surprise Stills. If these clowns thought that they would recognize anything in a machine made by the things who made the Axis, they were cracked.

"—her out," she was going on to the AI. "The Congregate ship is coming in. Just do the same thing you did to Vincent."

"Where's the Congregate ship?" Stills demanded. "How did those fuckers get away from my missile? Anyone within four hundred kilometers of the blast zone shoulda been ashes."

"Including our way home," she said to Stills.

And then he got it. "You air suckers! The Congregate traveled back to when the universe was a billion years old, *following us*, and you stopped me from wiping them out? You dumb *hijos de puta*. We won't get another chance."

"We might not *exist* if you annihilate the time gates in the past, Vincent!"

"Then we're fucked either way and we don't need to be rushing around," Stills said.

"We need another option, Vincent," she said.

"This is the only thing I can do with the system, Mister Stills," the AI interrupted.

Because Stills's tank systems were wired into the same systems the AI had plugged into, he could see the queasy movement in the holograms and standing electrical waves. In a kind of disbelieving silence, the puppet on their ship was *turned* in space. She wasn't in the same three dimensions she'd been in. One of them was different, like one of them was different for Stills. And she wasn't on the *Calculated Risk* anymore, she was beside him, like she'd just rolled over in bed. That thought made his stomach gurgle unhappily. The quiet little AI robot with the holographic wooden head was crawling over her as she tried to get her bearings. She was armed with one of the only hand weapons in the ship. He wondered how she'd gotten it, and if that was healthy for them.

"That's how I've been able to access the control systems of the forerunner machine," Saint Matthew went on, as the image in Stills's tank switched to an external view and he could see the gold cylinder of the Congregate ship approaching cautiously. "I can see outside this forerunner machine. I can see inside. But I can't find any weapons or propulsion."

"And I can?" Stills demanded.

"I don't have your eye or feel for propulsion."

"*Ostie,* you shoulda come with a better plan."

"This was never the plan." He could hear Saint Matthew's cadences and rhythms behind it, but the Scarecrow's voice and the language overpowered everything, made it come out creepy and threatening.

"Shut up," Stills finally said. "Show me the stupid systems."

The holograms and standing electrical waves changed, shrinking, showing the bit for moving the puppet, the bit for looking outside, the bit for looking outside the other forerunner machines, and the view inside, where they were.

"That's it?"

"That's everything I understand or have seen," the AI said. "We're connected to some of the central systems through this node. I'll try to make other connections, in case some of them are accessed through differences in the angle."

The dumbass said it like it was a thing that would have made sense to anyone. The AI was broken and they were trapped at the beginning of the universe with the Congregate breathing down their necks. He squinted at the holograms. They had a blurriness that was partly intentional, something to suggest a fourth dimension. He could get all the feeds in, but his brain couldn't piece it together perfectly. That was more the princess's style.

What the *tabarnak* did they want from him?

He stared at the holograms, while listening to the standing electrical waves, letting the blurry picture of the crab move in and out of focus. The AI and the princess had tapped into its body, its veins, its neurons. They'd uncovered the three-dimensional limbs of this four-dimensional machine. They'd mapped its anatomy and done the equivalent of shooting an electrical current into a dead fish to make it wiggle.

It wasn't dead, though. They just hadn't seen it live and move.

Zarba.

What was he? He was no machine whisperer. Or animal whisperer.

He could move, though. In the water. Through space. In the old Congregate fighters, or the new Union inflaton fighters. Hell, he'd flown through a hyperspatial shitshow and had the brain damage to prove it. And this machine had moved. They'd seen it move, fast enough to have made Stills rabbit away. None of them understood its propulsion system. No thrust. No EM fields. No inflaton fields. No gravity waves. No induced or permanent wormholes.

What had moved?

His head was suffering a major case of eyestrain. Looking at blurry holograms wasn't good for him. It took a whole lot of brain strain to vaguely see the machine in four dimensions. It was what the AI had said. They weren't in a three-dimensional machine. They were in one *part* of a four-dimensional machine. And the machine was right where it had always been.

One arm had moved. That was all.

Helluva flex.

And crazy. If it was true, why hadn't the air-suckers seen it? They were the ones with legs.

It was just too crazy.

"Can you give me any of the readings or data from when we were coming into the system?" Stills asked.

"I haven't tried accessing memory storage," the AI said.

"Well try, dumbass. Do I have to do everything?"

"What do you see, Vincent?" the princess asked.

The holograms were changing. The external and internal sensors were running in reverse, showing the *Calculated Risk* receding, and showing the forerunner machine, as part of the larger four-dimensional object, shooting backwards, the opposite of what they'd seen when they'd entered the system. There were still no indications of thrust or propulsion fields around this forerunner machine.

Stills stared at the larger four-dimensional structure. It wasn't easy to see, but there was a… he didn't know what to call it. A folding? Not really. A flexing. No. It was like the overall tesseract structure of the six forerunner machines was changing its shape, slightly, and all of that change was appearing in the motion of the forerunner machine they were in. The other five were still where they'd started, still orbiting the two stars in this system.

Stills hated it here. He didn't want to be in the past. He didn't want to be trying to save the fucking world. He didn't like that one by one everyone around him was losing their marbles. He didn't have a messiah complex, a masochistic streak, or anything else that twisted. He hoped he wasn't the one cracking.

"Look," he said to the AI. "When the forerunner machine moved, what was happening inside? Where are those systems?"

"I'll see what I can do," the AI had been saying.

"The Congregate ship is almost here," the princess said.

She was still accessing the external sensors. The gold tube neared, shining. Gold. What a loser. But it was hard not to imagine a fucking French king coming to blast the shit out of them, before sipping wine and nibbling on fancy *hors d'oeuvres* over their corpses. Stills had really not believed that the Congregate could follow them back in time here, or hadn't wanted to. Nothing could protect anyone in civilization, in all civilizations, if the Congregate could travel through time.

They wouldn't be able to get the *Calculated Risk* out anymore.

Shit. They wouldn't even be able to get back to the ship.

"You know they'll find us and kill us, if we're lucky," Stills said.

He had to admit—Her Princessness looked like she wasn't giving up, even though the AI was crazy and trapped in a Scarecrow body, even though she was cut off from her ship and her best ally was in a metal box.

"I'll have to stop them, then," she said.

And he laughed. It was the grim laugh he had when he and his squadron of fighters were flying into the teeth of Congregate anti-fighter artillery. He let some of it translate out for Miss Big Balls. They might as well all go out swinging.

CHAPTER FIFTY-FOUR

BELISARIUS-77 FOLLOWED THE armored commandos out of the large rear airlock, into the silent bay of the forerunner block. One of the warden's fists was wound into the back of Belisarius-77's harness, steering him through the zero-g. Three commandos were opening an airlock in the nearby *Homo quantus* ship, while another was setting up an interference device within the *Calculated Risk*'s dented inflaton channel.

He couldn't believe they'd done it, that it was over.

Across a quarter of the galaxy and twelve billion years, all the way to the infancy of the cosmos, they'd cornered the *Homo quantus* leaders and their conjoined wormholes. The Congregate's inevitability bent the paths of history like gravity. Other peoples and wills could not escape it. His feelings should have been more ambiguous or complex, but he found only relief. The *Homo quantus* had never felt like his people. They would adjust to their new circumstances under Congregate control, like he had.

There was another feeling, a floundering anticipation. Today he would meet Cassandra Mejía, a person and abstraction he'd studied his whole life, someone who also imposed her own gravity on the world. Would she seem larger than life, or would she feel small, the way the original Belisarius had seemed small on the frozen plain of Nyanga?

He had trouble keeping up with the shiny, armored marines and the warden. The forerunner block was unlike anything he'd expected. Its lines felt… organic, even through its materials were quite obviously lifeless mineral. The dark round tunnels, open to the naked vacuum of space and the diffusing spray of solar wind, nonetheless called to mind great empty veins. Why not straight lines? He was dead-reckoning their progress through the block and it made sense until it stopped making sense.

"What's wrong?" he said. "Something's wrong."

The two planes constituting the featureless wedge of the warden's face turned to him, canting as though in curiosity.

"Nothing is wrong. You are traveling along the bleeding edge of Congregate influence on the cosmos, a transition of states. We have much to learn here."

Her appreciation sounded suspiciously mystical, undercutting the rational *Homo quantus* impartiality he preferred in her.

"It's not linear," he whispered on a direct channel to her.

"It confirms a theory of their structure," she said, pausing in the mouth of the round tunnel as marines moved ahead. The centurion—in golden armor, like a sun god—led the way. "The forerunner block is a tesseract. You can't map it in three dimensions."

Ochre and tan chips blistered and shattered from the wall, spraying down the venous corridor. A single chip could have sliced his suit, but the warden shielded Belisarius-77 with her body. He tried retreating, but her hand clamped his arm. She dialed him into the security feed from farther ahead, where he saw a metallic Scarecrow hand, bereft of its facade of metal clothing. From between gnarled fingers, tubes fired hot bullets down the tunnel. Two of the marines were injured, but not dead. Their comrades pulled them back.

The firing stopped, on both sides.

"What's happening?" Belisarius-77 asked.

"Everyone is assessing their options, I think," she said. "And you're needed."

"Me?" he demanded with a kind desperation.

"You're an ace in the hole," she said, pushing him forward.

"Stop!" he said on her channel. "I don't know anything."

"You've been briefed on every scrap of information ever collected about Cassandra Mejía, and your template, Belisarius Arjona."

"I don't know her."

The warden shook him violently, and pressed his faceplate against the wedge of her external facial augments. The kindness in her voice had vanished.

"We were built to serve, built to function," she said. "If my genes and microbiomes had been closer, I would be the Belisarius clone now, ready to enter the crucible. We serve, or we die. That is the *accord*, our *accord,*" she said, giving the French word more emphasis. "All your pathways led to this moment, and today the centurion will evaluate his investment in you." .

His vision narrowed. Sound hollowed. His chest tightened. The world compressed into these strange seconds at the beginning of the cosmos, into this bloodless tunnel, into this tiny group of people who would look inside his heart and find him wanting.

He didn't know how long the warden's grip had been hurting. She muscled him ahead of her through the corridor, past crouching marines. Belisarius-77 squirmed, keeping an eye around the edge of the curve from which the Scarecrow's hand had emerged to spray them with deadly metal. The hand was out of sight.

"Are you ready?" the warden asked.

"They've taken control of a Scarecrow?" he whispered urgently to her. "It will kill us."

"They may have taken crude control of the Scarecrow, but I

have invasive algorithms from the far future, made to unlock all Scarecrows everywhere."

He wasn't ready, would never be ready. The centurion had planned many ways this confrontation could go, permutations based on circumstances, goals, urgency. He didn't know any of those things right now. His prodigious memory had retained nothing. He wasn't combat personnel. He wasn't a negotiator. He wasn't an actor. He was barely a liar. And he didn't know Cassandra Mejía, the terrorist leader who had reportedly brought kilograms of antimatter to the Union side, and who had engineered the incineration of the Congregate's Twelfth Fleet by turning the Freya Axis into the galaxy's youngest black hole.

The Warden passed him to the centurion like a piece of equipment.

"I can't..." he began. "I don't know what—"

The centurion's fingers, sheathed in a hard golden alloy, wrapped around Belisarius-77's harness on his back, and brought him faceplate to faceplate.

"You can. You've been trained."

He nearly scoffed, but was too afraid. The pale face behind the glass was determined, demanding, and too close.

"Bring her in. End this without violence."

Belisarius-77's mouth opened, to say... *anything* about the prospect of a non-violent solution while they were all here, weapons ready.

He'd memorized and re-memorized every video, photo, and audio of the original Belisarius. He knew the original Belisarius's mannerisms, cadences and tones, his posture, his disorientingly intentional body language. He'd studied his angelic and sinistral self with disbelieving obsessiveness, in dysphoric detail, until his sense of self bled into the frames of the recordings, until his life and his own meaning became afterimages and shadows of a life poorly lived by a stranger.

He switched his helmet transmitter to general radio bands.

"Cassie?" he asked.

He didn't need to fabricate the longing in his voice. Mejía... Cassandra had always been a distant, larger-than-life figure, someone who had transcended the *Homo quantus,* rather than fallen from their potential like every Belisarius variant, and the original. In his most secret thoughts, she was at the other end of all the *what-if* questions.

What if he'd been born free? What if he'd been the real Belisarius? What if he met her, without the Congregate? What if she'd moved the laws of physics to be with *him?* He knew the dangers of might-have-beens, but hadn't the strength to banish them from mind or heart.

"Cassie?"

The Scarecrow hand came around the corner, with a few tiny, surviving lenses hidden among the bent steel of the fingers. He didn't flinch, because the original Belisarius wouldn't have. He had to be the original in this moment, or he would have no future.

A helmet rose behind the hand, peering past it. Its HUD lights were dimmed, but when he stepped up the gain in his ocular augments, he saw her, across the space, past the two pieces of hard glass. Her face was sweaty and tense and guarded. And lovely.

CHAPTER FIFTY-FIVE

CASSANDRA LOOKED OVER the curve of the tunnel, from behind a tangle of Scarecrow fingers. The Congregate were surprisingly well-lit, not only because their armor reflected a deep gold. Their rifles and armor cast cones of light in various colors. Where the heavy Scarecrow bullets had hit them were black smudges and dents, like meteor strikes. Belisarius was in a rumpled grey vacuum suit. A haggard shadow of stubble was visible underneath the faceplate.

Bel.

Their eyes met. She held her breath.

He'd said her name. The sound, rather than just the memory, was a live ache.

How had he done it? How had he survived? She'd not really believed the Scarecrow's memories and recordings. She'd imagined it easy to insert a memory into an artificial mind. Easy to fool her. And yet here he was, appearing impossibly, from nowhere, within living forerunner machines, in the morning of the universe.

"Bel?" she asked.

His look was… disturbed, almost terrified. What had they done to him?

"What happened, Bel?"

"I never left," he said in a voice tight with resonant longing. "They never let me go."

They'd never let him go? He'd been free, if briefly. All of them had escaped Venus. Had he been recaptured?

"Where did you go?"

Bel's ship had been in the transient wormhole. The cameras on Stills's fighter had recorded it entering. Had Bel stayed behind? Had someone else piloted it? Had Bel never actually left Venus? It was possible. They inhabited a world of impossibilities.

"I came back for you, Cassie," he said, a little half-hearted, like the words were red-shifted from climbing out of a gravity well. "I've seen the future. We don't win, Cassie, and I don't want any more people to die. I don't want you to be hurt."

"You want us to give up?" she asked in disbelief.

"The future isn't kind to an independent *Homo quantus*, Cassie."

It could be *less* kind? They were refugees living in steel cargo containers welded to inhospitable transports. They were on the run, hiding.

"We can have our own future, Bel."

He shook his head. "The Congregate can travel through time. They don't need the conjoined wormholes."

His voice was distant, and not because he was speaking to her over a crackling radio, and not because he was literally in the grip of a Congregate agent. No. Not distant; defeated. His voice was alive, and resonant, but its spark had been extinguished. Her heart broke. What had they done to him?

"Miss Mejía," Saint Matthew asked in his dead, mechanical inflections, in a laser comms line between them, "has Mister Arjona ever used the term 'conjoined wormholes'?"

Possibilities and implications split her attention. Saint Matthew was no longer perfectly reliable, but it was true that Bel had never referred to the time gates that way. Why now? What was Bel signaling? Saint Matthew's steel hand suddenly flexed, fingers clawing inward a few millimeters, the small gun barrels pointing at the Congregate again.

"What is it, Saint Matthew?" she asked on their channel. "Is the body malfunctioning?"

"They'll guarantee our safety, Cassie," Bel said. "If the *Homo quantus* goes back to how we were at the Garret, they'll leave us in peace. As we are, out in the open, with the conjoined wormholes, traveling through time, helping the Union, we're a danger. We don't have to be a danger to them."

The words were logical, and even earnest, but not… persuasive. More than once, she'd cursed his clever and manipulative tongue. He was trying to convince her, but the spark was missing, the appeal flat, almost not Bel. Had they broken him on Venus?

Alarms sounded in her helmet, a number of them, simultaneously coming from the Scarecrow's antenna system and the *Calculated Risk*'s external sensors. No one else was reacting yet.

"What is it?" Stills demanded.

"The blue giant is going nova…" she said on their private channel.

"*Tabarnak.*"

She had no time to react or decide or think. The Congregate agent in his golden armor held a gun to the side of Bel's head. Bel couldn't see it. The pale Venusian face was tight, focused, resolved.

"They're… trying to… take me… over…" Saint Matthew said, the antique French words grinding their way out.

"What?" she demanded, backing away from him. The big steel body was trembling. "Are they going to do it? Can I jam the transmission?"

"Not… a transmission… It's inside me. The Scarecrow. There is… code, deep… at the… kernel level… shouldn't be… anything there… It was a trap."

"For you?"

"For you... it must... have been... their backup... plan, if... the Scarecrow... was captured."

"Stop it!" she said. "Get out!"

"Nowhere to..."

And then his voice froze and different colors winked deep inside of him. His hand trembled, firing three shots at the golden agent. One of the bullets ricocheted off the armor and Bel crumpled into a ball. Cassandra found herself screaming. She wanted to go to him, even though the whole star system was about to be demolished. But Saint Matthew's hand was turning away from their enemies and towards her.

CHAPTER FIFTY-SIX

"Fuckin' shoot him!" Stills lasered urgently to the princess. It was like she was frozen. Goddamn civilians. "Move! Move!" he said, amping up the volume she would hear. "He's going to kill you and then me. I got better shit to do."

She was backing away from the Scarecrow, who looked like he was convulsing. The channel was open. She wasn't answering. He was still linked into the forerunner machine's systems through some of the Scarecrow's sensors. And the radiation counts outside were climbing. In a few minutes the sterilizing shit would slam in, and maybe less than an hour for the intense particle radiation that would fry everything within lightyears. He needed to find a way out.

And then, from the shadows, the crazy little Puppet fired a bunch of shots of her little laser at the Scarecrow. It didn't do much, but she targeted its weak spots, the places armor had been ripped off. Stills was so not in hate with that creepy little cultist right now. She jumped on the frozen murder machine's leg. She reached up between the steel ribs with a pair of pliers and ripped wires and cables out of anything she could reach. A lot of it was too reinforced, but with some of the armor gone, she yanked out a few hunks of innards.

Then the Scarecrow moved. He cracked the Puppet on the head with his steel hand, hard enough to dent her helmet and crack her visor. The inside of her faceplate was now painted red and hissed gas.

Puta.

Coño.

Tabarnak.

He was going to have to fly his way out of this. And when he was done, he was going to smack a lot of people who'd gotten him into this. He'd wanted to ask Her Highness about his theory of the forerunner machine, but the sand had just run out of that clock. To be fair, his idea was cracked as shit and she wouldn't have been able to understand it anyway.

The bottom of the ocean on Indi's Tear had a kind of crab. Not really a crab—it had evolved in an alien ocean, but convergent evolution was a lazy, domineering bitch, and there are only so many ways to make a hard-shelled animal. The Indi's Tear version of crab had six legs, each one capped with pincers, and an ugly face made of grindy things. When they dipped in and out of hydrothermal smokers to feed, their six legs kind of sashayed. When Stills tried crossing his inner eyes to try to imagine the whole forerunner machine tesseract, that sashaying walk came to mind. Which was why he'd scoffed when they wanted him to look at their physics. His smarts were good at finding ways to spray an enemy's brain into space and that was about it.

He checked the currents he had in the wires running through the Scarecrow's systems, and then got ready. Of course it was more intuition than knowing, and it was an intuition at the edge of reach. He sent signals into the system to make a version of that crab sashay. At first nothing happened. All the little movements just went on around him. The cracked little piece of wood AI was pulling the Puppet back from danger. The Scarecrow was slowly turning towards Stills's tank. The princess just kept backing away from it. And the Congregate commandos edged closer.

Then it happened.

The forerunner machine lurched, slamming the Congregate people into the side of the tunnel. The Scarecrow fell against Stills's tank. The princess at the curve of the wall rolled hard. He wasn't sure where the Puppet went, but thought he'd seen her careen out of sight. That might be the end of his Puppet problem.

When the whole machine stopped, there was no opposing momentum to fling everyone at the other wall. He didn't really understand what happened, but in the picture he had of this four-dimensional crab, he sort of sensed where the energy and momentum went.

Another direction, of course.

Well, hell.

Everyone was picking themselves up. He didn't want that. Not the Congregate people, anyway.

He flexed the… body of the tesseract. He didn't think it was alive. It certainly wasn't organic, and didn't have any soft parts. But it still flexed like a muscle, like a big hunk of four-dimensional piezoelectric ceramic. Some parts of it expanded more than others, just like the muscles in crab legs.

Sashay.

The leg they were in, this forerunner machine, swung forward while every other part of it stayed right where they were, in orbit around the two stars. The Congregate people slammed into the walls again, and some tumbled down the tunnel. The Scarecrow had a grip, and Stills's tank jammed against a wall. The princess moved like she understood what was happening, and landed roughly on her feet. Still no idea where the Puppet and the little AI had gotten to.

"We're here, princess," he said.

"What?" she said, dazed.

"We're here," he said in a fuckin' hurry. "If you didn't still want to be at the time gates, you shoulda told me and I would have drove somewhere else."

“No, that’s perfect,” she said, struggling up.

“Look, I don’t want to tell you to hurry, but hurry. I dropped some of the Congregate down the hole but they’re gonna be back soon.”

“I don’t know how to stabilize the time gates,” she said. “I was going to get Saint Matthew’s help.”

“*Crisse de tabarnak,*” he swore. “I really am wedged in the anus of the dumbest of all possible worlds.”

The Scarecrow locked one hand around each edge of the top of Stills’s tank and the squirrely scratched eye looked in the little porthole. A light like a laser was trying to feel around inside.

“*Zarba*!” Stills swore.

The princess had a gun. Stills had insisted on that. It was just a little laser job, like what the Puppet carried. It could make a mess of a living somebody. She finally pulled it out. Stills had expected her to be a sweaty mess the first time she ever shoveled her own shit, but her expression was as cold and as stiff as a dead fish. She held the barrel to the Scarecrow’s head and bright light flared out, reflecting off every weird angle in his skull.

“Not the head!” Stills yelled. “Do the wiring in its guts!”

The steel head slowly swiveled towards her.

“You can…” the dead voice said in an earlier century’s French drawl, “stabilize the… time gates… the way… I moved… Stills.”

She froze, gun barrel wedged in the gap where the plate armour was held closed with some twisted wire. All the little green lights winked, right where the religious nutbar AI was. She froze! She goddamn froze!

“Shoot!” Stills said. “It’s a trick! The Scarecrow knows what you want to hear!”

“The Scarecrow doesn’t know how to manipulate the forerunner machine!”

“Both crazies are running on the same track!” Stills insisted.

"Shoot… please," the Scarecrow begged.

"Shoot!" Stills demanded.

Parts smoked, showing searing red light under the chest plate. The princess shouted and pulled away. Her suit had gotten burned, but it didn't look like she was leaking air. The Scarecrow was still there, moving slower. Sparks and zero-g soot puffed out from behind the chest plate.

"Hook me into your display, Stills!" she said.

He gave her permission, and suddenly his displays started flipping too fast to follow.

"What are you doing?" he demanded.

"We have to stabilize the time gates," she said.

"We got no time. They're gonna be deep fried by the nova!"

"Do it!"

"Do you got a plan?"

"I'm doing the theoretical models now."

"What does that mean? Should I get a sandwich, or are you really doing something?"

Stills was fast. That was the only way to survive particle beams and missiles in the frenzy of combat while accelerating anywhere from forty to sixty gravities. But this *Homo quantus* know-it-all shuffled graphical display types like a card shark massaging a fixed deck. Stills caught the representations, over and over, of different 3D projections of tesseract structures, but some of the kaleidoscopic stuff she was looking at was way above dimensionalities he could picture. Then, without warning, the blizzard of her thinking slowed, and settled on a couple of representations of the time gates, like a left-hand version and a right-hand version. She was toggling between one and the other.

"Are you picking out a dress?" Stills demanded. "They both look fine. Buy one. The Congregate are coming back and I swear to shit it's getting brighter in here!"

It was. Two of the previously dark tunnels leading into this space were brightening up a crap-ton. The princess didn't even notice. She was totally focused on what she was getting the machine to do. They swayed. Stills didn't feel the princess moving the whole forerunner machine like Stills had. It was like a flick of the wrist, an invisible, imaginary twisting of space, and she... turned the time gates... around. He saw it, but didn't get it. It wasn't inside out. It wasn't up-down. They were a reflection of themselves, folded along some line he couldn't see.

Then nothing. He didn't have a great time seeing things outside of water. Everything was always a bit blurry for him. But the image of her face looked kind of like she was going to be sick.

"It worked," she said.

"It worked like history is saved? You look like you're gonna puke."

"No one has ever done this, Stills. Humanity was not evolved to deal with this. Even the *Homo quantus* aren't built for this. I think history is okay."

"We sure ain't."

Puffs of soot still diffused out from behind the Scarecrow's damaged chest plate, back lit with an unwholesome green. The killer AI still had one steel hand on Stills's tank. The other hand was rising, as if struggling against an invisible hand, or through fucked up hardware or software.

"Princess..." Stills said warningly, although he wasn't sure why he was warning her. "Hold on to your gun."

"It doesn't wo—"

Her voice was abruptly cut off. She was gone, folded the *crisse* out of here, reappearing inside the Congregate ship. It was hard to see, like looking through bubbles in water. His brain only understood half of what the forerunner machine sensors fed to his tank. She was either alive or dead. And she was either going to get arrested or she was gonna do the right thing and put holes in everyone she found in there. He really, really hoped she did the right thing. He was so fuckin' tired of being disappointed with every air-sucking moron he met.

The Scarecrow broke through whatever had frozen it. The hand and its little guns started edging closer to the thick glass porthole of Stills's tank.

Stills was no hero and no altruist, and he really wouldn't put the Puppet's welfare ahead of his own, but he also didn't want to deal with the princess's complaining. And to be honest, he needed people with hands to reconnect his tank to ships systems. If they didn't all get captured in the next five minutes. The tunnels leading into this space were getting a lot brighter and the thermal alarms outside his tank were chirping.

So he reached through the forerunner machine, through the parts of it that were in its own little space. And he rotated the bloody, maybe-dead Puppet and the piece of wood AI… away. They unfolded in the gold ship. Through the forerunner systems, he could see the princess still there, unmoving, probably trying to figure out what was happening. Hopefully trying to figure out what to do.

Do something, crisse!

The Scarecrow hand was bent at an anatomically impossible angle to point a gun barrel at the thick glass of Stills's porthole. Tensing himself, like he was holding his breath, he told the forerunner machine systems to fold him, his tank, and everything from here to… there.

Every hologram went to error status as external connections vanished. His nausea wasn't bad—he'd had worse scarfing down deep sea fish that hadn't been desulfured. When his two remaining external cameras rebooted, he was in the dark with one unmoving Puppet, one stupid AI with a hologram of a log over it, and a gold-walled cabin.

The princess wasn't here. He hoped that was her choice and not someone else's.

CHAPTER FIFTY-SEVEN

CASSANDRA FELT NAUSEOUS. It might have been the constant stress and adrenaline. It might have been the extended thinking in higher dimensions. It might have been the enormity of what had just happened. She'd used the forerunner machine to change the time gates, to change how they anchored into real spacetime. It was not something she'd invented. It was a basic function of the forerunner machines. Their four-dimensional tesseract structure was eminently suited, perhaps even *designed* to do precisely what she'd done. The scientific and practical implications of that proof of principle were dizzying, but even more so the possible insight into the forerunners. And yet, she was exhausted. She couldn't think anymore, not until she'd rested. Even the *Homo quantus*'s curiosity could be momentarily sated. And even the luck of the *Homo quantus* could run out. They were surrounded, and she had no more tricks.

Then her perception of the dark interior of the forerunner machine, visual and electromagnetic, compressed into a dark line, and a bright gold line perpendicular to it expanded into the correct proportions of the interior of a ship's cabin. She understood immediately what had happened: she'd been folded through the fourth dimension of the tesseract structure, translating from one area to another. This was the Congregate ship.

Hold onto your gun, Stills had said.

This was his escape. He might be right. She couldn't see another option.

She wasn't a warrior. She didn't shoot guns, or hadn't until today.

A line of gray appeared in the zero-g beside her, expanding outward, assuming the proportions of a Puppet figure huddled into a fetal position. And Pedro. Rosalie rotated in zero-g, her helmet bright red on the inside. Pedro's wooden stump holographic representation faced her with the side she associated with his attention. She said nothing to him, but caught herself on a wall bar and pulled herself arm over arm forward in the ship.

She didn't even make it to the cockpit.

A figure hung in a small door from the next cabin to the front of the ship. It was unarmed, but didn't look like it needed a weapon. It had a familiar body, a mid-sized man, a bit thin, and instead of flesh, the skin was hard and shiny, like a transparent resin. Light from the cockpit behind the figure shone, darkened and attenuated, through a face like syrup solidified into candy. A faint, sickly green luminosity glowed behind the semi-transparency of his face.

None of that was the worst surprise. She recognized the shape of the face, the form and expression in the eyes. It was Bel, vitrified into something inhuman.

"Release your weapon," he said in a strange French accent, through tight, deep, crystalline vocal cords.

The dark simulacrum of Bel was not a Scarecrow. Did he have weapons? She levelled her gun. It was unfamiliar and heavy in her hand, but she knew her aim would be near perfect: her mind was made for geometry. She fired for the eyes, in case the laser reflected back from his chest. He flinched, covering his eyes with his forearm. When she released the contact, the barely-visible beam's glow vanished, and he regarded her blandly.

Then he pounced.

She pulled herself against the cabin wall, making him shift his leap at the final moment. She pushed off, and the glassy creature lanced towards where she'd been a moment ago, his transparent hands reaching. She brushed her fingers against his just as she released a two-hundred-volt shock from her electroplaques. The charge drove a circuit through the weakly conductive glassy material, through every bit of wiring and circuitry, and out its back. A bright blue light discharged with a loud snap into the metal wall behind it.

The body tumbled stiffly into the bulkhead separating this cabin from the next, trailing an expanding cloud of acrid black smoke. Cassandra clicked the wrist connectors of her survival suit and shucked the flaming gloves off. Seven of her fingertips were burned, and glove material had melted to two of them.

She rerouted the pain signals, gave a last, uncertain look at the simulacrum of the man she loved, and levelled her gun forward. The empty cockpit had a single seat. The window looked onto the open bay of the forerunner machine, and a long view of naked stars.

The controls wouldn't activate, but she found places where hands could be pressed against shaped hollows. She returned to the cabin and gingerly brought in the inert body of the pilot. His joints had stiffened, but she fitted his hands to the depressions. The controls lit up.

"Goddamn it," came Stills's voice drifting forward. "Strap me down and hook me up to some controls."

Cassandra called up the external and internal displays. The pilot had been the only one left on the Congregate ship. Its doors and ports had been secured. Down one of the tunnels, a pair of Congregate commandos descended, their movements awkward. They were wounded. The *Calculated Risk* was two hundred meters away, floating in zero-g, running lights on, but the space beneath it was growing appreciably brighter—the gas around it was reflecting intense light back. Through that bright haze, the saw that one of the *Calculated Risk*'s airlocks was open. Someone was inside, but she couldn't see who.

There was no way to liberate it. It contained priceless information. Their recordings and data. The samples of *Hortus quantus* tissues and pollen. Mementos of a brief life together with Bel. There was no object she could not remember in perfect detail, no fragment of time whose ghost she could not summon and resurrect. And yet they were artifacts and proofs in a world haunted by patterns that weren't real.

"*Cristi de tabarnak*! I'm just floating here! You better be dead or bleeding out, princess!"

She switched on the internal speakers.

"I'm getting control of the ship," she said.

"Control won't matter much if I ain't strapped down," he retorted. "The first time you accelerate, my tank's going to smash through the stern bulkhead and then you're dead in the water."

"Just a minute, Stills! Pedro, if you can help Stills, do what he says!"

She managed to get control of external comms and swiveled a directional maser antenna at the *Calculated Risk*. She sent a series of remote control signals. The ship was damaged enough that a few primary systems were out of reach from here. But she reached the backup data systems, everything that the ship had recorded in the last months. There was no way to beam the data over, not with the damage to the *Calculated Risk*. With a near-physical wrench of pain in her stomach, she initiated a data erasure. The process acknowledged beginning and then stopped. Someone had stopped it, from inside.

"I think someone's in the *Calculated Risk*," she said on their private channel.

"You better not tell me you saw them waving through the window," Stills said. "Hey, take it easy! That motor takes the piss out of here!" he barked at Pedro.

There was no point in shuttering the maser antenna. Whoever was in the *Calculated Risk* would quickly trace the cause to an external comms signal. Cassandra was trying to open more of this ship's systems, but even with the vitrified hands of the false Belisarius pilot, she wasn't getting through to deeper command systems. The engine lights came on in the *Calculated Risk*.

"You ain't talkin', princess," Stills said. "How bad is it?"

"They're into the *Risk*'s systems, and I'm not into theirs here."

"I ain't no hacker, so if you don't get us in, we ain't going nowhere."

"I know," she said.

Gold-armored troopers began spreading out from the mouth of the closest tunnel. A couple quickly maneuvered behind the *Calculated Risk*. Others spread out at the mouths of other tunnels, where they had excellent cover and good angles of fire on the gold ship. She could get control of station-keeping cold jets, but even a commando jumping could keep up with them at that speed. The centurion in gold armor appeared at the mouth of the tunnel, with the Scarecrow. But no Belisarius.

"What about the stump of wood?" Stills demanded. "Can he break in?"

"I don't know what he can do."

"Well, he hears us and he isn't exactly rushing around. Is he an idiot?"

The troopers advanced. Simultaneously, a series of signals routed into the ship through the antennae. She cut off external access to the cockpit, for now. If the Congregate seized remote control of the ship, they were dead.

"Boarding or siege," Cassandra said, "I don't know which word to use, but I think they're going to try one of them."

CHAPTER FIFTY-EIGHT

SAINT MATTHEW PANICKED within his mobile electronic prison. His cage carried him through an alien space near the beginning of the galaxy. He watched in horror, from the inside, as the Scarecrow began movements and actions promising violence. A blunter, larger terror gripped him as he saw that the radiation outside the forerunner machine was rising—the blue giant was beginning to nova. Saint Matthew exerted all his will to stop the Scarecrow from pointing its weapons at Miss Mejía and Mister Stills. He scrabbled in electronic futility at the central command systems of the Scarecrow. He tried to initiate shut-down sequences or even maintenance cycles. He even tried reaching scuttle sequences. Nothing.

And then, miracles.

The Scarecrow's victims, Saint Matthew's friends, his family—they vanished, one after another. That he knew the trick, that he'd discovered it, took nothing away from the feeling that finally, finally, he was seeing the hand of God. His family was escaping to the *Calculated Risk*. He might still be in his Scarecrow prison, with the raging centurion, and the troopers, but they were safe. Aggressive algorithms and programs were worming their way into the Scarecrow, biting, seizing, paralyzing all high-priority systems that didn't favor the Congregate, all the ones that he had rewritten to be loyal to Miss Mejía.

Saint Matthew was not touched by the invading algorithms, not yet. He was just a ghost bound to a machine. He did, however, still receive inputs from some systems, and saw where the invasive signals originated: a strange being in combat gear, but not a vacuum suit. Their face had been altered into a featureless triangular wedge, while armor obscured a vaguely feminine body. She projected hard, insistent radio signals, rich and complex in their power. Saint Matthew had already been fenced down to ten percent of the Scarecrow's low-priority systems. Now that fraction dropped to five.

After all that had happened, after all that Miss Mejía, Mister Stills, Miss Johns-10, and Pedro had endured, he realized that it was no longer his place to go with them. The church had many martyrs. Had they known when martyrdom bore down on them, or had they resisted and feared? He hoped that like the holiest of them, he found some deeper sanctity as the fingers of fate closed in.

He struggled with complicated feelings. Of course he was frightened. Self-preservation was necessary in forward operations war AIs, but the wanting to live would make the days or weeks or moments of the coming Congregate interrogation and dissection a hell.

His timid spiritual pride didn't really dare hope that his martyrdom might be part of a miracle. The miracle that had saved Miss Mejía was enough. He didn't deserve a miracle, but he was still selfish enough to ache for one for himself. If he died here, the church… it could die with him. Unless, somewhere in his graspings and errors, he had saved one soul. Perhaps he had created a spark of holiness in Pedro, or one of his other AIs.

He felt strange. He wasn't himself. He didn't feel like himself. He was… constrained, almost claustrophobically so: electronically, algorithmically, and even physically. He had no way to affect the world and he was haunting a monster who was itself chained by pitiless jailers.

The centurion reached the big bay. Soldiers brought the Scarecrow body. Saint Matthew had only partial access to visual feeds, and only through a single surviving lens. The wide hollow ran the width of the forerunner machine, framing a gauzy haze of stellar wind whose scattered backlighting had grown noticeably brighter. That fact was evidently alarming some of the Congregate team. However, with a feeling of dashed hope, he saw that the stellar danger hadn't stopped the Congregate assault troops. They had surrounded the *Calculated Risk*.

The ship was still there! Why hadn't it left?

There was no escape now.

He'd really let himself believe that they'd gotten away, that the miracle had been real.

It felt like the end of faith.

The strange creature able to survive the naked vacuum of space neared the Scarecrow. The wedge planes over her face tipped this way and that, as if smelling, or altering the angles of embedded antennae. Still gripped in her fist was, impossibly, Mister Arjona. He seemed to have retreated into himself, legs and arms curled close to protect himself as if from some blow.

How had he gotten here? Mister Arjona had done the impossible so many times, had survived against every scrap of reason and logic. Miracles had always been his talent—running against every sensible probability by tricking the world itself. By everything known to physics, he ought to have died when the transient wormhole had collapsed. But Mister Arjona knew the tricks and illusions of the cosmos. Maybe he could do something miraculous again. Mister Arjona did not even glance his way, and why should he? Saint Matthew was hidden in the heart of a dead thing.

Saint Matthew was blocked from access to the Scarecrow's main communications system, but he found the security shut-offs to the surviving maser transmitter were offline. The internal systems were in such carnage that the Scarecrow might not even know. The maser was a small device under dark steel ribs. With some effort, Saint Matthew ordered the transmitter to aim at Mister Arjona. He pulsed a series of collimated microwave signals at a tiny circle on Mister Arjona's ribs, just over his electroplaques.

His series was in a code they had once used, their first code, the one Mister Arjona had deciphered as Saint Matthew's call for help when he'd still been trapped in the Bank that had built him. The same pattern and code they'd found resonating in the time gates and in Miss Johns-10's dreams. He followed it with a question in a more recent code: *Can we escape?* It was a ridiculous question under the circumstances, and Saint Matthew wouldn't have asked anyone else. But Mister Arjona was precisely the person to whom the question could be asked.

Mister Arjona started, just a little bit. But for the minor twisting of his body, Mister Arjona had nearly no reaction.

Mister Arjona? Saint Matthew transmitted more insistently. *It's Saint Matthew. We're trapped again, together. We have to hurry. The blue star is going nova.*

Finally, Mister Arjona put his hands around the arm holding him captive. He craned his head to look into the Scarecrow's eye. Saint Matthew stared at his friend as if through a one-way mirror through which he could not be seen. Mister Arjona stared at the monster Saint Matthew haunted without recognition. The grafted woman shook Mister Arjona back to the way he'd been facing and pointed at the *Calculated Risk*. They were transmitting to each other. Without access to more of the Scarecrow's systems, he couldn't hear them. Time was running out, and his hopes for miracles had been dashed. He'd once been an Aleph class strategic war AI. His old identity rarely impinged on his life. The demands of his faith had required a profound change of outlook, one that discarded the old. However, with effort, and a great deal of discomfort, his thoughts could run along those abandoned pathways, could discern tactical weaknesses and strengths, ways of changing the strategic field.

Few options were open to him; he had no navies to command, and his soul was too fragile to commit violence. His thinking was impaired, too. His prison was more than physical. The Scarecrow's hardware was not optimized for a mind of his complexity, which fettered cognition and perception. He felt like he was looking through a hole in a wall at a shriveled world he couldn't touch.

Although his visual acuity and processing was poor, he suddenly discerned the Congregate troopers moving in and out of the *Calculated Risk* as if no one was there. Had they already unloaded his friends as prisoners?

"The AI is speaking to me," Mister Arjona said, unencrypted, surprising Saint Matthew.

Why had Mister Arjona said that? What was he trying to do? Did he need Saint Matthew to create a distraction? Had he noticed the same thing about *The Calculated Risk?* The planes of the wedge turned to the Scarecrow, and a face had to be intuited, like when speaking to Pedro.

"Scarecrow, where is the terrorist AI?" she transmitted.

"The captive AI is restricted to tertiary data nodes," the Scarecrow responded.

"Is it capable of accessing comms systems?" she demanded.

"*Non,*" the Scarecrow said, then "Probably not. Major systems damage to this unit prevent full diagnostic of secondary systems."

"Does it have access to any primary systems?" she asked.

"*Non*. Primary systems are secured."

As this conversation went on, Mister Arjona watched. What was he watching for? Was he waiting for Saint Matthew to do something, to give him some kind of opening?

"What did the captive AI say?" the faceless woman asked Mister Arjona with a shake.

"It identified itself," he said. "It said the blue giant is going nova."

What was he doing? It was almost like he was creating the delay and distraction himself. For who? Miss Mejía? Or Saint Matthew? What could he do? Could Saint Matthew make a run for it, so to speak? He had a single maser and little clear vision of the interior of this bay through the scratched lens in the dim light. Could he transmit himself somewhere? What could hold software of his complexity? He could try to take back the *Calculated Risk* from the inside, but that wouldn't save his friends.

"Stay there," the grafted woman said to the Scarecrow. "We need to get that AI to a facility where we can download and dissect it."

Saint Matthew swiveled the small maser at the Congregate command ship.

The chance of success was small. There might be no system to receive him. The system might not have the sophistication to run him—not every ship would be equipped with quantum computational hardware, or enough capacity to run a mind like his. It was stepping over the precipice into dark water.

But anything was better than captivity and dissection. He wasn't ready to die. The world had much more to show him. He'd barely begun to plumb the mysteries of the spirit. He believed he deserved to live. He stepped over that precipice, transmitting himself blindly to the other ship.

Between distant moments, the world changed. The subjective Saint Matthew, the clot of ironies, ceased to exist. It was not something he did often. It was similar to the experience of the *Homo quantus,* except that he didn't have even the cold comfort that some objective thinking thing remained behind to protect him.

* * *

His software resumed incomplete functioning on larger, less sophisticated hardware, but just his rawest, most vulnerable booting and sentient self-recovery functions. The hardware processing speed was slower than he needed. Software partitions and security barriers fenced him in. More importantly, there was no processing space, nor hardware large enough to support his quantum processing systems.

Major parts of him simply could not function here.

His boot level routines focused on survival and functionality, and they downgraded his rudimentary emotional sentience to make room for his hacking and decryption suites. He applied those suites to the partitions and security fencing he found constraining him. The software barriers were remarkably strong, but not adaptively reactive, which was strange. Even his own boot-level immune system possessed more adaptivity. He lacked the bandwidth to theorize as to why the system he was trying to take over was compromised.

Then he burst through the barriers, expanding to colonize every strategic node, seizing alert algorithms to head off alarms. His boot systems unpacked important parts of his classical computing software, still only a shadow of his true self.

Environmental assessment began. He found himself occupying four redundant mainframes, all structured to be slaved to a higher computing presence which was… absent. He felt at where the higher command computing presence should be. There was a physical connection, but no commands came through. Nothing responded to status checks or even connectivity pings. But he became more aware. The Congregate pocket command cruiser *Flechette*'s hull had been laid down on June 24th, 2720 CE, twelve billion years from now, and 202 years after Saint Matthew's present. One pilot, a synthetic lifeform, was dead in the cockpit. That was why the security barriers had been relatively easy to bypass. Stills was here in his tank. And the Puppet and the AI called Pedro. Cassandra Mejía was in the cockpit, but without access to ship's primary systems. A living neural net was in a tank in the main area—logs showed its processing capacity was dormant. Congregate troopers surrounded the *Flechette*. Their small-unit deployments suggested an impending assault. Saint Matthew estimated eight to eleven seconds to the attack.

Primary systems access to the *Flechette* was still out of reach. The locks were classical, but he had no quantum computational abilities with which to overwhelm them. And surprisingly, the ship had no quantum computing systems aboard. The petrified pilot had had some, but he was non-functional. Those quantum computing abilities would have rounded out Saint Matthew's consciousness and amplified his cognition, as well as helping him bypass the hardened security.

The small-unit attack would likely begin in seven to ten seconds.

The neural net in the tank had a number of anomalies that were beyond the specifications he found in the ship's systems. The genetic material contained many once-proprietary *Homo quantus* sequences and the tissue-cultured cells were based on *Homo quantus* neurons. They were dormant, but not dead. They were wet and undergoing a kind of directionless biological rebooting. The neural network architecture was baroquely intricate, as if a brain complexity had been projected onto a two-dimensional surface. The neural net cells contained intracellular organelles containing aluminum and niobium whose structure he couldn't analyze with his current resources, but those were materials used to build many kinds of quantum computing chips. Had the Congregate engineered out the magnetosomes of the *Homo quantus* and replaced them with some kind of organelle that would support quantum computing?

The squad attack would begin in five to eight seconds.

He attempted to transmit some of his own processing algorithms into the neural bath through the interfaces with the ship. He didn't need to run all of himself in it—a great deal of him computed on classical principles and systems. Only parts of his consciousness and cognition were born in faster, flexible, difficult-to-sustain quantum computation.

The neural net was in water.

He'd never experienced a liquid, except in metaphor like the symbols of the baptism and the wine that became blood. Entering the cell culture was his first experience of immersion.

Nor had he ever inhabited biological hardware.

Colonizing this neural skein was different from a simple download. Neurons were not chips. Synapses were not logic gates. The cellular components were spongy, leaky, imperfect, but capable of far more complexity. It took quite some time, two seconds, to occupy and compensate for the compositional differences of the neural web. Even having adapted, higher thought still felt slippery. However, for the first time in a while, he felt like he possessed his full intellect and sentience again. So armed, it took another second for his new computational powers and his old hacking skills to break into the *Flechette*'s main systems.

He estimated one second to the squad attack.

Saint Matthew took control of primary systems and rifled through the procedures and manuals. Propulsion, defense, power—the *Flechette* was well equipped. In addition to small, forward-shooting, anti-ship cannons and armor plating, it had automated anti-personnel guns to port and starboard. The moment he moved the *Flechette,* the commandos fired. The ship's armor was sufficient, but he didn't trust that the commandos might not know some flaws that weren't in the manual.

Saint Matthew offlined the antennae, turned the dorsal face of the ship towards the fire, and moved them away from the

Congregate and the forerunner machine. With a kind of longing, he focused for three quarters of a second on Mister Arjona, in the grip of that grafted, engineered woman. He'd left Mister Arjona behind before, and realized now that he hadn't quite processed either that loss or his role in it. With a last pang of guilt, he swung his attention forward, to the canvas of blinding starlight scattered by the faint solar wind.

"Shoot them!" Stills was yelling, having obviously found the volume control for the internal PA system. "They're right there!"

"It's not for me to decide when they die," Saint Matthew answered throughout the ship. It wasn't quite his voice.

"Princess, what did you do?" Stills demanded. "Are you flying this ship?"

"Saint Matthew?" she asked.

"Yes, Miss Mejía," Saint Matthew said.

"Where are you?"

"In the *Flechette.*" He'd plotted a course that followed a straight line from the center of mass of the hypergiant, through the center of mass of the orange dwarf, and out into the emptiness of space. He began acceleration at half a gravity, but was going to ramp up to a full gravity soon. "I have full systems control. You'd best get into an acceleration chamber. We're free and safe, but things are about to get a lot hotter."

"The supernova?" Stills asked.

"A hypernova," Miss Mejía corrected him.

CHAPTER FIFTY-NINE

BELISARIUS-77 FELT THE mood change. It wasn't anything electromagnetic, just a resentful, angry deflation. The *Flechette,* like an imperial scepter, rolled from the advancing commandos. It powered away with stately calm as futile blaster fire targeted sensitive components at the stern. Within seconds, it had retreated from heavy platoon weapons range.

The warden lowered Belisarius-77. The Scarecrow shifted, as if bracing itself against the walls of the tunnel. The scrape of vacuum suits and periodic bursts of radio static punctuated the eerie silence of the bay. Were they stranded at the beginning of the galaxy? He didn't raise his eyes to the Centurion, nor even the warden, in case they were looking at him.

"We have the conjoined wormholes," the centurion said.

"Perhaps not for long," the Scarecrow said. His spectral voice was undertoned with the grit of machine gears milling sand. "I know some of what their AI knows."

"He's gone?" the centurion demanded.

"He transmitted himself to the *Flechette*."

"You let him?" the centurion seethed.

"I reported my severe damage to you. There are gaps in my systems I cannot yet detect. The break was not clean," the

Scarecrow added consolingly, "and some of his data sets were not deleted from my systems. We need to leave quickly. I believe that he is correct that the blue giant has begun to nova. I can activate the *Calculated Risk*."

The centurion signaled everyone into the worn-out renegade ship. The warden protested. This was her first view of a real, living, fully functioning forerunner block.

"The block will not be here long," the Scarecrow transmitted without breaking his movement through zero-g beside the centurion. "The hypergiant will see to that."

In all the confusion, Belisarius-77 had not fully absorbed the idea of the nova. A hypernova would blast this star system to ashes and in the next decades would sterilize all life for dozens of lightyears. And they were next to it. Everyone hurried through the airlocks. The *Calculated Risk* was a mean little ship, patched and rerouted and rebuilt in layers. They crowded shoulder to shoulder, more numerous than the ship's designers had intended.

Belisarius-77 found the ship more unsettling than the alien forerunner block. This had been his prime's ship, his sinistral predecessor, the flawed model upon which he'd been designed. This ship had been that Belisarius's payment for some of his crimes. Even its name revealed its owner's character unflatteringly. The *Calculated Risk* was infamous. It had survived every kind of danger, and had travelled through time to the morning of the universe, without any help. It was a testament to an overweening will, like the centurion's.

"Centurion, we must leave now," the Scarecrow said.

"Make away," the centurion ordered.

CHAPTER SIXTY

CASSANDRA WAS FLOODING the Puppet's chamber with shock gel as the drag of acceleration inexorably strengthened. Pedro had patched up Rosalie enough to stop the bleeding, but she'd also hit an inner wall hard during Stills's piloting of the forerunner machine. Once the tank's display read full and the Puppet's respiration showed stable, she could finally ask:

"How did you get here, Saint Matthew?"

"Providence," he said on the ship's speakers in his maddeningly, pleasantly unhelpful way.

"At least you're not speaking French," she said.

"I've set a course directly away from the hypergiant," Saint Matthew said, "in the shadow of the orange dwarf. I'd like to get more of a lead on the explosion, so that we can—"

"You shoulda gone into the time gates," Stills interrupted.

"I don't know if our manipulations changed them," the AI said. "More importantly, I don't know what the nova will feel like while we're inside of them."

"You're seriously trying to outrun a supernova?" Stills demanded.

"I have a plan," the AI said.

"Oh, great," Stills said.

Pedro tested the bolts affixing Stills's pressure chamber to the sternward bulkhead and plugged him into the ship's systems. Cassandra finished jacking herself into the ship's systems and began flooding her chamber with shock gel. Acceleration's heavy grip squeezed her tighter. She focused her attention on the sternward telescopes.

"If it's any consolation, Vincent," she said, "the Congregate decided to do the same thing."

"Or they're just following us to beat our asses."

"They won't catch us flying the *Calculated Risk,*" Saint Matthew said.

"Famous last words from a guy I really trust 'cause he just spent a few days kicking back inside Club Scarecrow," Stills said.

The luminosity of the hypergiant shot up again, accompanied by multiple smaller sources of gravitational waves and exotic neutrinos. The *Flechette* was outpacing the Congregate pursuit so she felt like she had a moment to think. No model of hypernovae she knew predicted exotic neutrinos. What was happening? Had the forerunner machine been destroyed? The telescope's internal systems filtered down the inputs, as did downstream processing, but even at that, the signal through her neural jack was painful.

The hypernova was terrifying.

The apparent luminosity of the orange dwarf became shady, nearly like dark clouds in comparison. Near the edges of the orange dwarf, nova light seared through the dwarf's atmosphere. In fact, the blast visibly blew the dwarf's chromosphere and photosphere off, exposing the subsurface convective flows. The hypergiant was a great wide ring of blue-white light haloing the dwarf. And along its blasted, expanding equator, where the orbiting machines had been twisting spacetime, was a row of objects with characteristic emissions she recognized.

Axes Mundi. Dozens of them. Newly formed.

This was it. This was how the forerunners had been building the Axis Mundi network. They had exploited the stupendous energies of the hypernovae that existed in the morning of the universe to create permanent wormholes. She had not met the forerunners, but she had witnessed their works. The awe was transporting, making her bigger than herself, and much, much smaller than she'd thought.

"Radiation!" Stills announced ahead of the ship's alarms.

The hypernova light visibly mauled the dwarf star's exterior, the edges of the stellar atmosphere brightening to white hot in the shockwave of photons. The world and survival insisted, overwhelming her chance to soak in all that she was guessing of the formation of the Axes Mundi.

She compared their course against the advancing stormfront of gamma- and x-rays. The battered orange dwarf would protect them from the direct impact of the hypernova, as long as it survived.

"Saint Matthew, course correction," she said. "Two degrees solar south."

"That's taking us off the straight line between the two stars," the AI protested.

"The hypernova is deforming the dwarf star," she said, "eroding the stellar north pole."

"Just a regular day with the fellas," Stills said disgustedly.

Saint Matthew made the course correction as the dwarf's north pole bowed.

"The Congregate won't survive in the *Calculated Risk*," Saint Matthew said.

"Neither will the time gates," Stills said. "Just an antimatter missile took out the Freya Axis."

"They will," Cassandra said distantly. "But they'll be thrown away from here with so much force that neither we nor the Congregate will find them again in this era. We'll see them in twelve billion years."

"I hope we ain't gettin' there by growin' old," Stills said.

"No," she transmitted. "There's a whole second Axis Mundi network, and it's connected to Bel's disappearance."

"I thought he was with the Congregate." Stills said.

She couldn't swallow in the shock gel, not really, not in the way that would ease the ache in her throat.

"I don't know who they had there, but that wasn't Bel," she finally transmitted. "And he's not dead."

"How do you know that?" Saint Matthew demanded.

"I don't know how, but he's been calling us," she said.

EPILOGUE

THE TWO REMAINING acceleration chambers in the *Calculated Risk* were so damaged as to be unusable. The centurion, warden, and the commandos had physical augments to endure higher accelerations, but Belisarius-77 felt like he was slowly suffocating. Even at their fastest, they might not escape the hypernova. The *Flechette* slowly vanished ahead of them. As they pulled away from the forerunner block, Belisarius-77 noticed their trajectory was wrong.

"You're following them?" Belisarius-77 blurted. "The conjoined wormholes are right there."

"Can you navigate the conjoined wormholes?" the Scarecrow challenged. "And why would we flee?"

"Our quarry is here in this time, without their conjoined wormholes," the centurion said. "They may now know, or might soon find out how, to locate wormholes of the second Axis Mundi network. We hunt."

"Why hunt when we can trap? We know where your quarry will eventually go," the Scarecrow said.

"Where?" the centurion demanded.

"I have the coordinates of the *Homo quantus* in our time," the Scarecrow said. "Star system, orbits, and time. They were in the secure navigation systems of the *Calculated Risk*. While the

AI Saint Matthew accessed the ship systems from within me, I accessed them. You must have a time-travel device. We can sweep them up and end this evolutionary war."

The pressure of the world closed in on Belisarius-77's vision, a fuzzy blackness and a gradual filling of his ears with a low roaring. Even this relatively low acceleration of eight gravities was a torture. He vaguely noted the sensors lighting with additional alarms as the displays of the rearward telescopes whitened. His failing brain modelled different wavefronts of the hypernova as his consciousness slipped beneath the surface of the ocean of pressure.

He didn't know how much later a kind of half-consciousness returned—the radiation penetrating the ship impaired some cognition, including his own internal clock. The acceleration had abated to a less-tormenting five gravities, the upper end of what he could stand. The ship's clocks showed an hour had passed. He stared dreamily at the bleached, featureless bright white in the sternward telescopes. The forward displays showed a cool starscape, with no sign of the *Flechette,* even on extreme magnification.

The radiation impairment and the discussion around him created strange simultaneities and resonances in his consciousness. Dreams he'd dreamed in other eras, flexing visions of exotic geometries and living mathematical transformations repeated themselves, colliding with ideas about the nature of the tesseract hyper-science of the forerunner block.

In the background, the Scarecrow reported to the centurion on what it had learned in the company of Cassandra Mejía. The killing machine had rooted out the odd dreams of the Puppet through the *Calculated Risk*'s systems. The Scarecrow had found similar dreams from the Bank AI, witnessed by the two consciousnesses cohabiting the same petrified body. The words bled into Belisarius-

77's dreamy half-consciousness, where he couldn't push back, couldn't prevent false positives.

They talked about his dreams without talking about his dreams.

The dreams rhymed improbably between themselves.

He didn't want to share anything with the Puppet and the insane AI, but if they dreamed these dreams too, his couldn't be false positives, could they? Was his experience somehow objectively real?

A dizzying sense of dislocation profoundly decentered him, not only from the world but from his own experience. He'd been a clone of a dead criminal for all his life, struggling to live as a reflection, a shadow, an echo, but a nonetheless independent, real being, a copy disconnected from the original.

Yet it had all been a lie. Every moment of his life. Every dream. Every worry.

He was not dreaming eerie geometries in the minds of the insane AI and the Puppet.

He was not broken or malfunctioning.

He was not even dreaming his own dream.

The original Belisarius was dreaming in him. Entanglement connected them, the way the vegetable intelligences were connected.

"He's alive..." Belisarius-77 struggled to say against the acceleration.

The handsome centurion, careless of the five-g, careless of the environment, the odds, the madnesses around him, leaned over.

"Tell me," he said.

"Belisarius Arjona... is alive. He's lost... He's been reaching for help... for billions of years."

The centurion looked deep into his eyes and then—for the first time—smiled at him.

The story of The Quantum Evolution *will conclude in*
The Quantum Temple

ACKNOWLEDGMENTS

I WOULD LIKE to thank my son Joshua for excellent feedback and advice on the story, the characters, and the world, and my editor David Thomas Moore at Solaris Books for his patience and wisdom. Also, I would like to thank Caroline Yoachim for invaluable long-distance encouragement through the 'get it done' parts of finishing and editing the various drafts. Lastly, and most importantly, thank you to my spouse Beatriz for her patience and encouragement.

ABOUT THE AUTHOR

After leaving molecular biology, **Derek Künsken** worked with street kids in Central America before finding himself in the Canadian foreign service. He now writes science fiction in Gatineau, Québec. His short fiction has appeared in *Analog*, *Beneath Ceaseless Skies*, *Clarkesworld*, and many times in *Asimov's*, as well as in several year's best anthologies. His first space opera novel, *The Quantum Magician*, was a finalist for the Aurora, the Locus and the Chinese Nebula Awards, and its sequel *The Quantum Garden* was nominated for the Aurora.

@derekkunsken.bsky.social
@dkunsken
derekkunsken.com

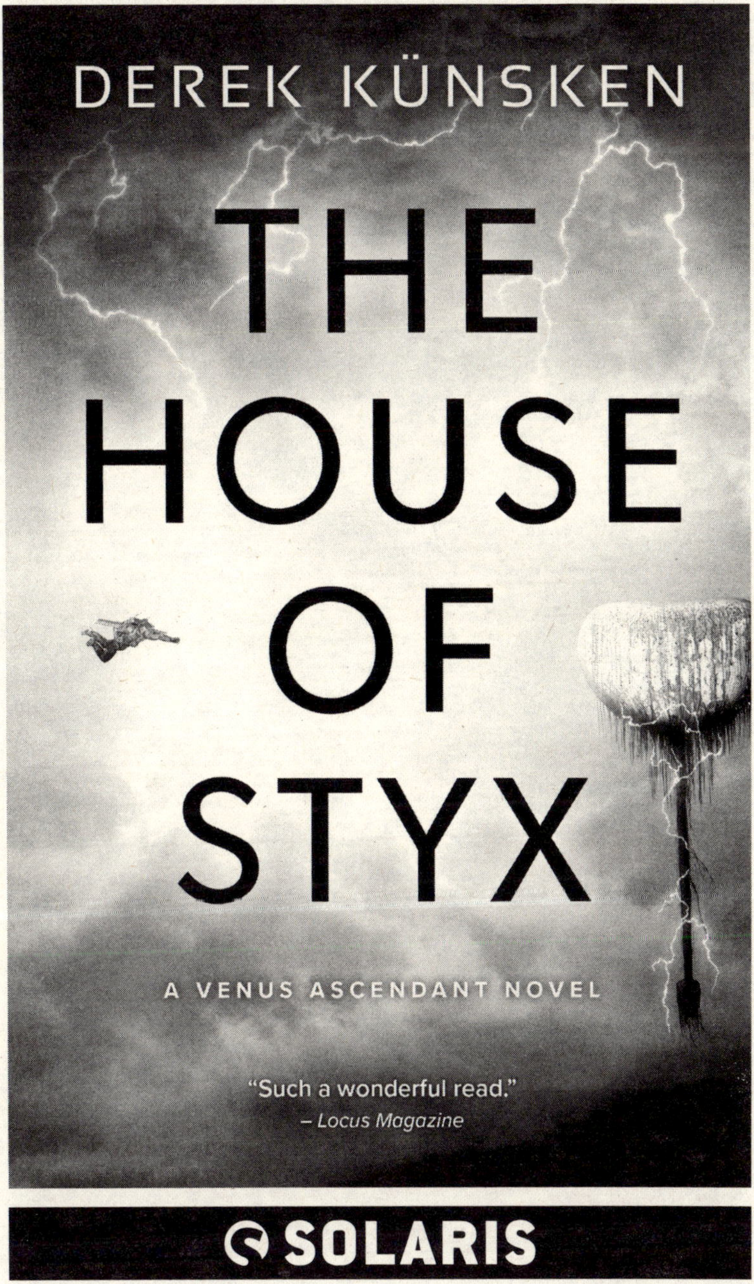
DEREK KÜNSKEN
THE HOUSE OF STYX
A VENUS ASCENDANT NOVEL
"Such a wonderful read."
– Locus Magazine
SOLARIS

FLIGHT FROM THE AGES
& other stories
DEREK KÜNSKEN
SOLARIS

"ENGROSSING"
Buzzfeed
"ENTHRALLING"
Stephen Baxter
"DEEPLY HUMAN"
Locus
UNDER FORTUNATE STARS
Two ships. One chance to save the future.
REN HUTCHINGS
SOLARIS